LOVERS AND DANCERS

Michael Feeney Callan

THE SHERIDAN
BOOK COMPANY

This edition published in 1994 by
The Sheridan Book Company
By arrangement with Random House UK Ltd
Random House, 20 Vauxhall Bridge Road, London SW1V 2SA

First published in Great Britain1981 by Hamlyn Paperbacks
Banda House, Cambridge, Grove, Hammersmith, London W60LE

Printed and bound in Great Britain by
Cox & Wyman Ltd, Reading, Berkshire

ISBN 1–85501–647–8

LOVERS AND DANCERS

In the pathways and yards there was much activity, and the cottage areas streamed with people scurrying about, carrying empty pails and spades and wearing jaded faces. But no one could be seen digging. Choruses of talk wafted out – Irish talk – cryptic and strange and somehow, today, disconcertingly loud. Crossing the granite prominence that gave onto the Devlin plots, Donna saw a broken line of police in the distance, marching through the fields, apparently interestedly inspecting the brown earth. Everywhere, as at all harvest-times, there were donkey slide-cars but now they stood idly, the sun-washed animals chewing rye grass by the tracks' sides. Donna fancied she heard crying and wondered if it was a man's wail or a woman's; it was not the momentary weeping of a child.

' . . . The lovers and the dancers are beaten into clay
And the tall men and the swordsmen and the horsemen,
where are they?'

W. B. Yeats *Curse of Cromwell*

*For Philip Hinchcliffe
and, of course, for Judith*

PROLOGUE:

1825

Rain fell.

In the silky light of the approaching evening and the storm Desmond Devlin dismounted and pulled the frightened mare into the tumbledown skeleton barn. Cloudy shadow darkened the far end of the sheltered area and he tied the horse in here, massaging neck and flanks, whispering reassurance. When finally she quietened he left her chewing the dry sparse grass and walked back to the doorway. Cobwebs of yellow light flashed across the heavens and all around leaves flounced in the downpour. Devlin's huge frame stood bent as if in pain, and he stared out blindly across the valley that swooped to the dead grey gloss of the Shannon, where it broadened to Lough Derg. He saw nothing. Not the patchwork half-fenced spread of Drumloch's potato farms, not the far apart, lightless cottages, not even the glittering jewel of Drumloch itself, seated near the river mud flats, shining in the black dark like the eye of God. Instead, his eyes looked inward – into the greater murk of his mind where another rain fell and no brightness offered relief.

Images came. He saw Kitty, his beautiful wife, in her fever sweat, belly swollen with the babe. She would be lying, he knew, on the straw bed by the rattling window, wordless in her pain. Carey, the old doctor who tended the less impoverished farmers for a shilling a visit, would be long gone. He would have come early and seen what he had seen last year, and the year before: the same febrile shaking, that unnatural heat, and the bleeding. Wherever he was now he would be thinking: She'll lose this one too, she'll be lucky to survive herself. And he could do nothing but soak her brow, hold her hand and pray for her. Across the low-ceilinged room, restless in his cot, would lie Colum, and the doctor would have looked at him and wondered why that young body wasn't enough, why it didn't fill the need. Had he asked, Kitty would have spoken: to live in the frame of a woman was to love, and wed, and bear issue; it was nature, pure and simple. Much as she cherished Colum, her dead sister's boy, her heart and mind revolved around a child of her own womb. And so, full of painful hope, she would lie in the chill with the rain spitting in from the rotted window frame, and wait.

At the big house Lady Janet would be waiting too. Devlin saw her in his mind's eye, her voluptuous well-fed body spread on a bed in Drumloch as big as his own kitchen. The swell of her belly would be pampered and healthy, swathed in satin, padded in fat. Her bedroom maid would be in attendance, and a constant doctor, one of the young London types with a bag of new medical remedies. She was safe, and without pain or anguish.

Devlin's mare started to whinny softly and he woke from his day dreams and peered through mizzling drifts towards the lighted honeycomb that was the manor. He counted the window lights and saw there were thirty. Then he looked to the whitewash tenants' cottages. Even though night was fast falling he could distinguish only three smoky lights. These illuminations would not be for reading by, or talking by, or for livening a room; they were the glows of range fires for cooking meals and warming the blood. They were the primitive fires of survival. For every tenant of the valley the bright lights of Drumloch were the greatest sign of immeasurable wealth and excellent living. More than anything the farmers coveted the endless light which at night so often seemed to mock them. And yet, because their existence here depended on the continued thriving of the manor, there was a place in their minds – hearts even – that revered the great lit house, and they had no wish to see any ill change befall Drumloch or its owner.

But change was at hand, as Devlin alone knew. With the

death of George Anderson and the absence locally of suitable candidates to inherit the role of agent, Devlin had become the estate's middleman. For a small gratuity this meant collecting rents, ensuring peace on the farms and acting as general go-between. The unlikely arrangement pleased both parties, though Devlin was always aware of the awkwardness of his position. But, as tenants' representative, he was privy to many of the intimate developments of the Drumloch household – an asset feasibly more valuable than money in hand. Sir Redmond Bouchard he found to be a feckless and unpredictable man, but one whose interest, however vague, in the well-being of the ninety-odd tenant families, seemed genuine enough. In spite of the occasional squalls of irrational behaviour and the reputation for drunkenness, Devlin quite liked the man. He was certainly a welcome improvement on his father, Edgar Bouchard, a tyrant who sponsored his decline by exaggerating rents and evicting tenants heartlessly. Rumour had it that Redmond had inherited his father's gambling traits and capricious wildness with money, but if that were true self-respecting status meant much to him too, and he had in more than twenty years of controlling ownership revealed no signs of defeat or indigence.

But now, at forty-five, a woman had entered Redmond Bouchard's life and patterns were altering. Below-stairs gossip bore many secrets but no one knew whence Lady Janet came and, from what the house servants gleaned, her personality and motives were as elusive as the halo round the moon. All Devlin ascertained for sure was that she was well-bred Ulster stock, with a wealthy foster-brother based in Lurgan, and Bouchard had met her in connection with the sale of some race horses he kept stabled at Newmarket. She had come to Drumloch only once, for the previous Christmas season, and had expressed her uninterest in the place during her one or two brief audiences with Devlin. She said the estate seemed too remote, and she found the people of the district unintelligible. Her remarks had been casual and dismissive but Devlin had guessed at the vehemence of her feelings. Then, during the summer,

Bouchard had fallen ill in London and decided to recuperate in Ireland rather than move to Hedgeleigh, his Kent estate. To Devlin's surprise Lady Janet had chosen to accompany him and set up temporary home at Drumloch. And there – like a cancer – she had permeated the machinery of the old manor, antagonising the staff and, when the best of them left, she carefully chose indifferent replacements who mismanaged the property and allowed the gardens and glasshouses to fall to disrepair. Bouchard blindly tolerated her interference and by late autumn it became apparent that she had impressed on him the difficulties they faced without adequate talented staff in so remote an area. The bad tidings had been almost expected by Devlin when Bouchard called him to his library and explained the problem. The considered option of selling out loomed large and Devlin, without tact, challenged it.

'If you go everything goes, don't it,' Devlin said. 'For as long as anyone can recall there have been Bouchards and their tenants here – a stable balance.' Bouchard nodded, his handsome face heavy in apology. 'So if this means a new landlord, it could mean a new agent, new rents, new boundaries,' Devlin went on.

'Can't say, can we?' Bouchard said. 'But *if* it comes to that, I'm sure whoever takes it on will be sympathetic to the problems.'

'I doubt that, sir,' Devlin snapped, irritated by his own anger. 'Speculators have been buying as much as they can round here. You said so yourself. And our land needs time. We had a partial crop failure last autumn. There's not enough food, not enough money. If rents go up people'll starve.'

'These lands would be better under forest. I've always said that. They're not good tillage lands.'

'But they're all we have.'

Bouchard's finely manicured hands pounded flatly on the top of the ornate desk. 'Anyway, much has to be resolved yet. Let us all keep level-headed.'

'But, sir, if there is a seed of thought in your mind, I implore you – '

Bouchard stared back at Devlin with a calm look of pity. At that moment Lady Janet had intruded. She was a plumpish woman, her sensual, mobile face almost comically the twin of Bouchard's, but with large alert eyes. There was a ruby encrusted with filigree gold on a chain round her neck and this somehow had taken Devlin's attention so that when she spoke the ruby spoke and the brittle words were as cold and sardonic as the sparkle of the gem.

'We expect no trouble, Mister Devlin. My husband considered it prudent to consult and advise you at an early stage in our plans, principally for your benefit.'

'I am grateful for his kindness, but I beg you sincerely, Ma'am – ' Impulsively he implored her as he had Bouchard, but her eyes froze him into silence and he was momentarily more frightened of her than he had been of anything in his life – either his own violent father, or Edgar Bouchard, or disease, or blight. He promptly backed down, bowed himself out and went about his normal rent-collecting arrangements. It had only been later – on his third or fourth meeting with the woman – that he realised she, like Kitty, was pregnant. That somehow repulsed him and her bulge seemed vulgar and mis-shapen compared with Kitty's pretty swell. But in the back of his mind he knew his view was a jealous one and he suspected her large fresh body would yield a fit son, while Kitty's hopes grew endlessly weaker.

Standing, watching Drumloch, his face dribbling in the soaking spray, Devlin wondered if – as had been the rumour – Bouchard had succeeded in transporting Lady Janet back to Dublin or London for her confinement, but he thought it unlikely. She had lasted out the summer and autumn here, missing the end-of-parliamentary-term parties and the early hunting season balls. She would stay now till the baby was delivered and the property disposed of. Like a good general in battle she would not leave the front till the shots of victory sounded and she got what she wanted.

Devlin's mare started up again, neighing deafeningly, and he turned to soothe her. The lightning had ceased and

11

he knew something else must have worried her. Just as the thought registered he heard the rhythmic gallop of an approaching horse. He untied the mare and went out to the high dirt path. The bull-necked figure of 'Swan' Duff, redoubtable tenant of the luckless River Farm, was instantly recognisable, thundering up the slope in the twilight. He called out a rough Gaelic greeting from a good way off and for no obvious reason it sent icy fingers down Devlin's spine. Duff reined his mount in excitedly.

'Many'd call you a hard-hearted man, Desmond Devlin,' he called down. 'A woman in the last days of expecting and you travelling out.'

'Work to do,' Devlin replied. 'I've seen a poor crop in again this season, like yourself, and here's my way to earning keep.'

'Some are greedy, I'm thinking,' Duff said smilingly. 'Haven't you a fortune in your live-stock. Or so you'd be telling us.'

'If I have it's no more than I've been advising the likes of you to make way for. The crops cannot be trusted. It pays to buy a sow.'

Duff spat into the dirt and washed his face with rain. 'What work be you doing here?'

'Measuring land.'

The fat man's voice dropped a key. 'Oh. Why? Someone selling?'

Loyalties divided, Devlin was unsure of how to answer. 'Haven't heard officially,' he said.

'There's ghosts of rumour.'

'Always is,' he shrugged. 'What takes you up here anyway? Is it free potatoes you're after?'

'I'm an honest man,' Duff beamed. 'No,' his voice wavered, 'it's Carey sent me.'

'Kitty . . . ?' Devlin's voice was loud, making the mare jump and whinny anew. 'Is Carey with her?'

'Yes. Says the time is now. You should come.'

There was more in Duff's face than in his words but the night and the rain stood between them. Devlin mounted the mare, his heart beats racing, a stiffness slowing his movements. Kitty was in trouble. In the normal way of a birth – even for a dead child – the doctor would not attend. One of the farmer's wives would be sufficient. Duff's wife, God rest her, had assisted last time when the girl had been born dead; Devlin had expected Cara, Duff's eldest girl – who in turn had tended her mother through a birth and illness – to assist now; no mention of Cara had been made, but Carey was there and it was nightfall – well past visiting time – and the omens were not good.

Following Duff he rode down through the valley, crossing the half-clad potato plots, picking out tracks wherever possible in the close dark, but for the best part taking the most direct routes, whether through grazing fields or half-dug crops. In less than twenty minutes they reined in outside the four-room stone-and-mud building with the roped-thatch roof that was Devlin's home. With its neat outbuildings and chicken-coops it was the envy of every farmer in the valley, though it was Devlin's own enterprise and not, as some suggested, the privilege of his position that had established so acceptable a dwelling. Now, as Devlin tied his horse and Duff shuffled aimlessly in the yard, the back door of the house opened and a young red-haired girl rushed out and started drawing water from the well. Cara Duff saw Devlin but made no attempt to converse. His momentary surge of spirit died. Bracing himself, he walked in.

Kitty was lying as he had pictured her during the day – a slender body beneath a pilotcloth blanket on a straw bed. Two lamps had been lit and a fragile fire twinkled under the canopy chimney. Large pots of steaming water hissed, intensifying the silence. Carey sat, listening-tube in hand, crouched beside Kitty's head. When Devlin entered he jerked round nervously, then shook his head sharply as if to command quiet. Kitty seemed unconscious, her face oddly yellow-coloured, like souring cream. The doctor gripped Devlin's sleeve as he nudged closer to the bed.

'I don't want her to die,' Devlin murmured heavily.

'There's life in her yet,' Carey whispered. 'If only she could deliver it. But she isn't strong. There is little I can do.'

13

'How long will it be?'

'The Lord God knows. It should have been by now. She has the will, but . . .'

'She has the will,' Devlin shot. 'It is enough.' He took Kitty's hand and brought its cold dampness to his face. 'Kitty,' he said, kissing the words into her veins, 'be strong now. Be patient for both of us.' He mumbled an Irish prayer.

'I thought she'd be dead before I got back,' Carey said, half to himself. 'The young lass called after me. She'd lost blood. I had to get laudanum.' He paused for a moment. 'There is great desperation in your desire for a child.'

'Kitty's need,' Devlin said. 'Me, I have hungered for an heir as all men do. The honour of carrying on traditions. Now, I think twice about the lifestyles and traditions I would have carried on for future generations.' He kissed his wife's fingers again. 'If she survives this, I will teach her new sense.' He appealed to Carey. 'What can we do?'

'Keep her awake – she is still – and help when she starts pushing. I think she has a chance once – '

Devlin heard the door behind him open and, thinking of Cara at the well, he did not move. A man's voice muttered out behind him and the doctor rose to his feet.

Suddenly Carey's voice spoke out, his hand tapping Devlin's shoulder. 'I'm sorry, friend. I must leave now.' Devlin swivelled. He saw Pearson, Bouchard's servant, standing in the flickering firelight. 'Her ladyship is ill. They think it is the baby. And her doctor is in Dublin tonight.'

'No,' Devlin said disbelievingly. 'You can't go yet.'

'I must. There is urgency.'

'But she'll die – they both will.'

'Maybe not. If she has strength – ' Carey stopped, his mellow eyes boring into Devlin's, asking forgiveness and help. An order had come from Drumloch, there was nothing he could do. Devlin found no answering sympathy. He said evenly, 'I hope to God her ladyship dies.'

Pearson held the door and Carey pulled on his cape. Neither man looked back to the straw bed. 'I wish you both

God's grace and luck. *Dia dhuit,*' the doctor said; then he left.

Three architects had died during the construction of Drumloch. The resultant grey stone mutation reflected no particular style of design and yet looked attractive in its general appearance of contrast and incompleteness, and it was volubly admired by all cultured visitors.

Dr Phineas Carey, who saw himself as a man of culture and society who knew the masses but enjoyed the select, had never been able to attune himself favourably to the manor. Drumloch had its own doctor and Carey rarely called for professional purposes but he had many times dined with Bouchard. As with the house, Carey neither particularly liked nor understood Bouchard, but he blamed himself for this, suspecting the prejudices and inconsistencies of old age. Years ago he had known and disliked Edgar Bouchard – but at least that villain was as straight as a die, and aspects of his blunt openness were almost endearing. But Redmond was a chilly fish, masked perennially by a bumptious *bonhomie* that seem to cover no more than spineless weakness. Like the house with its colonnades and swaggering Palladian plan, Bouchard's extrovert behaviour was all a cover-up and if one ever scratched that surface, one might find insurmountable rot beneath.

Carey thought these things as he scurried through the rain to Drumloch. He had heard strong rumours of the domineering Lady Janet, but had chosen to ignore them with the wish that he would never meet the lady. He grinned wryly to himself. Had any woman tried to assert her power over old Bouchard, by God she'd have regretted it. Edgar would have leathered her backside in view of his drinking friends!

The housemaid opened the door to the doctor. From the vestibule Carey was led into a rather stunted Great Hall from which aisles led to connecting rooms. Above, a boarded vault that framed the gallery gaped down on them. In spite of fine French chandeliers and attractive art pieces, the immediate impression was one of vacancy and the immensity of space.

Bouchard was sitting in a book-lined room with a solitary oil lamp at his elbow and a half-full glass in his hand. Carey saw his arrival had startled the man, that the small expressionless eyes were redshot and the mouth drunkenly slack. Bouchard quickly fumbled the drink aside and turned up the lamp. 'Forgive me,' he mumbled. 'I have been dozing. My wife – '

'She isn't well? Her pregnancy has some time to go, I am reliably informed.'

'Quite so. But, you see, she had been horse-riding this afternoon.' Bouchard's eyes avoided the doctor's.

'Most undesirable in her condition. You know that?'

'She is . . . a stubborn woman, sir. I'm sorry you haven't met her up to now.'

'Well, I had better not delay. If she is ill – '

'Not really *ill*,' Bouchard began quietly. 'It's just that her doctor is away and that troubles her. She is accustomed to close attendance.' He coughed, turned away. 'And she's had some discomforting cramps. You may go up to see her now.' Bouchard shook the maid's bell.

'I had a rather urgent case down the river – Devlin's wife.'

Bouchard had boldly retrieved his brandy glass and was gulping it thirstily. 'I regret upsetting your work, doctor. How is Devlin's wife?'

'Alive. Not well.' Carey's words were sharp. Bouchard hung his head and muttered, 'When you attend Lady Janet inform me of her condition.' Carey nodded, excused himself silently, then rejoined the maid and followed her upstairs. Slanting rain hammered the mock lancet-windows of the upper chambers but, despite its vastness, the area was snugly warm. Carey eyed the heavy Italian wall tapestries and deep-pile carpets with a critical closeness. The maid opened the door to a brightly lit bedroom and retreated. Carey entered, aware at once of the fussy splendour of this place and, simultaneously, of the rounded beauty of the woman in the bed. He could see nothing of the cold obstinacy that some said was in her face.

Briefly questioning her personal maid and the midwife in attendance, Carey abandoned them brusquely and formally introduced himself to his new patient. Lady Janet stirred the coils of her rusty brown hair spread on the pillow and pulled herself fractionally up. The silvery chemise she wore, scarcely covered by a muslin overdress, seemed grossly inappropriate to the doctor, but its scant appearance brought a flush of pleasure rather than embarrassment to his cheek. She looked, he saw, perfectly relaxed and quite fit.

'You experience some discomfort, m'lady,' he offered.

'It started and stopped,' Lady Janet said. 'But I wanted you here for the sake of safety. They tell me you are a sound man.'

Bewitched and disconcerted, Carey stuttered out an inept reply and began his rapid examination behind the pre-set screen. Lady Janet co-operated dutifully, asking an occasional polite question and answering the doctor's with equal ease. When the check was completed Carey stood back and frowned down at her. Her smile and her gentle perfume softened his words.

'You have no signs of contractions and, from what I can judge, there are some weeks yet to delivery.'

'But the pain. Distinctly. In my side – here.' She whipped back the blanket to clasp her hip.

'You were riding. That's not sensible. There seems to be a little inflammation there. I'll leave some lotion. Your maid can rub it in and you should be your usual felicitous self after a night's sleep.'

'*Should be*! I'm afraid, doctor, that is not good enough. It's my child you are talking about, remember. One cannot leave these things to chance. I know what pain I felt. I want to be quite certain my baby is born healthy and safe.'

'It will be, we must not doubt. But your own doctor did inform me – you have some short time to wait still.'

Lady Janet's smile had been replaced by an angular expression that bared her teeth and made her look almost intimidating. '*When* the birth happens remains to be seen,' she said harshly. 'But I will expect your assistance till

Doctor Appleby returns from Dublin. You may have his rooms in the meantime.'

Carey felt indignation burn in his throat. Too many beautiful women in his experience – wealthy and poor – used the pride of their looks as weapons. He would stand his ground. 'You may not know my schedules, m'lady,' he said. 'I live in Banagher, which is all of six miles away. My clients are the good folk of Laurencetown and thereabouts. Only very occasionally do I work this area.'

'And you are working it now.' She hesitated, inhaled noisily, as in pain. 'Thank God, sir.'

'I have a few patients in the valley, true. But –'

'I seek no explanation nor argument, doctor. You know it is a case of dire Christian need. You will speak to my husband and make your services available here.' Her face momentarily bloated and she crossed her hands over her bosom. 'The spasms I feel are quite real. They have returned, I assure you. Not contractions, just pains.'

Carey began reassurance but Lady Janet interrupted him. 'I want an heir for Redmond, a strong boy – a strong-willed boy – who will grow up and bring some real honour back to the Bouchard name. I must have it. They say the first time is the best. Fail now, and I shall always fail.'

'The Bouchard name is well respected, my lady, don't doubt that,' Carey urged. Lady Janet closed her eyes and buried her head back in the pillows. 'By who?' she asked. 'The Devlins and the O'Tracys and the Duffs? Peasant farmers whose ignorance enables them to do no more year after year than dig the same earth, plough the same trough. Respect from them is nothing because this country is nothing. Hundreds of miles of barren earth – bog, estuary, dead fields. And beggars. Everywhere penniless women, naked children, scavengers. Wasn't it your Dean Swift who said Ireland's misery and desolation could hardly be matched this side of Lapland? By God, how right he was.'

'If you dislike this country so much, why do you stay on?'

'Stay on!' Lady Janet laughed shortly. 'My dear doctor, all the tea in China would not keep me here one day more than was absolutely necessary.' Her expression tightened, the eyes opening to stare fixedly at the chandelier overhead. 'What remains of the Bouchard eminence?' she asked, almost questioning herself. 'A useless pitch in Kent that no one wants to visit. A decrepit house in Doughty Street. And this – acres of waste that pay not at all.' Her head cocked quickly towards Carey and the eyes blazed. 'Did you know these people, these so-called farmers, actually rose up against Redmond two years ago? They besieged this house, by God. The glasshouses were destroyed – '

'It was all misunderstanding,' Carey explained. 'Groups of farmers from Abbey were complaining that their lands were being annexed for pasture work. They rely on tillage. And they mistook Drumloch – '

'What does it matter?' Lady Janet snapped. 'The peers are good enough to help them in the first place. I mean, these are *our* lands. Every beggar among them could be turned out in the morning. But patient idiots like my husband maintain them. And all they get is abuse in return.' Her eyes closed again and her voice resumed a restful monotone, deceptively peaceful. 'Anyway, I am reconciled to leaving. So is Redmond. Drumloch is a waste. There is no future in Ireland for anyone. When King William bestowed these lands on Jean Bouchard a hundred and thirty years ago he was giving an empty box. There was nothing anyone could put into it, and nothing to take out.'

A light sweat, shimmering like small diamonds, coloured Lady Janet's brow. Carey stood over her, head bowed solemnly, hands joined behind his back. He contemplated her tone, not her words. The gist he understood totally. Lady Janet had baulked the Bouchard ascendancy and the Huguenot line at Drumloch would be no more. She was after all, he decided, a formidable woman. Her mildest conversation was charged and brittle; he would not like to incur her wrath.

He waited as she lay silent and still, and at last she opened her eyes again. 'The discomfort has abated,' she said. 'You had better see my husband and settle matters.

Appleby's quarters are, I'm told, quite agreeable.'

Excusing himself and calling the midwife back to her side, Carey left Lady Janet and retraced his steps slowly to Bouchard's ground-floor study. As he entered he pulled back in surprise at the sight of Devlin, hollow-cheeked and frightened-looking, standing by the lifeless hearth. Bouchard sat quietly in the comfortable wing-back chair, his flabby cheeks burnished red in the glow of the oil lamp. Before Carey had closed the door he spoke in a voice that lacked masculinity and verve.

'Her ladyship, I take it, is managing quite well?'

'I find no signs of complications,' Carey said. 'I should imagine you can look forward to a bonny boy in two or three weeks.'

Bouchard grunted. 'You. . . .' He paused nervously. 'You found her in good spirits? She talked much?'

'She is not a shy person.'

'True.' Bouchard rose and seemed to privately debate another glass of brandy. 'Devlin wants your advice,' he mumbled over his shoulder. Carey looked into Devlin's wild eyes and the naked fear he saw unnerved him for a second.

'She is unconscious,' Devlin choked. 'Can you come?'

A minute of silence passed. Neither Carey nor Devlin dared to commit themselves further to words. Devlin was shaking in fear and fury and Carey caressed his knuckles tightly until the joints made small audible cracking noises. His back to them still, Bouchard said, 'I think one must see that Kitty Devlin requires immediate assistance.'

'Your lady said – ' Carey began, then ceased. Bouchard was pouring more brandy.

'My wife should not have been horse-riding. I apologise for her stubbornness.' Bouchard twisted towards Carey. 'Go on, do not tarry,' he said. 'I will look after Lady Janet.'

The tremor in Devlin's face died. He pulled himself upright and shoved a hand out to grip Bouchard's arm. The men looked blankly, warily, at each other. 'I thank you,' Devlin said. 'I will repay this blessing.' Then he turned and led Carey from the plush room.

*

One thin scream let Devlin know his wife was still alive.

He sat in the old outbuilding they used to store their potatoes, occupying himself methodically – peeling and soaking tomorrow's ration, washing the grime from his face and hair in the old, cracked wash-hand set deserted there. And all the time the loud rain fell – a powerful tattoo that gouged the earth, drilled the roof and might flood his remaining crops; but he diverted his mind from this; instead, he set his thoughts to the fantasy that was the future, and allowed the water-drumbeat to lull him.

No better world lay ahead at Drumloch. God alone knew what the motives of the next landlord might be, but evidence of a hundred others in bordering counties suggested that he would be a freebooting speculator interested only in investment and profit, caring not at all for the tightrope of poverty that every tenant farmer treaded. The Government was encouraging pasture-farming and he might throw out half his tenants and convert from tillage. If that happened open warfare among farmers would begin. Or he might turn to forestry, or might lease land to his titled friends for building. Whichever way, the farmers would suffer. They needed their potato crop because it was all most of them understood, and it fed them and kept them alive and even helped them earn the few shillings that they had to pay for their land rent and for the tithes that helped support the Church of Ireland, an institution largely believed to be heretical. These oppressive rents and cess taxes the farmers found punitive and unfair but they had little voice against them; the landlords were the demi-gods and the tenants could only pray for one that possessed some traits of humanity. In Redmond Bouchard they had been fortunate enough, but luck comes sparingly to beggars and all believed a new owner would mean real distress, and a fresh tide of poverty. For Devlin himself the prospects of change augured a little better than for his fellow farmers. As middleman, the assumed trustworthy native, he might expect to move to a like position with a new buyer; but that in itself guaranteed nothing. For, if there were no tenants – if the man sold his land for forestry or construction – there would be no dues to collect. Devlin's work would be no work. His lands would go too, and all the selfless labour he had put into developing his plots and decorating his home would be wasted. The earth beneath his feet would be sold, and within twenty-four hours he would be instructed to pull up his potatoes and leave. And where could he go? In a country of eight million people, claimed by the learned to be the most heavily populated agricultural lands in the world – and one of the poorest – hundreds of thousands were landless, workless and starving. Some said there were opportunities up north, in the cottage industries and flax fields; others declared America the place to go, an un-claimed paradise of ample work and full freedom and no taxes (or so said the shipping agent in Portumna); and others again said there was no way out, that the situation country-wide with work and land occupation was just the same, and America was a fools' kingdom.

So all that existed between subsistence and starvation was a landlord's will. And Devlin, like millions of others, lived on that soul-rending knife edge. Some farmers at-tempted to provide for their future by fathering huge families, trusting in filial devotion to sustain them when their crops rotted or their lands were taken away. But such recourse wasn't there for Desmond Devlin. Ten years had given no children and this fruitless marriage seemed to foretell a barren future. If Drumloch was no more, what would there be? – road work somewhere, with a weak wife begging? And if Drumloch survived, if the lands re-mained. . . ?

An hour passed – an hour punctuated by tortured screams that scythed through his body – and nothing changed, only thunder laced the rain.

He fell asleep and woke to find Carey shaking him excitedly with wet hands. 'Come on,' the doctor said. '*Brostaigh*! Quick.'

Devlin hurried after him, head numb with sleep, tripping through the mud and animal dirt. The lights in the cottage were up full, its opaque windows glowing like harvest moons. It looked, he thought insanely, opulent and glorious, like a miniature Drumloch in a fairytale dream. Elbowing in the door after Carey he was aware of many things, unusual things: the glaring light, the scent of sweet lotion like rambler roses, and a heat like the closeness of animal flesh in a packed byre. When Carey moved he saw the straw bed, saw Kitty lying quietly, her face not sweating and her eyes closed. At first he thought she was dead, then he saw the red fullness of her lips and the stir of her heart under the sheet. He looked again. Huddled in a neat bundle beside her, in the crook of her arm, lay a child – a puckered, pink-faced child, expressionless in slumber.

'Alive?' Devlin said, whispering. Kitty blinked, moving her head off the pillow. Carey held Devlin back, gently cautioning. 'Easy now,' he urged. 'She is weak and tired.' Devlin leant over her, kissing her roughly and touching the smooth skin of the babe's face. It fluttered with life under his fingertips. 'A boy,' Kitty murmured. 'A perfect boy.'

'You're all right, *mo chree*?' he asked tersely.

'With sleep and God's grace,' Carey put in, 'you shall have a strong wife and an excellent son.'

The door crashed open, swept in by breeze and the force of a man's hand. Young Cara Duff screamed in fright and Kitty reared up. Devlin jumped round. Two men from Drumloch stood behind him, their cloaks and faces streaked with mud and grass. Their pallor was alarming and Carey put a hand to his mouth as if to stifle a coming shock.

'Our back-to-back lost a weel on the river road,' one of the men gasped. 'I fear we are too late. Lord Bouchard requires you to come urgently. Her ladyship has delivered prematurely – '

'And?' Carey snapped.

'She is dead, sir.'

Devlin crossed himself and Carey blustered out into the night. As he closed the door to the hurrying men he saw that the rain was fading. Not long after, it ceased.

'Now that I see the south for myself,' Samuel Mortimer said, 'I am assailed by confusion.'

Hoar-frost crackled under their feet and their breathing

steamed the morning air as Bouchard led his deceased wife's foster-brother from Drumloch's moss-grown graveyard. The small service, attended in small numbers, had just concluded and Mortimer's coach had arrived at the very moment Lady Janet was being laid to rest. Polite inquiries had elicited Mortimer's firm intention to move on directly; much as he would like to stay a day or so, there were pressing business engagements in Waterford, engagements he had delayed far too long already. Bouchard scarcely knew the willowy, hawk-faced man and a stiffness stood between them. In Newmarket and Belfast it had been easy – the mutual passion for horses – but here a common tie of warmth seemed elusive.

'You prefer Lurgan?' Bouchard said, not greatly interested one way or the other.

'I have never travelled the midlands. I admit some vistas seem unnervingly like hell itself, but I wonder was I hasty in concurring so readily with dear Janet and advising a move. I've seen some pleasant houses down here. Clearly someone believes in worthy prospects.'

'Some do. It's been said the bogs are masked goldmines. Few realise that. After the turf has been worked and used up, new tiers of highly fertile pastureland or tillage ground are exposed. There *can* be profit here, certainly.'

'And room for industry, I'll wager, with all that energetic labour.'

'Maybe.'

They had arrived on the manor forecourt. Mortimer's discerning eye roved the grey stone building, frowning unashamedly at the broken pantiles and wind-pitted pillars. He pulled his sable-collared cloak about him as the breeze sang. Bouchard swept a hand towards the entrance. 'Some refreshment, at least?'

The lean lined face creased into an appreciative smile. 'Deuced kind, but no. We breakfasted at the Coaching Inn in Athlone. But – perhaps – some other time.' Mortimer hesitated as he took a hand up into the carriage. His black brows met in question. 'Tell me,' he grimaced. 'Did you not consider burying dear Janet elsewhere?'

Bouchard looked bewildered. 'Elsewhere? Why, no. Drumloch estate seemed – well, fitting.'

Mortimer seemed to suppress a grin. An evil spark lit his eye. 'I believe Janet hated here.'

Bouchard was devastated. 'No, sir. *Hated*? I really cannot agree. Her moments of unrest perhaps, but – ' He shook his head rapidly so that the fat jowls shivered like jellies. Mortimer concealed reaction: he shook Bouchard's hand and listened to a wary inward voice telling him he must shortly review his image of this passive Irish gentleman. He sat back in the carriage with Bouchard at the door.

'What of Westminster?' Mortimer asked as he gathered rugs about him. 'You still hold the Kent seat and prosper?'

'While Liverpool is in, yes. But I have become rather distanced from events in the political sphere. I have my business interests and, as you will know, political life pays not at all. I may not contest Kent again.'

'The Tories will be disappointed, eh? A family seat moving away from the Bouchards.'

A troubled mist crossed Bouchard's face. He prodded a change of subject. 'And life in Lurgan? Does that excel, as ever?'

'Labour problems never desist.' He puffed his cheeks. 'They talk of labour *force* now, I'll have you believe. Villainous. But I have expanded nonetheless and opened a new factory.'

The carriage horses were shifting uneasily in the intense cold. Mortimer decided an end to the talk. His hands slipped into a muff and he sank back in his leather seat. Bouchard banged the door and the groom released the lead. Mortimer gave a curt wave, and the carriage was gone.

Back in his study, Devlin was awaiting interview with Bouchard. He had been sitting for forty minutes and the smell of raw peat that wafted from his clothes heightened the atmosphere of the small room. He was as conscious of it as was his landlord. Bouchard immediately engrossed himself in a large cigar and a glass of claret. Devlin waited in silence. It struck him as odd that his master's mourning garb allowed for a fashionably gay and colourful stock.

'You came with the land map I requested?' Bouchard started.

'As you say, sir. I have been thorough in my survey.'

'You were fortunate to get some small Dublin education that enabled you to be thorough,' Bouchard wanly smiled.

Unsure of the mocking undertone, Devlin retorted stoutly, 'I was fortunate perhaps that there were still lands to survey.'

Bouchard's grin became grim.

'I was sorry about your wife,' Devlin said swiftly. 'She was . . . she seemed . . . a very strong woman.' That seemed inadequate as an obituary. 'Admirable,' he added.

Bouchard had taken the rolled map from Devlin's hand and stood now by the window, idly perusing it. He said absently, 'They tell me your good lady recovers remarkably well, and the boy is healthy.'

'Indeed. We call him Robert.'

The enthusiasm in Devlin's voice made Bouchard lower the map and beam a smile. 'Robert,' he repeated. 'A name I enjoy. I had a great-uncle Robert whom I remember for his generosity with bon-bons and sweetmeats. I must visit you and look in on this boy.'

'I owe you thanks,' Devlin blurted.

Why are farm folk so damnably predictable?' Bouchard said. 'I considered it an unhappy inevitability that you would associate the successful delivery of your child with my wife's unfortunate death.' His tone became sombre. 'And the link is not as you might believe, I assure you.'

'You allowed Carey to tend to her.'

Bouchard hid his expression behind his claret. 'I misunderstood circumstances perhaps,' he said. 'So many things could have happened.' His lips quivered momentarily, as if with cold. 'We must be thankful the children survived. And your woman too. That is enough.' Devlin fancied he glimpsed some of the passion of that statement in Bouchard's tense posture: as soon as he recognised it, the moment was gone. 'So,' his lordship said brightly, 'I continue to enjoy 1500 acres of potatoes, with some corn, hay, poultry, pigs and turf thrown in. And ninety happy families?'

'Map's the same as last year,' Devlin said. 'But your efforts to get the people to grow corn and keep poultry haven't worked. Why should they bother? It costs them too much in labour and money – and anyway, the more they have, the more tax they pay.'

Bouchard shrugged. 'That is lazy thinking. If they expanded their crops they would be better fed and better off financially. Which, of course, is convenient in its way for me.'

'And what happens when their landlord pulls up the pegs and tells them to shift out? They cannot take corn fields with them. What good has the labour been then?'

'So they do not wish to better their lot?'

'They have no lot, just borrowed ground.'

Devlin's fierce tone sprung Bouchard's ire. 'I know the position, don't try to preach to me,' he smarted. 'I have been liberal with them, never evicting, never penny-counting rents.'

'But now you wish to sell.'

Bouchard calmed, stared impassively.

'This *is* a sale survey?' Devlin asked, pointing to the map.

'That is quite right. A proposed sale survey which I am entitled to carry out whenever and however I desire. After all, these are my lands.'

'So the Crown says.'

The ice in Bouchard's stare melted. He smiled again. 'You are lucky to have me, Desmond Devlin – a fair-minded man. It may now please you to know that – again acknowledging my prerogative – I have decided *not* to sell Drumloch.'

'Not to?' A wave of relief flooded Devlin, making him slump in his chair.

'I am sure that will still the whispering rumour which has been circulating – that Redmond Bouchard has been challenged and bettered by a . . . woman.' His eyes were faraway, fingers flexing hard around the claret glass. 'No, I have reconsidered the value of this land and decided – like my father and grandfather before me – that it is worth retaining. As well as all else, I have a new generation now to provide for. This land will be a sound investment later on, when the Government puts more money into Ireland.' Bouchard grunted smilingly. 'Don't betray yourself by looking so absolutely pleased,' he chided. 'My decision is not solely and entirely for the purpose of spiking someone's memory. I recognise the value of this earth now. But I may not always feel so. Circumstances change and you must face up and accept it now: by tradition this is mine, I can dispose of it when and how I like.'

'Let us not argue the distant future, then.'

Bouchard considered that seriously.

'The tenants will be relieved, and pleased,' Devlin said. 'Just as they are pleased for you now, that you are a proud father.'

Opening a wall cabinet Bouchard withdrew a wine bottle and a fresh glass. He refilled his own goblet and poured a good measure into a glass for Devlin. 'Let us drink then to the new offspring,' he said quietly. Devlin took the wine and raised it.

'And to the memory of your wife.'

Bouchard smiled slightly. He drank, then said, 'Whenever I see your face, Mister Devlin, I shall think of my wife's death and the Williamite heritage at Drumloch. In a wild way, you are part of it now, part of its continuance.' He began tearing up the survey map, throwing its crumpled pieces into the fireplace.

Devlin was unsure whether to be pleased or not. 'We native farm folk have always been part of the heritage, sir,' he said. 'But in a different way than you mean. We belong.'

'I do not challenge that,' Bouchard tipped his glass in toast. In spite of the dark undertones in Bouchard's statements, Devlin's feeling of relief and satisfaction surged. He finished his wine. 'I hope your child grows healthy and true,' he said.

'Child?' Bouchard grinned ironically. 'Then no one has told you?'

Devlin shrugged non-understanding.

'It wouldn't have pleased dear Janet to *die* and leave me an heir. Knowing my frequent unease with females, she would have considered them more appropriate. As life deprived her, so she would smite me.' He paused and looked suddenly overwhelmed by sadness. 'She left me girls – not one, but two,' he said. 'When I die Drumloch may well be theirs.'

He stared squarely to Devlin. 'God save us from women with power,' he said.

PART ONE:

ENGLISH DECLINE
1835 – 1843

CHAPTER ONE

An icily sober Redmond Bouchard sat with his daughters in the carriage that took them southwards, towards the place of their birth. He had not planned a shared sojourn; but the girls' resident nurse-companion at the Lennant Academy for Young Ladies in Ashford had fallen to a sudden apoplectic stroke and he had been forced to reconsider his summer arrangements. The sale of a plot of land on Drumloch's periphery had – because of complications – necessitated his return, and he had hoped to stay for some of the fruits of the salmon season; but the responsibility for the girls, with only Nurse as a buffer, would be a marked encumbrance now. They were strangers to him and would prove awkward at card parties and drawing-rooms and hunts. But, without reliable trained companion, what choices had he? Gloom overtook him. He had posted cards for a Welcome-home at the weekend; that had seemed important after so long an absence. But how could he fairly cope? A dithering servant-maid, a house full of incompetents, two noisy children – *and* this fund of personal troubles.

Conversation was short but the day was glorious and the sun shone on them gently while refreshing breezes from the Irish hills cooled the sweaty discomfort of long journeying. Bouchard had expected the long trip to worry and exhaust the delicate-complexioned girls but, as they rounded the small fir forest that led them within sight of the manor, it was he and not the girls who breathed massive sighs of relief and mopped perspiration from weary eyes.

The girls huddled sleepy-faced but alert on the bench opposite, obediently hushed, their gazes trained beyond the window. From the corner of his eye he surveyed them: Letitia, tall and cream-skinned and intense-looking; and Donna, a graciously pretty child who would grow to beautiful adulthood – the last babe delivered, the one, according to the doctor, who had caused the complications that killed Janet. Of the two, Bouchard guessed, friendship with Donna would be the harder.

Irate, he pushed the notion from his mind. Girl children were time-wasters. How unfortunate Janet had not yielded an heir. And Bouchard was getting no younger. He would have to cast thoughts on that issue soon too. Life was fraught with problems and paradoxes: one wanted an heir, but the process of pursuit was – with the necessary involvement of women – so disagreeable.

Drumloch's small resident staff headed by housekeeper/master Pearson greeted the carriage, effusive in the normal Irish fashion. Bouchard was impressed. They displayed what proper deference should be paid to the Sir, setting sound example for the newcomers. Letitia sidled around, wide-eyed, but when he asked Donna what she thought of her birthplace her stiff, controlled answer was that it reminded her of Lennant without the flag on its roof. Nurse admonished the frostiness of this response, but Bouchard brushed it off. He liked candour, he said. His lie annoyed him. He disliked outspokenness, especially in women. Watching Donna parade through the lofty hall and into the drawing-room, he was sharply reminded of her mother, the iron ramrod of will and ways. Memories rankled. Dismissing Nurse, Bouchard announced his intention of having a brandy in the drawing-room before bathing and sitting to a meal. As Nurse hurried off to help Pearson search out the desired bottle Bouchard found himself for the first time quite alone with his daughters. Both stood by the huge, arched windows, gaping out at the new landscape. Distantly houses could be seen through the forest, cloudy-coloured, cheap buildings.

'They're ranches,' Letitia said, 'for farming folk. But where's the cattle and hens?' Donna shrugged her sister off.

'Those are the homes of some of my tenants,' Bouchard pointed above them.

'They're poor,' Donna said dully, staring straight ahead.

'Not really,' Bouchard answered testily. 'But of course they do not have the resources we possess. That is why I am their landlord and they farm the ground.'

'Where do we play?' Letitia asked.

'There is a nursery upstairs which I requested should be rearranged. We shall see it presently. And there is this – the Doon Lawn and forest. . .'

'Can we go to the far fields?' Donna put in. 'It looks exciting there.'

'I think you will find quite enough to amuse you in the lawns, Donna. Some of the Anderson family children come here to play, I am told. Their papa was once my agent, rest him, and they are good stock – '

'But I like it beyond,' Donna said. 'Where it's wild.'

'It is unsafe. Or unwise, m'dear. The gardens are enough.' Donna was gazing at him, no challenge but a strange gravity in her large eyes. He touched her curls and heard himself stammer. 'However, there is plenty of good space and clean air. You will enjoy it and Nurse will take care of you. You will not be bored.'

'But *why* – ?' Donna insisted. Bouchard overrode her. His brandy had arrived and, annoyingly, he felt badly in need of it. He quaffed the first goblet and poured another. He looked at Donna and saw Janet again.

The similarity once seen lingered in his mind, lasting through supper and beyond. In his dreams the traditions of Drumloch frittered away with a fading smile on Donna's young face until, by the end, she was scowling. He woke in a cold sweat and drank four glasses of brandy before sleep found him again.

Before breakfast next day he despatched Pearson to summon Devlin, and he was relaxing with yesterday's *Times* when the servant tapped at the library door and announced Kitty Devlin. Bouchard fumbled to his feet and invited her in.

The door closed and he stared into the eyes of a

35

frightened doe.

'You have cut some of the breeze from my canvas,' he smiled, 'I'd been anticipating your husband.'

'*Dia dhuit*, sir. Desmond's ailing. His mare threw him last Shrove on the *sliabh* bridge. He's been prostrated since.'

'Good God, I'm sorry to hear of it.' He halted, eyed her from head to toe with some warmth. 'Well, it's been a time since I saw you.'

'Five years gone.'

'Desmond will get better? Who tends my collections?'

'Some of the neighbour farmers helped out. Now Colum, my other lad, looks after it. He sees Mister Halifane, your Dublin attorney, every few months – to deliver.'

Bouchard laughed. 'And he a mere mite! No one told me.' He held a chair for Kitty to sit. She had aged considerably since he had last seen her: the small body was slow and arthritic, it seemed, the once-lush hair silver-flecked. 'I am at a loss,' he said smoothly, 'to face you with my query. It seems unkind, with you burdened by troubles.'

She did not meet his eyes. 'I think I can match your request with one of my own, sir.'

'Really?' Bouchard was on his guard. He sat opposite her on a twin chair of bog oak. She said nothing for many minutes so he began:

'This tithes war that seems to have so unanimous a support from the farm folk is of grave concern to me – not in my official capacity as a parliament member, but as an Irishman and investor in these lands. These Ribbonmen groups that have been wreaking such havoc do no good. I feel *they* should be the concern of all reasonable and law-loving citizens.'

'Why do you address me with this, sir?'

'You know I have upped for purchase the river flat you call the Welsh Fen?' She nodded. 'Its value, I am informed, at current land price is a thousand pounds.' He spread his fingers as if to demonstrate that multitude of pound notes. 'However, because the troubles in neighbouring counties

36

have edged into ours, that valuation is threatened. Already I have lost one potential purchaser outright and the boat-builder who I had been negotiating with through Halifane now suggests a much diminished price. This, there can be no doubt, results from the tax war.'

Kitty's intelligent eyes narrowed towards him. 'You want Desmond to try to prevent any support for the Ribbonmen here?'

'He owes me a favour,' Bouchard said lightly. When he saw Kitty's seriousness he frowned and added, 'And, very earnestly, I *must* see my full valuation on that land.'

'Black Hand O'Tracy still lives in Eyreton. I curse no man, but decry his friendships and his ways.' Her eyes flitted nervously. 'Whatever trouble shadows these lands arises in no home within Drumloch's boundaries.'

'I trust you speak truth. It's wise to damn these devils, you know. And it's not as if the farmers were not getting the power and voice they so long sought anyway. O'Connell has forced the Emancipation Bill. What else do they want?'

Kitty ignored the question. Very coolly she said, 'It is now my turn to feel confused with my question. My request.' She breathed sharply. 'You see, my son has been arrested by the sub-inspector.'

'Robert? But the boy is only what? – eleven, twelve years of age?'

'As your good daughters, sir – eleven years.'

'What occurred?'

'There were gale day troubles. O'Connell is against the principle of Protestant rents. A row started.'

'O'Connell is a misguided fool who scraped into parliament and was lucky to win a little support. Now he charges at every red cloth like a half-blind bull.' Bouchard pounded a fist on the padded chair arm. 'Don't tell me the child got involved in anything sordid!'

'I swear, no. There was a fight on Major Middleton's lands. Black Hand was behind it, they say. My boy was just there.' Her face took on defiant pride. 'Robert knows right from wrong. He has the honour of his own mother.'

'Aye, but that doesn't stop him fighting other people's fights, I suspect. Major Middleton, by God! I'm not surprised the sub-inspector was engaged. I know old Middleton's retired, but I think you were lucky the garrison troop was not called. Rob could then have found himself on the high seas to New Holland.' Bouchard fought back genuine annoyance. During his summer visits to Drumloch over the years he had interestedly watched the progress of the boy, had several times visited the Devlin houshold and had *liked* the child. He stood to pace, turning his grim-set face from Kitty's. 'Surely Desmond's influence and wisdom could have stopped this,' he grunted. 'A mere child!'

'He is to be charged with obstructing lawful collecting,' Kitty said, matter-of-fact, 'but everyone knows his innocence. Children follow Black Hand, his adventurous ways excite them . . .' She hesitated, surprised by her landlord's intense anger. 'Robert is in the Banagher jailhouse.'

'This is an atrocity. I come here at expense and trouble to warn against the influence of the Ribbonmen and their dastardly ways and I am told of a child of the estate imprisoned.' Bouchard took firm hold of himself, breathed quietly for a minute.

'You know the Chief Secretary in Dublin, sir. You could appeal to him – '

'No, no. It need not come to that, I'm certain. I can speak to the Major and the sub-inspector. Argue that the child is no more than a juvenile misled by this O'Tracy villain.' He contemplated in silence, chewing his fleshy bottom lip. Then he turned and levelled a penetrating gaze to Kitty. 'This must be a conditional arrangement. Rob is a good boy, I observe that. Without casting doubts on your rearing, I recognise the pitfalls that he may encounter. I'm sure we must all provide against his fall. I trust Devlin, and one day Rob may be my trusted agent-in-charge – '

Kitty bravely met his gaze but its flinty light confused her. 'What conditional arrangement does your Honour's Sir have in mind?'

'Rob must come into this household. As a surety of many kinds. Here he can be educated and trained in the proper ways. If nothing else, the lad deserves it – a good opportunity for him. Pearson, my master here all year round, is a brilliant and gentle man. Rob can learn under him and later . . . well, later there may be funds for a formal education, in England perhaps.'

'You mean, Rob living with you?'

'As a groom or knife-boy to start with. Pearson can look after him and fix him in Banagher schoolhouse. He may still go to your home, of course, as is his right, but we must train him acceptably to inherit a proper agent's role.'

'What kind of a surety is this for you?' Kitty asked coldly.

Bouchard waved her question away with the sweep of a hand. A smile broke on his face. 'Do not think me sinister, dear Kitty Devlin. I mean surety in the nicest sense. A happy guarantee for us all for the future. Consider it an investment in mutual understanding – for the manor and the tenants.' His eyes bent from her now piercing look. 'Anyhow, it is something I had given much thought to of late. The boy deserves this.' He frowned. 'But let us pray firstly that we can resolve things with the police satisfactorily.'

Without awaiting invitation to rise, Kitty stood. In a calm, smooth voice that riveted Bouchard she said, 'I am confident in the Sir's facility in seeing his wishes obeyed. And I'm sure he'll meet this request if only for the favours he owes me.'

CHAPTER TWO

A blue-backed ant, fired by curiosity and the smell of warmth, crawled through the hills of Nurse's skirts and commenced its climb on the mountain of her bosom. Letitia and Donna sat in the couch-grass of the Doon Lawn and eagerly watched its progress across the sleeping torso.

Donna took a stray blade of grass and poised above Nurse. 'I should take it away,' she said. Letitia pulled her off. 'No,' she hissed, 'wait and see. Perhaps it will crawl into her mouth and down her throat – '

The wise ant didn't; but Letitia was not to be disappointed so easily. Scooping the creature up on a loose page from her picture book, she balanced it gently whilst curling the paper into a funnel. Then, with the measured deliberation of a doctor administering, she tilted the paper and shook it. The ant wriggled free, glittering like burnt honey in the hard sunshine, and fell neatly into Nurse's open mouth. Nurse gave a little groan in her sleep and swallowed obligingly. Donna stifled a cry but Letitia's expression blazed, ordering silence.

'There is a lesson for you,' Letitia whispered. 'Never trust friend or family.' Donna shook her golden hair in distaste, not wanting to hear any more of Letitia's precocious wisdom. It was always this way with Letty – an angel incarnate before her elders, but a creature of swaggering knowledge and sly action when backs were turned. Her manners astounded Donna, who knew herself to be the truly shy one, the cat's-paw puppet who frequently suffered the brunt of her sister's cleverness. It was irritating, humiliating, and Donna knew she must some day rise against her sister's trick-playing.

These thoughts floated through her mind now, succeeded by a sudden burst of single-minded ruthlessness. She faced Letitia:

'Nurse told me Doon Lawn means, "the lawn of the ringfort". The old warriors of Ireland had a stone palace here, she said.'

'A lie!'

'It's true. These are sacred grounds. Kind of. See the broken-down wall there – ?' She pointed to a straggling line of eroded stones that curled round the fir forest and beyond. 'That's the edge of the fosse of the fort. Beyond is the fort building, where there may even be unfound treasure.'

'No.'

Donna was on her feet. She started walking towards the dark trees. The astonishment on Letitia's face, she thought gleefully, was fully ridiculous. The girl was shocked by Donna's outspoken resolve. 'You're not . . . you're not going down there, are you?' she queried Donna. 'Papa made it clear – '

Donna's pace quickened. 'Why not? I might find treasure. I want to see the fort.'

She turned and ran, her heart pumping uncontrollably in her chest, her cheeks stinging red. The stubbly grass of the lawn gave unto thick rye clumps choked with towering nettles that lashed her thin calves, drawing weeping, tickly welts. She flinched, but ran and ran. Behind, in the misty distance, she heard Letitia's wild surrendering call and knew the bait had been taken, but when she glanced back over her shoulder the edge of the forest had crept between them and there was no sight of her sister. She raced in pursuit of a yellow butterfly winging in huge loops from larkspur to thistle, then fear nudged into her thoughts and she stopped to take quick stock. Penetrating silence, the like of which she had never experienced before, settled down round her. She remembered her sister's pursuit and opened her mouth to a full-throated shout:

'Letty! *Letty!*'

The reverberating call drifted on the air, lingering. Then suddenly, with the sharp crack of a trap springing, a rough young voice croaked out of nowhere:

'*Shut up* in the field of the pishogue – or ye'll waken them as well!'

Donna started in fright, blood draining from her face. A small head popped up from a bank of hawthorn – a black-eyed, scrawny-faced gossoon wearing a cut-down frieze 'trusty'. He looked, she estimated, maybe twelve, maybe more. The self-possessed demeanour and harsh look reminded her instantly of older men.

'Field of the pishogue?' She spoke without thinking.

'Fairy-ones, y'know. Silence.'

In spite of herself she stole forward. 'What are you looking at? The fairies?'

The boy crouched in the hawthorn. He did not look away from his task. 'Bees,' he said. 'Free food, if you're willing to take a few wee stings.' Donna craned over to watch. The boy had edged open the top of the hive and was gingerly exploring with two flat sticks, trying to pull out the caked honeycomb. Donna gazed in mute fascination. Only a few uninterested insects floated round the boy's dirtied hands and the hive appeared almost deserted. 'There's some more below,' he said, 'but I think they're swarming, looking for a new home – so I won't get too many pinches.' His tone hardened. 'But they'll have taken lots of honey with them too, so I won't be getting as much of that either.' Donna went to speak but suddenly the boy's movements became jerkily animated. He whipped a slab of something from the hive, dropped it on the ground nearby and quickly pulled a length of muslin across the vanquished nest. The noise of the bees within grew loud and angry. The boy cheered, revealing snow-white, uneven teeth. He fell to his knees to examine his spoils. Donna curled down beside him, full of ardent questions. 'This is for eating,' the boy answered casually, 'and for healing sores and for making medicine. My mama does it all – everything. She knows bees.' Carefully dusting the honeycomb of splinters and leaves, he began wrapping it in cotton. In mid-stride he stopped and looked keen-eyed to Donna – first to her pale face, then down along her fresh-clad body. By contrast his clothing was crude hand-me-down. He twitched his nose. 'You smell,' he said.

'Of bathing lotion.'

The urchin giggled. 'Don't tell me then, Missy. You're rich and you're English.' She smiled and he remembered something he had heard Swan Duff or one of the other grown-ups say, that it was always better to 'brazen out' a woman; so his grin broadened. 'Vis'ter to Drumloch manor, are you? I didn't think there was room in big houses like Drumloch for new ones. Don't they say fifty bedrooms only fit five Englishmen – everyone knows that.' He made an effort to laugh at his joke, but he had aired it too many times before and laughed at it too often. Amused at his body-shaking humour, Donna laughed along. He froze and stared. 'What you want out on the pishogue anyway? If the fairies catch you they'll stew your guts.'

'I'm not afraid. Nurse says all this is my papa's land.'

'Your papa is the Sir, is he?'

Proudly, Donna nodded. 'I was born at Drumloch –' She was gazing, bewitched, into the dark directness of the boy's eyes; 'So I'm really an Irishwoman.'

The boy appeared perplexed. They started walking, out towards a dry-looking potato field populated by a few thin chickens. 'But you couldn't work like an Irishwoman, I bet,' he boasted. 'See this ground? Ten acres – and every bit of it could be sown of a season by Mrs Dwyer and her boy Jack in two days.' He rambled on stoutly for a moment, then said, 'Or maybe three.' Donna chuckled again, and he looked keenly at her. The black eyes softened into friendly warmth. The boy sensed he no longer had to wave his knowledge and good wit like a flag; this idiot girl was impressed. 'They call me Colum,' he beamed, hefting his booty from one shoulder to the other. 'I work the Devlins' farm – my dadda's,' he added in blustering voice.

'You cannot,' Donna replied honestly. 'You're too young, surely.'

'To work? No one's too young for that,' Colum snapped. 'I been working the ground since I were four. Me and me kinda-brother. This time of year there's nothin' on the farms and all the potatoes are gone and we're down to the last of the food. So we go labouring – get road work, building the new road to the coast maybe, or in May and June we work the bogland. That's where I'm goin' today – to earn a bit diggin' for the farmers with big plots, like Anderson, the Irish Prod who lives yonder at valley's edge on the corn farm.'

'But what about school?' Donna gasped, appalled and excited at the prospect of tough, adult living.

'I go sometimes. That's where I learnt to talk English – with help from my dadda. He believes what O'Connell says – that Gaelic is the tongue of the past. There's a school-house on Finnegan's farm, but the master is poorly, so he can't always learn us. Don't matter. You learn more on the turf in the digs than you get from no stupid book . . .'

They had come to the crest of a hill, a rolling ridge that bisected the valley. On either side lay a multitude of lifeless farms, criss-crossed by thin pathways. Drumloch itself winked distantly in the sun. Colum slumped to a seated position in the dirt and Donna stood by him. 'Looks like my honeycomb,' Colum whispered, watching the manor. 'So sweet and tasty.' As if to remind himself of the similarity, he unwrapped his treasure from its cotton and inspected it. 'I captured this from the bees. Maybe one day I'll capture Drumloch from you.'

'You wouldn't like it much,' Donna said. 'It's too cold and too ancient.' She crouched by him, warming to her thoughts. 'But if *I* owned it, it would be different. I would give lots of party balls and have lots of happy children round it. I'd cut down the forest and dig up the Doon Lawn and invite every neighbour in.'

'Huh,' the boy growled. 'I'd chip every stone down and give 'em to the bog workers to build new houses.' He laughed aloud at this new joke. Donna thought of Letitia, somewhere in the forest behind, seeking her out. She suddenly felt wickedly confident. 'I like the freedom of the open fields,' she said, touching the boy's sleeve. 'Take me up to the turfland, let me help you work.'

His eyes were avoiding hers. 'What for? To carry my slane? Or just stand there like an overlord and bring home funny stories for the Sir?'

Colum had sprung to his feet and was staring across the distant plain, a hand cupped above his eyes for shade. His body tensed forward, like a young animal's. 'It's Rob,' he said. 'He's come back. They let him go, then.' Donna followed his vision. Far away, quivering in the heat haze, two figures could be seen moving on foot across the valley fields.

'Who's Rob?'

'Me foster-brother that got taken by the police for nothing more than helping Black Hand talk out agin' Middleton's upping rents.' He grunted angrily. 'But they got the wrong 'un. It was me that was shouting out for Black Hand – but I fled away. And look what they do to poor Rob – lock him in irons.'

Colum turned to Donna, his expression both ironical and questioning. Suddenly Letitia's voice was riding on the breeze, calling her.

'I hate people like you,' Colum said, and he swung his honeycomb across his shoulder, spat, and raced off down the hill towards the far figure of his returning foster-brother.

Transfixed, Donna stared after him until Letitia hurried up to the ridge and flopped down beside her. 'You little witch! I'm all spent of breath. Whatever are you gaping at, you moonstruck idiot?' Donna pointed to the little group and explained her encounter in a few swift words. Letitia clucked indecorously, upset that her sister had uprisen and beaten her to an adventure.

'I want to meet this rascal and his criminal brother,' she said, charged with determination. She ran down the slope in Colum's tracks. Donna watched her go, saw her intercept the strangers and fall in step with them. Knowing Letitia, she would smooth Colum's ruffles and make friends quickly. Donna frowned. Laughter came back to her on the afternoon wind. She steeled herself to say, 'Damn!' quietly, then shook out her skirts and strolled back towards the Doon Lawn.

Two weeks in Drumloch, on the eve of the lavish Welcome-home in preparation under the combined directorship of Pearson and Nurse, Bouchard received young Rob Devlin into his house. The boy came at dinner time, his gaunt and craggy young features showing fair sign of respectful preparation. The black hair was shorn and combed, the thin face scrubbed pink, the overlarge waistcoat and old breeches meticulously dusted. Bouchard admired the boy's sense of propriety and knew it to be real, spontaneous and self-designed; in his visits to the Devlin home since the day the lad could speak, Rob alone addressed his Sir as unchallenged master. Or so it seemed.

Bouchard shrugged inwardly. Perhaps age dulled the senses: perhaps he was seeing only what he wanted to see.

'You caused me a deal of trouble, Rob,' Bouchard began, stout-voiced. 'I was forced to seek a mandate from Dublin Castle in order to persuade your release. I'm not at all sure that Mister McClune, the sub-inspector, has forgiven me. I was obliged to invite him to sup with me tomorrow to try to make small amends and repay his blessing. I am not a man used to compromise and settlement.'

The boy had pluck, and Bouchard admired that too. He spoke out: 'Sir, I admit my fault in being present on Major Middleton's lands when the shoutin' started, but I raised no hand against me fellow man. On God's honour.'

'So.' Bouchard sat before the boy and prodded a large finger into the small chest. 'Do you or do you not support this tax fight, m'lad? Mature and grown gent that you are.'

'I support right, sir.'

'Which in this case means. . . ?'

'Means any sort of trouble is wrong, sir.' The dark beady eyes gazed straight ahead, delightfully imperious. Bouchard rubbed the grin off his lips.

'Tell me, lad. What do you want from your life? You will know what proposals I delivered to your mama?'

'Indeed, sir, I seek an honourable life.' He faltered, swallowing hard. 'And – ' He paused again, the unspoken words building up like engine steam.

'On with it,' Bouchard encouraged.

'And wealth like yours, sir.'

'Well now. Wealth like mine!' Bouchard patted the boy's bony shoulder. 'What would your dear dadda say about that, eh?'

'My dadda believes that ambition is a virtue. He went to Dublin for a time to educate his'self. He said to us, we should do like. He's a farmer, but he says farmers will be beggars in years to come. I want a big house and money, I want other things.'

Impressed with the verve, Bouchard said, 'They're handsome plans, Rob. Fitting for any young buck. And

46

here I intend to allow you some chance to see them through. You will join my house this week, helping in a variety of tasks. We have a small staff, as you may know – the best of them have come from Dublin and Kent. You can learn much from them. You will be turf-boy and groom, helping Tartan O'Neill with the stable. He is very old and ailing, so I will expect compassion and hard work from you. Mister Pearson is master in my absence here. He will lend you benefit of sound experience and a good brain. Next week he will arrange for your schooling at Banagher House, together with his nephews and the rest of the brightest young lads locally. Appreciate that, m'lad, because few get such gilded opportunity.'

'Why me, sir?'

Bouchard's jaw dropped. He clapped his hands. 'Let's side-step impertinence now and begin our habits of good manners early. Yes? I am opening my doors to you. In the past I have engaged your father as middleman because I felt I could invest in him. His silent tongue and straight honesty have proved me correct. Now let me see my intuition proving right again.'

'Sir.'

'In time – who knows – you may come to England with me. There your ambitions might yield fruit.'

'I am honoured, sir.'

There was silence. Rob saw that his audience was over. He barrelled his chest out and took a deft step back, his brogue heel loud-cracking on the parquet. Bouchard halted him. 'One more thing, m'lad. As employee at Drumloch, your loyalties stay here. You understand?' Rob bowed briefly. 'You may move with all freedom and visit your homestead when not labouring, but you must recognise divisions. Farmers may be your associates, but they cannot be your friends.'

Rob bowed again. 'I understand my obedience is to the manor only.'

'You may be ambitious, Rob. You are also wise.'

Leaving the manor by the garden door Rob met Nurse and her charges fleeing a cloudburst that had disturbed their embroidery on the Doon Lawn. Donna ignored him but Letitia trailed behind when the others had slipped indoors and, though he kept his back to her and marched unwavering towards the coach-house, he sensed her skipping after him. The short tug on his sleeve turned him round and he looked shyly into her bold, arrogant eyes.

'You were not up on the high road with the labourers yesterday,' she said. 'You told me you would be.'

He reddened. 'Dadda's abed still. I told you. There were errands to do.'

The bunch of violets in her hands was pushed forward. 'I suppose you will say no to this offering from a lady too?'

He hesitated a fraction, urgently revolving all the master had said in his brain, then reached out and took the bouquet. He stammered out, 'I . . . I refuse nothing a lady graces me with. I – ' He recalled what he had said to Bouchard and the response of naked pleasure it evoked. 'I am honoured.'

'We must play again,' she said. 'Up on the bogland, or with your labouring friends.'

He laughed, then Nurse's call intruded and she was gone.

CHAPTER THREE

Papa looked grand and cruel whenever he dressed in formal clothes, Donna decided. Now he stood before the sisters in the Great Hall, clad in gallant evening dress. In the drawing-room the bustle of final preparations for the Welcome-home was audible.

'I have no inclination to scold you both,' he was saying, 'and anyway I do not know who the true scoundrel is. But if I hear whisper of this again, I will be obliged to return you both to Lennant Academy forthwith.' He slapped the back of one elegant hand into the open palm of another to emphasise the threat of punishment. Letitia looked at him with bold directness; but Donna, largely innocent of the charge but frightened by it, lowered her head in embarrassed shame. Bouchard caught sight of that.

'Am I to assume then that what Nurse says is true? – you have been cavorting with those labourers building the new Athlone road?' His eye fixed Donna accusingly. Letitia curtsied and said in a soft voice:

'I promise, father, I have not been disobedient or disorderly. Both Devlin boys came up to the Doon to speak to –' She paused ' – to speak to both of us. We have been polite and mannerly to them. Have we not, Donna?' Donna nodded, unable to muster the courage to deny Letitia's calm explanation, to pour out the truth of it – that her sister had been enjoying a day-by-day relationship with the Devlin boys that entailed diverse games in the forest and sallies to the bogs and even to the work sites of the new north-south road. It seemed that, whilst Donna's hour of madness had broken the ice, once again Letitia's cleverness was allowing *her* the fun of the waves and eddies beneath. Donna was jealous of Letitia's ease in these relationships, but she had been concealing it carefully, busying herself with reading, puzzle-making and embroidery. And now, for these innocuous pursuits, she was to suffer papa's admonition.

'Do not misunderstand me,' Bouchard said. 'I regard the Devlins and many other of the estate families as kindly folk. But they are our employees, our tenants. I insist on an awareness of correctness and caste.'

'But father –' Letitia demurely started.

'Are you telling me that what Nurse says is wrong? That her informants lied? That you *never* were on the new road site?' Bouchard arched his eyebrows and Letitia hung her head. 'Ah – !' he snapped. 'A confession in gesture. It really is not good enough.' His eyes were again on Donna. 'I warned you. I have no objection to your association with the likes of the Anderson children. They have property and position and excellent lineage and friends in Dublin.'

From the tail of her eye Donna saw Letitia's smug half-grin. Suddenly her blood boiled and before her father had ceased speaking she exclaimed, '*I* have nothing to be ashamed or apologetic about. Nothing!'

Bouchard regarded her through narrowed eyes. 'Very well, my dear ladies,' he said, still addressing Donna. 'As you obviously need a time to consider the error of your judgement, I must confine you to your chambers for twenty-four hours. Beginning now.'

A grunt of annoyance escaped Letitia's lips and Donna drew herself up. 'It's not fair, papa. I . . . we did nothing *wrong*. How can conversing with people be a sin? Please – tonight is our first evening's entertainment since we arrived in Ireland. I wanted – '

With a firmer resolve Bouchard raised both hands. 'I'm sorry, then. What *you* want cannot be. I expect obedience.' He looked at Donna's fury and saw Janet. Brusquely he turned away from the children. 'I will ask you to consider: ignorance must listen to wisdom, and women must listen to men. That is the way of life. Down every other avenue there lies only trouble. Goodnight to you both.'

It quite shocked Bouchard that only Letitia wept; but on reflection it did not surprise him: whatever intensity pervaded Letitia's character Donna could match with hidden strength.

The guest list for the dinner party had expanded astoundingly. Large nearby estates would be represented by Major Middleton, Squire Stephens and possibly one or two others; professional society by Doctors Carey and Appleby and the Reverend Jacey-Fox; some of the military garrison people had been invited; and Halifane, Bouchard's Dublin-based attorney, had foisted on two special guests – possible purchasers of the Welsh Fen. To these was added sub-inspector McClune, the canny and hard-hearted Scotsman who, despite his rank, had undiminished control of the police-agents between Drumloch and Shannonbridge. Though Bouchard had only made the sub-inspector's acquaintance a year ago and actively renewed it so recently in the incident with Rob, he had no doubts that the Scotsman despised him with earnest vehemence. In McClune's eyes,

Bouchard believed, he was an officious and pompous cad who used his waning political swing like a battering-ram. A warm invitation to a dinner party would not necessarily neutralise that, Bouchard felt, but it could do no harm.

As the guests arrived and he received them in the drawing-room Bouchard could not but help notice the chilliness of McClune's greeting, a mood perpetuated by the subsequent arrivals of Major Middleton and two lieutenants from the garrison. Clearly word of recalcitrant associations with trouble-makers had passed around. After these, it was with honest pleasure that he greeted the first of Halifane's discoveries – a Frenchman called de Doubalier, in company of his daughter, Alexandrine. De Doubalier, it seemed, was in Ireland principally to speculate on investments in canal developments and railroads. Bouchard instantly liked the man, liked the smell of wealth that seemed to surround him, and he extended a profusely warm welcome. Most red-blooded men would dearly have liked to welcome de Doubalier's daughter with open, eager arms.

Just as dinner was announced, Halifane arrived belatedly with his second prospective buyer, the American Mrs Cabbot, widow of (according to the attorney) the renowned construction engineer. Bouchard took his place at the table and found himself facing de Doubalier's daughter. Alexandrine was a large-breasted girl with a graceful neck and slanted eyes that reminded one of an antelope. She sat resplendent in a saffron-yellow dress of shimmering silk, making polite conversation with verbose Squire Stephens and his diminutive wife. Bouchard found his own eyes, like the eyes of so many men around the table, seeking her out from time to time. He was attracted to her, to the generous breasts, the masculine strength of her French-toned voice, and her dimpled smile. Many men could desire this woman for many things. She had grace, intelligence, conversational charm and humour and a positive presence that assured you she was not a fake. Bouchard promised himself a talk with her later.

While the Reverend Jacey-Fox effectively splintered the table talk by absorbing himself in rapt chat with the Major,

51

McClune and their womenfolk, Bouchard turned to the American woman on his right. Josephine Cabbot had the appearance of a robust ornament, with pallid leathery skin and grotesquely doll-like features. She sported petticoats of grassy green and a band of thick emeralds above the lace ruffles of her bodice. Bouchard suspected some Irish heredity and questioned her about it. The upright old lady was amused by this keen observation.

'True indeed,' she drawled, 'though indirect. I had Irish great-aunts, but my stronger call to this emerald isle comes from my dear deceased husband's family.'

'Your husband was a notable engineer?'

Mrs Cabbot detected and disdained her host's ignorance. A deep-set frown puckered her brow. 'Theo was *the* foremost construction designer, sir, known worldwide. Some of the great engineering problems of the last ten years were solved by him alone. Concrete inlaying for railroads across mire, iron stressing on free-standing buildings, the suspension bridges – ' She barked out the achievements, slapping fingers against the table top in a most unladylike fashion. Bouchard shot a glance to Halifane, who smiled without humour.

'My husband's mother, bless her, was Irish – from outside Ballinderry, a mere pitch from here,' Mrs Cabbot was saying. 'The enduring bond he felt all his later life has passed on to me. I'm a traditionalist as much as anything else. Hence, my mellow years imminent, I seek a property or land for building near the Shannon, near the cradle land, you see.'

For some reason Bouchard could never imagine this hard little woman in 'mellow' mood. Neither could he imagine himself as neighbour to formidable Mrs Cabbot. His glances towards Halifane became critical and grave.

'You travel alone?' he asked her.

'No. With my son, Paul, and a scatter-brained daughter called Emma. But for all that, I might as well be alone. Tonight Emma has a minor fever, so chooses to lie in in our hostel at Athlone. Paul supervises.' She craned forward conspiratorially. 'Emma is quite useless, but Paul might prove good. You see, someone must take the reins after me. The Lord knows I have carried the weight. Too long.'

'You interest yourself in the business end of things?'

'Sir, I was fifteen years my husband's book-keeper and organiser. Without me – ' She waved a dismissive hand. 'I was the one who turned his talent to fortune. I was the one who guided a solitary genius towards the acclaimed financial success of Cabbot Industries. First, by establishing reputation in construction in out-of-the-way, pioneering areas – areas where others shied away, fearful of profit losses. We built, sir, wherever people wanted building. And five years ago I saw the rise of the railroad concept of communication, so I insisted on investment in iron foundries.' She jangled her heavy jewels. 'I bless and recognise my deceased husband's talents, but I am sensible enough to see how *I* contributed. Today I alone direct Cabbot's contracts, but at sixty-two there is tiredness.'

Bouchard tensed as Halifane leaned forward to say, 'Mrs Cabbot has already inspected the Welsh Fen. She insisted on doing so before we came, since the evening was fine and the light good.'

'You . . . like what you saw?' Bouchard asked.

'Too small, too low-lying,' Mrs Cabbot promulgated loudly. 'Not good land.' Bouchard shuddered as the Frenchman de Doubalier swivelled to regard their group. 'I appreciate its nearness to the Shannon – a requirement I insist on – but the acres are not attractive and building on soft ground entails injections of concrete and difficult hammer-packing.' She shook her head adamantly. 'However, I like this house. I would buy here.'

There seemed only one way to answer that: Bouchard laughed; but the hairs on the back of his neck crawled in indignation and his fingers beneath the table laced tensely. Blethering women! Problem was, they never knew their place.

'At times I think the world wishes to lure Drumloch away from me,' he said politely. 'But the greater the attempt at seduction, the more I resist.' He grinned. 'Though Squire Stephens's might, by chance, be for sale.'

Stephens, at Bouchard's other elbow, turned to answer the charge. Bouchard enjoyed his neighbour's derangement – all the more so when Mrs Cabbot rejoined enthusiastically to say that she had seen the Squire's estate house and, despite its *dilapidated* countenance, quite admired it. The Squire's plum-blotched old face displayed alarm. 'Dear lady, Fork Estate would be unfitting for you, back of nowhere, by God – '

'I am accustomed to far-flung locations,' Mrs Cabbot persisted. 'For a creature who survived fiteen months in Michigan, I assure you, Ireland is lavish and socially grand.'

'I have three hearty sons and a contented wife to account for,' Stephens returned, 'so I must withdraw whatever offers my good neighbour has been making, regretfully.'

Everybody laughed, but Mrs Cabbot was serious. 'I may not succeed on this trip, but in time I shall procure that ideal property. They say it is a buyers' market now – but that is not my experience here. It seems I shall have to try harder.'

Bouchard was relieved when the meal ended and the groups retired to the drawing-room. He found himself in conversation with de Doubalier. The Frenchman's talk was intelligent and informed and Bouchard quite gladly joined in comparisons between the recent progress of French history and Irish events. Though the Frenchman's health was not good – he suffered chronic heart spasms – his mentality was keen and youthful.

Several de Doubaliers had died by Louis's side but he fled to England, abandoned his religion, and married a Scotswoman and, in 1810, Alexandrine was born. In 1830 revolution in France drew him back to Paris and, with the proclamation of Louise-Philippe as 'King of the French by the grace of God and the will of the nation', and the establishment of a safe and acceptable monarchy, he decided to stay on and rebuild the de Doubalier line. His cousins had joined in and, despite set-backs, he could cheerfully report to Bouchard that France was at last succumbing to peace. But, in his view, no such peace lay ahead for Ireland.

'Respectfully,' he began, 'the peasants and farmers here have a far heavier load than ever the non-nobles had in France. But the basis of their unrest, I judge, is similar – they are deprived of privileges here, just as the non-nobles were denied access to high offices in state and church. That in itself might be enough, but there is also this heavy taxation and reports of military suppression – no?'

'Much is exaggerated,' Bouchard said. 'The talk of subversion and unrest I hear is pure nonsense.' The lie echoed in his own ear.

'Do not think I accuse *you* of any misdeed, friend – either in your parliamentary capacity, or as member of the gentry. You – like me – inherited a situation in which, under God's very eye, all we could do was temper conditions, wait and hope. No? But what I see in Ireland distresses me greatly. My friends in London encourage me to come, saying how fruitful investments could be with the new roads and waterways. They say the Emancipation Bill has appeased the Catholics and all is well.' He paused to sip port. 'I see it all, and I see none of it. It seems to me the Irish are burning and O'Connell is driving them on.' De Doubalier squinted at Bouchard, conscious of implied criticism. 'A recently acquired mutual friend, Sir Myles Rossitor, tells me you speak of retirement from public life? Do you contemplate retiring fully to here?'

'Since Wellington abnegated power, these last five years, I do not think one might describe my career as *active* public life. Maybe I am growing old, but the thinking of these modern times goes beyond me. Many of the Tory ideals I grew up with have dissipated and faded. My belief in the *status quo* seems somehow no longer fashionable. I still hold my seat in the lower house but, I sadly confess, it is friendships that have really kept me there.'

'You dislike political life now?'

'Oh, I like it well enough,' Bouchard hurried a laugh. 'If for nothing else, its associations assist my stock market games. Ideally one should achieve the respectability of politics before dabbling in the pirate world of business.'

De Doubalier joined the hearty laugh. 'So you will keep a finger in the business pie and retire to charming Drumloch?'

'Why not, I suppose? I have the happy distraction of a good court life in Dublin – well-placed friends and the like. I inherited this –' He spread his arms for emphasis, 'just as I inherited my Tory seat, and why should I not keep them? That is the basis of my thinking, I confess. As for this alleged unrest in Ireland, well, the people now have more than they ever did. And with the Education Act and the work of Peel's State Commissions, their lot will gradually improve. *I* have no objection to that.'

'Yes,' de Doubalier agreed, 'but like the *roturiers*, their lot will improve so much and then they will want their fair share of *this*.' He crashed his boot on the floor.

Bouchard shrugged. '*This* is a Williamite inheritance. Mine alone, I assure you. And mine in a hundred years.'

De Doubalier's heavy expression softened and he looked over Bouchard's shoulder. 'Anyway,' he told Bouchard, 'you are still a businessman, like me. A businessman always has a second home. A spiritual home.' Bouchard's eyebrows raised. 'A good investment is a good home,' de Doubalier grinned.

A swish of silk turned Bouchard's head. Alexandrine excused herself and stood over her father's chair, massaging his thin shoulders. '*Mais non, chéri*,' she chided, 'I hear you talking business and that means I hear you worrying. Please – tonight is for relaxed talk, and new friends.' Her dark eyes shone into her host's and his pulse quickened.

'Ignore me,' de Doubalier said. 'Go on – find some profitable enterprise. Look. They're beginning to dance inside. Ah – and they are not the barbarians they try to make themselves seem.' He winked cryptically to Bouchard. 'Go on, my lovely.'

Alexandrine hesitated and Bouchard heard himself say, rather coyly, 'If my excellent guest will allow me his daughter's company. . . ?'

'By all means, dear fellow. Go. Go.'

With cumbersome care Bouchard led Alexandrine out to

the parquet apron of the pianoforte and, wrapped in the heady scent of her body, he gripped her firmly round her strong waist, leading her into a smooth waltz movement. The music was gentle and accurate and they danced on the edge of the apron. Alexandrine allowed her body rest into him, but her head remained erect and away from his and, without looking, he knew she was regarding him in a cautiously appraising way. At length she said, 'Squire Stephens suggests there is some small mood of *déplaisir* present this evening.'

'Why should there be, pray tell?'

'Major Middleton hints that you sympathise with the agitating farm folk – that you had arranged a house sale some years ago and cancelled it to support some farmers and stop the threat of a forestry takeover; that you are a friend in London of the Liberator O'Connell; that you employed a young criminal in your household –'

'What balderdash!' he protested. 'I'll hear no more. I shall have to take the Major aside and explain myself to him. None of these accusations are true.' Bouchard reflected worriedly: Middleton was no valuable enemy; his wealth and sway were much respected in Dublin, his kinship with the former viceroy known.

'This criminal employee – ?'

'A bright and energetic lad, no more. And from good reports, the "criminal" incident you speak of was rather less than that in the first place. Certainly I effected the child's release, since he is son of my estate middleman; but criminal? – no. I cannot see myself, I assure you, as noble redeemer of prodigal souls.' There was genuine dismay in his voice.

When she did not speak for a time he thought it better to change the subject. 'You will stay long in Ireland?'

'I doubt that. My father's hopes have yielded little. Conditions, he feels, are not compatible with investment in his field.'

'He has seen my Welsh Fen?'

'Not yet. But his interest in transport development along the River Shannon is reduced by the knowledge that there is already a barge service from the upper loughs and the existing canal traffic in the midlands is poor, so a possible new canal would seem superfluous.'

Bouchard nodded glumly. 'Then perhaps you would not accept my hospitality for another few days?'

'The invitation, I'm certain, will please my father. But I know he has commitments for next week. I myself enjoy what I see of this land and would like to travel more here. Though I cannot admit,' she added darkly, 'I would much care to spend a lifetime.'

'There are jollier places on earth,' Bouchard suggested agreeably. 'But do not judge too soon. Do not allow rumour to quell your interest or enjoyment. I have a happy relationship with my farmers. Remember there are two sides to many stories. One must see that whatever has been said to you tonight could well have been sparked by a green spot of jealousy. Jealousy from those who enjoy less settled peace.'

'Maybe,' Alexandrine said uncertainly. 'But perhaps you are a trifle casual about your status here, may I venture. One must never be seen to weaken.'

Bouchard covered the surprise he felt. Alexandrine's candour might easily have been insulting, but her innocent-faced admissions were somehow only intriguing. He felt as if he were speaking to a wise, experienced friend and the warm, distracting pressure of her body nullified any sense of challenge. He boldly remarked on the incisive strength of her thinking. Alexandrine smiled. 'I accept the compliment,' she said.

'Then I accept your wisdom,' he replied. 'Perhaps I have been away from Ireland too long. I shall ruminate tonight on my relationships here. Work more at the friendships, and perhaps play a little stronger as overlord – '

'Do not ruminate tonight. Tonight is for pleasure – ' Her breasts crushed demandingly into his chest and he held her tighter.

The music was about to cease and Bouchard to speak again when, like the explosion of a cannonade, a massive jagged rock crashed through the casement windows and

58

slid across the polished floor. A chorus of screams – not all female – soared. The pianoforte hit a flat C and died. Aghast, Bouchard released Alexandrine and moved towards the gaping window. As he did Alexandrine mumbled out a warning. Before the words registered, the rattle of shattering glass rang out and, in quick succession, a flight of stones pounded into the room. Bouchard jerked back as fast as he could but a shard of glass caught him full-face and scalding blood burnt his eyes. He staggered, tripped backwards. Another blow hit him – a rounded rock this time, grazing across the forehead. Alexandrine cried out and he heard her voice clearly and felt her protecting arms embrace him.

The blood was salt in his mouth and his vision was gone. Then consciousness ebbed.

CHAPTER FOUR

She was dressed in pearl-white and the colour somehow lifted his spirits.

'The doctor's gone,' Alexandrine said. 'I hope you do not consider me too improper and impudent. We have been worried, my father and I.'

She sat by his bed, tense with concern. Bouchard tilted his head so that his right eye could observe her. The left was, as it had been for twelve hours, bandaged and blind. Doctors Carey and Appleby had said they believed the pupil itself was perforated and quite possibly destroyed. His lordship must prepare himself for that, and later today must transfer to an eye surgeon's in Dublin. The best Fitzwilliam Square practitioners must try their tricks; but optimism was inadvisable.

'I feel quite numb,' Bouchard said, his voice slurred with too much brandy. 'I apologise to your father and to you for this appalling ordeal.'

Like goosedown, Alexandrine's warm hand encompassed his. In a firm voice she said, 'Think not of us. We are just filled with regret for you. Everyone was so distressed. Mrs Cabbot fled immediately, though *vraiment*, I fancy she was the least alarmed.'

Bouchard's fingers closed lightly on hers and he drew strength from her strong hand. 'McClune still claims it was the tithes fighters, does he?'

'Those are the words I heard.' She paused. 'You doubt that?'

'I am recalling all you yourself recounted last night,' he said gravely. 'The dissent among my neighbours.'

'You have refused the sub-inspector permission to interrogate tenants on this estate? Is that because you believe . . . someone else responsible?'

Bouchard washed the tacit accusation aside. 'I denied McClune because I saw the fire in his eyes. He is out for blood in his campaign against these so-called Ribbonmen. Any excuse befits him.' His voice diminished. 'Perhaps he seeks my blood too – but I will not be ordered about like a beggar.'

'Major Middleton explained much to me. He and other landowners have increased rents in recent weeks. He suggests this assault could be warning of sorts for you.'

'I am numb,' Bouchard repeated. 'I do not know what I believe to be true. I trust my tenants. Maybe I have been a fool to be so trusting.' He shook his head miserably and looked at her. 'I am an old fool too used to the calm order of sedate London. *You* would have me employ a new tough agent and fortify my high position and live in Westminster – no? Perhaps you would advise me to abandon here?'

For a moment he thought the naked directness of his question had frightened the girl. She lowered her head and spoke, addressing her hand entwined in his. 'If you did me the honour of asking, sir, I should advise nothing other than prudence. A gentleman like you deserves a distinguished and untroubled existence.'

At that moment a shallow knock came, and the maid directed de Doubalier into the chamber. Bouchard saw the man walked now with his stick and, despite the warmth of the sun through the opened window, his face looked drawn and grey. De Doubalier gratefully took a chair. He thanked Bouchard for the overnight hospitality and expressed profound regret at the sad happenings. Then he hurried on to say that he must leave this afternoon and return to Dublin. One day's survey had been enough, coupled with the interesting facts he had gleaned from the estates' agents and businessmen he had met in the midlands. He had decided there was nothing for him in Ireland. New development on the canal or Shannon would be premature and the restless rumours of growing rebel trouble discouraged him. It was unfortunate, but the prospects for Ireland boded evil.

'Perhaps you do yourself an injustice,' Bouchard said. 'You have been here so short a time. Allow a day or two more to judge. Please. I would be distressed to think that this gross deed further tainted your image of this land. As a Frenchman you well know – we live in violent times. We accept a kind of permanent danger.' He sighed. 'Though I confess I personally have experienced nothing till this.'

De Doubalier pressed Bouchard's arm in a fraternal way. 'I envy you your good faith, *mon ami*. I admire you. But we cannot impose – '

Alexandrine smiled agreement.

'You do not impose, I assure you. Please stay. You give comfort to a depressed spirit.'

'Depressed, but not defeated,' de Doubalier said. 'You are rich and victorious in all things, sir. You are a gentleman.'

*

The stone which the builders rejected
The same is become the head of the corner
Whosoever shall fall upon that stone shall be broken
But on whomsoever it shall fall, it will
grind him to powder.

Opposers to social order like the elusive, far-spread Ribbonmen, it was said, found Divine encouragement in God's bible. Desmond Devlin sat reading Luke and remembered the impassioned speeches of Black Hand O'Tracy up on the bogland, decrying landlord power and imploring aggressive resistance to tax and rent increases. Black Hand, tenant of a neighbour estate, was Major Middleton's worry, but the growth of his influence transgressed mere physical boundaries and affected every farmer. Devlin, at heart a peace-loving man, found laden clouds of unease darkening his thoughts.

He closed the old yellowed bible to drink water from a china cup, one of the few passed on to him, chipped and aged, from Drumloch's pantry. Then he stood to walk, to assess the stiffness in his legs that the fall four months ago had brought on. After a dozen steps his knees became weak and he crumpled back into his chair by the cold grate.

From the low door that gave on to their bedroom Kitty observed her husband's collapse. She bit back the anguish that rippled through her own body.

'Where's the boy Rob? I did not see him last night. I was asleep before he returned from the manor.'

'He left shortly after dawn. There was work to be done in the forge this morning,' she said proudly. 'The toil excites fair enthusiasm in him.'

'And Colum – where is he?'

Kitty's muscles tensed. She seemed always to be acting in the foster-child's defence. Almost angrily she said, 'He is all right, Desmond. He has chores to do.'

'Schooling? I'll wager that comes low on his list. One day a month is not good enough, you must see.'

'Do not worry for him.'

'I worry because I hear dangerous rumours. I can guess the truth of what was behind Rob's arrest. Colum's young eye lights to the adventures of Black Hand and his sort. *He* led the lad there, I am certain. And now there has been trouble at Drumloch manor. The sub-inspector blames renegades and Colum is intrigued.'

'He is an impressionable boy, full of dreams.' But she cautioned, 'You must not be unfairly suspicious of him.'

'I know the legends and stories of fosterage, woman. I

know how a boy can grow with twice the cunning and half the heart. Colum lacks something in his small world – there is a passion which is fanned by jealousy of Rob's position, not only in the home but now in the manor.'

The kitchen door swung and Colum edged in, crooked under the weight of a sack of summer-dried firewood. He lowered it by the hearth, unspeaking. Devlin glanced out at the sun shadow on the flags beyond the door. It was gone midday, he saw. Colum sat opposite him, wheezing. 'You want some bread?' Kitty asked. The boy shook his head. Devlin stared at him with inward-looking eyes. Colum saw the abstraction. He stood up, crossed to the water bowl and scooped out a drink. He looked back at Kitty, seated across from Devlin. The room was silent, odourless, bleached and warm in the sun. He was not wanted here. 'I can go get some bream from the river seller,' he said.

Devlin did not reply but Kitty smiled her motherly smile and nodded. Colum sauntered out into steamy sunshine and ran. Down through the black-earth potato plots, skipping the wild-grass pathways, veering away from the hunched cottages. Ahead lay the meadow and forest that were Drumloch's garden and, like azure satin beyond, wound the river. The farms around were vacant, their tenants departed for road work many miles away since early dawn. Only invalids and their nurse folk lingered and they, like dadda, sat indoors to hide from the tantalising heat of the sun.

Colum's pace slackened. Ahead, sitting in the shade of the fir trees that screened the wing of Drumloch, sat a girl. As he drew closer, he saw it was Donna. Closer again, he saw she was talking to someone and as the screen of trees opened up he recognised his foster-brother. Instinct told him to turn away but in another second or two both Donna and Rob had spied him. Rob was propped on an elbow, looking clever and mature. Donna smiled from beneath shimmering gold curls as he approached.

'Letty's gone,' Rob said unhappily. 'Angry at me 'cause I said I knowed what man smashed her papa's house, and it weren't Black Hand. It were the Major's men, vexed 'cause the Sir got me out and engaged me. They say the Sir won't play the game – so let him feel what real trouble is.' He frowned. 'Letty didn't like that. I don't think she cares for the rebel folk or anyone who knows them any more.' He was watching Colum closely. 'She won't speak *to you* again.'

Colum eyed Donna. He was surprised this quiet girl had stayed to listen to outspoken Rob. But a new look, a look of hard defiant strength, coloured her lovely face. Rob seemed mildly vexed that the girl was showing so little reaction to his blunt assertions. Donna set her attention firmly on Colum. 'I am leaving Drumloch today,' she said. 'Papa is quite well again. We must sail for England.'

'Enjoy your journey, then,' Rob said, rising up to pull on the groom's jacket Tartan O'Neill had loaned him. 'Perhaps we shall meet again across the water in fair England.'

Without a backward glance, Rob made for Drumloch. Colum turned to follow him but Donna's words held him back.

'Papa said people like you and us should never be friends.'

Expressionless, he turned to her. 'Does he now?' he said, almost in a growl. 'And you'll obey him, of course?'

'He says you are our manservants and we must keep apart. And he looks at me, as if I intend to ignore his wishes. But I do not. It is Letitia who is your friend, not me.' Her eyes drifted off. 'Papa hates me,' she said.

Colum approached her, moving close. 'Your papa is not to be disobeyed,' he said. Donna looked up. His eyes, she saw, were grey-speckled, like a bird's egg. His breath was sweet. 'So we cannot be friends,' he said. His arms moved quickly, surrounding her. One hand clamped fiercely on her bottom, tight enough to hurt. His mouth pressed onto hers, hard and wet. As quickly, he pulled away. The muscle of her backside stung and her lips instantly felt swollen.

'Do you still hate me?' she said, breathless.

'With all my heart,' he shouted, and he ran.

CHAPTER FIVE

The further few days de Doubalier proposed to stay on had become a few weeks and, apart from Bouchard's temporary removal to Dublin and hospital, the new friends spent much time together while, under the Frenchman's careful eye, the relationship between Alexandrine and their host grew deep and solid. Everyone seemed appropriately surprised and pleased at this development, none more so perhaps than Bouchard himself. In Dublin an eye surgeon's assiduous endeavours established sadly that, because of damage to the retina and lens, it was probable that the impaired left eye would remain permanently blurred to the point of blindness. When the Frenchman called in his hired carriage to collect Bouchard at Fitzwilliam Street and the news was conveyed, Alexandrine wept and, despite himself, Bouchard was profoundly touched and felt overwhelmed by desire to embrace and soothe her. He did so, and her father nodded his approval.

They spent four days in Dublin, and wined and dined in the splendid Merrion Square houses of London-based associates. The former Chief Secretary treated them to a gala evening at his Stephen's Green town house and, wherever possible, Bouchard introduced de Doubalier to businessmen friends whom he guessed might proffer worthy advice for the Frenchman's plans.

On Bouchard's insistence de Doubalier stayed on till the beginning of August and an arrangement was made for both families to return to London together. On the morning of their planned departure from Drumloch, de Doubalier took breakfast with Bouchard on the terrace that looked towards the Shannon, and made a proposition.

He began warily, 'No matter what future acquaintances may say about me, I am not an excessively wealthy man.' Bouchard did not believe that, but nodded co-operatively. De Doubalier went on, 'Single-handed I have re-established my family in our beloved land, and that has cost me more than a little, I assure you. But – ' He winked and tapped his nose, 'I have a sense for good business and I seek it out. I have excellent banker and business friends. My experience and advice has proven invaluable to them and they, in turn, have profited from my sagacity.'

'And do you suppose Ireland to be unready for your investments?' Bouchard joined.

'As you know, trans-shipping, the conveyance of travellers, hostels – these have been my concerns. Initially Ireland looked like a suitable fertile field, but the problems are many, not least of which being the government control on such developments as canal building.' He spread his hands. 'Alas, but that is how it is. But there are many other promising markets open to me now. My friend the celebrated genius Sequin in France is following Stephenson with steam rail inventions and work is afoot with tubular boilers for lines from Orleans to Lille and Marseilles. An investor there – in either design or construction – will earn a fortune, believe me. And I know many.' He smiled with a look of satisfied wisdom. 'You may even be looking at one now,' he beamed. 'But I am certain,' he continued, 'fortunes are to be made in advanced transport systems. I have recommended many to Sequin. But equally I am recommending my friends to steamship investment.' He paused to guage Bouchard's reaction. Encouraged, he pursued:

'Fulton is not alone in his passionate confidence in steamboats. With the success of the scheduled run of the Canadian *Royal William* there is a burning interest in development in England. The Atlantic crossing is easy. That is well proved. What we need now are faster vessels with larger engine capacities. A man called Cunard in America is talking about steam postal service. Napier, the designer, is at present working on advanced cutwater bow designs. The possibilities are limitless and the field wide open. And a few shrewd men are forming companies to invest in genius.'

'In genius?'

'To foster development,' de Doubalier enlightened. 'To pitch one's pennies in with people like Napier or Sequin.' He paused. 'I know many such investors.'

'And you would advise your good friends to pitch in too?' Bouchard was guessing what was coming, squirming uneasily in his chair. If the Frenchman wanted a well-heeled supporter, he was drifting on the wrong tack. The Welsh Fen was to be sold at last to a river vendor who wanted sheds for his boats – but the price Halifane had wangled was an unsatisfactory eight hundred. What great bounty would de Doubalier see in that?

'You are too swift for me, *mon ami*,' the Frenchman laughed. 'Yes, I suggest you – and whatever worthy acquaintances you have – invest. Moreover, I suggest – if you will excuse my candid approach – that you invest in *my* company. The Liverpool First Steamship Company. We have brilliant design men and cunning accountants and we recognise the one challenge: that people want to get from place to place faster and faster. The Atlantic trip has been done in twenty days. If it can now be achieved in fifteen, we have made ourselves millionaires!' He ceased speaking but Bouchard said nothing for a time, just gazed unblinkingly at him. Mindful of the danger of insulting his new friend with so direct a proposition, de Doubalier quickly made it clear that it was for Bouchard's benefit alone that the notion came to mind, that on hearing of his unfledged intention to leave political life and concentrate on business it had seemed opportune to speak of expanding concerns.

'How much of an investment would you suggest?' Bouchard asked thoughtfully.

De Doubalier became openly candid. Very genuinely he confessed that the First Steamship Company *needed* an investment of hard cash, that innovative design work was eroding the working fund and, while breakthrough ideas were on the drawing-board, finances were desperately needed to allow practical research. Given the opportunity he would offer and advise a partnership deal for his friend, but he had already entered into a three-way partnership, so some difficulties were obvious there. The next best alternative would be – from both their points of view – an interest-free loan now from Lord Bouchard with a *pro rata* share in profits of the company over an agreed period of time. 'I absolutely guarantee you,' de Doubalier said, 'that the projected profits are far greater than any proportionate accrued interest.'

With a frown of discomfort Bouchard said, 'My dear fellow, I do appreciate your generous offer and it intrigues me – '

De Doubalier interjected persuasively, 'It would be wise, I'd venture, to invest *away* from Ireland just now.'

Bouchard ignored that. 'But I am not a very wealthy man myself. Only some months ago a banking firm I had interest in came undone and I lost quite a bit of finance. Quite a bit. Naturally I am eager to fill that gap, but – '

'Then allow my maturer experience to help you do so,' the Frenchman begged. 'Trust this,' he said, tapping his slender nose. 'It will lead you back to the road of generous profits.'

'But – '

'Come, friend,' de Doubalier laughed, spreading an arm to illustrate the fine silver and glass of their breakfast table. 'Do not pretend you have so little treasure in your bank vaults, eh?'

Bouchard was reflecting seriously on his banking position, on the problems with Hedgeleigh, with gambling debts. But the Frenchman's proposition was twinkling like a bright star in the bleak darkness. With a titled name and sound friends and a seat in parliament there were always ways. . . .

Quaffing his wine, Bouchard decided suddenly. 'Very well then, consider me convinced. Let me see my banker in Dublin *en route* for Kingstown and discuss this loan.' He lapsed for a moment, remembered Alexandrine, remembered the pervasive thoughts of the last few weeks: with the insidious gathering gloom of Ireland it really was time he found an heir. Women present problems and marriage may intensify them, but . . .

He set his glass down with a bang and his eyes frosted. 'And in return, perhaps you will allow me the benefit of *your* immense treasure?' De Doubalier's forehead twisted into a thousand wrinkles. 'I would like,' Bouchard said, 'to seek the hand of your daughter in marriage.'

The Scotsman McClune rode up the Doon Lawn as the leaders were being reined to the carriage and Bouchard came out to meet him, rather heavily supporting himself on a rosewood cane, a gift from de Doubalier. Cursory greetings were exchanged, but Bouchard saw impatience and aggression etched on the sub-inspector's face.

'A day for travel indeed,' McClune commented, watching ghosts of cloud disperse beneath a hard sun. He looked sternly to Bouchard. 'One hopes you took the precautions of departure.'

'Precautions?'

'There were notices circulated to all estates by my men. The gentry need take heed of the stirrings of organised Ribbonmen. No one must see that more than you.'

'We spoke of this before, you and I. My lands are safe –'

'Safe? Then how do you account for the savagery that may leave you maimed?'

'I try to think little of it, Mister McClune, for otherwise dark spirits grow in my mind that leave me in sorry doubt about all humanity.'

McClune drew himself upright in the saddle. 'If there is unease and doubt in one's mind, and sense of divided loyalty perhaps, one might be better off departing these shores –'

Angered, Bouchard cut in: 'Sir, my family possessed this ground for generations. *I* am master here, and decide for my own present and future. Neither peasant nor police will alter that. These are uncertain times, we all know. At this moment I am still in some shock over what occurred but my disposition, blessedly, has always been one of fast and full repair. Other more pressing matters absorb me.

Commitments in London face me now and it is my marked intention to forget this dreary place for a time – and forget your frown of criticism.'

'Forgive me if it seems so.' McClune was not apologetic. 'I speak boldly only for your good. This estate alone enjoys an undesirably lenient control –'

'What nonsense. You speak so because I came to you to request a farm child's release.'

'Your rents are out of step with neighbour estates. You possess no fitting agent-of-the-gentry. You spend three-quarters of the year abroad and then return to preach to *me* on the errors of Irish society.'

Bouchard blazed. 'By God, sir, I will ask for a civil tongue. How dare you speak so, and from horseback to a parliament member!'

McClune did not retreat. His chest inflated a little and his words speeded. 'I have no wish to be uncaringly rude. But I suggest the Sir lacks understanding of the gravity of the situation. In a year there have been 300 murders. Parliament's records, if nothing else, will show you that. Not too long ago Prime Minister Grey spoke out in the Commons –'

'I need no reminder of unchallenged records.'

'Only last week two bailiffs from Nenagh were attacked and killed, and they were going about their lawful duties.'

Bouchard turned his back on McClune and moved to walk away. 'One moment,' the sub-inspector called. 'I do not come to harangue you with known facts, Sir.'

'Speak, then.' Bouchard twisted back irritatedly, the ferrule of his cane rat-tatting the gravel ground.

'I seek interview with Robert Devlin.'

'Not possible. I have decided the lad will accompany my household, to be schooled possibly in Kent. He is pre-cocious and mature beyond his years and will make me an excellent employee.' Bouchard spoke with open confi-dence. 'He has had a few weeks at Banagher and is pre-sently preparing departure with the three members of staff who will accompany me abroad.' He stalled, suddenly aware of McClune's amazed disgust. 'You frown so,'

Bouchard said harshly, demanding explanation.

'It is my right to see him. I am in course of a criminal inquiry. Last evening at the sliabh bridge the daughter of Lord Ormond's agent was set upon and ravished by three young men dressed in the white shirts of the rebels.'

'Ravished? My dear sir, you seek Robert Devlin for such an inquiry – a gossoon not yet twelve years old?'

'It is said they were young boys.'

'I am sure. But, for the Lord's sake, let us use some sense and look intelligently at the vestiges of the crime. Twelve years old! Bah!' Curtly Bouchard swivelled towards the manor. 'Mister McClune, I give you my solemn word that Robert Devlin was within my household *all* yesterday evening. That will be sufficient for you, I know. And there the matter ends.' He began to walk away. McClune tarried.

'You do yourself no justice, Sir Redmond,' he called. 'You are protected by your own ignorance at the moment, I detect. But see how it will be when you come home to reside in retirement. Things may seem different when the tamer sleeps among his lions. And what is more, be careful that you have friends left for your return.'

Bouchard turned back and addressed McClune fiercely, his face contorted in fury. 'I live by the instincts God bestowed on me,' he spat out. 'They do me well enough. And now they tell me I have tolerated an arrogant man on my land too long.' He lifted his cane and prodded the sub-inspector's mount till it sidled away in fright.

As he stomped across the drive McClune's voice floated back to him:

'Be careful of your friends, Sir. Nothing more surely brings about ruination than the wrong ones.'

CHAPTER SIX

The attendance at the wedding at St Peter's in Sandwich and the celebratory luncheon afterwards was not good.

71

Bouchard smilingly explained this away to his new wife by claiming that, at fifty-five, the appeal of the quiet social function was the sweeter, but Sir Myles Rossitor, longtime associate of Bouchard's from Westminster, now retired, elucidated further. On his insistence, the reception was held at Pegwell Hall, his residence by the sea, and it was here on the balustraded balcony that gave such magnificent vistas to the Channel that he confided further in Alexandrine.

'Redmond's a veritable pack o' cards,' he told her. 'Salt of the earth, mind, but apt to keep too much to himself. Truth is, his scope and position in Westminster's much dulled.' When Alexandrine's eyes widened in alarm, the old man laughed hugely. 'Do not misunderstand, my dear. I speak of a natural process of – ' He searched for a word, 'growing old in politics. Tory life is different from what it once was. Old buzzards like Redmond and I are swept out by the brooms of new revolutionaries like this devil Peel. That is the way of things. For a time now Redmond's interest – and grip – have been unarguably slipping.'

'He is respected still, surely – ?'

'Oh, without question. No, do not allow me to mislead. Redmond is much the man he always was but, when one's politics go out of date, well, maybe slowly and surely one follows oneself!' He laughed again at her confused expression and tweaked her arm. 'I say this to you only to dispel any unease you may feel at so small a turn out.'

It struck Alexandrine suddenly that here was a generous and amenable confidant, a worthwhile key to her husband's past perhaps. In a roundabout way she questioned Sir Myles about political life and, less directly, Bouchard's career.

'Retirement soon is the foregone conclusion,' he stated bluntly. 'Not because Redmond is less popular with his party now – though, with Peel's supporters, there might be some touch of that – but because it is accepted that it's time to make room. There is some pressure from within for him to move on, and I'm sure a sound candidate to inherit the traditional Bouchard Kent seat is fit and ready to jump in.'

'That sounds quite appalling.'

Sir Myles grunted and his mouth curved into an inverted smile. 'Redmond knows the lie of the land. *I* did when, four years ago, I waved goodbye to a plum position as minister with portfolio at the Foreign Office. But one cannot complain. Redmond would be the last to say his years in parliament have not served him well, business-wise.' His gaze was, all of a sudden, severe. 'Mind, he might have extricated himself with greater aplomb – though I must not be critical.'

'You mean – ?'

'I mean, sweet lady – and forgive implied indignity, none intended – that Redmond might have sired an heir sooner, and passed on his seat more deftly.'

Alexandrine blushed furiously and hid her face briefly behind her fan. 'There is much I do not clearly comprehend about social life in England,' she said. 'Papa and I must be indeed grateful for your friendship.'

'Ah, but the pleasure is truly mine. I enjoy hosting all good businessmen who pass through these parts, and it is an extra pleasure when alliances bloom and I succeed in seeing new partnerships, new romances.'

'Tell me,' she rejoined nervously, her eyes drifting from his. 'In your wisdom do you see Redmond's *business* interests suffering by this poor timing?'

Sir Myles temporised. 'The division between business links and political ones *should* be clear. These are separate worlds you speak of. But – ' He hesitated to consider her posture and gaze. 'Let me say this – advice to a pretty young bird about to make her nest: Redmond has a good brain. In the past he has made some inordinately good investments, and that is his metier, playing the shares game. There is no reason why he should not once again choose some winners.'

Once again? Alexandrine's narrowed look widened. Did that imply Redmond's present, relative, difficulties. Why had Sir Myles taken her aside? What lay behind this volley of reassurances? Before these thoughts found order in her brain Sir Myles was speaking again.

'Will you live in Ireland?'

'Ireland? Live?' The question oddly startled her. She hurried on: 'Not in the sense of ten or twelve months a year, not at all. Obviously there are plans Redmond has yet to put to me, but I envisage a life in England and – '

'France?'

'*Non*. Certainly, no.'

The old man mentally interpreted the emphasis of her words: the lady had spoken enough about her intimate life. Even for a sophisticated and informed Frenchwoman, the limitations of etiquette stood. He called for more port and refrained from further personal debate.

Across the balcony the ubiquitous Squire Stephens watched with his fat wife and eldest son, William, while young Adam Rossitor pointed out the white cliffs of Ramsgate across the bay. Donna and Letitia crossed to join them. A full term at Lennant had passed since the girls had met the Stephens family, on visits to Drumloch after papa's 'accident', but Donna was intrigued by the new William who, in return, very obviously admired her. His career at Radley Public School had been checkered with incident, it was no secret, but by all accounts he was now settled comfortably in Trinity College, and a distinguished future was in the stars. According to the Squire, young William displayed 'temperament, no one will deny, but real genius'. In her childish way, Donna fancied she saw through that pomposity, detected in William calculated, cold counterfeit. He dressed in *bon ton* finery, affected an imperious look – but there was fear and self-doubt in hiding behind the young, shallow eyes.

When, by chance, they landed together in a corner sipping their mineral water wines, Donna felt the urge to blurt out her suppositions. The fear in his face kept her at bay. But she felt smug and competent under his gaze, not at all child with a young man.

When, in cheeky voice she asked, 'What will become of you after Trinity?' he stammered, bridled, then said:

'The world's my oyster. I might choose commerce or the academic field, that I've yet to resolve. Education,' he added loftily, 'opens all doors.'

'So Nurse says about young Rob Devlin.'

Aghast, William pulled himself upright.

'I mean no insult, William. I merely recount what Nurse says, that sound schooling comes first in gentle folk,' Donna explained. Letitia had drawn close, unwilling to allow her sister benefit of uninhibited talk with a boy. Now she heard William say:

'Very well. But please resist numbering me among serving staff. Young Rob Devlin is servant, not gent.'

'You are envious of his looks perhaps,' Letitia put in with insolence, intent to win over the conversation from Donna.

'What unadulterated *rawmaish*! My dear, such comments are ill-befitting a mere child such as yourself, and if you suppose they foster fun, be warned they do not. That is what is wrong with society now – no honour in class.'

The admonitory toughness did not deter Letitia. 'Rob now works at our London home,' she said. 'His schooling continues and, I'll vouch, he grows as upright and handsome as the best beau.'

'What romantic idiocy.'

'Romantic, perhaps,' Letitia grinned in defiance while William blushed madly. 'But isn't it said the best suitors should possess the gifts of both worlds: the manners of gentry and the strength of simple men.'

'Simple men, you say? Pah! My dear, you must go and *live* in Ireland for a time. Sample then the simple men.'

'You are jealous.'

William would have no more of this child's play. Nurse was passing, and he caught her eye and signalled his chagrin. In minutes she descended on them, scattering ranks. Donna fled to the safety of Squire Stephens's complaisant old wife. But Letitia stood her ground till William himself melted away and Nurse pulled her aside in vexation to voice her wrath. Chattering so outrageously freely to young gentlemen with arched expression and glass in hand! It really was not good enough.

'But it's only playful divertissement,' Letitia insisted.

'*Divert* – what! Where do you hear such nonsense,

colleenóg?'

'Alexandrine – mamma, I suppose – I positively heard her say –'

Nurse chewed on her lip to contain herself and took a firm grip of the child's shoulder. 'My little lass,' she started, 'I really do not know what they teach you at this academy but there's a measure of good manners lacking. Please consider your words when addressing older, wiser folk. There is no honour in overhearing adult conversation and you betray dignity by speaking like an old *beán*.'

Nurse turned away to Alexandrine's call, but there was no remorse in Letitia's green eyes, just haughty disgust. When later Donna rejoined her, Letitia told her:

'Being a girl, it seems, is as lowly as common servitude. What freedom does one have?'

'Nurse warns for our own good. Papa would be annoyed –'

'Papa has *his* fun. *I* am annoyed.' She nodded to Alexandrine, engrossed in laughter across the balcony. 'Must one put on the airs and graces of a slatternly hag like that to command an ear? By heavens, if that is the game, I shall learn to play it. Then when I have lord and lady at my feet, I shall choose what *I* want, and settle for no less.'

The vehemence shocked Donna yet excited her in some strange way. There was truth in her sister's fury. The charades of the drawing-room really were complicatedly spurious and, with the memory of a coarser way of life in mysterious Ireland, somehow unsatisfying. She thought of Colum Devlin. He might admonish her in his gruff way for many things – but not for laughter. She reconsidered that swiftly. She scarcely knew the boy, and her fancy was running away with her thoughts. In a year, or two, or ten, she would grow up in body and mind, blossom perhaps with the grace and lace and rouge of the lady who had wed papa. Then she would inhabit a graciously elegant drawing-room world and sup with the gentry . . . She tried to imagine herself in that fantastic setting but the opaque windows of the future denied her a clear and reassuring vision.

*

76

The first jolt in the married life of Bouchard and lovely Alexandrine came with the Whig Melbourne's fall from power and the accession of the New Tories under Peel in '41. For many Peel's victory presaged the dawn of a better, stronger England, but almost immediately there was acute pressure on Bouchard to relinquish his seat and influence. Old Wellington – though still a minister without portfolio – was gone, and the new tide seemed keener than ever to wash away the stanchions of his old guard.

In their first few years together Alexandrine had never admitted knowledge of Bouchard's declining position. Her life had been pleasantly undemanding: at Hedgeleigh and Drumloch she had been powerful and honoured chatelaine; at the old Doughty Street house, hostess to the long stream of titled gentry who passed through during the London season; she had ridden to hounds and mastered the Kilshowen Hunt. In Kent she was spoken of warmly, in Ireland with solemn respect. Her life was a desirable balance of varied vacations, it seemed, but two factors perpetually jarred: not only had she little opportunity to discuss career with her husband but, because of the frequent absences he enjoyed, there was little chance for intimate talk of *any* order. This rankled.

So too did the fact that their efforts failed to produce a male heir.

These gloomy weights seemed tolerable until, with Peel's new victory, Bouchard's spirits crashed and within the course of a few days Alexandrine found herself sharing Doughty Street with a new and desolated personality. Bouchard's new mood so startled her that she confronted him stoutly, risking anger. To her surprise, he confessed at once:

'Peel collared me at Windsor,' he explained. 'He had asked me to accompany his committee of report to the Queen on O'Connell's Repeal of the Act of Union campaign. I'd had little association with it, and I sensed his purpose. We had a pleasant audience and tea afterwards and I rode in his carriage. He did not procrastinate. I knew the picture well. By God, I was insulted. "Wellington's in his sixties," says he, "and you too have sat in the house for a considerable time." I saw the insinuation. Wellington in his sixties, by God! And what of Peel? Is not he just a pitch away from that esteemed age?'

Alexandrine gave careful indication of her prior knowledge of the situation, then said, 'But I fail to understand the alarm this excites in you? All right, as Wellington's man you are *démodé*. But they cannot surely *force* you out?'

'They can, with great ease. So many of my friends are retired or dead – or brainlessly inactive, like Wellington himself. Already I see the shadows of cold opposition within the party – the sudden disappearance of personal support, the lack of invitations to good functions.'

'But, Sir Myles has said to me – is this not the way of political life?'

'Perhaps,' Bouchard snapped, 'but this happening at *this* time perturbs me.'

'Without an heir to take your place in Kent?'

'There are shades of that, maybe, but that is not all.' His attention temporarily shifted to the wine in his hand; he refilled his glass with trembling fingers. Fury or fear, Alexandrine wondered. 'I cannot expect you to understand how much a benefit is a house seat and a foot in the right political circles. It means much, very much, to a man who has little else. Doors are opened to a parliament member that would otherwise remain permanently closed.'

'If I have failed you in any way – ' she began.

'Everything has failed me,' he cut in. 'The world is changing to sand in my grasp. Maybe Peel is right, I am old inside my head. The *status quo* traditions are gone. Ultra-Toryism is dead with Wellington and high pedigree government is no more. I said and did the wrong things at the wrong times. Gambling on Wellington was a waste. Not joining sufficiently in the fight against O'Connell was wrong. Not having a male heir to share the burden and pander young blood – that was wrong. And now I will be edged out, and my reputation and credit in good circles vanishes out the window.'

For some reason Alexandrine's spine crawled. Credit in

good circles? What possible relevance could that have? What standards of their life were dependent on *credit*? Had not papa established the fair extent of this Irishman's wealth.

'I will fight Peel,' Bouchard was expounding. 'It may suit him to be surrounded and supported by young swells who've laboured at this miserable game and waved flags against O'Connell more than I, but it suits *me* to retain a high post now. Damn the man. I will not quail.'

'Is there . . . something else, Redmond? Something I should know apart from the affairs of parliament?'

Ignoring her, he whipped out his timepiece and flicked it open. 'Six o'clock already. I must meet old Rossitor at the Pall Mall Club. A card party.' He looked at her without focus. 'You remember I informed you – ?'

'Another gambling spree?' Indignation fluttered up from her breast. 'Redmond, I am obliged to warn you about excesses of drink, and of gambling – '

'Nonsense.' He was on his feet, summoning a footman with a jab at his bell. 'A trifling wager game, no more. Pray do not flurry. There is enough on my plate just now, you'll agree.'

When he had gone, black despair beset Alexandrine as surely as a cage.

CHAPTER SEVEN

The letter that stunned Alexandrine arrived in the morning delivery at Doughty Street:

Lady Bouchard
Permit this urgent and solicitous approach. I see no need to be identified but believe that in entreating you, pressure may be brought to bear on your husband in this matter of needy settlement.

79

These seven years I have sat to game in a number of clubs with Sir Redmond and, in spite of former small difficulties, have always enjoyed fair play and honest payment. Be it known then that, when on April 19th he and I engaged with others in a game of high-stakes Napoleon at the Pall Mall, the losses incurred by your husband and payable to yours truly were never honoured.

Informed as I was then of Sir Redmond's financial difficulties – a state which had evidently absorbed him for some nine years – I agreeably extended the arrangement for promised payment. However, promises were broken and I felt obliged to pursue and investigate his position. The resultant alarm I felt, you will comprehend. I was not aware I had sat to gamble with a virtual bankrupt whose decline in Tory circles had been precipitated by a sequence of frequent debts and gambling rows.

I am sorry, my lady, to address you so crudely, but my own state of affairs allows little patience. I have waited long for your husband's settlement of this fifteen hundred pounds – a great sum, you must see – but time will hold me no longer. Therefore I appeal to you . . .

Alexandrine skipped the pleasantries in rage. Bankrupt! Nine years of debts! At first the accusations seemed so preposterous she could not bring herself to believe them. Then the worrisome hints of the last months filtered into her brain and the rage that had faded to confusion turned to a smouldering, bitter ferocity.

She struggled to contain herself. Donna and Letitia's arrival from their final term at Lennant occupied her afternoon and preparations were afoot for a spring vacation at Drumloch. Bouchard spent that night at his club but, next evening, her opportunity for confrontation came. They sat in their carriage trundling home along the Strand after a visit to the theatre and, concealing the stormy emotion she felt, she explained the missive. Bouchard reacted oddly, she thought – unmoving for some minutes, then smiling grimly, then nodding like a weary old sage.

'I see no fun in this,' she snapped. 'Accusations such as these constitute libel, do they not?'

'If they are defamatory, yes. It depends on how one chooses to translate them.' He swallowed a deep breath. 'In the circumstances they are correct enough neither to defame nor worry me.' His voice became shaky. 'Although I would like to know what unnamed scoundrel revealed private details of my banking position. Such villains should not hold posts of trust. I shall report this to my banker –'

'Do I hear correctly!' Alexandrine gasped. 'Is this all you wish to say? – that the accusations are true? What of this claim, that you are a virtual bankrupt? *Mon Dieu*, explain!'

Bouchard grew rigid beside her. 'Dear woman, recognise your place! I explain to no man – and assuredly to no woman. You ask for it. Well, the truth is that, these many years, I have carried the burden of uneasy debts, debts that accrued as a result of optimistic investments in the wrong offered shares –'

'And gambling!'

'That is no business of yours. Hold your tongue, woman. I have provided well for you –' His tone became pure vitriol, 'and have given you far more than you have returned. Six years ago when you and your father accepted my hospitality in Drumloch you were more than pleased to do so. Six weeks ago when you curtsied before the King of Belgium at the Lord Mayor's Hall you were equally pleased. I have opened these avenues for you and you have been blessed with a good life. All by my grace, remember.' The anger seemed to weaken him and he flopped back on his cushioned seat.

Alexandrine demurred. 'I concede the truth of much of what you say, Redmond. But if this situation is as grave as this cad makes out, had we – you – better not prepare measures of precaution to ensure a continued good name?' She stalled. 'Or is that too late?'

It seemed as if she had already divined the answer. Bouchard said quietly, 'Hedgeleigh has been heavily mortgaged these six years, Doughty Street even longer. Word has escaped, it seems. I have seen the blooming complications over a time now. A very real and sour shadow has been cast on my character.'

'Hence you suffer Peel's pressure – ?'

'I am troubled,' he confessed, his head slipping into his hands. 'Extraordinary, isn't it? Once I recall my father swearing that every member of the gentry was unimpeachable. But it seems times have changed.' There was glum irony in his smile when he turned back to her. 'Whether or not there has been some political or other campaign against me I cannot tell for sure, but it is certain that my status here is . . . well, lessened. Greatly lessened. And this monstrous debt must be settled.'

'One could sell Hedgeleigh,' Alexandrine ventured.

'For what benefit? To pay off the mortgage?' He frowned distractedly. 'Though that must follow soon, I regret. My bankers are pressing me for huge interest on that loan.'

'Drumloch,' she suggested. Why hadn't she thought of that first? What loss in dank, miserable Ireland? She could cope with less good hunting.

'No.'

'Why not?'

'There are problems involved.'

'What problems?'

He closed his eyes and shook his head gruffly. 'Enough questions, woman. Grant me some peace of mind.'

'But Redmond, I am worried too, desperately worried. My entire being depends on what you next choose to do, realise that.' His face in the light of the passing street lamps turned to molten lead and a jaded sound rattled in his throat. 'You must have some *real* money. Did you not freely invest two-and-a-half thousand or more in papa's company?'

'And went in debt to my bankers to do so, increasing the Hedgeleigh loan with a false surety.'

'Then the simple truth is we have nothing and are solvent only because of bankers' loans! The ignominy of it!'

'Not ignominy. There is always the distant world of

Ireland. You perhaps do not understand these things, but society here and in Ireland turns on different axes. I am down but not out. I retain sound contacts in Dublin and my estate is one of the largest in the midlands. What I must do now is utilise those strengths. Utilise them cleverly.' He was ranting now, muttering to himself. 'Act fast. Resign when parliament sits again, befriend old Peel, sell Hedgeleigh, pay off that gambling creditor – '

'But how can you? There are no funds – '

The carriage was rumbling into Bloomsbury, slowing down as heavier night traffic narrowed the city's arteries. Bouchard spoke in a firm, final voice. 'The money I need will come from your father, from the dividend I am due from the Liverpool First Steamship Company. I estimate, from what he has written me of its progress, that it will be vastly up on the last one paid two years ago. That one was only pennies, but this time I will have all I require to repay most of the mortgages and settle this villainous cad.'

'When is this dividend due?' Alexandrine said, a touch nervously.

'On July 30th,' Bouchard replied.

The dividend due from the First Steamship Company did not arrive in July.

In December of the year a liquidator was employed to salvage the shillings left in the rubble. The towering success of the passenger service run by the British and American Steam Navigation Company, and of Samuel Cunard's breakthrough steam mail line, had crippled the long-foundering company.

De Doubalier's shaky empire – if empire it ever was – had crashed around his ears.

CHAPTER EIGHT

Dermot Halifane, the attorney, reminded Bouchard of a large preening ginger rabbit; from the smoothly hairy visage to the indolence of the eyes, everything spoke of smug, well-trained domesticity. Bouchard liked such serene and mild qualities in his associates; they allowed him a sense of inflated power, though self-admission of that fact would have surprised him. Overtly Halifane's appeal lay in his shrewd and loyal dedication to inherited 'family clients', and his unfailing trustworthiness.

The first port of call on arrival back in Ireland was Halifane's spacious office at Dame Street, near the old Irish parliament building. Alexandrine and the girls had travelled separately to Drumloch – the result of one of a sequence of virulent arguments that had succeeded the First Steamship news – and Bouchard had taken the opportunity to indulge his drinking for three days of journey. Alcohol fuelled his mood of despair and by the time he faced Halifane his temper was on a short fuse.

The hard facts, effusively poured out for the attorney's benefit, seemed more desperate when articulated. For the first time in his memory, Bouchard saw the ginger rabbit stir. Halifane's eyes twitched in shock and his fingers drummed the fine Irish oak desk.

'You should really have informed me of the strained nature of your position sooner, Sir Redmond. As adviser to your family for – '

Bouchard cut in: 'Let us not waste time on bumptious prating. I have not come home for the Christmas season to make merry and entertain, Halifane. I am chased out. Chased, dammit. There is the pressing matter of this fifteen hundred due, and I see no credit source open to me.'

On written instruction a fortnight before, Halifane had commenced the sale of Hedgeleigh – a move loudly resisted by Alexandrine; but, then, he had had no knowledge of exigency. Now he said, 'What about Hedgeleigh? You will fetch perhaps fifteen thousand on that.'

'Fine, fine. That will balance the sum I drew as mortgage from Locke, the banker. I would not be embarking on that course only that, through some evil channel, word is out about my troubles, and Locke is demanding settlement too.'

Halifane sank in his padded chair and examined the chandelier overhead. He looked, outrageously, quite perturbed. 'You must consider every course very carefully.' A bankrupt of such prior eminent standing within his client book would be quite unacceptable. His face flushed brightly, the roots of his ginger hair highlighted a pallid pink. 'Is it true that you have resigned your seat?'

'Had to. Leave it longer and a conspiracy to shift me would have drawn up. At least, this way, I retain dignity and *some* valuable friends. I am a victim of changing political trends, dammit.' He pounded down a fist. 'Why did this have to happen now?'

Halifane refrained from reminding him that acute crisis might have been avoided had he been consulted honestly earlier. Instead, with rigid control he said, 'Am I to take it when you say you have lost much money in, er, uninspired chance investment, that you mean it is entirely irredeemable?'

'Of course, you fool. I do not mean I have cash tied up in lame companies and bad scrip lists. As you know, since my marriage and in order to enjoy a continuing standard of good life, I have sold out all of my developing shares. The rest – and those few you did not know about – went down with idiots like the deceiver de Doubalier. And whatever else I speak of as 'uninspired chance' refers to –' He paused to choke on the fury of his own words, 'dammit, the horses and card games I have dabbled with.'

The attorney changed tack quickly. 'Clearly one must look to Drumloch estate as a way out. As you yourself have said, Ireland will afford you an alternative in lifestyle and standing. Word of the true state of things need go no further than here, as far as anyone is concerned. But we must consider borrowing on Drumloch.'

Bouchard sighed, exhaling the residue of alcoholic verve.

'I cannot.'

'I appreciate honour, sir, but –'

'Nothing to do with honour. You see, Doughty Street and Hedgeleigh were not alone.' His voice fell. 'I have deceived my wife by not yet telling her the truth, but I took mortgage on the manor at the time of the First Steamship Company investment. I fought hard to get it, for at the time – as now – bankers were reluctant to advance on properties in the west midlands because of the imminent troubles.' He touched his covered, damaged eye. 'I sacrificed, I promise you, to get that cash. You questioned me before about my reluctance to pursue investigations when that violent attack on the manor occurred. I had a number of reasons – but one of the main was that, in fostering investigation, I would have been raising waves for myself with the banker I was negotiating with. And then, when de Doubalier convinced me about this great sum he needed, I sought further monies. And was in even less of a position to chance problems with neighbours and tenants.'

'You have not confided in Lady Alexandrine?'

'A whim of mine,' Bouchard snapped. His reasons showed a weakness of character, and he knew it: in spite of the perfidy of her father, a continued calm marriage seemed important to him; with career and money gone, the loss of an attractive, noble wife would indeed be a final straw. He would have to face Irish society, and word of one obvious failure would insidiously give way to word of another. He was determined not to allow that happen. But he knew Alexandrine well enough to know how this alternative of long and singular life in Ireland would affect her: one season more than usual might be tolerable, but the real prospect of a continuing existence here would repel. But in that course, Bouchard sensed, lay the lifeline and he must cajole and persuade her agreement. As time went by she would learn the wisdom of his ploy, but for now it seemed simplest to present her with an uncomplicated *fait accompli*. So the facts were simple: Hedgeleigh, Doughty Street, England itself carried the stigma of debts and complex mortgage loans; Ireland was free. That was the basis of his planning, but beneath it lay another nub of firm resolve. All else he had he had earned, wagered and won, but Drumloch was heritage, the blossom on a proud tree that stretched back scores of years. Edgar Bouchard, despite his wayward life, did not lose it, nor did his thriftless father before him; neither would he. No banker, nor Peel himself, could deny Redmond Bouchard that. He would retain and preserve its *status quo*, and in a hundred years it would reign just as it did now.

Halifane knew of the Bouchard passion for the estate and guessed at much of the background of his client's thinking. He went on:

'Do you propose retirement now, pure-and-simple? A settled life with your lady?'

'Dammit, man, you know better than to suggest such nonsense. How can I step back and forget the world with these debts? I must find gainful employment in new sound investments. But let this be my smokescreen for the moment.'

'You must find capital for investments.'

'And so I come to you.' Bouchard collapsed back into his chair and prodded accusingly towards the attorney. 'You presume to guide. Guide me now. Where should I go? To whom should I pander? Leave me to build the smoke-screen, I can cope with that. But where might I turn for money fast?'

Halifane resisted a display of rude anger. He stood and crossed his arms busily, focus drifting purposefully to the ormolu clock on the Empire fireplace. Bouchard played games with trust it seemed; at least, records showed, old Edgar had respected the Halifane traditions of loyalty and candour. But this man blew hot and cold, chose to conceal his patently insane gambling and reveal only when un-avoidably pressed. Well, such whimsy was an insult to professionalism, to Halifane himself. It really was not good enough.

Bouchard saw Halifane's eye on the clock and stood smartly. 'I engage you overlong, it seems,' he grunted. 'Am I to assume this attorney's existing involvements are so great as to preclude interest in long-time friends' troubles?' He hesitated, then pushed on darkly, 'If such is the case I must consult my Castle friends. Old Shepherd – he comes to you, does he not? And Sir Davis Ross? Shall I inform them – ?'

Halifane was not impressed by the childish threat. He shrugged it aside and said flatly, 'I shall need to see papers of these mortgage loans and all your private correspondence relating to them; this gambling debt also. Then I must begin my own rapid inquiries on possible credit sources. Clearly Locke is out. So too would be Meehan and Kiely, your old people in St Stephens's Green.' He frowned in thought. 'However, there may be other fish in that particular sea. Then again, there may not.' A brighter thought crossed his mind. 'You must consider this de Doubalier. He surely owes you a favour.'

'He is in Boston. On his death-bed, they say. His weak heart has been greatly strained these last months – and I can see why.'

Sincere concentration still twisted Halifane's flabby face. He scratched his whiskers. 'Very well, that is a route closed to you. But you are a clever man, Sir Redmond – you do not need *me* to suggest methods of chicanery or wiliness. What I would recommend now is a close consideration of all *possible* assets – friendships, former associations, whatever.'

Bouchard grimaced, questioning.

'For example Squire Stephens. Is it not said that his son William is continuing his excellent career in some lucrative field?'

'It's a time since I've seen old Stephens.'

Halifane shrugged. 'I may be wrong. But it is said he has benefitted enormously by the business acumen of young William. If perhaps *he* owed you a favour –' The attorney's uneasy embarrassment showed again. Bouchard said nothing: the old Squire of Fork Estate was a good, if stolid friend, but more known for geniality than generosity. What was more, there were no favours owed.

'If that may not seem worthwhile, what of Lady Alexandrine herself, of her contacts?'

'Contacts?'

'Well, you said this de Doubalier was of good birth – yes? There must be allies there. Why not propose to her – ?'

'To travel to France and cadge off old acquaintances?!

And in my name! What about scruples, sir?'

The attorney scotched Bouchard's scowl with a wry 'What about alternatives?'

Letitia, with her ear to the drawing-room door, had overheard much of the unchecked argument of her father and his wife. In a state of hot excitement she fled through the Great Hall – judiciously carrying shoes in hand – and upstairs in search of her sister. In the large dressing-room Donna used as a work and study chamber the sketching boards of her favourite pastime were propped, ready, on their easels, but there was no sign of Donna. Letitia ran to the bedroom window and pulled the shutters. Below in the coachhouse yard a small figure could be seen, drawing-pad under arm, traipsing towards the forge. Letitia opened her mouth to cry out, thought twice of it with papa just below in the drawing room, and ran out.

The forge was empty but she found Donna in the connecting stables, perched on a stool in rapt contemplation of Zephyr the chestnut stallion, finest remaining stud horse of her father's diminished team.

'You will not believe what I have just discovered!' Letitia rapped out, startling her sister.

Donna's pulse raced in surprise, then slackened. She sighed with petulance and turned back to the horse. Six weeks they had been back at Drumloch, and Christmas had come and gone, yet this restless mood of bickering and half-hidden excitements persisted. It was clear that papa and Alexandrine's relationship was under some strain, clear too that an uneasy hiatus in the normal business of seasonal life and further schooling was being forced upon them. After Lennant a finishing course had been proposed. But months had passed with no further move. It really had all become rather dreary and tiresome. Nurse would admit to nothing amiss, Pearson was tight-lipped as ever and, for reasons unexplained, Hedgeleigh and its trim acres had vanished from their lives like melted snow. For Letitia, whose relationship with father allowed easier approach, this time had been no less frustrating: rumour and hint had been elicited, but no crisp facts. All that remained certain in Donna's sharp mind was that *nothing* was certain. Perpetually there was this feeling of imminent departure, of unheard plans.

Letitia said, 'Mamma is going to France.' Her eyes shone with delight. 'Who knows – perhaps she will take us.'

Donna concentrated on Zephyr. 'I would rather stay here, thank you.'

Deflated, Letitia sat beside Donna and poured out the gist: 'I heard shouting in the Great Hall. They were storming about like young lovers. Papa claimed her father had cost him his fortune. He said she must go to France to speak to whatever friends her father called dear. At first she refused bluntly, then he started badgering her like an old hound, I swear. He said he had doubts about her honesty and nobility and she became – naturally – extremely indignant.'

Creeping intrigue held Donna. She twisted round and stared in awe at Letitia. Such ungentlemanly accusations, she could never conceive the like from upright, scrupulous papa.

'He went on, sweetly cajoling, pointing out that *this* was but a temporary set-back, and she must assist in overcoming it – for both their good. "Realise this," says he. "What future has the separated wife of a former parliament member, drifting about under the shadow of debt?" '

'*Debt*!'

Letitia's green eyes widened. 'Of course – can you not see? That is the dilemma. Papa is in trouble for money. Alexandrine has been persuaded to depart for Paris and pursue loans from her family's friends urgently.'

Donna's knuckles brushed her lips and her thoughts tumbled wildly. That explained much: the reduction in house staff in London, the diminished stable, the jumbled travel plans, the rumours and hints. . . .

A boot scuffing earth made both sisters turn. Robert Devlin stood in the doorway, an apparition from the past. It was more than six years since, as carefree children, they had played in the fir forest and the uncharted fields beyond, and fully four since last either sister had seen him – on vacation in Kent when his schooling there had allowed him time to resume household work at the estate. And in the vacant years he had grown powerfully – in stature and spirit, it seemed – and now stood before them as a right young gentleman: brogues with a beeswax shine, breeches as neat as a Regent Street dandy's, fine woollen jacket and well-cropped hair. The face had matured too, had become rugged and full, though not handsome. Donna looked deep into the eyes and saw the strange, fox-like cunning she fancied had always been there, but Letitia only gazed admiringly.

Rob bowed and set down the old minstrel's clarsach he had been carrying. 'Forgive an intrusion, my ladies,' he said. 'I had come to borrow tools to mend this harp for Lady Alexandrine.' He allowed his eyes to survey the girls from head to toe. He saw dissimilar twins, two unlikely flowers from like buds: Letitia slim and prettily angular-featured, with russet hair; Donna smaller, fuller of body and face, with huge eyes and ring-curled blonde locks. Both attracted him, as lovely women appeal to all men, but his eye fell on Letitia and he recalled her pleasing – if arrogant – directness, so glaring a contrast to Donna's moody shadows.

'Pray enter,' Letitia said, 'and be welcome, Rob Devlin. We did not know you were numbered among us again.'

Rob walked in and began a dutiful search for tools. While he did, he spoke: 'Sir's generosity and nothing else has kept me from Drumloch. I have busied myself at school in Banagher and in Kent – ' The soft accent evinced that. 'Then for a time at a stud in Sallins Sir once held partnership in.' He spoke with bold pride. 'I have learned the trades and occupations of good men and I am pleased to be back here – '

'A gentleman yourself now?' Donna could not resist the invitation to prick Rob's bubble. Letitia scolded her with a violent elbow jab.

Rob faced Donna, lop-sidedly grinning in a way that momentarily frightened her. 'If it please my lady,' he said.

Then: 'I think not a gentleman in the sense you mean, but hopefully one may humbly aspire to same with lesser blood and greater effort.'

Letitia clapped her hands as if applauding a performance in a circus ring. She stood down from her stool and moved closer to Rob. Her fingers tripped over the heavy cloth of his coat, testing quality of material but gauging the young muscle beneath too. 'Is papa pleased with your endeavours, then?'

'Thankfully, yes. My training will allow me to take over as chief groom and coach-keeper now that Tartan O'Neill is dead.'

'A task that pleases you?'

Without insolence Rob answered, 'For this moment. But other functions will open to me. Sir Redmond has indicated a promising and worthy career.' He stalled to meet Letitia's gaze squarely and return the look of warmth. 'The barriers of servitude are not what they were. I expect within time to hold my head up in the best drawing-room or hunt.'

'Bravo,' Letitia cheered.

'And Sir Redmond is the one who will open these doors to Society for you, is he?' Donna queried.

'Yes, he is.'

She gathered her winter shawl about her and slid her drawing-pad under her arm. 'Then, were I you, I would prepare for some delay in procuring my golden key.' Letitia spun, disgusted shock on her face. Donna stood her ground beneath Rob's ironic grin. 'The Sir may be preoccupied a time with matters a little more pressing than . . . playing patron to spoilt children.'

Before Letitia could challenge her, Donna was gone. Rob had found the tools he sought and wrapped them in a skin while Letitia wavered uneasily at the door. When she did not speak, he took the initiative. 'Miss Donna dislikes me, I observe. Perhaps it distresses her to see peasant dress as gent –'

'She is merely contrary,' Letitia reassured. 'I do find her mysterious at times.'

Suddenly the salt-sweat smell of his body was beside her,

invading her senses like a delicious intoxicant. She looked nervously around and found his shoulder right by hers. His eyes held hers in mesmeric closeness. The cruel hardness set her heart a-flutter. 'Or perhaps my gaze perturbs her,' he said.

'The gaze of intent and ambition?' Her voice was uneven, hoarse; her eyes wet with fear.

'Of desire – in presence of two exquisite ladies,' he grinned.

'You *are* outspoken, sir,' she stammered, her face aglow.

'No, just truly ambitious.' As she stood frozen his hand struck out somewhere behind her and, sickened with shock, she felt its fingers dribble along her spine and under her arm, nimbly embracing the smooth satin of her bodice. She shuddered, her head reeling till she almost swooned, when the fingers stretched and encompassed one soft breast. For a second he lingered . . .

'I must go,' she gasped. But by the time she reached the manor the blood was back to her cheeks and the thumping in her chest had transformed to throbbing pleasure.

CHAPTER NINE

For Donna the estate lands of Drumloch and their rhythm of life had a bewitchingly fairytale quality. Less mercurial in temperament than her sister, Donna found it easy to win the trust of Nurse and Alexandrine and, at this maturer age, greater freedom of the lands was allowed her. Very frequently she rode out with Brenda, the senior housemaid – often along the banks of the Shannon and far beyond the distant estate boundary – and often she walked the fir forest and hills, carrying sketchbook, all alert for the petrified images of pure Ireland. And though the rule was chaperonage at all times, she had her tricks, and often walked alone. The colours and shapes of the land, the songlike voices of the people, the strange language and gestures, the very quality of air – all won her over until, in a few short wintry weeks, the world receded from her thoughts and native Ireland dominated. Fleeting friendships were struck, with fisherwomen strolling out at early light for their eel nets, with pedlars, and bards and dirty-faced children. And what amazed her more than anything was that the fantasies of her Lennant tuition, of William Stephens and papa, seemed baseless. There was no limbo of communication. The farm folk waved to her cheerily whether she strode out in flounced satin and lace with her hair in tulle lappets or concealed herself beneath a broadcloth cape; and when they addressed her they did so with sunny warmth and frankness. This freedom and the fun of new-found casual friendships elated her and she fancied suddenly that she could be truly happy here, were it not for the shapeless ghosts of doubt that walked Drumloch's passages and the querulous face of papa.

Things were easier with Alexandrine abroad and papa flitting so often to Dublin. Donna's favourite walk took her north of the manor to the wedge of forest between estate boundary and the Shannon. Here, screened to east, south and west by forest, manor and river banks the land was uncluttered and only one abode – the Protestant Andersons', a houseful of children whose father had once been Drumloch's high-placed agent – stood out of the landscape. Donna came here to sketch the last firs of the forest, and the gushing waters of the river and the sun sinking on the far deserted plains.

On this chilly afternoon, with a briny breeze blowing from the south, her attention had fallen on the old Gothic house that was the Andersons' and she sat shivering in her heavy shawl and tracing its outline on the pad on her knees. Her brain was intent and serene, but suddenly her eyes drifted up from the paper and the figures of two young men interposed the scene, heading in her direction. She looked round, saw nothing but the trees bending under wind and long skeough grass rippling on the fens. The far-off wing of the manor gazed blankly back at her, with not another soul in sight. Slight fear bubbled: only last night Pearson had related blood-churning tales of ancient peasants' rebellions and the almost mythical Ribbonmen and Whiteboys; and now evening's dimness was softening the air and the wind beginning to howl like the banshee.

Donna pocketed her crayons and scrambled to her knees, but the men were almost on her. For a minute she recognised neither, then she identified the lean face and wavy hair of young Anthony Anderson and a dart of relief jabbed her heart. Anthony was eldest of the Widow's clan, a cool and uninspired twenty-five-year-old whose lenient and gentle ways, Donna often shamefully reflected, befitted best an aged, soulless servant.

'Am I to suppose you grace *us* with your artistry?' he grinned. She nodded brusquely. 'And the cold sweeping up from the South Pole? You really should be home by a crackling fire, Miss Donna.'

'As you came I was setting on my way.'

Nervously he offered his arm as she drew to her feet. She glanced at his companion, frowned inwardly, then let out a little gasp. 'Is it Colum Devlin?' she asked.

'At your service, my lady.' He did not bow, nor did his eyes quiver from hers. There was nothing of Rob's blood in him: no powerful girth of waist nor broadness of face; instead his body and features appeared finely and girlishly chiselled, and in perfect proportion – the eyes far apart and lustrous brown, the nose small and neat, the mouth full, the body more sinewy than muscular. His longish hair of peat brown flailed in the breeze and the skirt flapped and billowed against his creamy skin.

Anderson observed the tight exchange of glances with a grin. 'I be accompanying Colum to the Duffs. Their sedge thatch collapsed in the storm just gone and there's only the lass Cara to help.'

'Let me not delay you, then.'

Anderson nodded. 'Aye, there is some rush. The night may come down wet.'

The loose pages of Donna's sketchbook caught breeze and suddenly tore from her hands. Colum immediately

95

scurried after them. Anthony Anderson, with a knowing grin, bowed to Donna. 'Permit me to hurry on ahead, Miss Donna. Colum may follow me up.' Before she could protest he was calling out to Colum to assist as he please, then follow on. A distance away, Donna could see Colum falter and half-turn; she knew he had no wish to be left with her, and the realisation was irksome and alarming all at once.

When Anderson was gone she hurriedly grabbed the few items at her own feet and, without waiting for Colum, turned for the manor. In seconds he caught her up, gruffly pushing the retrieved pages into her hands. His face burned red and his hands were unsteady, revelations of a wariness that, because it equalled hers, consoled and warmed her.

'I am . . . am pleased to see you so healthy and well,' she stuttered. Had he really grown so tall, taller than her by all of six inches.

He marched by her side in awkward step with her. 'And I, you. Is it true they say you are here – home – for good? That the Sir has resigned his seat?'

'You are educated in such matters?' As soon as she said it, she regretted it, and the mild hauteur of its delivery.

'I keep informed,' he said harshly. 'Just because I am a farmer does not mean I lack awareness of parliamentary affairs.'

'Of course. I am sure.' There was open apology in her smile. She risked looking at him, risked the depthless brown pools of his eyes. Briefly she recounted the position, revealing only as much as conversationally concerned him. She concluded with: 'Given my own choice I would say now that my education has run its course and I am quite content to embark here on – ' she stumbled over the words, 'an idle life.'

'They say the life of the gentry is never idle,' he grinned, 'what with Society balls and hunt parties.'

She shrugged. 'I will have my share of it, I'm sure. In a week or two papa presents my sister and I to the viceroy at Dublin Castle. In a way that grand occasion is the opening to Society for us.' His quizzical glance made her blush. Such talk really was out of place between daughter of

Society and peasant. She ceased talking bluntly.

After a time he resumed, 'Your art work does justice to our lands. Perhaps you'll grow to be a celebrated landscape painter who'll exhibit in the world's best galleries and place on record the life of Ireland.'

Donna giggled. 'I think not. Though it gives me recreation and comfort. I love to paint those things that are so distinctly Irish – like the Andersons' home, a building the like of which one would not see in England.'

'Or the Doon maybe?'

'Do you know, in all my days here I never did find and locate that famed Doon. Beyond the fir forest, don't they say?'

Colum nodded. 'Its stones are secret and sacred. Within them Celtic kings died and, it's said, on his way to find a site for building his Seven Churches, St Ciaran rested here for seven days. So says the Book of Lismore.'

Courage rose in Donna, though the wind was whistling loud now and the laden clouds of a coming storm blackened the heavens. 'Show me,' she said, her voice even and calm. 'Perhaps I may sketch them tomorrow, and record them for posterity. Bring me to the Doon.'

He hesitated, trapped in confusion. The seriousness of her proposal was obvious – but what of Anderson, and the chores that awaited him back at the farm, with a hundred-and-one things on every plot to do and a father abed almost daily these six years? And, too, how safe was it? What if Bouchard heard of this, cavorting about with the daughter of the manor, and evening fading to night?

When he did not speak she said, 'Clearly you hate me still – I am so different from you in life and religion and aspiration.'

'No.' He spoke with parched, unconvincing boldness and his step changed, striking away from the manor towards the shadowy recesses of the forest. 'Come then if you will, I will show you an old glory of Ireland's, from the days when every inch of soil was true Irish and no barriers stood between people.'

His eloquence amused her and her heart beat fast. There

97

was only Nurse and Pearson and Brenda to answer to; she could easily contrive some convincing yarn, or perhaps steal in unseen after full dark. With a bounce in her step, she followed him.

It took all of thirty minutes to find the secret spot, a valley of growthless grass and a ring of smooth round stones centred with a fallen Holy Well and cairns set about forty paces apart. The ground underfoot was spongy bog and, Donna guessed, whatever majestic fort once stood here had long since sank. In the dip of ground, protected from the wind, they walked side by side in silence. Colum sat by the twisted heap of the Holy Well and she joined him.

'I come here to meditate often,' he said. 'When the labours of the farm tire me too greatly.'

'Tell me about your life,' she said. 'Your papa is still middleman?'

'In name only. His fever illness never died since that Shroveday fall. He lies abed and reads and the farm folk visit him and listen to his wisdom. Sometimes he ventures forth, but not often now. And mamma, she is old and tired.'

'You work the farm alone, then?'

'I am pleased to be a farmer. God made my work.'

'You do not . . . envy Rob his fortune?'

Colum strugged but his voice was fierce. 'Fortune? To play games of Society and pretend one is what one's not? Perhaps I am simpler in heart than Rob. My ambitions are small against his.' He thought for a moment. 'Perhaps I envy Rob, perhaps I do not.'

'You disdain Rob's desire to be a gent, and possess good finery and live in a manor maybe – and yet you befriend the Protestant Anderson?'

'Prod, Catholic – what does it really matter? Anthony Anderson is my friend, a friend to all farm folk – for he himself is a farmer. He must work his plots like the rest of us though his house be bigger and colder. He is the one lad, and must support the colleen sisters and the Widow.'

Donna detected an undertone of bitterness, but did not oppose it. Instead she sat quietly, her thumbnail shredding blades of grass. 'Why do they call this the Holy Well?' she questioned.

The mantle of unhappiness sloughed off him and he sighed. 'There are many legends, and it is true that wishes are granted for those who believe here.'

A few large drops of cold rain spattered the earth and Colum slipped off his waistcoat and wrapped her sketches in it. He gave her his hand to rise and she pulled the hood of her cape across her golden hair. 'Tell me some of the legends of the Well,' she said.

'It's the Love Well,' he told her. 'Those who seek the Bed of Honour soon come to sit here and they win a love match, not an arranged one.'

'Pray, what's this Bed of Honour?' she blushed.

His face was above hers, just inches away. She could smell, almost taste his breath, sweet as summer strawberries. His hands held her forearms strongly. 'It is marriage,' he said.

Thunder rumbled just then, and they ran when the heavens opened.

Bouchard was ready for Alexandrine when her carriage snaked up the drive and she swept into the Great Hall. The journey to Paris had not, it was clear, tired her to any excess and she sat to port with him in the drawing-room looking freshly pleased with herself.

'You succeeded with your papa's friends?' he launched eagerly.

Giving swift succinct account of her trip, she concluded, 'And so this Monsieur Lucien, Guizot's business associate and papa's former friend, has promised to advance one thousand, through a Dublin solicitor, not later than the end of the month.'

'It is not enough.'

Alexandrine's anger flared. 'Hold your tongue, Redmond. Please understand I expected gratitude, not abuse for my generosity.'

'What generosity? You had little choice if you wished to continue to live with the pride and style you are accustomed to.'

'So what have *you* achieved in my absence? What advance have you made?'

'Little, little.' He stood and paced heatedly. 'I have been flying about Dublin, entertaining like a clown and trying to befriend the right folk. I swear this worry will be my undoing. Hedgeleigh has finally been sold – ' She squirmed in her chair and gritted her teeth; Bouchard would not be put off. 'But the proceeds have been disappointing. Fifteen thousand to the penny, which clears one debt and still leaves me with the others. And interest is well overdue.' He stomped a foot down. 'And I will not be made bankrupt, nor see a scandal.'

'The money I have procured will assist – '

'It will pay this gambling cad a measure, that is all.'

'Do not raise your voice at me again, Redmond, I warn you.'

'How dare you, woman! You *may not* warn me! Let me remind you of something: I may not be in this position at all but for the meddling greed of your crook of a father!'

'How can you say that, you vicious man! And papa on his death-bed in America!'

'Aye, earning the wages of sin – death.' He fumed, 'Do not try to deceive me any longer with your innocence, my dear. I have had time enough to ruminate. You and your papa toured these islands with your bag of tricks those few years ago, searching out a suitably well-off suitor. And the fun of it is you thought you found one in me. I have inquired, I have established that you called on so many great houses and tried to sell your potion!'

Alexandrine crashed a spiky heel on the floor and her face flooded with fury. 'Be careful, Redmond. You have retreated from London for a time to rally. I have invested my efforts in helping you and you still possess the threads that can save you. But do not cross me further. All right – I have my stakes in you, but I recognise too the stakes you have in me, the ways in which you need me at this time. Now *I* warn *you* – insult me in this manner once again, and you will live to regret my departure. Take heed. Next week we go up to Dublin for the Presentation Ball. Do not have me make fun of your name by starting a scandal here and now.'

His anger was cooling. He raised placating hands. 'All right, all right. Hush, please.'

'And one more thing.' She jabbed a finger into his chest. 'We none of us intend to languish here forever – neither your daughters nor I. Understand that. This is your opportunity to redeem a position and make good socially and business-wise. Do not miss out on it.'

'Meaning?'

'Meaning if this Irish existence does not blossom and fruit in my eyes, we shall sell out here and resume in Doughty Street – ' She bared her teeth. 'And to hell with the Bouchard reputation and heritage. At least in London we may live without this incessant stink of turf and lifeless vistas.'

CHAPTER TEN

Fur-hatted guardsmen in tunics of scarlet and blue stood immobile by the State Apartment door and footmen scurried about like busy insects as the carriages rolled up. Inside Dublin Castle brass lanterns winked gaily and bubbling laughter filtered out to the wet and windy night. Bouchard craned forward as the carriage prepared to set down and saw already familiar faces from his part of the world. There was Sir Davis Ross, the great Dublin Tory; and Major Middleton with his rather ugly daughter Amanda; and here and there were faces from the local garrison, officers and their wives he himself had many times entertained.

'Are you quite certain my petticoats are even?' Letitia demanded of her sister. 'I do want the quilted satin to show above the straw plait, but the whalebone rather tugs it upwards.'

'Be quiet,' Alexandrine ordered, for the nervousness of her step-daughter was wrestling into her own brain, and she was tense enough as it was. For the hundredth time she found her reflection in the carriage window and patted her carefully piled curls into firmer place. She looked quite splendid, she knew, in her oyster satin gown with large-jewelled intaglio at the throat carefully set to draw emphasis on her broad breasts, but she knew too that any woman would have her work cut out to surpass the attractions of her step-daughters. Letitia had taken greater care in her preparations and took pride in her snow white dress with Limerick lace, but Donna positively radiated in jewellery and dress of gold.

As they stepped from the carriage and swept into the ball room, the glances of unabashed admiration the girls drew did not pass unnoticed by Alexandrine. Shunning the protocol of Castle pageantry, the viceroy and his attendants met the guests at the foot of the massive stairway to the State Apartments. Through the ballroom leading to the stairway a huge procession of people thronged, noisy with chat and laughter at the rear of the column, but fearfully quiet near the head. Bouchard and his family took their place in the queue and edged forward. By coincidence, Sir Davis Ross's party was channeled in behind them. Bouchard in his former life, before his marriage to Alexandrine, had known and socialised with the Rosses and jauntily now introduced his family and commented courteously on Ross's pretty daughter and son in uniform. Instantly, with a cold breeze on his spine, he knew something was amiss. Sir Davis's manners were faultlessly correct and his brood responded pleasantly, but an icy vagueness of chat alerted him. For a moment he contemplated a possible breach as a result of his resistance to Peel; but that seemed unlikely. Fair enough, Sir Davis was Peel's man, but as such for many, many years had enjoyed Bouchard's hospitality in Doughty Street and elsewhere. And what cause for political grievance had he now? Bouchard was, as Peel wanted, out of the game; and the likelihood of *detail* of his debt position circulating now was slight.

'You do not ask me how I prosper in my new base?' Bouchard jokingly nudged.

Sir Davis's expression was arch. 'Oh? Quite. It goes well?'

'Exceedingly. I ride better than ever and have the pitch on every fox west of Naas.' He laughed; Sir Davis's daughter grinned, but no one else joined in. 'You must come to weekend with us,' he proffered.

'Pressures of parliament,' Sir Davis commented mysteriously, looking over Bouchard's head.

'Budgetary deficits still?'

'Um.' Sir Davis glanced around, turning his back to Alexandrine much to Bouchard's annoyance. Suddenly he perked and took his daughter by the arm. 'Oh, excuse us, would you? I see a colleague.' Without waiting for response he led off his group.

'What the devil – ?' Bouchard hissed. 'I could rightly draw a pistol on that fellow. Treated me like a damned peasant, did he not?'

'You over-reacted, *chéri*,' Alexandrine said, but she too sensed reproach and insult.

They were distracted at that instant by the bellowing voice of the chamberlain announcing them and, as the crowd before them dispersed, the viceroy and vicereine stood forward. The Chief Secretary, another close associate of Bouchard's, was standing nearby in bright court dress but as the girls stooped forward to receive the viceroy's kiss, he vanished among the surrounding groups.

Presentation over with, Bouchard led Alexandrine into the ballroom with a heavy heart. 'I tell you,' he mumbled, 'there is something odd here. Did you see the Chief Secretary in the plum robe, did you see me signal to him? Absolutely ignored me, by God.'

'The viceroy was attentive and warm –'

'Dammit, lady, that oaf would not know a live human being from a Lecoq sketch. My concern has nothing at all to do with him. Look – ' He was becoming quite aggrieved as he summoned a footman for drinks. 'Where are hospitable friends? I cannot stand alone in a corner all damned night, can I?'

'Better that than make a fool of yourself by raising voice and drawing attention.'

A few young bucks from the Shannonbridge garrison in red uniform with twinkling braid and epaulettes caught sight of the twins and, like chess pieces in a master game, manoeuvred their way through the crowd, moving from garrulous knot to knot until they came to engage Donna and Letitia. Alexandrine, to her husband's disgust, entered their fun and joined the talk. Bouchard dallied politely but his interest floated off to other groups – groups of former acquaintances who, by his estimation, *should* have been entertaining him. Finally, unable to control his curiosity, he spotted Major Middleton in solitary conversation with an aide-de-camp and stalked over.

As the assistant moved off Bouchard descended on the surprised Middleton. Cheerfully clamping his shoulder he began, 'Fine turn-out, what? I always say the Castle beats any state house in England.'

Middleton's walnut face smoothed over and the crafty eyes beneath tufted brows narrowed. He stared at Bouchard, but said nothing at all.

'I see you've brought your lady daughter up. Lovely girl, lovely. A long time since I'd seen her.' The void on the other's face remained. 'I had just recently been saying to my lady how we must again have you to dinner.'

'These are not times for entertaining,' the Major said flatly. 'Whilst the Ribbonmen problem persists who would consider it safe to walk out after dark?'

Bouchard frowned. 'I really had not heard of Ribbonmen – oh, for some months.'

'One hears what one chooses to hear, is it not said?' The Major decided to qualify that. 'What concern can the Ribbonmen be to you, a supporter of theirs and of Repeal and – '

'One moment, sir. You insult me without cause. I am no supporter of Ribbonmen, nor of O'Connell's Repeal. This fallacy may have been aired by my opponents, but it carries no truth.'

'Did you not argue against Peel – ?'

'Sir, respectfully, you are no politican. If I argued with Peel it concerned matters of Toryism quite removed from O'Connell's campaigns. If you ask me, I do not, nay, support Mister O'Connell. My record will show that. And as for supporting the Ribbonmen – '

'You have engaged a rebel in your household. You refuse investigation of your tenants' subversive work by the police. You fall purposely out of step with other landlords by not in the last years increasing your rents. . .' Middleton coolly itemised while Bouchard was seething. 'And, to crown it all, you encourage a whore of a daughter to prance with a Catholic farm boy.'

Bouchard was stuck for words. He gabbled fiercely, then calmed. 'Such cheek! Sir, firstly regarding my attitude to Irish issues of politics, I suggest you consult Hansard, wherein you'll find a full and proud history. Secondly, we live in a free world, thank God, and *I* am free to employ what staff I choose. And thirdly, why increase rents when the end-of-sheet figures you're talking about are mere shillings, and at a time of land wars and unrest one is encouraging uprising?' He attacked with venom. 'Unless that is what *you* desire, sir: uprising and civil war?'

'Ridiculous, man – '

'I am not finished, Major. Hear me out. I demand apology for any insinuation that an offspring of mine is any other than virtuous and chaste!'

Middleton's face barely twitched. 'What can I say but the truth? Mine own eyes have seen your lass – the blonde-haired one – in the arms of a peasant. Young Devlin, I think, the fosterage boy. And if you doubt my word, ask McClune. We rode together one afternoon not ten days ago.' At last Middleton's creased face showed emotion: he grimaced as if repulsed by the recollection. 'As we found the track to the river, by the Doon, there they were – he most evidently with passion about him, she no less.'

'By the devil!' Bouchard had to hold himself from striking out a fist. So this was it, this was the source of censure: the Major's resentment had germinated ten years ago, in jealousy that his neighbour's lands enjoyed a tranquillity his did not, and year after year, fanned by incidents mis-interpreted, resentment had grown to insurmountable, unquenchable bitterness. And now at last, with some extraordinary incident, evidence for reproach and reason for revenge had been proved. Bouchard held no doubts: Major Middleton had put word around – Bouchard was a dissenter.

'No, sir,' Middleton announced coldly. 'I will not accept offer to dine with you, as I suspect many, many others will not in the months to come. In fact, it is my wish not to know you again, as friend or acquaintance.' His eyes rippled round the room. 'A sentiment shared with many, I'd venture.'

Bouchard snapped.

His right hand shot out and he caught Middleton heavily beneath the chin, knuckles screaming with the crack of pain. Middleton went down like a leaf in wind, clearing space for a fall with the wide sweep of his spread arms. As Bouchard pulled back and a wall of sound rose up the first face he saw approaching was that of the Chief Secretary. His head swam and his legs became weak. The Chief Secretary was gaping at him, shocked to his very toes. Gradually the horrified screams of women died down and an aide-de-camp clasped Bouchard's arm tightly. He swayed, shaking his head to revive himself. 'I need air,' he gasped. 'I feel quite ill.'

'So it would appear,' the Chief Secretary grunted, appalled. He nodded to the aide-de-camp. 'Take Sir Redmond outside and summon round his carriage.'

Around them in the great ballroom people groaned and hissed, and made jokes.

Halifane's note came six days later.

It had been almost expected, and Bouchard did little more than pause to curse into his brandy as he scanned the content. It amounted to this: no City banker was prepared to double-mortgage Doughty Street nor Drumloch. Other credit sources – even Cohen, the Jewman of Usher's Quay – had been unsympathetic. But that was not the crux.

Meehan and Kiely's wanted now quick discharge of the Drumloch loan of six years ago, plus interest. A time limit of three months had been extended to Halifane, but that was all. If no settlement was made in that time, Bouchard's affairs would be in the hands of the courts.

Bouchard took the attorney's letter and locked himself in his library with a full bottle of brandy. There seemed little he could do, all resources were drained. In London his name carried no weight politically and a marked foul odour permeated gambling and Society circles; and promising Dublin looked little better now. Oh, he had done what he could to make amends after the fiasco of the Presentation Ball. He had apologised to the Major and written to both Chief Secretary and viceroy. He had sent flowers to the vicereine and appealed to mutual acquaintances of the top men. But the fact of it remained: Middleton had been passing rumours about him and his estate and, in tackling the accusations with violence, he had seemed to validate them.

He had confronted Donna squarely after the debacle and she confessed tarrying with a farm boy; that it was Colum Devlin she denied, but he had sensed a lie and beaten her all the harder for that. Across his knee she had gone and before Alexandrine, whose rage was no lesser, he had whipped up her petticoats and leathered her with the studded belt of his breeches. If nothing else appeased the anger he felt, her plaintive screams did and as he lashed her he recalled Janet, recalled the oppression of women, the callousness of neighbours, the pressures on Drumloch, the supercilious strength of this very girl on his knee, and his thrashing became more vigorous. He would teach her, by heavens! He would knock her into line, hone and shape her like the girl Letitia, who at least had respect and honour!

The last travelling cases were packed, but still the snow fell heavy in slanting, thick cascades.

Donna stood by the window-seat, snug in a long cape, and looked out on the forecourt of Drumloch. From time to time, wordlessly, she leant forward and scrubbed away the grey condensation. She was bathed and dressed since nine, ready for the promised carriage, and her heart was heavy and glum. The clock chimed eleven, but still there was no sign. Nurse had suggested that some of the new bogland roads might well be buried under the dense overnight cover, so delays of all kinds must be borne.

As Donna watched, the lithe figure of a young man approached, inadequately dressed for the cold in a thin cloak and without head covering. Halfway down the drive Pearson was organising the dig party. Various work implements were being distributed among the group of casual labourers who had come to assist clearing the snow in the avenue. Donna saw the young man approaching was Colum Devlin and her breath choked in her throat. In two weeks she had seen nothing of him, but thought much. Now, watching him so close, thrilling innocent memories flooded her brain. She closed her eyes. The last weeks had been strangely complicated, a time of mixed emotions but – in spite of papa's thrashing – no regrets. She had done nothing wrong, merely met and talked with a boy on a level of straightforward frankness. And her blood sang to that memory.

As she moved away from the window, the figure in the court seemed to see her. She saw him bow, run lean fingers through his long hair, then stoop to spade. She stayed by the window, excited, remembering long ago when he had boldly kissed her, recalling every second of that sensation.

Down the avenue a carriage was sliding slowly through the half-cleared passage. She called Letitia and together the girls watched as muffled footmen ran down to meet the arrival.

'Our time is here,' Donna told her sister.

Letitia sighed. 'Now that we must move again I am filled with trepidation. Imagine – Rouen, in France – the school of the Mesdemoiselles Parat. A comedown from Corley, I do not doubt.'

'Do not be so gloomy, Letty.'

'I am, 'cause it's true. At least we shall be finished for another while with dull old Ireland.'

'I shall miss it.'

'Not at all. You shall only miss the villainy you have been enjoying.'

Donna ignored the wicked smile of her sister's. 'I shall miss the sun on the Shannon and the greens of evening.'

'Silly girl.' They stood in silence, then Letitia resumed, 'What will become of us, Donna? I fear papa is quite unsure of the future.' She shuddered. 'Let us hope he recovers contentment soon.'

'Will he go back to London?' Donna felt a stab of fear in her heart. 'Maybe sell Drumloch?'

'Who knows? It seems everything is being thrown to the four winds. Lord knows where next year will find us.'

The snow passage was cleared and Rob the groom was gingerly leading the horses through. Nurse's step could be heard on the stairs and Letitia had suddenly remembered something she had forgotten to pack. Donna did not move. Her eyes were on Colum Devlin, but her mind was as blank as the driven snow.

PART TWO:

IRISH DISASTER
1843 – 1845

CHAPTER ELEVEN

The open Bianconi coach rumbled over good roads that paralleled the Dublin-Belfast rail line then turned west, towards the flax fields and towns.

The journey from the station was rocky but fast and, in less than twenty minutes, Bouchard was set down at the crossroads dividing Samuel Mortimer's fields. Away to the north the chimney-and-hutment bulk of Lurgan could be seen and ahead, up the hill, stood the flat-roofed spread of what Bouchard guessed were Mortimer's storage sheds. Grumbling dully he made for the sheds. Ireland's northern lands had so far surprised him. The roads were better, the cottages larger and more frequently seen, and fewer beggars dogged one's path. There was no evidence of wealth, but the land did not exude that air of poverty which marred the southern territory. It was many years since Bouchard had seen Mortimer, many years since he had guessed at his wealth. Now, with palms damp and tension in his spine, he wondered just how well his former brother-in-law's factories had succeeded.

He found Mortimer in the first shed. The men greeted each other coolly, each seemingly rapidly assessing the other's appearance and recent fortunes. Mortimer shook Bouchard's hand firmly and politely admitted that he had received the letter of herald. Then, hooking Bouchard's arm, he led him out into refreshing sunshine. As the two men walked together Bouchard could see the wary watchfulness in hiding. Mortimer suspected a problem already, and was steeling himself for it.

They crossed through the blue-decked flax fields and saw the labourers inspecting the flowers. They were following a high path and Lurgan's outlying houses and huts stood before them. Mortimer pointed to a squat monster of a building, not a mile away. 'This was the first of my two factories. My rebirth in business, as it were. When cotton went down I turned to linen. Then, when the factory system proved so effective, I borrowed and built. And today I have quite a large industrial concern.' He looked sternly to Bouchard to underline his sincerity. 'It should make me an extremely wealthy man, but it does not. Oh, I do well, I cannot deny. But the government still intervenes in many unfortunate ways. I don't think they have a full awareness of how many difficulties a man like myself encounters. Labour is always a problem. True, there is plenty of it – and cheap too. But I have always striven to *increase* output and better my investment. But the more one pushes labour, the more problems one meets. And for some extraordinary reason, the attitude of your average five-shillings-a-week worker changes in the atmosphere of four walls. They band and fight. The dissent can be quite a worry at times. One has to just throw them all out and start again. It really is that bad.'

'Faithful servants are never easy to come by,' Bouchard agreed carefully.

'That's it. And I am sixty. I am too old for the struggle and the problems the government pitches against me. I tire easily. But sometimes I think I would like to put to use the lessons I have learnt on this estate.' He winked proudly. 'I dabble in local politics, you know. Your own neck of land, eh? I'm a businessman's politician. Sometimes I dearly wish I could stand in the Lords and point out a thing or two about Irish industry. That's where they err, you see. Rather than encourage the likes of me – English-bred respectable businessmen who want to tap Ireland's natural resources – they put us down. And that makes us strive harder, which in turn causes a rebellious rise among workers. *That*, mark me, is this land's trouble. Give me five days in government and I'd tell them what to do with Health Commissions and whatnot *and* I'd treble my own and many other factory-owners' profits. Not to mention putting the native trouble-makers in their place.'

'You are ambitious for a political career?'

Mortimer shrugged and his face turned back to Bouchard. 'They say you have fully quit that sphere?' he said suspiciously.

'Indeed. I began to find it tiresome. It was really – ' He faltered, then saw nothing wrong in candour. 'I was neither good at it nor, in the end, specifically interested. Though I may not admit that to many.'

'You are no businessman, then,' Mortimer quipped. 'To me political life is where every young chappie should start. That's where real power lies.' He kicked the dirt and his rich Northern burr became fierce. 'If I were younger – ah, doesn't bear thinking about. But – ' He sighed. 'I am not young. My wife is dead, my son at Marlborough, and all I may do is strive to make the factories yield a little more . . . and get on with enjoying whatever scant pleasures remain.'

They entered the factory-mill and spent an hour pacing the maze of gangways between power-looms and ancient jennys. Mortimer's tongue had well and truly loosened and he prattled on and on about development plans and government disappointments, but Bouchard's attention was taken by the crowds of serried labourers, sorry-looking entities, half-clad in the airless heat. Some were as young as eight years old, others aged and bent, women and men. Their produce was fine lace, canvas, sewing thread and fishnet, and the asthmatic smell, perked by an endless breeze of urine odour, sickened him until quite breathlessly he asked Mortimer for a place to sit awhile.

Chuckling aloud at Bouchard's weakening mettle, Mortimer drew him up a flight of steps and into a spacious office. He sat Bouchard down and spoke briefly into a pipe. Then he returned and gazed out through an observation window at the dizzy workers in the factory below. 'Too hot for you?' he grinned. 'I cannot understand it,' he went on. 'You've seen it yourself. Everything is quite in order.' Bouchard said nothing. 'And yet the damned Sadler Committee come along and tip the apple cart with stupid rumours of exploiting children and paying them tuppence. Silly fools.'

A dark-eyed, well-dressed girl whom Mortimer introduced as Miss Prendergast, his personal assistant, entered bearing a tray. There was coffee and a decanter upon it for which Bouchard thanked God. The lovely girl beamed coyly, eyeing her employer admiringly. Bouchard guessed she was eighteen, no more. He noticed Mortimer's overfriendly response to the girl, saw him wink to her secretively, cup her waist with a big arm. Bouchard wondered what kind of distractions took his fancy in Belfast and Lurgan.

They both took whiskey and Bouchard boldly spoke. 'No doubt you will want to know what grave hurry brings me to you. As I suspect you guess, I am in some debt. The detail of it is unimportant, but suffice to say unfortunate investment and not squandering was the root cause.'

Mortimer raised his brows. Janet had relayed more than one dark secret about her husband's predilections. He cleared his head and listened.

'My estate at Hedgeleigh is sold and that will ease the burden. But my income from Drumloch, you must see, is insufficient to offset the demands of creditors who are former partners of mine. To be frank, Samuel, only months of consideration and the greatest pressure of these particular debts bring me to you. I require, until my business ventures take me back on my feet – ' He grinned. 'And do not think because I am a grey old man with no more claim to politics, that I am fully out of such games – I require an urgent personal loan of some magnitude.'

'How much?'

'Five thousand, at least.'

'A fortune!'

'I know. I know. Please do not think I dare confront you for a *baseless* loan. I can offer security.'

Mortimer seemed unimpressed. He had sat down, absorbed in his own thoughts.

'I have rented out Doughty Street and decided to stay here. I will be less tempted to spend extravagantly, you'll agree, and general living expenses will be cheaper by far.'

'What of your wife and daughters?' Mortimer asked. For a second Bouchard thought there was a hint of a smile.

'My wife has been most helpful and understanding, of course. An acquaintance of hers in Paris has kindly forwarded some small money which has enabled me to placate some pressing people. But full settlement of these remains, and interest due on a large mortgage – hence this five thousand.' The last words were stated loudly, pleading reaction. When Mortimer did not immediately respond, Bouchard pushed on. 'My daughters have been residing at Rouen, at a school of sorts, but its standard and class troubles me and I do not wish to foster dangerous education. I may be forced to return them to Ireland – though I am not sure even this is the right thing to do or the right place for them. Especially Donna, the wilful one.'

'The problems of children. I know.' Mortimer blew out a loud sigh. 'I do not wish to depress you with my problems, Redmond – and I have no wish to seem unsympathetic – but all we spoke of today concerning the state of the linen industry here really does rather make things awkward for me. I am striving to fight my way out of a hole and money is not actually my greatest weapon at present. I have succeeded financially, to be sure, but my real talent has always been industry itself, not money matters.'

Just like Janet, Bouchard reflected with anxiety. Struggle to the last, say black is white, plead penury if necessary. Rather harshly he said, 'What more can I say, Samuel? I am absolutely confident that whatever you may generously allow will be returned in a short period of time. I had a good attorney and sound friends in Dublin Castle, as you know. And there are good investments around now. But, should you seek references –'

'Five thousand is so much,' Mortimer said, 'and I know nothing of your lifestyle or family situation. I have never believed in attorneys or accountants, just as I have never believed in agricultural advisers who tell me when I may and may not plant flax.' He filled himself another whiskey. 'After all,' he pursued quietly, 'after dear Janet, you are a stranger to me.' His rheumy eyes were remote.

117

Eagerly Bouchard took him up. 'Please, please,' he implored. 'If it might at all help, allow me to offer you my home and the estate income as collateral. Please come south if you will and visit with us. Examine for yourself.'

'They say there is much trouble brewing in the midlands – with the Liberator O'Connell urging rebel risings.'

'Not at all, my dear fellow. Take it from one who knows. Whatever else might be said about the man, O'Connell does not urge violence. And things are peaceful now. See for yourself. I cannot promise you a house of luxury, I'm sure, but you will enjoy the Shannon's fair air. And an excellent cellar. Please.'

Mortimer stared Bouchard. A year ago, next year, he might have given a blunt refusal. But Bouchard had come at an opportune time, saying intriguing things. Yes indeed, Mortimer would like to see the virgin south. 'Very well,' he agreed slowly. 'I shall journey south and observe your home. Then perhaps we can inspect income sources and the like – and see.'

A weight of fear passed off Bouchard's shoulders. 'Excellent,' he said. 'Consider my home and all in it as yours. My wife will enjoy greeting you as truly I will.'

'I look forward to greeting Lady Alexandrine.' Mortimer stood and tapped the window, gazing down into the factory. 'Now,' he grinned, clapping his hands explosively, 'let us repair to Meadow Hill, my manor house, and talk of pleasanter matters – eh?'

Bouchard was auctioning an Ingres nude from the Great Hall together with some *objects de vertu* under pretence of a planned redecoration and Squire Stephens, having caught wind of it, was among the first to arrive.

Before the auctioneer had shown himself with his choice clients, the blustering Squire was pacing among the ranked bric-à-brac, huffing and puffing his interest like a sow at swill. The Ingres was either too pricey or indecent, but eventually the Squire's attention came down to an attractive matched arrangement of Honduras mahogany side tables, Bouchard spoils of some foreign war.

The Squire examined the pieces carefully while

Bouchard fussed over him, pleased at his presence. Stephens alone among neighbouring gentry had maintained an attitude of friendly warmth these last few difficult months, it seemed, and Bouchard was grateful for it and encouraged it. He was mindful too that indications showed the Squire's formerly indifferent fortunes had improved greatly since his eldest son William's final desertion of academic life and entry into stock brokerage.

Having discussed the merits of the goods at length and decided his purchase, Stephens joined Bouchard in the library and drafted a cheque. As he scribbled he said, quite unexpectedly, 'My dear chap, will you consider me obnoxiously rude if I ask boldly when your daughters may be returning from France?'

Bouchard stammered, hedging lest he reveal a chink in the armour of pretence. 'I am undecided.' Then, truthfully, he added, 'I am concerned about the girl Donna, the difficult one. It is difficult to see a future for her here. Letitia has sense, but she is wayward and hard.'

Stephens blushed and blew warm air on his cheque. 'I come, in truth, to ask about young Donna.'

'*You* – about Donna?'

'I wondered was there any likely suitor fixed?'

'N-no. Such thoughts had scarcely entered my head.'

'Well, she is surely of age, and quite lovely, I'm sure.' He frowned. 'I am intrigued to hear you call her an awkward child. I would have thought she was quite the opposite. Many's a time I encountered her out strolling and was taken by her courteous kindness.' The Squire hesitated. He had heard rumour of an alleged association between one of Bouchard's girls and a peasant; till now he had supposed it to be false, just some concoction of spiteful Middleton; but Bouchard's nervy reaction gave him second thoughts. Still, the matter wasn't primarily his concern; he was but agent of communication.

'Do you, by any chance, object to the notion of a marriage?' the Squire asked.

'I'm at a loss, friend. Of course I do not object to marriage – ' He chortled. 'Though a wedding of Donna to yourself might seem a trifle odd.'

Stephens stood and addressed Bouchard seriously, the cheque poised like a card of bargain in one hand. 'I speak for William, dear chap. This inquiry comes from him. These few years he has admired your girl and now, with a sound career opening for him, he is frankly contemplating the idea of marriage. You may have heard of his successes. His broking partnership in London is going on famously and his associations specifically with the railways people are the envy of thousands.' The Squire craned forward to whisper. 'I will confess *I* owe much to the boy. His sagacity has fair dumbfounded me. The scrip lists he advised me to quite appalled me at first but, by the Lord, I have made a fair few shillings from them in no time at all.'

Bouchard stalled, his thoughts jumbled. *Does Stephens owe you a favour?* Halifane had said. *Consider and utilise all friendships.*

'You are suggesting an arrangement for William and Donna? My dear fellow, I know not what to say. That Donna should be so lucky.' He paused to sit. 'Of course, one must not presume that I can give any undertaking without speaking to the child.'

'Naturally, naturally. As I say, I am merely the vanguard. If you are in agreement, then perhaps the girl can be allowed home and a courtship can begin.' Stephens was leaving no areas of grey doubt. 'Followed by engagement and, after a suitable time, wedding.' He shrugged his sloping shoulders and pulled the waxed ends of his moustache. 'Damned children, never understand them. Due respects, Redmond, can't see what is wrong with fifty other women the lad knows through varied respectable channels.'

'Donna is, I suppose, very lovely in appearance.'

'Yes, yes. That's it. Never was attracted to glitter myself, but the ways of youth – all unmanageable desire and dizzy thoughts, eh?' He passed over the written cheque and gathered his cane and cape. 'Anyway, the boy will be delighted to know we have a meeting of minds. I shall tell him you will speak to the girl – ?'

'I shall have her home within a fortnight.'

'Excellent, excellent. William will be beside himself.'

The Squire became conspiratorial again. 'They say times have been . . . unkind for you, these last months.'

Bouchard thought of denying it, but saw sympathy in the other's gaze. 'A change of lifestyle is always hard. I have been accustomed to one world that, it seems, no longer exists. But I am back on my feet –'

'Money in the stars?'

Bouchard considered Mortimer, due next week. 'Yes. I see signs of ease.'

'Do you know,' Stephens tugged his friend's sleeve, 'money begets money. And – take it from one who has been down that rocky road – gambling horses wins nothing in the end. Use your money, but wisely.'

'If I had the right kind of expert advice, that might be much easier.'

The Squire stood stock still. Bouchard's remark had been calculated and intense and Stephens understood it. 'Let me put it to you this way: William's brilliance I have no wish to share with anyone, for the danger of causing landslide investments negates the very reason for high returns on unlikely lists – you understand?' Bouchard nodded. 'But his enthusiasm for your girl is very real and means much to me as a consequence. I want to repay the lad for his caring attention to my fortunes, so I wish to give him what he desires. Now, should you persuade this girl to reciprocate fairly, I think I can offer you a promise for this money you have in the stars.'

'High returns, short term?'

'Given William's inside information – a double-your-money deal over a mere month or two.' The Squire laughed excitedly. 'You see, this is the genius of it, Redmond. *Now* is the time for making money on railways. Now, while the boom is on. Because there is only so much ground to cover and so many towns to service. In five years there will be a surfeit situation and shares will plummet, no matter what the line. William knows.'

Bouchard bit back his eagerness. 'Let us see how things progress from here,' he said and he thought, Let us hope Mortimer comes up with the goods.

CHAPTER TWELVE

To Bouchard's chagrin, Mortimer did not arrive in Drumloch till October. The summer had been fraught with problems – keeping Halifane interested but at bay, placating creditors who were ever-increasingly threatening law actions, bringing the girls home from France and carefully prompting Donna towards William Stephens while rigidly controlling chaperonage and respectability. By winter Bouchard felt himself in a state of exhaustion, sensed his grip on Drumloch was slipping and even the brickwork of his marriage was beginning to erode.

On the first day of Mortimer's arrival Alexandrine was confined to her rooms with a seasonal chill that Bouchard neither witnessed nor believed: she was, he was certain, trick-acting, resolved to play no further part in the recovery of 'a position' in Ireland. When, the following afternoon, she revealed herself as they were departing on a survey ride through the farmlands, Bouchard saw that she looked the picture of health. She was dressed in her finest taffeta gown, trimmed with sable – a dress more befitting a Russian princess in July than impoverished gentry on a bitter Irish day. Her exchange of greetings with Mortimer was cordial and they stood for many minutes laughing in reminiscence of a previous encounter in London – an encounter tailored by de Doubalier, Bouchard did not doubt – excluding everyone from their talk. Bouchard was somewhat relieved by their ease of friendship but her insistence on joining them for the ride somehow rankled. Mortimer, however, took heartily to the idea and Alexandrine went indoors to change clothing and returned wearing a heavier velvet dress, cut too low over the bosom by far, Bouchard thought. But Mortimer admired it, saying that she looked as pretty as a Mayday colleen.

Rob Devlin as guide led them up first to the high ground overlooking the valley. Mounted on Zephyr and in his finest young squire's dress, Rob impressively contributed his local knowledge of the pastures and plots, confidently speaking with optimism as if he had divined the necessity to win over this hawkish Northerner. Bouchard was delighted. Even the sun deigned to shine for them, spilling over the undulating fields in butter-yellow, healthy lakes, lending a uniform appearance of fruitfulness. And the farm workers were out in good numbers, busily digging their crops and labouring with dedicated determination. Mortimer drank all this in, face impassive.

'In conclusion,' Bouchard said, 'I have before me 1500 or so of the best acres south of Athlone and settled tenants.'

'But no agent.'

'Since old Anderson, no – not in the sense of an overlord. But Devlin, this lad's father, has been a superb and worthwhile trustee. A keeper of the peace in every sense, since he is so respected by farm folk. And of course Halifane gets my rents when due.'

Mortimer faced Rob. 'A desirable situation, do you think?'

'You ask me, sir?'

'You grew up on a farm. Is it wise to allow so loose and lenient a control, without enforcing agent?'

'I do not contest Sir's wisdom. The valley has had peace. It speaks for itself.'

Mortimer reflected on that. 'Interesting but – ' His mouth curled downwards. 'I really think an agent-of-the-gentry would be better.'

'If that is what you advise,' Alexandrine said, 'we must see to it, I'm sure.' Bouchard glared savagely to her but Mortimer's glance riveted him.

'We cannot allow weak links in the chain, you will agree,' Mortimer said, and tugged his mount's reigns to angle down to the farm tracks.

They trekked down through criss-crossed paths across fresh-dug plots and Mortimer noted interestedly that the

123

potato seemed the staple crop of the tenants. 'They resist new ideas,' Bouchard explained. 'Which carries virtues too, I suppose. But I have tried to educate them into pasture and animal rearing, with little success. Very few even pursue corn and fewer bother with chickens and pigs.' They joned the river track and passed the house of Swan Duff. 'Yonder, the Devlins' farm,' Bouchard said, seeing the bent figure of Desmond shuffling across his yard.

Devlin looked up to the approaching party with a mixture of clear pride and mistrustful concern. Rob was virtual stranger to him now, though the lad visited with dutiful frequency when working from the manor, and Devlin had the sudden unnerving feeling of not knowing his son at all. It was as if, of a sudden, Rob showed greater kinship to this cloaked, cold-eyed newcomer.

'*Failte*,' Devlin said. 'Stay to drink.'

Bouchard shook his head. 'Be easy, old man. We ride to show our guest the face of the valley. A happy one this season, it seems?'

'The crop has been good, sir. Thank God. I complain not at all.' He brushed his eyes and raised both hands, arthritic and shrunken. 'Sight and memory are denied me occasionally and I cannot myself work long in the plots, but I have a strong lad to dig and plant for me and we have food and roof.'

'Your wife is well?'

Devlin smiled with benign expression. 'She is healthy in spirit, but suffers the ailments of age. She awaits God's call.'

Bouchard understood. 'I am sorry. Convey to her my warm sympathies.'

Mortimer cut in, 'What do you hear of O'Connell? No doubt he's popular among the farmers.'

'The Liberator is a legend, sir, like CuChulainn. The stories we hear are wild and glorious, but they do not feed us or dig our lands.'

Bouchard sat back contentedly in his saddle, well pleased. Mortimer pushed: 'Where I come from people talk of these parts in the same way they discuss warring Austria. One hears of continued agrarian distress – '

'With respect, sir, such rumours may find truth elsewhere, but no one seeks war for satisfaction or pleasure. If you are asking me what troubles these lands have suffered, I will answer you: none. But why should they? What reason have we farm folk to complain? We have our needs, we have all we've ever had.'

'I think it will rain,' Alexandrine broke in rudely, pulling the strings of her sable collar.

'You're right, m'dear,' Mortimer agreed. 'I think we must find shelter.'

'Lead the way home,' Bouchard ordered Rob. Zephyr cried out shrilly as Rob whipped him round and headed for the river path.

Devlin stood gazing after the party, assailed by a sudden sense of grief and loss.

Donna sat by William Stephens on the gilt-edged confidant and nervously eyed the corner cushion just vacated by Nurse. William, at last seeing his opportunity, grasped her small hand and tugged it to him. Careful of alarming her, he kept his conversation circumspect, questioning her about Rouen, about the friends she had acquired.

'I had little time for associations,' she said tartly. 'Never expecting to be taken home so quickly, I had given all my free hours to sketching.'

'I should love to see your sketches, then.'

Donna politely pulled her hands away from William's and suppressed an angry exclamation. 'Really, William, some other time, I think. As I said last evening, I am still studying my French and rather want to spend more time at it.'

The young man stood and tramped across the room indignantly. 'My dear Donna, I think you play an unreasonable game. Come now, be fair. I feel as though I am playing tagtail in the dark. I have made it quite clear to you these last weeks – my true emotion for you. Blessedly everyone approves –'

'I am sorry, William. But if it is courtship you are after, I suggest you turn to Letty whose interest in love-making is rather more keen. I have no wish to tease or disappoint you, but my mind is in a muddle about such things.' She stood herself and paced the fine Persian carpet, her fingers gently massaging each side of her head. 'All this excitement and unease has me quite unbalanced. One minute Rouen, then back here – nothing seems settled from month to month.'

'You are becoming quite unreasonably excitable, Donna.' William disliked squalls of temperament in any young woman's tone. 'All I ask for is your time and easy co-operation.'

'But, don't you see? – I would be unfairly encouraging you.' She crossed to him and touched his arm. He stared her levelly. 'Why pretend? I like you, William, but that is all. I have no interest in couch games or future planning –'

His hands reached for her and he felt a pulse throb in his forehead. The scent and sight of her intoxicated him so – the delicacy of her touch, the smell of her hair, the huge dishes of her sapphire eyes. A nerve snapped somewhere inside. He had come this far, found the Squire's and her father's approval; he would not surrender. He crushed his body against hers, throwing her back to the wall. She struggled heatedly but did not call out – a sign he took of clear encouragement. 'Come,' he urged. 'You can have a good life with me. I have funds beyond your papa's, I believe you know. I can take you to London, free you of this dull ritual of Drumloch.'

'I like it here, William. I like Drumloch.' She used her elbows to prod him away but his lips were at her ear already, nibbling into her. 'Please, sir –'

The door squeaked and, in a burst of energy, she flung him from her. Both swivelled round, faces burning red and clothes askew. Bouchard sauntered in, conscious of their embarrassment but casually indifferent. 'Ah, William. Didn't know you'd come again to visit. Splendid. Pearson should have informed me. Take a drink with me, eh?'

'Really, sir – no. Not this afternoon.' William was visibly shaking, his face draining of blood and looking waxen and ill. 'I have much to do before I return to London at the weekend.'

'Oh, you go back, do you? For a short time, may we

hope?'

'Much depends,' William said mysteriously, correcting his stock with a jerk of the wrist. His skinny neck squirmed in its starched collar. 'Perhaps we will have an opportunity to chat and drink before I return.'

'Let us hope so,' Bouchard said earnestly, frowning. He looped an arm around the young man and led him out.

Donna sat by the fire, gathering the French study books she had been perusing about herself again, hoping for Letitia's intrusion and praying that papa would not come back. But back he came.

Very purposefully he closed the drawing-room doors behind him and marched across to face her. Before he spoke she said:

'I will not marry him.'

Bouchard held his patience. This stringent self-confidence so appalled him. 'Let me get this clear with you,' he said. 'Whether you suspect it or no, the funds of this house are very low at this time. I do not possess the wealth – nor the inclination, I should add – to send you on a Grand Tour. Neither do I any longer possess the connections that might have put you into the household of Lord de Grey at the Castle or somebody of his ilk. My *advice* to you now is – content yourself with what God offers. You are fortunate to find yourself courted by a lad as celebrated as William. The stories one hears of his business prowess leave little to be desired indeed.'

'But I do not wish to go back to London, nor marry just now.'

'Why?'

'I wait for . . . love.'

'Love, m'dear, means lust.' Bouchard gasped out the words, quite shocked. 'Whores may climb abed for it, but sensible women seek finer arrangements, I'll have you know. If this is the nonsense you have been taught in Rouen – ' His hand raised, uncertain of whether to hit her, but at that moment a short knock came on the door and Alexandrine led Mortimer in.

Bouchard glanced sharply to his wife, signalling that she had come at the wrong moment, but Alexandrine was not troubled. With determined ease she said. 'Fetch wine, Redmond, dear man, and draw our good guest a seat by the fire.'

Four weeks Mortimer lingered – eating well, drinking well and progressively expressing himself more and more enchanted with peaceful Drumloch. He had met new people, made a few new friends – yet still he sat on the fence, avoiding the final commitment of money.

With time running out the pressures opened rifts between Bouchard and Halifane, and with his staff, and most significantly with Alexandrine. No longer able to talk congenially with her, he lapsed to non-ending drinking and a depression she had never known before. But it was only in these moments of drunkenness could he ever face her. Then, tranquillised and benumbed, the explicit look of distaste on her face became merely a blur that he understood not at all. Their conversations were taut. Repeatedly she would call him spineless and wasteful; he would ignore her acid, stolidly wondering aloud why Mortimer withheld decision.

'Are you so stupid that you cannot see?' she snapped. 'Mortimer is a businessman first and last. He detects the subtle ramifications of your position and enjoys playing you like a salmon on a line.'

'You mean, our . . . marriage dispute?'

'I mean, the fact that he is your final hope. He knows that. And so he can afford to consider at length. Doing that, he may persuade the best exchange deal from you.'

'What d'you mean? I shall arrange to repay him honestly through Halifane. We three have already met to discuss that. From my income he shall be paid.'

'He likes Drumloch.'

'What does that mean?'

'It means, dear Redmond, that, were I you, I would observe his greedy eye closely. He tells me he admires these cheaply-managed havens of the south. After the money-consuming industrial strife of Lurgan, they seem desirable properties. The people are ill-educated and labour is cheaper. Mortimer is too shrewd to pass by the promise of that.'

'Well, if he likes the south so much let him purchase out the Major's pitch and start growing flax on the hell bogland. That has nothing to do with me or Drumloch.'

'He seems politically ambitious too. I note how he persuaded you to drag together the vestiges of your old power and get Cavendish, the old Tory, down from Dublin, and Sir Myles Rossitor to call as well. Was I correct in assuming he was keen for them to visit?'

'One must entertain a distinguished guest. And I cannot burrow myself into a hole just because Middleton wants to destroy me and the Chief Secretary thinks I'm a devil.'

'Mortimer is interested in borough-mongering. Perhaps he hopes to *buy* your assistance to help him into government.'

'Don't be ridiculous, dear lady. I have nothing to offer Mortimer – except fair repayment.'

'*Nothing*?' Alexandrine laughed darkly. 'I say these things only to instruct you to plain sense. All your life you have been fooled by people, your judgements have been outrageously wrong. I feel nothing but pity for you now. But, sadly, I still carry your name and your absolute destruction reflects on me. I do not want that but I must inform you I stay on more in confidence of Halifane than of you. All I say is, beware of Mortimer. He has what you want. *You* may well have possessions *he* wants.'

After a few more days, unable to sustain patience, Bouchard bluntly approached Mortimer while at dinner, requesting a decision on the loan.

'I will give you my answer in the morning,' Mortimer responded, excusing himself from further debate by professing a headache.

What could Bouchard say? Courteously he gave way. Then, with the household retiring early, he took a decanter into the library and settled to contemplation of a misty future. As events were resurrected for the fiftieth time and revalued it suddenly seemed as if the train of ill-luck had begun, not with intemperate personal gambling or any weakness of character, but fairly and squarely with Alexandrine. She had come along like some Nemesis and started the rot. At least with Janet, in the end – whether by providence or his actions – he had won. But this black angel was casting her spell still.

It had been all of three months since he had shared his wife's bed but now, in his drunken rage, he saw that gradual agreed separation as another of her ploys to some dark end. Cursing aloud, he staggered to his feet and sought the parlour-maid. Informed that Lady Alexandrine had retired Bouchard clambered upstairs after her. She had probably turned in early to read some nonsense novel, he guessed, for such were the atrocious French habits he had come to know. He pictured her, perched up in the pillows. He found himself suddenly feeling excited. He had neither touched her bare flesh nor embraced her for love-making in more than six months. Distorted images flickered into his head now, images of her in naked abandon in the better days, and his heart raced.

Crossing to the connecting door of her bed chamber in his own room he twisted the handle. The door was locked tight. He shook it angrily. What game was she at now? Bouchard spat an oath and stormed out to the landing. Still unstable on his feet, he moved into her room by the main door. Only the small fire that she perpetually had lit showed life, casting moving fingers of brightness across the floor. He moved to the bed and edged aside the canopy curtain. The firelight sprayed in but the pillows were smoothly virgin white, untouched. Bouchard reached down and took up the leather-bound volume lying there. His mind tried to focus, but was too tired and too inebriated. Vaguely he imagined she must be in her dressing-room, making her toilette. Perhaps he should creep upon her? Tear the silken dress from her shoulders. . . .

Moving with uncertainty towards the dressing-room, a low sound from within momentarily checked his step. He stood frozen still, listening. Was she weeping? Had she cried out, moaning? A rustle of cloth sounded, then the noise again: this time very distinctly a groan. Impulsively he moved away, but now a voice stopped him – not the voice he might have expected but a deep bass man's voice.

The words spoken were indistinguishable but their effect on Bouchard was as piercing as a million cries of terror. He turned back and, in stunned silence, opened the dressing-room door. Its draught-protecting curtain had been drawn and now, with shaking hands, he tilted it back. He stood in darkness, but two candles had been lit in the inner chamber. As the gap of vision opened he saw two tangled bodies, not fifteen feet away, on the small bed-couch. In his confusion at first he recognised neither. The man was lying stoutly atop the spreadeagled woman, half-off the stirred bed. His bedshirt had been hoisted above his waist and his naked buttocks pulsed powerfully. Neither spoke. Then they both stiffened and twisted awkwardly onto their sides. Bouchard dumbly stared. Mortimer was getting up now, pulling down his shirt and quietly pouring water into the basin on the nightstand. And Alexandrine lay still, her thighs splayed apart and facing Bouchard's line of vision. Mortimer leant across and handed her a dampened linen. She sat up on the bed and Bouchard saw that her big breasts had been released from their stays. He swallowed hard and tasted bile on his tongue. Then Alexandrine spoke softly:

'Am I to take it then, from your conversation, that you will extend this loan to Redmond?'

Mortimer had concluded washing his hands. He smiled, pinching her exposed nipple playfully. 'Wait and see, my poppet,' he grinned. He kissed her. 'You are every bit as excellent with the motion of your splendid body as I had hoped,' he said.

'Then that is payment for the thousand pounds you forwarded in answer to my appeal in May.' She pressed a forefinger against his eager lips. 'But that is to be our secret – remember. For Redmond believes it came from Paris.'

'You are an artful woman, and ambitious,' Mortimer said.

'And you are an ambitious man,' she laughed. 'But for what, I have yet to fully understand.'

Convulsive feelings of sickness in his gut made Bouchard reel back and he fled the darkened room.

CHAPTER THIRTEEN

Thirty years before, in a moment of exorbitant fancy, Bouchard had commissioned the building of a neo-Roman belvedere on the Doon Lawn. He had had problems with funds then too and, halfway through, the builder had quit his task. Because of the odd shape of the roofless result, the structure had become known as 'the mule' and, though scorned by everyone, it had attracted Alexandrine's whimsical eye from the start. She visited often and it was here next morning Bouchard found her when, rising from his whiskey-induced sleep, he could resist confrontation no more.

She was swathed in her winter furs, a book of verse open on her lap, and her posture did not shift as he buffeted into the mule and screamed her name. He stood swaying over her, his fists curled tightly. She rose slowly, a look of injured dignity washing over her. Bouchard's control was gone. He lashed out a half-open fist and struck her full on the face. The blow sent her hurtling backwards, crashing over the bench and against the marble wall.

'Whore!' he shouted. 'In all my days I have never witnessed such wanton lewdness. In your own marriage chamber! *Whore!*'

The words seemed to surprise them both. Bouchard slunk back, massaging his bruised hand, and Alexandrine rolled onto her knees, mustering calm. Her eyes were dry but wide in stark fright. 'How dare you!' she muttered shakily.

'I saw you, slut. Lying open for Mortimer, repaying his loan – *his* loan! – with your body. I heard every word you said, so do not try to deny it.'

She recoiled as he lurched forward, covering her face with her hands protectively. 'You stole in on me,' she gasped, deaf to his words but reasoning his anger.

'Behind my back you wrote to him, begging money. And you told me the money in May came from Paris. My lady, I am sickened. You have conspired with the devil behind my back.'

Courage came to her in a heady rush. She kept the brick bench between them and rose to full height. 'Conspired to save you, you fool. Had that money not come when it did, Meehan and Kiely would have had this ground from under you by now. Consider yourself blessed that I bother to grace you with my intelligence.' She bared her teeth in fury. 'But do not believe I do it all for you, or for your precious daughters. I do it for me, Redmond. *Me*. I must live with the decisions *you* make and the inglorious world you create. But I refuse to tolerate endless squalor and shame. From now, I help myself. And you are fortunate to benefit from that.'

'You help yourself with a whore's craft!' Bouchard pounded the earth, words spilling from his lips unchecked. 'I see it all now: your reluctance to have Mortimer come, your "illness", your initial embarrassment.'

'What if it is a whore's trade, Redmond? How does it differ from your debased games – from your card-playing without funds, your plan of bargaining Donna with the Squire? –'

He hit her again, but this time her responding evasive speed of movement reduced the blow to a mere clip. She steadied herself rapidly and raised a sudden tight warning fist. Her anger flared. 'Take heed,' she cautioned. 'Consider carefully *all* the actions you take this day of decision. My reasons for staying by your side diminish day by day. Hedgeleigh you sold to spite me. Little remains. And now Samuel has made his decision. What actions will you take in the face of this whore's act? Take issue with him?' She grinned. 'Chance that, Redmond, and I'll venture Samuel will lose all sympathy for you.'

That, of course, was the obvious truth. He drew back

from her. 'Words cannot express the disgust I feel,' he muttered. 'A wife of mine, an honourable woman – '

His retreat, and the clear weakening of his aggression, charged her boldness. 'Not *honourable*, as you have so blindly believed, dear man. You really have no sense of judgement when it comes to women, do you? You see, such acts of whorelike behaviour as you witnessed last night are not foreign to a woman like me. You called my dear papa a villain and cheat – well, I must certainly accept those laurels too.' She paused to allow fuller impact of her words. 'I am no more a daughter of aristocracy than dear papa. I'm afraid le Comte de Gauston or Monseur Guizot might claim knowledge of my existence on quite a different level than you have been led to believe.' She laughed. 'They might recognise me on the boards of a singing tavern but not, I think, in the drawing-rooms of the King. Oh, I must not complain. There have been rich and well-placed friends, like dear Lucien. But you must see I was in no position to chance involving them and perhaps allowing my guise here to slip. Far better to search out new gentlemen, new patrons.'

Bouchard was speechless for a time. He twisted slowly to her, his florid face suddenly white. 'A dancing-tavern girl?' he said. '*Me* – opening the lineage to a harlot.'

'Your judgements – of people and gambles – have never been sound.' Her fingers slid through his hair, teasing. 'So what course lies before you, Redmond? Throw me out? I'm sure Samuel wants me. Perhaps he will take me back to Lurgan. Challenge him about last night's play? Relinquish everything?'

'You are a demon woman,' he mumbled.

'And you a fool. From now on, Redmond, you will listen to me and hear out my proposals. *If* survival matters to you. I can play Samuel *my way* and you had better be thankful for that.' She picked her book off the ground and pulled her fur wrap about her. The cruel deriding grin on her face remained. 'This is my land as much as it is yours now. In marriage you took me for better or worse. It suits us both perhaps best to retain that.' She moved towards the doorway and turned sharply. 'But remember this. You have no place in my bed from now on. I have no more wish to feed your dreams of a male heir and I have no time for ugly drunken brutes. And if you raise a hand to me in violence ever again, I will see you in hell.'

Five thousand pounds.

Just three simple words that rolled off Mortimer's tongue with ease. Conjuring no more perhaps than a few months' income for him but drawing pictures of degradation side-by-side with subsistence in Bouchard's head.

They sat for an hour in the draughty library, Mortimer fresh from sleep and light of humour, Bouchard blethering over map sketches and ancient accounts books, endeavouring to persuade and win over. It took great effort to subdue the rambling, bitter memories that paraded through his brain, but Bouchard knew this was the last hand, the final deal, and he must maintain dignity.

'I've agonised over this one,' Mortimer stressed, 'because I consider it an investment outside my normal field.'

'A loan,' Bouchard reminded.

Mortimer shook his head. 'So vague a term irritates me. No. I am investing in you, Redmond.' He patted the closed accounts ledgers. 'Investing in Drumloch's continuing prosperity, investing in the wisdom and power of your control here. I have been impressed by what I've seen over a period of time. Young Rob convinces me too. These lands and the available workforce would be the envy of many. The pity is that they are allowed so free and easy a control.' He squeezed Bouchard's arm. 'But you will start tightening strings there, eh?'

Bouchard stared in confusion.

'A proper land agent, we want – yes? That will be half the battle. Help regularise rents and develop a realistic turn-over for the estate in years to come.'

Bouchard recalled the notoriety of certain agents, the troubles that changes in appointments had given rise to over the years. 'I had in mind some postponement of that notion,' he said. 'Perhaps just till Devlin goes –'

Mortimer was emphatic again. 'No. Be safe. Engage a good man now, someone with experience and position in society. Foolish to allow sentiment to come into it. All right, Devlin has been convenient – but Halifane has pointed out the difficulty of regulating rents when a native middleman of local residence collects. It is just not wise.' He leant forward, so close that Bouchard could smell his harsh breath. 'And I do so want a *happy* arrangement with you, my friend. These last months have been an education, I'm pleased to say. We are now closer acquaintances, we understand each other. The friends-in-politics you introduced me to fair intrigue me. I have had good dinners and good wine and good companionship. A vacation indeed. From now on I shall view these lands with friendly warmth and close interest. I shall consider this a home from home and shall visit often, and make merry with your fascinating friends.' Mortimer stopped speaking at this juncture and looked questioningly to his host. Seemingly satisfied, he went on, 'In spite of our differences in life styles, I feel you and I share similar aspirations and that alone encourages me to say – *Yes*, I will give you your five thousand.'

Bouchard's heart fluttered in his throat. 'I will repay six-monthly, on the terms suggested by Halifane,' he said.

'Whatever,' Mortimer beamed. 'Tomorrow we can meet again with your Halifane and settle it. The important thing is that I am happy and that you have your money. And –' He hesitated to smile strangely. 'You and I have become friends who will extend whatever assistance to the other as needs be.'

The words sounded ominous to Bouchard's ear but he banished the frown from his face. What did it matter if Mortimer cherished fancifully obscure plans for government and, in reality, coveted Drumloch? In Lurgan he would be a million miles away and Bouchard too had his plans. He had money again, that was all that mattered.

The silk-ribboned purse landed on Squire Stephens's desk. Bouchard craned forward expectantly and searched the Squire's reactions. Stephens sighed massively and shook his long white hair.

'Three thousand for those prime lists William promised,' Bouchard restated. 'I entreat you earnestly, Squire.'

Stephens displayed open distress. 'My friend, hard cash excites me as much as I'm certain it excites you. But I can offer you little encouragement in your porposals here. Perhaps, if you discussed with dear William yourself. But, as you know, he left for Dublin yesterday – '

Bouchard cursed under his breath. The last week had been a terrifying strain to him – first badgering Mortimer, then skipping to Dublin and avoiding Halifane's pursuit, then placating Meehan and Kiely with a thousand and a promise. With Mortimer's cheque in his hands the plan hatched weeks ago had seemed irresistibly workable. Alone, Mortimer's loan presented only a fraction of the answer to his troubles: future growth must be considered and five thousand would not lift him clear of Drumloch's mire and the ever-fastening control of Alexandrine and Halifane. The gambler in his character stirred to the challenge: a portion of that five thousand would buy him a mighty spin of the wheel; he must go for it, go for freedom. Young William Stephens's record was checkered and odd, but evidence of his recent success decked this very room, apparent in the new furnishings, in the Honduras tables that stood beneath the arched windows – Drumloch tables, lost heirlooms.

Stephens twined his fingers on the desktop. He was patently embarrassed. 'The fact is, our, er, arrangement hasn't absolutely succeeded. Your girl has no mind for marriage.'

'What nonsense. William must not listen to such indecent hogwash. The girl *will* marry him, you have my honest word.'

'But if this is so greatly against her wishes – '

'No, no.' Bouchard stood up and turned from his friend to hide his annoyance. 'Had I but known this fear lay behind your own and William's reticence to come forward these last weeks! Do not heed Donna. She plays tricks, betimes. I will sort her out and William can plan a summer wedding. I swear to you.'

The Squire's reservations were passed aside for a moment. His fat fingers toyed with the ribboned pouch before him. Three thousand! What commission would William allow him? Five, ten per cent? 'There *are* one or two superb investment lists open just now,' he ventured coolly. 'Myself, I have enough stock – but William heartily recommends a few foreign lists.'

'Foreign?' Bouchard sat again. 'I am interested, as I told you, in fast turnover. But far flung investments –'

'America,' Stephens said, wagging a forefinger. 'Land of opportunity.'

'It's a distance away –'

'You trust the lad?' The Squire's tone was quickly fierce. Bouchard nodded with enthusiasm. 'America's another universe to you and I, maybe. But William is well versed in its language and business.' He rummaged in a drawer and unearthed a sheaf of rolled papers. In a minute he had found the one he wanted and he pushed it across to Bouchard. The ornate heading announced the Mid-East Rail Company and the promotional leaflet comprised a report on the first annual stockholders' meeting in New York, share projections over several years, proxy voting forms to designate management and varied news clippings from American journals. 'That one's a gem, by all accounts,' Stephens boasted. 'Penny shares and huge prospects.'

'Just another rail line?'

'Just another! No, my dear chap, no. *Not* just another. You have heard of the Baltimore and Ohio?' Bouchard said no. 'Well, there's few in the world of high finance who have not. The two companies whose tenders won home are both sweeping the market and the dividends are superb, truly superb. You see, New York is bursting its banks. Progress westwards is inevitable. Ohio first, then it will be Illinois, Missouri – oh, endless. The frontier lands are opening every day and astute investors are riding close behind every inch of new ground. *That's* the secret in American investment.'

Bouchard consulted the paper in his hands. 'This is a company building a line to Philadelphia, north from Baltimore.'

'Humph.' The Squire suspected insulting contradiction in Bouchard's voice. He blew out his cheeks pompously. 'Augmenting the Baltimore-Ohio, my friend. A business line of perfect timing, I'll wager.'

'What is the present shares price? And the market trend?'

Stephens shook his head wearily again. 'Perhaps I move too fast, eh? William might not thank me for so casual an introduction – '

'Please,' Bouchard cut in. 'The promise I give you comes from my heart. Communicate with the lad. Assure him a wedding will be arranged and he will have the warm acquiescence of my daughter Donna.' He slapped the money purse that sat before Stephens. 'Then ask him respectfully to procure for me three thousand worth of Mid-East.'

The sweeping boldness of the request made even Bouchard light-headed. A fragment of vagrant thought flashed into his mind: he could imagine the tempest of abuse that would greet this action from Alexandrine and, in roundabout means, from his attorney. His knees were suddenly shaky. He had never gambled so much on one throw before, but then neither had there ever been so much to play for. Solvency or scandal? Who would not quail at such a risk game.

A dart of pure greed absolved Squire Stephens from any self-doubt. His big hand raked in the purse of money and he said simply, 'Deal done.'

CHAPTER FOURTEEN

There seemed no end to the exhausting intrigue. The full facts of the gamble could not, of course, be revealed to

Alexandrine but Halitane, whose spies in the woodwork flourished, had to be admitted. At first Bouchard had procrastinated; then, as the news of part-payment for Meehan and Kiely filtered out, he had conceded a long written report on his stratagem. Appalled and offended, the attorney had at first washed his hands of all further association. Mortimer's 'gravest misjudgement', Halifane boldly declared in his return missive, had been the sudden and thoughtless drafting of a personal cheque. At first angered, Bouchard was subsequently alarmed. Friends in Dublin court and society life could now be numbered on one hand and, despite his failings, Dermot Halifane had his compensations: though rigidly loyal to the confidences of his work, he was unarguably popular in Dublin and held the ear of well-placed folk he represented – people like Sir Davis Ross. Quite simply, at this time of ebb tide, Bouchard could not dismiss the possible value of that. Perhaps he had been rash but the deal with the Stephenses was in the brew now, and that was that. But, with time on his hands, the appeasement of the attorney became the next demanding challenge.

To that end Rob had been dispatched to Athlone, where Halifane was overseeing some land transactions, to convey copies of the promotional papers for Mid-East. Bouchard would have liked to forward the shares certificates for the attorney's perusal but, though he held the Squire's receipt for cash and a letter of promise from William in London, no confirmed word on the purchases had come through. It was game tactics, Bouchard felt, and a greater ease of coagency would come when William returned at Easter and the plans for the July wedding could be finalised. For now, it was best to be trusting and easy. And when doubts assailed, one had only to examine the Mid-East charter to feel confident again.

Rob had risen at dawn to ride north for the delivery and it was late afternoon on a short spring day when his track took him back through Banagher along the river road that would lead to Drumloch. The sun was long down and the leaden colour of evening was intensified by heavy blankets of raincloud. At Banagher the rain was merely threatening, but on the river banks the heavens opened. Rob rode with the measured care of an expert horseman – and expert he was, for all his time outside schooling these last eight years had been spent in stables and forges. That interest in horses was more calculated than truly felt, for was it not true that horse-racing was the sport of kings, and the graceful animal itself the best friend of all gentlefolk? Rob – nothing if not ambitious – saw expertise in the stable and stud as a call card for good drawing-rooms; and already he had been proved right. Eighteen months ago at Newmarket Bouchard had taken him into the paddock and, quite without shame, introduced him to the nobility as his groom and adviser; a short time later at Sir Myles Rossitor's Rob had been installed as organisor at the stud sale. Now, with Tartan O'Neill gone, he had assumed full control of Drumloch's transport and, by his education and his lordship's fondness for him, the highest place in the household – second only to ailing, aged Pearson – was his. But for Rob, that was only a beginning. To dress in worsted finery, to have the stables' best horses under his thighs, to run errands of importance for the Sir – these were not lucky perquisites but signs of a blossoming gracious future, a future of gentlemanly luxury. It was all merely a question of pitching your fate in with the master, and biding time. This was not conjecture, it was certainty.

Rounding a rock crop in the blinding rain, Rob quickly reined Zephyr in. Ahead, blocking the dirt road, stood a gig, its horses immobile and the passengers idling under shelter of a bent oak. Tom Og, youngest stablehand from Drumloch, was busily working under the crippled gig, stripped to the waist and levering its wheels from a deep-dug pit. Rob immediately saw that the pit had been carefully centred in the middle of the track and a sacking cloth covering drawn over it, scattered with dead leaves and rushes. Nurse and Letitia waved despondently from under the bare tree.

'A trap?' Rob called down.

Tom Og grinned like a wily elf. 'Ribbonmen, *a cairde*.

Who else? This track serves Lord Estelle's manor and they'll be thinking they'll catch 'im.'

'You want assistance?' Rob was off his mount, burrowing under the wheels with the stablehand.

'Gettin' her up'll be easy enough,' the young man pointed out. 'But the shock of the drop means it'll need two axle-pins.' He carefully placed more splinterwood for traction. 'I can whittle out a makeshift, but it'll take me an hour.'

Rob clambered to his feet and joined Letitia and Nurse. A garrulous and bitter account of a simple afternoon's jaunt was related by Nurse, punctuated throughout by Letty's sneezing. 'I do think,' Nurse observed, 'that Miss Letty should not be forced to await this repair work. Might she take Zephyr home? She can take my travel rug and you can accompany her.' Nurse fussed insistently, drawing her woollen rug over Letitia's shoulders and slicking back the tails of wet hair from her forehead. 'We really must not permit a chill, colleen. Remember your last one – ?'

Rob walked the horse over and helped the girl into the saddle. Mindful of offensive actions before pernickety Nurse, he desisted from mounting but took the bridle and prepared to pace the animal. 'Be watchful, Rob,' Nurse warned. 'An old *bean* like me has little to fear from Black Hand O'Tracey and the Ribbonmen, but a lady of the manor might do.'

'Fear not. Am I not a native of this dirt?'

Aye, but a traitor friend to a landlord in the eyes of many insurgents, Nurse reflected unhappily as she watched them depart.

The rain lashed relentlessly, soaking Rob's thick hair and even through Letitia's cape hood, rippling in rivers across their faces, flooding into their clothes. After a few minutes, out of sight of Nurse and the damaged gig, Rob ceased caution and mounted behind her. His hands found the reins and the heavy cold weight of her haunches sat upon his thighs. As he leant forward to guide their path his cheek touched hers and he jolted slightly at its steamy heat. Two days before, she had wandered down to the food stock

142

room behind the scullery that he had transformed into quite a little office, from where the affairs of the stables and the staff were directed. For hours they had conversed and, he fancied, her flawless charm had been couched to seduce and win him. But yesterday when finally he had succumbed and tried to kiss her, she had side-stepped mercilessly and disappeared. Then, there had been others around – and one could never be careful enough of prying Nurse – but now the world was theirs.

'Even the birds are gone,' he whispered, cajoling, and she listened hard and heard nothing, nothing at all but the drum of rain. 'You tease me unkindly,' he went on.

'When!' The voice was unconvincingly petulant and her body writhed for a second between his tight arms.

'Yesterday, the day before. For weeks now. Perhaps since the days we first met.' His lips trickled through the exposed hair above her ear and he nudged back her hood to allow a fuller touch.

Her breathing came fast. 'You do me injustice. I tease no one. I am not so cruel.'

'Cruel you are.' His teeth found her ear and he bit so fiercely for a second that she cried out and squirmed from him.

'Please, Rob. One must behave properly. If Nurse –'

'No more games, Letty. Time is too short. God knows when my master will take you off again, or me back to London.'

'That's as maybe. And when the day comes I will be pleased enough to go. This horrid weather tires me so.'

'You would happily leave your beloved friend?'

'Beloved? Be reasonable. Love is a sacred commodity one may not jest about.'

'Is it too much to hope that you could . . . love me?'

She was enjoying this, he knew. Her back arched into him and her breathing calmed. Her voice when she spoke was purring, playful: 'My love will go to someone like Adam, Sir Myles's son.'

'Adam Rossitor?' Rob laughed genuinely. 'The feckless art dealer? Why, he's twice your age and quite

143

'unattractive – and quite penniless, I'd venture.'

'I like him.'

'You know not your own mind.' He nibbled her ear again. 'Perhaps you seek a love of social standing and class. In time, I can give you that. Believe me. But for now, for a lass so young and healthy and lovely, love begins not in the head but here – ' His right hand dropped the rein and descended to her, bunching her skirts and tightly squeezing her groin through heavy petticoats. She felt weak, but propped herself firmly against him. The horse's pace had slackened and the rain was heavier than ever. His hand drifted away from her belly but continued its bold exploration, sliding over her bosom and down along the soft swell of her hips. The magic of the touch transfixed her but her brain rattled along swiftly: this was a dangerous dalliance; Donna had suffered a whipping for a hearsay incident with a farm boy that, knowing her, must in truth have been innocent in the extreme; it had cost her dearly and now, as a punishment, she was to be bargained off to the first gent who wanted her; Letitia must be careful of a like fate, she had laboured hard to win papa's affection and must at all costs keep it till she needed it no more.

But now both Rob Devlin's hands were working over her and a rich sensuality she had never known seeped from every pore of her tense body. It was true what they said: peasant stock, dress them how you will, were barbarians. Adam Rossitor would never caress her so, no gentleman would. But the callous ferocity was unbearably delicious and she spread her knees complaisantly when his hand fell to her lap again.

Suddenly, decidedly, she came out of her swoon and took the rein herself. In a deft movement she pulled Zephyr towards the evergreen bushes by the riverside. Some dangers, she had concluded, were deathlessly worthwhile.

In the night dark of Donna's boudoir, with a single secret candle burning beside them, Letitia bathed her sister's weals and bruises with a solution brewed on hyssop and comfrey. Donna did not cry out as the astringent sting of the wounds began, but silent tears flowed. When the ablution was ended Letitia took the compress she had been chilling against the window-pane and pressed it gently on her sister's bottom. 'You're a fool, Donna,' she said. 'To vie with papa openly as you do is to invite trouble.'

'I do not vie, Letty. I am what I am. I say what I feel. He must see reason – were I to marry William Stephens it would be flying in God's face. I fair detest the boy.'

Letitia felt no great sympathy for Donna: such subtle emotions found little place inside her. Instead tonight she was filled with the pervasive afterglow of love-making, a joy quite new to her though she had dallied – with less abandon, true – with boys at Rouen and Lennant. It was ironic really. Papa had kissed *her* goodnight, and here was poor honest Donna, humiliated and in pain, suffering for nothing at all.

'You must grow up, child,' Letitia urged as Donna twisted onto her side and pulled down her night shift. 'A woman must live by her wiles. Even Alexandrine has said as much to me. The dream world of your painting and your poetry will not sustain you. Every woman has her place and one must *manipulate* it.'

Donna frowned question.

'Honesty pays no dividends. You could have so much more fun by simply using your brain, acting sensible. For instance,' she persisted, 'what foolishness made you confess to papa that you had been idling with a farm boy those months ago? Why could you have not denied it, called the informant a rogue?'

'Because I did no wrong, I –'

Letitia hissed impatiently. 'Donna! You do so sound like a five-year-old. Are you so dim that you do not see the signs: that papa has a constant suspicion of all women? That stubbornness he interprets as evil? That he despises change in these lands? That the farm folk are so very different from us?'

'What has that got to do with a harmless conversation? –'

'I'll tell you,' Letitia cut in. 'Simply by being obedient and courteous one can purchase fortunes from any man – for that!' She clicked her fingers softly. 'You may wish to dabble with farm boys . . .' she paused, 'as I might. But sooner or later a suitable match will come along and a marriage will be arranged. I accept that, as must you. By doing so and not complaining I can therefore enjoy my farm boys where and when I want. Let them be fun now, for in years to come our opportunities will disappear. That is the right attitude, the one you should adhere to – quickly before it is too late. And by accepting things, and having my fun in secret, I can pacify papa and assure myself a good dowry and a sound share in this inheritance.'

'Inheritance?'

Letitia spread an arm wearily. 'This, and London, and whatever else remains.' She shrugged. 'Oh, not much perhaps – but it has, I'm sure, a market value.' Her eyes grew foxy and dark. 'Consider the situation here, and be wise. The strain of the marriage to Alexandrine shows. They no longer sleep under the same canopy. Papa gets no younger, and it seems fair to guess there will be no male heir. When he dies – '

'Letty! How can you!'

Letitia wasn't perturbed. 'When he dies, as things are, he may well dispossess you.' She paused to consider that, then added, '*And* her.'

Donna covered her ears. 'I will not listen. That is evil thinking, devilish.'

Letitia pulled her sister's hands down brusquely and whispered vehemently, 'See if I'm not right. It is generosity of spirit that makes me reveal all this to you, Donna. Your naïveté only makes you suffer.'

'Honesty.'

'Call it what you will. But *you* are the one who will be beaten every night until you accede to William, and *you* are the one who, in the end, will lose legacy and family. And fun.'

'I will not marry William.'

'A date is set for July, is it not? The banns will be read

146

soon.'

'I will resist to the end.'

Letitia sighed tiredly and watched Donna roll onto her stomach again and bury her golden head in the pillows. 'You say you like this hell country. William is Irish and he will spend a time each year here. Does that not please you? Or what more do you want? The passion of some brute like Colum Devlin?'

Donna's burning embarrassment was hidden in the pillows.

'You can have Colum Devlin for a rub, but not for –'

Donna exploded. 'Leave me!' she burst out, disregarding the fragile peace of the night and elbowing her sister off the bed in a violent lurch.

'Aha, the truth will out!' Letitia stood and whacked an open hand hard across her sister's torn bottom. Then she fled the room on soundless feet. Donna bit her lip until the scream in her throat died and the welter of tears within began to flow.

The mellow, calm weeks of spring that followed were not destined to last. For Bouchard they were weeks of composure after frenzy, relaxation after gnawing fear. His peace with Halifane was made (though the attorney still flatly declined all involvement with the Mid-East ploy), Alexandrine was quite remarkably well-behaved, and Donna – astoundingly – submissive. Creditors were lying low, a bulk of back rents had come in from Colum Devlin and old Cavendish, his last remaining active political friend from Dublin, had been persuaded to visit again. As he opened the mail Rob had transported from Banagher this eve of Palm Day, Bouchard basked in the early sunlight through his library window and speculated on the prospects of the coming week. Sir Myles Rossitor and his idle son Adam were due for the holiday; they were always joyously easy company, though the recent knowledge of Sir Myles's alleged financial problems somewhat darkened that anticipatory pleasure. More importantly, William Stephens was due home and Bouchard felt he could chance optimism on that count. Blessedly, the girl's obdurate insolence had been broken and, by all the Squire's accounts, share certificates and good news on Mid-East could be hoped for.

Bouchard began surveying his mail cheerfully but by the time Alexandrine entered five minutes later, a mask of manic fury had replaced his cool serenity. Undeterred, she strode into the small room and placed herself before him.

'Before Sir Myles arrives,' she began, gasping as though in effort of self-control, 'I wish to know if the word I have from Mrs Stephens is true or nay.'

'Word? What word?' Bouchard's attention was bent to the three-page letter on the desk before him, the content of which had just ignited his wrath.

'This treachery with Mortimer's money.'

Bouchard pounded to his feet. 'Yes, yes, it's true, woman. Investment! I chose, with the Squire's good advice, to invest the most of it.'

'But three thousand, Redmond! My God, I might have conceded five hundred on a shares gamble, but never this. Your bankers will damn you.'

'They have a promise. I will not let them down. They will get their full due plus a good gratuity, that is what I have undertaken to offer all my creditors. Do not pester me, woman.'

'Are you aware of what you are saying or has drink destroyed the last vestige of intelligence within you? Redmond, there are many *many* people who would not trust William Stephens one inch – you must know that. The boy's career has been, to say the kindest, irregular and unsure.'

'You knew my plan.'

'I knew you planned some fast turnover investment with Stephens, conditional to your allowing Donna's hand. I was thinking in terms of a few hundred –'

'Don't you see a few hundred's no good!' Bouchard's shout rocked the paintings on the walls and scattered robins from the window-ledge. The chair he had been sitting on toppled over with the sweep of his movement and crashed onto the floor. 'I've got to bid for freedom. I cannot go on borrowing from one to pay another. Look, look what your precious Mortimer needles me with in return for his paltry few shillings!' Bouchard crushed the letter on the desk into a ball and flung it at her feet. 'A blackmail weapon. He has been courting Belfast Tories and Dublin Tories behind my back, cunningly utilising the introductions I opened to him – using old dogs like Cavendish. Now he's marshalled support, it seems. Certain people are saying his nomination for the Tipperary seat can be foisted on Peel provided a guarantee of local votes can be made.' Bouchard cursed and stomped a heel down. 'The villain must have been working at it even before I approached him in Lurgan. God knows the background of his efforts.'

The fire of Alexandrine's anger abated. 'So my warning comes true? He seeks your vote, and your tenants', and the Squire's and Estelle's and all those derelicts you still number as friends.'

'I will not have it. I have scruples.'

'The impoverished have no room for scruples, Redmond,' she retorted viciously. 'And you are impoverished in spirit and mind. You are destroyed. This recklessness with William Stephens is the last deceit I will stay to witness.'

'Nonsense.'

'I am pregnant.'

Bouchard stopped in mid-stride and collapsed into a chair. The mental calculation of incidents and timings was over in a second. It had been too many months since he had lain with her. His jaw drooped. 'How – pregnant?'

'Come now.' She was grinning, he fancied, but the morning light from the window behind her blinded his eye. He turned away.

'The child will be mine. A boy child. A male heir. . . .' He prattled in fever, rising again to pace the floor. 'At last, a male heir – '

Her brittle voice cut him to silence. 'I am at the end of my patience, Redmond. I want you to surrender these shares with Stephens and pay off your creditors as much as possible.' She stooped to retrieve Mortimer's letter. 'Then perhaps *we* can utilise Samuel's need. If he truly wants

149

Tipperary he will grow more desperate as the election nears. Use that, as he uses you. Ask for a further payment – a gift, say – of two or three thousand. I know he can afford it –'

Bouchard gazed at her, his head spinning and icy tension contracting his chest. What was she saying? Pass full control to her and abandon all hope of freedom? Sell out to borough-mongering, become a penny-servant of Mortimer and Peel, a purchase vote, the lowest of the low? Where would that leave him in a year's time: a servant of Mortimer's languishing in a rundown estate?

'No,' he blurted suddenly. 'It must be my way. I must build up a reputation of dignity and grace again. I must remain a free agent and independent money is the answer.'

'Very well. Play that game and I will leave you. Together with –' she hesitated, 'my child.'

'And go where? To Mortimer?' Bouchard snickered. 'He would see you in rather a different light were you to arrive at his household heavy with child. In fact, if I construe the method of his trickery accurately, I would guess *you* are only good for Mortimer while you reside alongside me. In his vanity he probably believes his seduction of you can assist the eventual persuasion of me, that you will work in his favour, entranced by his love and kindness. Alone, he will see you as no more than any other slut.'

The tips of Alexandrine's fingers were trembling but her face revealed no sense of insult. 'Clearly this remains to be seen.' She drew herself up with pride. 'You have made a lifelong pursuit of gambling and now you gamble again.' Her hands clasped her stomach and Bouchard saw already the swelling beneath the satin. 'I may possess the one thing you so surely want for Drumloch and the Bouchards, regardless of consanguinity – a son of the household. But I am resolved not to take second place to you again, Redmond. So decide now and forever. What do you want? To obey me – or to sacrifice your claim to this?' She patted her belly.

'Mortimer will throw you out – you'll see.'

'Which, Redmond?'

Bouchard's jaw hung and he stared her without speaking. Alexandrine bowed gently and said, 'Very well. I must take *my* chances. I have seen enough senselessness and I have no wish to calmly sit aboard a fast-sinking ship. As soon as Easter is past I shall leave.'

She walked from the room and Bouchard lurched from his chair to follow her but his feet turned to stone and before he had reached the doorway he was stock still, weeping the emasculating tears of despairing frustration.

CHAPTER FIFTEEN

It was Rob who brought word of the new agent's appointment to Desmond Devlin. It had been Halifane, not Bouchard, who had found and engaged Nim Mackie, the hardnecked Dubliner who worked Estelle's estate ten miles north. Extraordinarily, Rob felt, Bouchard had not faced him with the facts, rather the story of the appointment had escaped from old Nurse and, true enough, this very morning he had seen Nim ride to the manor, upright and thin as a ramrod, carrying his fat leather accounts bag. The sight and the word had depressed Rob – principally because he knew he was of an age and standing now to inherit the legitimised agent's role – but the implications were far darker for old Desmond.

Rob sat in the shadowy bare room, Desmond huddled before him in a basket chair, the bandages on his forehead concealing the leeches at work on the new swellings of his illness. To a weaker disposition the sight of the timid, ailing man would have been pathetic, but Rob's conversation made few concessions for infirmity or weakness. Without embellishment he poured out his story, almost relishing the omens of change in the valley.

Only Devlin's eyes twinkled with life and he watched

his son unblinkingly, absorbing every quick inflexion in the voice. When Rob had finished he said, 'The mysteries of the past years are explained to me. The Sir's gradual diminishing interest in this household, his infrequent calls.' His face was momentarily full of tragedy. 'He has taken all he can from Desmond Devlin – son and all – and now he needs me no longer.'

Embarrassed, Rob shifted on his stool. He was suddenly aware of the disparity of their dress – Desmond's rags against his own good-tailored garments – and his persistent discomfort. 'One must feel gratitude and no more for Sir Redmond's interest. He has given me an education and a . . . home that many would envy.'

Desmond Devlin was silent for many minutes, his hands idly caressing the clay pipe in his lap. 'What are the prospects? Will you and the Sir stay at Drumloch a while longer, or return to England?'

The searching power of Devlin's gaze unnerved Rob. For some reason arrogance burned within him and he hedged, unprepared to show his ignorance of Bouchard's intimate plans. 'Ireland is convenient for now. Sir Redmond has retired from political life and requires a time for solitude. He has affection and ambitions for this estate, as you know.'

'I am afraid for him, Rob. And for you.'

'Afraid?'

Devlin shrugged. 'The world is yours now. I am an old cow to pasture, no more. But – ' His forefinger rose and touched the side of his head. 'I still have visions. I still see and imagine. People come to visit and tell stories, and I know what goes on in the world beyond my plots.' He leaned forward for emphasis. The Sir must be wary, as must you. The world is on the brink of some drastic and enduring change. The life I knew as a child is no more. Look at yourself, at the world that has opened to you. I knew the day you walked from this room and took place at the manor that the seeds were irremovably sown. Sir Redmond has striven so long to retain a life and order he believes to be right, but in his foolishness – or God's wisdom – he invites this change himself.' Devlin paused and allowed a small smile. 'At last.'

'You confuse me, dadda.' *Dadda*. So long since that word had been aired. Rob hurried on, 'Do you speak of the Ribbonmen, of possible insurrection?'

Devlin's mouth curved downwards and he frowned. 'You realise O'Connell's call for change must lead to that? The Ribbonmen scheming of the last years has become an earnest fire that burns in every peasant's breast. There is resentment of the landlord system, the taxes, the endlessly oppressive rents –'

'Why do you fear for me? I play no part in taxes and rents?'

'Come, Rob. You have jumped the stream. You reside there now, a gent in every way. And these signs of change in Drumloch manor bode evil. A new agent, you say? Meaning new rents quite probably. What fun Black Hand O'Tracy will have. At last he will be able to step across the boundary of Middleton's estate and say to Drumloch's people, Now see the suffering your indifference has wrought, now see the error of your ways. Rise up, *make war*.'

'A new agent does not necessarily mean new rents.'

'Nim Mackie's reputation precedes him, my son. And it could be that the Sir's scope of business is not what it was.'

Rob was suddenly, unreasonably, indignant. 'What do you mean by that?'

Devlin sparkled a smile and sighed. The yard door swung in and Colum entered, his face smeared with the dirt of a day's toil in the potato plots. The relaxation of his posture vanished as he saw Rob and Devlin recognised a fleeting glance of acid bitterness. He understood it, and wondered for the thousandth time if the jealousy would be any less were they blood brothers. Colum walked to the milk keeler in the cooling corner and scooped out a ration in a mug.

'How go the crops?' Devlin asked.

'All right. And mamma?'

'Poorly. Rob brought a dram or two.'

'That be kind of Rob.' Colum was striding back to the doorway, hefting a cluster of sacking wraps he had found in the corner. Devlin checked him to ask his purpose with the sacks. 'The potatoes've had enough rain. The skies are heavy again and it'll be wet by night. I'll cover the Irish Apples.'

Rob stood. 'I'll assist – if brother will permit?'

In silence the young men walked into the yard together and Colum bundled the sacking onto a turf slipe no larger than a child's winter sledge. Then with deft movements he reined the old workhorse to the slipe and pulled it round towards the plot track. Rob fell into step behind him, painfully aware of the other's agitation. It seemed prudent to avoid retelling the tale of Nim Mackie just now so Rob chose a smattering of local rumour and incident instead, sticking to innocuous tales gleaned from Tom Og and the housemaid Brenda, stories that opened no gulf of class or position. Eventually the incident with Letitia's gig on the river track was recounted and Rob laughingly decried the foolishness of such Ribbonmen tricks.

'What joy's in it,' he joked, 'when only the likes of poor Tom Og and Nursie suffer? Who wins?'

Colum was grave. 'The point is, you and I talk about it. The campaign of the Ribbonmen gets known.'

Rob took exception to his foster-brother's grim acceptance. 'Seems to me we all know enough about the legends of the Ribbonmen. Murdering sheep, daubing property, molesting daughters of agents. It's been going on for too many years and now appears aimless, just tomfoolery for the happy distraction of idlers.'

'You speak from another world, Rob. *I* have lived here these last years. Foolery there may be, but its direction is very clear. The Ribbonmen want to underscore the injustice of oppression. Punitive rents must cease. The final answer will be self-government for Ireland and a redrawing of the tax and tenure laws by people in a Dublin government who understand life on the land here.'

'Dear me,' Rob grunted. 'I was unaware your affinity with such societies as the Ribbonmen persisted. I thought your affection for derring-do and Black Hand was a passing foible of childhood.'

Colum would not be shaken. A dark smile crossed his handsome face. 'I pledge myself to no society, if that is what you insinuate, brother. I am a farmer, that is all. My life's work is the maintaining of these crops, and looking after my parents.' He glanced challengingly to Rob and saw coy evasion.

'You think me unkind in not visiting more than I do?' Rob said warily.

'Your life's your own. Dadda always taught us that ambition was a worthy friend. Yours has always been an ambition to take you away, to win you new kingdoms. I have my own ambitions, but I believe I will find my new world here.'

Rob did not try to answer that quizzical remark. They had reached the Irish Apple plot and, disregarding the wet mud of the ground, Colum knelt and began spreading out the sacking cloth with great care. Even as they spoke the mizzling rain he predicted began, drifting soundlessly onto the fertile earth, painting a glossy pallor on the heads of the tiny shoots. 'Will you visit again over Easter?' Colum asked. 'Mamma may not last the spring out.'

'I shall try. The household will be busy with visitors, and William Stephens will be back from London to court Donna and set the wedding plans – he too will be a guest. Then – '

Colum swivelled up, a look of mild alarm glaring. 'Donna and William Stephens to wed? You jest.'

'No.' Rob took stock: was it true then what Letty had hinted, that Colum and Donna had enjoyed some secret trysts that she had later been punished for? Stoically up-righteous Colum, the stay-at-home dullard? It had seemed so unlikely then. But now, with the mention of her name, what reason for this frenetic naked resentment?

'It can't be true, I'm quite certain. William Stephens? Who would trust that devil long enough to consider him a worthwhile suitor?' The words tumbled out breathlessly and Colum's face glowed red.

155

'I know not my lady's motives, brother. But that is her destiny. Marriage to William.'

Rob leant awkwardly to assist the business of cloaking the plants but Colum's interest had waned. He sat back on the rickety slipe and allowed the reviving rain wash over him.

The Easter Feast popularly celebrated the day after Easter Day by open-air fêtes on various estate lawns coincided with the first farmers' horse fair each year. As a consequence the mood of unbridled merriment that succeeded the pious tranquillity of Holy Week filtered through all ranks and classes and those who did not participate found themselves labelled by the cadgers of gossip either unfriendly or unwell.

For Bouchard, in no frame of mind for frolicking despite the company of the Rossitors and the Stephenses, the Feast presented just another headache. The Mid-East certificates were in his hand at last and Donna was towing a line, but the greater problem of Alexandrine's imminent departure and the misty threat of Mortimer's interest stood in the way of everything. But the façade of congenial respectability must be kept up, he knew. Bearing that in mind, the forced introduction of Nim Mackie served him well. Through Nim's offices a family invitation to Lord Estelle's Feast was made – a timely offering, thereby releasing Bouchard from the obligation of designing his own fête.

On the day stomach cramps and a high fever laid Bouchard low, but the family contingent headed off, Adam Rossitor and William partnering the girls and Sir Myles with the Stephenses accompanying Alexandrine. A glum party they made, with Alexandrine's wordless depression and Adam's loquacious idiocy, but Donna refused to allow her spirits to sink.

As they neared Estelle's canal-side lands, swelling groups of gypsies and farmers slowed their carriage down, sitting on the road, drinking, shouting, bargaining with skinny animals and cartloads of last season's crops. They carefully nudged through, the ladies blushing wildly at the hollered calls of indecent endearment from toothless nomads. On Estelle's lawns a sight not greatly different met them. At the rear of the great house, where its lawns sloped to the canal banks, food-laden tables had been set and a multitude of loud-voiced people — distinguished from the gypsies by their elegant attire only – clustered about. Dogs screamed choruses while overfed children played noisy Catch-me and conversation droned with kettledrum intensity.

Letitia and Donna endured a few unresponsive introductions, then Donna took the first possible opportunity to flee and explore alone the action along the canal's bank. Here most of the younger folk had gathered and cheering groups sat with their drinks, whooping to the swimmers in the water and the horse-selling gypsies across the far bank. Donna sauntered on, shaded from the soft summery sun by a French parasol, and wallowed in the clamour and jollity. Across the water some lusty Irish voices called out admiringly and, incredibly, she found courage and waved a cheeky hand.

She passed a knot of dead grey alders and suddenly a new voice – solitary and intense in its low key – reached out for her. She turned, knowing before she did that it was Colum Devlin.

His eyes were wide in fear and she swiftly saw he was wearing his best Sunday clothes, plaid breeches and an aristocratic stock. The tendency to giggle at this preposterous sight was suffused with a surge of warmth.

'At Feast there are no fences,' he grinned nervously. 'Lord Estelle might welcome me with open arms.'

'Then so will I.' She saw he sought the shelter of the spring foliage so went forward to join him. Her heart pumped unsteadily and her palms in their gloves were wet.

They stood facing each other, the white sun hiding their blushes. Colum did not move towards her and his hands remained firmly in his pockets.

'I wanted to write to you,' he began, 'but thought better of it. So many weeks have passed since last we

157

walked and talked and I was unsure of your sympathies.'

'My sympathies?' she smiled softly. 'How sweet you talk.'

He stammered. 'I mean to say, I believed we were friends. I would like to believe I could speak with you as . . . equal friend.'

'Yes, of course.' She resisted a crazy notion of stretching out a hand and touching his. 'I do not mean to make fun of you. We are friends.'

'I tried to see you many times. I thought – '

There was no sense in burdening him with the Castle incident. She interjected, 'Papa's plans have had us in some turmoil. The rhythm of the house is different now, I get out to walk much less frequently.'

He stared her with huge, worried eyes, saying nothing, just drinking in her beauty. At last he rejoined, 'You cannot be marryin' William Stephens.'

A flood of unexpected relief filled her head: silly and infantile perhaps, but she had so wanted to see him again, and so dreamt of this candour. 'Did you follow our carriage?' she asked.

'Hear me out.' He had no mind for roundabout talk. He stepped forward at last and gingerly took her arms. 'I know I have no rights to address you this way, but I speak from the heart. It would sadden me beyond words were you to marry William, for I know him to be a waster, a dreamer.'

She watched his arms, keeping her eyes away from his. 'There is no shame in being a dreamer. The Stephenses are respectable.'

'And I am not? I, a mere farm boy.'

She darted her head up. 'You know I do not say that. I meet you eye to eye as I did the day we first met. I make no distinctions of society, if that is what you think.'

'You want William?'

The pressure of his hands was tighter, demanding. The sting of a tear was in her eye and she dropped her head. 'You ask unreasonably intimate questions,' she said. 'All I can say is that a marriage has been agreed.' She tore herself gently from him and strolled away a little, still under

158

shadows. Her mind sought to be free of his persuasive stare, but her heart did not. She sat in the grass and he knelt beside her. At length she said, 'My marriage is not of my choosing. My father no longer wishes to have two unwed daughters – so he pushes me out of Drumloch.'

'Then spite him – leave before a wedding.'

She jerked round to him, eyes blazing. 'Where might I go? Be sensible.'

'Maybe London.' He touched her shoulder, caressing her for the very first time. 'If you like,' he muttered, 'I could take you.'

She wanted to laugh. It was madness, this talk. A laugh tickled her throat but her insides had turned to liquid – bubbling, longing. If some things were different . . . If perhaps he were of good family. . . .

'You would give up your home for me?' She said. Decided, she shook her head. 'No. It is foolish. One must never run away. I could not live like an exile and forget what I am.'

'I have saved money,' he urged. 'My work has improved the farmland we posses. I have pigs now and a new horse, and I've earned money fencing neighbours' land. With what I have and the sale of my own animals I would have enough to start somewhere –'

She shook her head, trying vainly to rebuild convincing logic. 'But it would be no escape. You must see that. Our past lives would be closed to us –'

'You mean you could not live with the shame of running away with an ill-educated farm boy of different religion and background?'

'No. I mean, such insane action would close the door on this land for both of us forever. I cannot let you ruin your life and I cannot convince myself that a risk that might deny me Ireland forever could be worth it. The truth is, I like it here.' She shrugged her sadness away and, with a galloping heart, took his hand. 'Colum, words can never express my gratitude for your selfless offer. But I will not destroy another's life.'

'You need make no promises to me. We can live as

159

brother and sister until you find a route to fuller freedom – '

'No.' Her voice shook and she recalled her sister's winning advice 'Better you take me and love me now and forget me. *If* you care for me with any passion.' She pulled his hand to her and laid it on her tightly corseted breast. His reaction stunned her. He whipped his hand away, as if stung by hornets, and his face became pale. A confusion of Letty's bedtime tales assailed her; was it untrue then that physical pleasure was the soul of love in men?

'The affection I have for my country only matches the affection I have for you,' he said seriously. 'I seek only to see you happy. I know William is wrong for you. Please, please allow me to take you away. If you care for me at all, put trust in me. Perhaps now I do not have the style or grace of Rob or William, but I can toil and I have a good brain. I will make no demands on you now, but in time if you come to care for me I will offer you a proper home.'

She gazed at him without speaking. What should one do? – Letty had advised . . . But then in some matters Letty could be seen to be wrong. Maybe honesty, self-honesty, was the truly first virtue she believed it to be.

'Do you want to kiss me?' she asked.

'I want you to come with me,' he said. He looked at her confidently but she could not know that that veneer covered absolute terror. What he was suggesting was irregular, sinful and quite probably unlawful.

In the distance she saw the slim figure of William approach, his head bobbing like a hunting sparrow's, searching her out. She watched his poise and the arrogance of his bearing and in that moment she was decided.

CHAPTER SIXTEEN

Halifane's arrival with portentous news and determined expression in mid-May was ill-timed. For days Bouchard and his wife had been savagely arguing and the bold bluff he was attempting was clearly failing fast. For the first time the real strength of Alexandrine's character was showing but her iron no-compromise resolve to take control of affairs was resisted by him inch by inch. The impasse was painful because the carrot she dangled before him – a possible male heir – he wanted passionately. Nonetheless he withstood her warnings and braved her out. But now, today, she was leaving. Nurse had been summoned to pack her heavy travelling cases and an atmosphere of disorder hung heavily, the great house lapsing to an eerie silence.

Halifane wasted no time arriving at his point. 'In Dublin last weekend I dined with some friends of note, among them Cavendish and the Chief Secretary,' he began. Bouchard sat up in his chair.

'I trust they remember me happily?'

There was little time for pleasantries. Halifane waved the remark aside. 'Samuel Mortimer joined us for liqueurs, down from Lurgan for the old Tories reunion. We talked. When one comes to know him he is quite a splendid chap, very full of good stories and intelligent observation.'

'On with it.'

Halifane was not to be unnerved. 'May I say that, when I oversaw this loan arrangement, I assumed it was one of mutual goodwill and earnestness. Like you, I was quite overcome by Mortimer's generosity.'

Bouchard frowned. This was the language of the law office, and he was in no mood for it now. With luck he could eject the attorney before lunch and confront Alexandrine again, perhaps revert to physical force. . .

'Let me get down to it, Sir Redmond. Mortimer tells me that a straightforward request for simple aid from you has been bluntly and *rudely* dismissed. As referee in this loan arrangement and longtime adviser to your family, sir, I feel I must request most earnestly that you reconsider your decision.'

It was the wrong time to come singing Alexandrine's song. Bouchard leapt from his chair. 'You know what request this man has made? Vote buying.'

'I understand the sense of a friendly vote. All he wants is your assurance of a warm hearing – '

'Nay, sir. He wants guarantees. Guarantees that I can gather him enough votes from Stephens and Estelle and whatever other sources I am prepared to get on my knees for.'

'You spoke to me before of this estrangement with prominent associates you have experienced. Perhaps this is the way to reopen friendships – use your influence to assist the Tory cause.'

'Ah, but you have not walked down the corridors of political life often enough to understand that a borough-mongerer is next of kin to Satan in most "respectable" eyes. The game goes on, to be sure, but no one wants to confess their own deceit, no one wants to advertise their association with such scurrilous villains.'

'But this is a ploy of *Samuel Mortimer*'s – '

'Aye, but he lives in the background while I canvass votes – *I* am seen to do the dirty work. No, sir. I will not have it. It may surprise you to know after all these years that I have some honour. I have seen too much muck raked over old graves of faded politicians.' He faced the attorney with a look of appeal. 'Don't you see that I am trying to rebuild *my* life, my career? I cannot *sell out* to Mortimer for a mere few pounds. I must think of next year, the year after.'

'Forgive me saying so – ' Halifane sucked air and flinched at some anticipated blow. 'It almost seems to me you refuse Mortimer to spite him. You speak with such fury.'

Bouchard regarded Halifane seriously, his breath coming in short, restless gasps. 'Mortimer frightens me, Halifane. I reflect on conversations, on the events that brought this arrangement about, on all the Tory work he must have embarked on behind my back – I reflect on it all and wonder what great plan he nurtures.'

'Great plan?'

'I now see the greed in his eye.' Bouchard swept one of Nim Mackie's new accounts books off his desk and shook it. 'This agent, for example – what does this mean?'

'A surety that enables you to get regular rents and thereby, as planned, repay him bit by bit.'

'Ha! Maybe. Or maybe a ruse to put the farmers under the boot of steady control and prepare them for tuppence-a-week factory labour.'

'You cannot mean you expect Mortimer to dig himself in down here and –'

'Yes, unseat me. Why not? His northern factories are a strain. He said so himself. Labour here is more plentiful and cheaper, no doubt.' Bouchard's fist pounded the bog oak panelling. 'Maybe Drumloch manor would convert to a fine factory for scutching flax. And with a seat in government he can then safely urge the bending of rules to suit his businesses. Damn the workers, pay them a penny if tuppence seems too much!'

The roar of Bouchard's voice had Halifane unsettled, but he was not yet prepared to retreat. 'Personally, my own judgement of Mortimer would be quite to the contrary. But this is all conjecture. The fact is, you needed money and he advanced a loan.'

'An investment. Use his damned phrase.'

Halifane shrugged. 'And by the by, I am obliged to tell you to your face, sir, that I feel the way you discharged that money was unwise.'

Bouchard shuffled to his desk again and pulled out the wallets of certificates. His manner softened somewhat. 'Here,' he offered. 'Examine for yourself. Mid-East already shows profit. I could have sold last month for a seven per cent profit.'

Halifane shook his head and kept his hands in his lap. 'I have stated already, sir. That gamble investment rests on your head alone. I have seen too much disappointment in railway shares already. The market is up, but can only go down. I advise extreme caution.'

'You've met Stephens and his lad, you know their honesty.'

'That is beside the point, respectfully. For you that money represents a vital lifeline. And this brings me back to Mortimer's request. All I can do is counsel you. I am concerned only that Drumloch returns to its former glory. But I believe the retention of that friendliness with Mortimer is important. You must see he holds the reins now.'

'In a few months Mid-East will have given me the key to escape. I'll pay him off and be glad to see the back of him.'

'What if it is more than a few weeks, Sir Redmond? And what if Samuel Mortimer reneges on his promises – as he legally can, I don't doubt – and asks his money back *now*.'

'I do not wish to discuss it anymore, Halifane. You are welcome to stay to lunch, if you like. There is some good venison in – '

'I would rather persuade you agree to make your peace with Samuel Mortimer.'

The door creaked open and Alexandrine peered in, her long travel cloak already laced at the throat. Halifane stood smartly but she did not offer her hand or enter the room. 'I bid you *adieu*, Redmond, Mr Halifane,' she said. 'Do not disturb yourselves to see me to my carriage. Good day.'

The intensity of the woman and the parched pallor of Bouchard shocked Halifane. When she had gone he quietly asked if the lady was well and whether her absence would be long. Bouchard poured himself a brandy and neglected to answer, as though the questions spoken had never been heard.

When Halifane left the manor a half-hour later and the great carved door sighed closed behind him a terrible sense of foreboding beset him. Sir Redmond's lack of response to reason was staggering and in the curious abstraction of that last thirty minutes Halifane sensed a final loss of grip.

'Will her ladyship return?'

'That is a strangely impertinent question from you, Rob.' Bouchard slumped jadedly against the row of banding irons and watched Rob, stripped to the waist, labour in the forge. As they spoke Rob wrapped a skin round his hand and drew a short shoe out of the fire. A few quick hammered strokes had it in shape, then he stooped to Zephyr's foreleg and began charring the hoof before scraping its thickness.

164

'I speak out because there is word in the household that we will return to London soon.'

Bouchard sighed. The years had proved that Rob was a sound man. He had blossomed, Bouchard reflected, beyond reasonable expectation, had grown to demonstrate an innate pride of bearing that once seemed too much to hope for. All things considered, one was obliged to view the diligent lad with affection and admiration: all this pleased Bouchard greatly, but did not serve to erase the pangs of sour sorrow felt in his company. Bouchard shoved aside a moment of mawkish sentimentality.

'I am bound to say Lady Alexandrine might not return. Ever.' He watched Rob, sought offended horror. But Rob laboured without pause and his face was cool and expressionless. 'London, I am unsure about. In a few months maybe, but the time is wrong now.' He sat on a stool and contemplated Rob's work. 'This toil is no longer fitting for you.'

'I like it, sir. It keeps me fit.'

'Without question.' Bouchard slapped Rob's hard-muscled shoulder. 'But grace and poise are more important for the man of drawing-rooms.'

'Would that I were one.' Rob grinned and gathered nails to start the shoeing.

'Your ambition has always been well stated, my boy. And the assiduous care you've taken to achieve it much respected.' He halted to catch Rob's eye. 'Perhaps the time has come to take you a step nearer to the drawing-room.' He slapped his hands on his thighs. 'Temporarily I am without companionship in this great house, it seems. Old Pearson still takes the helm, but I feel it no injustice to him if I now appoint you personal secretary and companion.'

'Sir?' Rob's hammering stopped and he looked wide-eyed at his master.

'Dammit, why not? You're a good boy and I don't doubt there's some sound blood in you. You have the manners of a gent and you move well. Your language is excellent, your honour impressive.'

Rob felt a kind of victory inflate his chest. He stood

upright and bowed. 'I am grateful, sir – and rather speechless.'

'Not at all, not at all. Nothing will change. You will simply attend my correspondence now and accompany me on whatever business or other travels that arise.' He stepped forward and extended an open hand. 'We will be companions, and friends.'

Rob quickly wiped his soiled hands on the skin and took Bouchard's. In his satisfaction his eye met Bouchard's bravely and each sought to penetrate the shadowy depths of the other's. 'It gives me great pleasure,' Rob said, 'to serve you and live my life with the benefit of your wisdom.'

'Um.' Bouchard found no comfort in that. He wandered around the forge, hands tucked deep in pockets. Rob resumed his work self-consciously. 'You like Drumloch?' Bouchard asked suddenly.

The question unbalanced Rob. The truthful answer might be a nebulous 'no', but he said without hesitation, 'I owe much to this estate. I hold it close to my heart.'

Appeased, Bouchard smiled. 'Then we share a vital similarity of thought. I too care for Drumloch. Until recently I never realised how much I cared.' His hand found the intricate stonework wall and caressed the furrows and swells. 'When all's said and done this is the cradle of the Bouchards, the monument to our family. Generations have maintained it and I will not be the one who loses it.'

'Why should thoughts of losing even enter your head, sir? Who can deny you a family heritage.'

This conversation would hold Bouchard no longer. With a gruff and mysterious, 'The world is changing, Rob,' he quit the steamy forge and marched out into the eye-smarting heat of the summer sun.

The momentary depression of wild thoughts lapsed as he saw Squire Stephens's carriage approach and the Squire step down in the forecourt. Donna had been passing and as Bouchard watched Stephens approached her and they conversed. There were five weeks till the wedding and there at least the smooth continuance of the planning offered peace and pleasure. Crossing the cobbled coach yard Bouchard shouted a greeting to his friend. Bellowing loud, Stephens excused himself from Donna's company and strode over. He looped a hand through Bouchard's arm and they walked together in the sunshine, Tom Og's stable dog yapping at their feet.

'You heard about the villainy last night at Parson's Bend?'

'Pray tell,' Bouchard frowned.

'One hundred sheep slaughtered and cottages burnt. The Ribbonmen again, taking revenge on the poor farmers on Estelle's lands who had quite willingly gone along with the increase in rents instituted.' Stephens shook his head despondently. 'Three people died in the cottage fires. Children, all.'

'It's an ill day.'

'O'Connell and his blasted Repeal have much to answer for. Whether he likes to admit it or not, *he* fires such passion.' The Squire puffed out his cheeks. 'But what worries me is the proximity of these disturbances. You and I and Middleton and Estelle stand side-by-side along the Shannon. Up till now we've endured our discomforts with these devils, but such extremes of violence are new. Clearly the dreams of this Black Hand O'Tracy character are coming to fruition – he has gained control of the farm folk and convinced them to violence. For this butchery last night was not the result of one man's work, or two.'

'The sooner the better O'Connell takes my example and retires.' He laughed but the Squire did not respond.

'The fact of it is, Redmond, we – all estate owners – must band together and frustrate these peoples' aims. McClune summed it up when he said, strength in numbers. We must all agree a uniform system of rent increases and turn to the police for the assurance that, once implemented, our increases are forced through. We must support Middleton and Estelle and – '

Bouchard took the note of personal criticism in the Squire's voice. He spoke sharply: 'I regret I was never one who functioned best in a group, Squire. Like my father, I have stoutly individual aims. And Mister

McClune's heavy-handed tactics inspire me not at all.'

'Easy to say that, Redmond, when your estate suffers no unrest.'

'My estate suffers no unrest because I work at it.'

The Squire did not believe that for one second. He shrugged. 'All I say is, I go along with the idea that people need dominant, careful control. Allow them their freedoms and – ' He made a solemn low whistling sound.

They walked a distance across the overgrown lawns, until the tracks before them opened into the farm plots. Bouchard motioned to go on but Stephens stopped, as though arrested by the implications of last night's violence. He looked over the patchwork lands with their scattered cottages of plaid-thatch and latticed windows. Bouchard glanced to him and was alerted to some further bad news by the flowing riddles of sweat on the Squire's fat cheeks. The eyes, he saw, were wet and nervous too.

'I bring some further unhappy news,' he began after a time. 'News that lays my very spirit low – but it must be told.'

'About Mid-East?' Bouchard knew not where those words came from. His head swam.

'You are not alone in your ill fortune,' the Squire smiled lamely, 'if that provides some consolation. *I* have lost some money, it appears. Many will have.'

Bouchard slowly disenaged the Squire's grip on his arm. 'What trouble do you speak of? The shares are dropping?'

'Young William is distraught. He felt sure – '

'Tell me, for God's sake.'

'It is early to be alarmed. There is still hope. If one sticks with it, one might gain. This new concern – '

'Mid-East has sold out, is that what you are saying? Why was I not informed?' Stephens's head was low, not answering. Bouchard's gall rose. 'For the Lord's sake, speak. Where do I stand now?'

'It seems Mid-East's officers were rather, well, cavalier about the whole enterprise. The chairman and treasurer have vanished and the working capital has been seen to be rather less than was advertised. A sell-out and merger were

168

the only and obvious answers. A majority vote carried the move but the sell-out value on certificates was small indeed. On the other hand, investment in the newly-formed company could work out well. They're involved largely in road work – speculative, some say – but who knows? Just now their stock is worth little but – '

'Damn you,' Bouchard hissed. 'I should have known so far-flung an investment would deny me up-to-the-minute knowledge of developments. I should never have trusted you or your damned William.'

'Really, sir!'

'Tell me, then – how much is my money worth? Out with it, come!'

'Today, on sell-out price – five hundred, give or take.'

'Five hundred!' Bouchard reeled.

Stephens became effusively apologetic. 'What can I say, my friend? Miscalculation. William feels quite disappointed. But he is equally determined to guide you on to better lists.'

'Guide me! After this? You bloody fool. What is it you seek – another few thousand from me? Another commission for yourself to help purchase the ground from under me?'

'I shall ignore your insults, Redmond. The heat of the day has gone to your head, it seems. But I would appeal to you to bear dignity in mind. Now that we are to be linked in a wedlock we must join forces in peace with each other.'

Bouchard's voice spiralled to a full-throated scream. 'Do you know what this means? Three thousand gone!'

Mumbling inanities, the Squire laid gentle hands on Bouchard's shoulders. 'You are upset, naturally. But in time – '

'Damn your eyes, don't you understand? I have no time left!' Stephens babbled but Bouchard could take no more. He struck out swiftly with a young man's zest and caught the Squire full-fisted on the chin. The fat man fell heavily, dust billowing round him. Blood welled at his mouth. Shaking in fear and rage he scrambled to his feet, shook himself down and limped across the weed-scarred lawn.

Bouchard stood, aghast, and stared out over the rich plots of farmland. A flash of clear thought cut through his panic: these were the only thin treasure left to him.

CHAPTER SEVENTEEN

The apple orchard behind Major Middleton's – unvisited for three-quarters of the year – was the meeting place in their weeks of planning for Donna and Colum.

Here each found comfort in a frankness of conversation never touched before, but the terror of the gulf between them did not abate. They spoke without touching, romanced without embracing, and always there stood this wall of fear, this weight of guilt with every smile, every new plan voiced. The sickening reality of the sin of running away with a man of alien and peasant blood never ceased to haunt Donna but news of papa's sudden baffling decision to withdraw the marriage agreement did not alter her determination to flee. Colum, on the other hand, responded with relief and seemed quite prepared to forgo escape plans. In the summer moonlight of the orchard she challenged him.

'You are young,' he responded, 'and have time now to grow and decide your own mind. My prayers have been answered thus.'

'I know my mind. A future under papa's guidance promises nothing but pain and humiliation.'

'But you yourself said you had no wish to leave this place forever, and fleeing with me would surely mean an end to it.'

'Perhaps. I felt that truly until you convinced me otherwise. And anyway, fleeing does not necessarily mean an end to Ireland. We need not choose London. We could move south to Cork perhaps and –'

Colum twisted from her and walked away, his hands

busily running though his long hair. 'It is no good, Donna. These last weeks have had me in torment of conscience. I have no religious fervour, but each night I've prayed for some Divine help. Tonight's news seems an answer to my prayers.'

'You do not wish to take me away?'

He kept his back to her. 'I *wish to*, indeed. But we have made plans without fully discussing a future life. What would that life be for you? I have been selfish. I have seduced you into believing my desires were just and true. But it's all a dream – all a useless fairy fantasy. In leaving, both of us would lose family and roots forever and only *I* would gain, winning your everyday companionship. But what would it be for you? A false life with a peasant "brother"? – '

She walked to him and turned him to face her. The moonlight shimmered in his clear eyes. 'I too would gain much,' she said. 'I thought by now you would know that.' Her voice wavered as she went on: 'I am young, but not so young as to deny my heart. I think I could not live with you as brother and sister for long.'

Colum sighed loud and avoided the pools of her eyes. 'We might struggle forever and never find a respectable life.'

'I have courage. Love is sacred – is that not respectability in itself?'

Their breathing was in unison now, fast and shallow. Her eyes bored demandingly into his and the soft weight of her body against him drowned all wandering thought. He held her in his arms fully for the first time, his senses afire. The scents of her wafted up to him and he felt the promising nudge of her breasts and the concave, exciting sweep of her belly. He kissed her hair, then she lifted her chin and their mouths met – infinitely softly at first, then her lips parted a fraction and his gentle exploration began.

When they broke he whispered, 'My darling, I only want to keep your best interests at heart. There is no place for selfishness in the affection I feel.'

'Then take me away. This idiocy with William Stephens

will only be the precursor of others. I fear for papa's sanity sometimes. Now, more than ever. The household is desperately unsettled, and mamma has been absent these many weeks. Letty talks to me of papa's grave debts and all sorts of possibilities of travel and change.'

He held her close, drawing her warmth into his bones. 'All right, give me time then. I will help you to your freedom, but I need more weeks. My mamma is ailing, close to God's call. I must bide by her and serve dadda. She cannot have many weeks, and dadda cannot be long in following her.'

'Are you sure, Colum? – are you sure you truly want me, want a life that may well deny you your land and your friends?'

He hugged her and kissed her then, for she began to cry without reason, sobbing endlessly into his shoulder, tearing him to her. The answer to her question took form in his head, an aching sorrowful answer. He watched the yellow moon and thought: Would that I could have her *and* my farmland and live forever by the Shannon.

Like a bushfire, in mid-July the word went round that Nim Mackie's first act of command was to be the redrawing of the river plots, together with reassessment of the small-holding rents. The inescapable likelihood of evictions on one hand and increased suffering on the other immediately drew frenzy and scorn from the valley farms. Accustomed to the informed involvement of Desmond Devlin, the farmers were at a loss to interpret this shocking move. The majority view was that Bouchard had pitched his lot in with hard-hearted profiteers like the Major, as a punishment for the increased activity of the Ribbonmen. Few even entertained the notion that the Sir's new policies were dictated by his dire financial circumstances.

To answer the repeated worried inquiries addressed to him, Devlin detailed Colum to call on Sir Redmond and investigate the situation firsthand, but when Colum visited the manor Bouchard was absent, riding. On point of being turned away from the Great Hall, Letitia floated out and directed Pearson to allow him the visitors' drawing-room. There, cap in hand, he sat before her and watched ruefully while she affected her mistress role.

'Papa would expect the house to extend courtesy to a visiting representative from the tenants,' she explained.

Declining refreshment, Colum outlined the purpose of his visit self-consciously, while her narrowed eyes raked over him and a ghost of humour flickered on her lips. When he had finished she said, 'From henceforth, I'd imagine, such queries can only reasonably be addressed to Mr Nim Mackie, who carries on his offices from Hollow Lodge, on Lord Estelle's acres.'

'Indeed, I know the location,' Colum came back. 'But confirmation of Mister Mackie's function and plans is what I seek.'

'Does not Rob provide Desmond Devlin with the advice he requires?'

'We rarely see Rob, mistress. His toil here keeps him from the plots and it's been many a week since he called.'

'How thoughtless of him, I'm sure.' Letitia stood to circle Colum's chair like some predatory beast. Aye, that was it, he reflected: her gait, her poise, all gave her that singularly animal air of menace; she didn't frighten him, merely discomfitted him – while leaving room for amusement. How absolutely unlike Donna she was. How bold, and unsubtle.

'It is pleasant to have you here,' she resumed. 'We seem to entertain new people here too infrequently. And I do believe this is the first time I have encountered you within these portals.' Her hand traced the back of his chair, brushing the edge of his shoulder. 'You do look the part of the drawing-room gent, in your good Sunday garments.'

'I visited as a child, with dadda,' he said, blushing.

'How awful for you: to come as an outsider, while brother Rob calls this home.'

'A man cannot live in ten rooms at once.'

'Jealousy.'

Colum stood and bowed sharply. 'By your leave, mistress. I am obliged for the time you allow me. I shall return

173

to my father and explain your information. Perhaps I shall call again in hope of speaking to the Sir.'

'Good. We will be pleased to see you,' she purred, joining her slim fingers as though in prayer, nibbling at their tips. 'Though I must forewarn you that papa may not view your call with any great sympathy.'

'Whyever not?'

She stepped close to him and he smelled her lavender powder. The gaze of her eyes was piercing, knowing, and he bent away. There was suggestive humour in her words when she spoke: 'Did you not dally with my dear sister those months ago and earn her the whip? You were seen together, down at the Doon.'

Colum pieced together puzzling parts of the last months – his vain efforts to see Donna after her return from France, the altered rhythm of household life. She had spared him that, spared his share of blame. 'I know and respect your sister.'

Letitia grinned shyly. 'Whatever of Rob's educated traits you lack, sir, you do not lack the gentlemanly gift of tact.'

The breeze of a door opening made Colum turn. He started as Rob strode into the room, weskitted and elegant, like some storybook squireen. His foster-brother's ease of movement through so grand a house surprised Colum, as did the expression of ominous distaste. Rob's eyes flew from Letitia to Colum and Letitia drew back slightly, her cheeks aglow.

'Pearson informed me of your arrival,' he started bluntly, his voice overloud. 'I had no idea Miss Letitia was entertaining you.'

Letitia bristled. 'In my father's absence, Robert, yes *I am* entertaining Mister Devlin. Permit me to ask how I can assist *you*?'

It was Rob's turn to blush. He stood, shaken, between them and his jaw worked soundlessly. Finally he blurted, 'Perhaps I am better equipped to answer whatever queries may be advanced.' He stared Letitia in a way that seemed to Colum possessive, almost proprietary. 'That, I'm certain, would be your father's wish.'

Colum sensed the tension in the air and found no desire

to solicit information from his foster-brother. Explaining succinctly his desire for conversation with the Sir, he announced that he would call tomorrow, then took his leave.

Rob faced Letitia as the door closed behind him and glared his anger. 'Kindly refrain from addressing me with such obvious supercilious disdain,' he whispered. 'Especially in front of –'

'Servants and tenants?' She arched her fine eyebrows accusingly.

'I am entitled to some respect. As secretary to your father –'

'*Musha*,' she chided, 'you are entitled to just as much or as little as the family of this household allow. Please remember that you are a servant too.'

He stood frozen, confused. Then his manner thawed and he walked boldly to her and swung his arms round her waist. She pulled back in alarm, glancing to the doorway with anxiety. 'Beloved,' he muttered, 'is this how you treat one who serves you love? – with open derision after just three or four sweet embraces?'

'Three *or* four? You forget the count already, when I give you my innocence and my caress.'

'Four, then!' He bit into the soft white skin of her neck and ran hungry hands over her body.

'Leave me,' she surged, struggling to subdue his passion – and her own. 'If someone sees us *here*. The coach house is one thing, but –'

Rob held her fast, relishing the moment.

'I had never thought of it before,' Letitia mumbled through their embrace, 'but your Colum has quite the face of an angel, has he not?'

Rob exhaled sharply, twisted her to him and kissed her till the breath was gone from her body and blood tasted on her lip. 'Never make fun of me,' he warned her.

Bouchard's plans, it appeared to Rob, had about as much sensible immediate direction as a feather on the wind. As travel compnion Rob now accompanied him everywhere, but the pattern and purpose of their journeying had taken on a decidedly worrying aspect. To Athlone, in pursuit of Halifane (who evidently evaded them): to Dublin, in search of old Tories for purposes unknown; to Belfast, in search of ancient associates; back to Dublin, to speak to some banking folk. Week after week new travel engagements came and with each venture, it seemed, Bouchard's spirits sank. Rob was careful of his new position, and careful of his own buoyant form. In carriage and rail coach they sat side-by-side, Bouchard speaking with less and less frequency; but Rob recognised an ever-present need to retain calm and good humour. The infectious strength of his master's nerviness he resisted, but the mood of the suddenly sprung journey of the last week in July ate into his resolve.

In a drunken moment in Drumloch's library on the night before their departure Bouchard confessed his purpose in Dublin was to meet Alexandrine – and buy back his heir.

CHAPTER EIGHTEEN

Quiet attempts to trace and chart Alexandrine's progress after leaving Drumloch had failed, a factor which increased Bouchard's despair. The obvious line of inquiry to Mortimer yielded nothing, for letters addressed to Lurgan were returned unopened. Clearly Mortimer had decided that only personal representation could amend damage done; but Bouchard would not budge. Finally Alexandrine's efforts, and not his, brought about renewed communication. In a letter from the Royal Inn, Dublin, she curtly requested interview with her estranged husband.

In company of Rob Bouchard drove north, steeling himself for battle. But nothing could have prepared him for the shock of his wife's plight. From the Royal he was referred to a rather seedy doctor's rooms in fashionable

Morehampton Road. Somewhere along the line her high hopes for a new life had perished and according to the doctor-proprietor of the private clinic – a phlegmatic ancient crab of a man who, it seemed, took his fifty shillings and asked no questions – her body was riddled with the pox, decaying in life and clinging tenuously to the child that grew within.

Bouchard entered the dark cryptlike room at the corridor's end and found her perched up in a dishevelled bed, her frame shrunken and bent, obscene around so fat a belly. A permeating stench of ether and rot made his stomach churn, but he approached the bed and sat by its edge and waited till her misty eyes focussed and lit with life. 'My time is near,' she said helplessly. 'Are you not pleased?'

'Mortimer turned you out, did he?' His voice was dull and flat, without a trace of the bitterness that burned in him.

She winced in pain and her small limbs curled under the single sheet. 'His life, it seems, is full enough as it is. There's a lady called Miss Prendergast – '

Bouchard recalled the factory assistant, a dark-eyed girl of eighteen, a mere fledgeling. He almost snarled a laugh. 'Then I was not wrong, it appears. Mortimer is the mercenary genius I always guessed he was.'

'Do not doubt that he wanted me,' she said unnecessarily, without conviction. 'But I will not play second fiddle to some harlot. I can exist just as well without Samuel Mortimer, without any man. I am independent in spirit, like all Frenchwomen. I need no one.'

On impulse Bouchard stood to stretch, but she feared his leaving and grabbed his hand. Her body tensed in the bed and her breathing winged. 'Please. Allow me a time.' He sensed the pleading nature of what was to come and felt himself grow desperately cold. 'Let us at least talk like friends. We have had many years together. Let us build on that.'

'You are in fever.' He avoided her eyes. 'Remember that *you* walked away from me. Where's friendship in that?'

177

'That you have travelled this far proves you feel some benevolence towards me.' She gripped him harder. 'Please, let us repair what gap has opened between us. I shall forgive the error of your ways, you disregard my flight.'

'You should know Stephens's investments have not gone well –'

'No matter,' she said. Her body craned forward and a tremulous smile spread on her face, nervously unstable. Bouchard smelt her foul breath and turned away. She recognised his disgust and suddenly became grave. 'I pursue your help only because of the child,' she said. 'The doctor says I have but a week. I . . . I have little money of my own left. A few shillings, no more. If the delivery is delayed, if the child requires a nurse and care – there will be nothing to cover the costs.'

He sighed mournfully, gazing into his cupped hands. His heart within felt chilly and dead, like a stone. The smells and shadows of the room urged him out, but the thought of the child held him back. Alexandrine's well being mattered nothing to him now. She had thrown in her treacherous hand, and he had no desire to allow her the game again.

'I think only of you,' she croaked. 'It was you who said this child would be yours.'

'Ha! You change sails, it seems. You cannot sell it – or yourself – to Mortimer, so you come back on your knees to me.'

'Please!' She was shivering now, her stomach heaving in an alarming way. 'I am desolated. I have neither money nor home. My health no longer bears me up. This illness –' She gripped her head and rocked herself in the bed. 'I feel I am losing my mind at times. What can it be? Just weeks ago I was well, but now this fire within. My God, will I live?'

Bouchard did nothing to soothe her. He sat upright, regarding her with calm. Eventually he said, 'Very well. I am a christian man. I will tell you what I will do. I have not much finance, but I shall pay you a sum, say one hundred pounds, when the child is delivered. You shall then take that money and go back to your beloved

France and cross this land no more.'

She recoiled. 'Pay me? But what of the babe?'

'The child I will take. I can, I am certain, provide *him* with a better life.'

'What if I fail to deliver, or it be a girl child?'

Bouchard stood. He tied his cape at the throat and dusted off his sleeves. 'I stand to no advantage having you exist, whether in destitution or not, in Dublin town. Your presence may threaten embarrassment ever after. I will see you a fare to France.'

'A hundred?'

'A fare to France, my lady. Be grateful for that.'

She cried out and reached for him, but he stepped back. 'You are still my husband,' she demanded. 'Have you no obligation to stand by my side?'

'Had you no obligation to stand by mine?'

'I can defy you, Redmond. I can deny you this deal and allow your child to be born into poverty and squalor.'

He turned from her. '*My* child? Make an end to this game, Alexandrine. I am free from conscience in the matter of this child. I make you a fair offer. Take it if you wish, if not –' He shrugged. 'We neither of us stand to gain by stubbornly standing away from each other.'

'You could take me back.'

He shook his head slowly. 'No, I could not. I am too old to recommence that kind of gambling. I have had my fill of card games and women's wiles. I want to spend my mellow years re-establishing the Drumloch glory I have watched fade. I need not the interference of women.'

'It is too late for you.'

'Make your decision, Alexandrine. Do you want a fare to escape?'

She slumped back in her pillow, nodding. He could endure the oppressive room no longer, and he fled.

Two days later an agent of the doctor's came to Mr Gresham's Inn in Sackville Street, where Bouchard had his room. A child had been delivered.

Bouchard rode across the airless city with a fast-beating

179

heart. As he entered the Morehampton clinic the tension within him was such that he had to draw his flask and sip brandy on the steps to the upper corridor. An aged and senseless old nurse directed him into the familiar room and he crossed to the big bed haltingly, his feet like lead.

Alexandrine lay amid twisted sheets, open-mouthed and breathing with a grating rasp. Her pallor was startling, her neck and bosom blotched red. The cradle was propped at the far side of the bed but, for some obscure reason, some sense of duty, he sat by her and looked into the tortured face. Slowly she opened her eyes, and a smile touched her dry lips. 'One hundred,' she said.

'A boy?'

'You are pleased with me? Perhaps you can forgive now. I have given you an heir for Drumloch.' Pain splashed through her body as she spoke and Bouchard drew back as she suddenly gritted her stained teeth and grunted a scream.

He moved quickly to the covered cot and pulled back the silk sheet. The child's skin had the pink lustre of health, a lustre that satisfied his very soul. A wet nurse entered then and took the child from the room. Bouchard stood at the foot of the bed, confused by the tangle of emotions coursing through him. Astoundingly, she was laughing. 'A son for Redmond Bouchard,' she chided. 'A gift for Midas! Just watch him destroy it as he has destroyed everything else that crossed his path!' Her eyes sparkled with febrile heat.

He walked to the door, wary of her building fury. The forced merriment was already transformed to aggression. She knifed forward, grabbed a jug of water, and flung it towards him, her face distending in some agony. Her hands gripped her stomach. 'Animal!' she shouted. 'Spineless fool. Dare frown upon me! Dare act as though I were among your chattels. I could devour you now as I did the day we met. I could twist you round my fingers and make you dance like a doll. I could save you or destroy you, and yet you are too much the idiot to see –'

He left the room and closed the door to her. His limbs

were a-quiver. Passing a drawing-room he saw the young nurse unbutton her dress and feed a breast to the writhing child. A hand rested suddenly on his arm. The doctor stood by him, morosely staring. Alexandrine's muted screaming still rung in his ears, louder than the child's cry.

'I am tempted to suggest your lady should be moved to a hospital with adequate facilities,' the doctor said apologetically. 'There is not a great deal more I can do for her. You see yourself this fever that grows in her. It is not something I can properly tend or cure.' He looked away from Bouchard. 'In fact, I think one must boldly say that her body is so diseased that likelihood of recovery is slight. Aside from her venereal disease, there are tumours. Her resistance is poor and the surgery of this early delivery has weakened her.'

'Thank you, doctor. You have done all you can.' Bouchard was matter-of-fact. 'She requires no further attendance. I am well pleased with your work and advice. You can allow the affair to settle in my hands now.'

'She will certainly not live without treatment of some kind.'

Impatience clearly showed on Bouchard's haggard face. He shook the doctor's hand with rough deliberation. 'All right. I have attended with interest. You have served her well these last two weeks. She has her own maid in lodgings nearby who will join her soon, I'm sure. I will retain the wet nurse for the child, if that is agreeable.'

The doctor nodded, perplexed. 'You have a son, sir,' he said quickly. 'I wish you God's luck and I congratulate you.' He hesitated. 'And your brave wife.'

Brave? Bouchard could think of his wife in many simple terms – clever, domineering, resourceful, self-interested – but never as brave.

The doctor moved away and Bouchard went through to the drawing-room and spoke to the nurse. Then he left long written instructions for Alexandrine and her maid. On Sunday the child was to be dressed and made ready for a journey; the nurse would accompany.

He then prepared an envelope for Alexandrine. Into it

he put one hundred pounds. It was all the money he possessed.

CHAPTER NINETEEN

Eviction notices were served the week of Bouchard's return. Thirty-one of them, delivered to the farmers' front doors by agent Mackie. Their arrival cast impenetrable gloom over the funeral service for Swan Duff's second daughter.

The morning was one of dry muggy weather, with the Shannon low on its banks and no breeze in the air. The bards had ceased singing but the high mood of the wake the night before persisted, providing a strange but fitting litany to the knell that sounded from the little church two miles down the valley.

Kitty Devlin's illness denied her attendance, but Colum helped Desmond along to the small Catholic graveyard by the church, where they joined a throng of mourners. Swan Duff stood to the fore, his great fat bulk heaving in sorrow, unashamed of his tears. The loss of his second daughter meant the loss of a possible son-in-law, a likely provider for his old age, and left him only Cara, a daughter alone and – being without wife – necessary housekeeper.

As the ceremony ended and the priest blessed the Brighid's Cross above the grave, Nim Mackie rode up the valley track and dismounted, checking a written list in his hands. Colum watched the agent disappear among the crowd and held his breath. Desmond Devlin, seated on a knuckle of rock beside him, tugged his sleeve. 'Can it be this fearsome news I have awaited?' he asked his foster-son.

In Mackie's tracks Anthony Anderson, son of the former agent, was approaching. His figure was out of place at a Catholic funeral, but Colum quickly guessed at the cause of his concern.

Before Anderson had reached the gathering a hushed turbulence rippled through the mourners. Colum scrambled up on a rock to peer over the heads of people round him. Leaflets like snowy kerchiefs were fluttering about and Mackie was already pushing a path out of the crowd, bound for his mount. A voice or two of bitter venom rose up and someone balled one of the leaflets and hurtled it after Mackie. Momentarily Colum was pitched off balance by the swaying of the group before him and he slumped down. Just then Anderson elbowed in beside him, muttering a stern-faced greeting. 'It's true then,' he said. 'The Sir is selling off some land?'

'My heart will not believe,' Devlin said but Colum nodded gravely.

Swan Duff suddenly broke out of the crowd before them, his hand clutching a torn document. His pudgy face was smeared with dirty tears and he spoke through bared teeth. 'Aye, and what can this mean?' he growled. 'Thirty-one of us out, an L-shape from the manor to the river's edge – an' me right in it. But not Desmond Devlin – no.'

Colum read the insult and his face drained of blood, but Devlin merely shook his head.

'And what advice do we get when we seek Desmond Devlin's precious counsel? Have faith, be easy. Trust the Sir. Aye, well, that be easy when you have a son residing in his lordship's manor and when the plans for evictions are drawn your own property is safe.'

Colum angrily lurched forward but Anderson pulled him back. 'No,' Anderson urged. 'Not on a funeral day.'

'You roost together, is it?' Swan persisted, his tears drying in rage. 'Prods and friends of the manor. By God, if only we'd have listened to Black Hand and his boys years ago. There's no freedom in obeying the Bible. Damn the gentry, damn those who support a word they say!'

A wry cheer rose. The crumpled eviction notices flicked into the air like missiles. Devlin waited while the shouting died.

'We stand on blessed ground,' he said, 'so what I speak I speak in God's eye. These last weeks I have offered what

183

advice and wisdom I could offer. But I am no longer a young man, nor a middleman for the Sir. What I told you was spoken from the heart, without prejudice.'

'Aye, well, can your wisdom stop Nim Mackie now? What of the farmers here and elsewhere who will go home to find the black cross on their doors? What words of comfort have you got for them?'

'Circumstances have changed. There is nothing I can say that might ease your or my sadness.'

'Nothing more to say because in speaking out you might jeopardise yourself, eh?'

Colum's patience vanished. He darted forward and gripped Swan's arm fiercely. 'Withdraw your allegation, Swan Duff. I respect your sorrow this day, but you cannot ply insult like that. Neither my dadda nor myself nor anyone else knew of these evication plans for sure. And believe that the association of blood with Rob permits us no favours.'

'You may speak, you with your pigs and corn and overdone cottage. You are secure. What of me? One daughter not bid for, no wife. A crop of potatoes and an old horse. What can I do, where can I go? I cannot call to the manor for tea, like you.'

'Our lease is like everyone else's,' Colum said. 'We share the same insecurities with every man and woman here.'

Cara Duff came on the scene, a long-limbed and powerful looking girl whom, as a child, Colum had romanced in the thistle field. Colum knew and understood her and now saw that Swan's accusations appalled her. Without ceremony she tore her father away from Colum's side, her flushed face beaming reprimand.

'This is an ill day,' Swan pursued. He pulled away from Cara and stretched to face the farmers. 'Let no man lend ear to the wisdom of the Devlin clan again, and let no man speak out against the Ribbonmen.'

''Tis reckless talk,' Devlin intruded.

'You speak from the lofty position of privilege, while we suffer,' Swan shouted again.

A rumble of discord ran among the gathered group. Cara

and Anderson called out in defence of the Devlins, but others took sympathy with the sacked farmers. The parish priest tried to take charge. Jumping onto the graveyard gatepost, he entreated peace. Colum decided to take advantage of the distraction and assisted Devlin to his feet. Anderson pushed a passage through the knotted groups. Suddenly a splinter log spun from the crowd and crashed across Colum's shoulders. The dart of pain made him jerk forward and he almost fell, but Anderson caught him. The priest was shouting loud now, demanding calm. Colum stood and for a fleeting second saw a blur of movement that seemed to herald another attack. He lashed out to counter it and struck the man before him square on the chin. That was a signal for fight. In seconds friends and clans were banding against each other and the jeering and elbowing of imminent outright battle began.

Colum pulled Devlin from the fray, but Swan Duff was not about to see them escape so easily. In a wild sweep of his leg, the old farmer thundered into Colum's side, knocking him across the pebbly earth and sending old Devlin tripping. Colum curled up to protect his body from further blows and watched from the tail of his eye while Swan set upon another farmer whose protestations in defence of the Devlins rang loud.

A gunshot sounded.

The struggling groups on the edge of the hubbub froze. Colum shinned forward and helped his foster-father through the maze of legs, hauling him to his feet. A swift side-glance showed him a cadre of mounted police-agents, conspicuously armed with sparkling percussion-lock guns. Sub-inspector McClune sat at the head of the team, his pistol drawn and smoking.

'Arrest that armed man!' McClune cried out, and a few of the horsemen slid to the ground and drove into the gathering. A scuffle ensued, but Swan was overpowered, the club of splinter wood wrenched from his grip. Stunned, the crowd fell to total silence. Cara Duff alone stood forward and challenged the sub-inspector. This was a funeral day, she pointed out heatedly, and emotions were high; what went on in the church grounds was the priest's business and none other's.

'You have been disorderly,' McClune barked down. 'But that's just a biteen of the story. There are posters all over every town, from Athlone to Neenagh. Public meetings are agin the law. Anyone taking part is liable to imprisonment.'

Devlin understood. The Liberator O'Connell's country-wide tours had stirred whirlpools of dissent: Repeal was the keyword still and every town and valley had its champions-under-O'Connell, passionate and eloquent men who stood upon turf stacks and appealed for support. Their success, Devlin saw, could be measured by the ever-increasing wariness of the authorities' reaction.

Swan was being bundled up onto a horse when Colum addressed McClune. 'If you arrest one man, arrest us all. For no one is more guilty than any other.'

'I seek no explanations, man. You people have terror-ised these estates for too long. I am the lawman and I will take it on myself to do what needs be in order to quell such criminality.'

'Sir, you may not speak of our folk as law-breakers. These grounds have seen no blood spilt, no sorrow.'

McClune was positively grinning, relishing the shocked confusion that held the crowd. Cara's voice alone now soared up, wailing her distress, calling her father's name. Colum took her in his arms and gave comfort and Anthony Anderson smoothed her scraggy red hair. McClune ob-served Anderson and his eyes widened. Devlin fancied he saw the sub-inspector's smugness wane.

'Mister Anderson, seems you are out of place at rowdy gatherings,' McClune said.

'I'm among friends, no other.'

McClune's face grew grim. '*An shea*? Well, Satan sleeps with kings.'

Anderson ploughed a hand through his fair wavy hair and ignored the slight.

'Seems high time I rode these lands more,' McClune resumed. 'These past years they have been a closed book to me, but now there are evictions to be enforced and Nim

Mackie asks my guidance, wise friend. Seems all along ɪ have been passing by a nest of snakes.'

Colum jerked forward but Devlin and Anderson held him. McClune turned and gave orders for Swan to be escorted to the jailhouse.

'Spare my father,' Cara screamed.

McClune's hard lined face did not soften. 'Your father faces some months detention for law-breaking, depending on the magistrate's judgement.' He gazed over the heads of the crowd. 'And let this be a lesson to all here. Lawman McClune now rules these grounds, with the blessing of Mister Mackie. All discord will be silenced!'

The posse began turning back for the valley track and McClune caught old Devlin's eye. He craned down to him. 'I have waited long for you to step down from your throne, Mister Devlin,' he whispered. He grinned and jerked his rein and the horse veered round and tramped off. Under the clamour of hooves he did not hear Devlin mutter, 'You will rue this day, *cairde*.'

Cara, insensible in grief, sat by the church gate with Colum before her, wiping her tears. Anderson and Devlin looked on disconsolately as the crowd dispersed, passing among themselves the copied eviction notices. 'What will become of me?' Cara implored. 'No family now, and no home. A few weeks to pick up our potato crop and sell our chickens and move – to where? A work house? A bowl of skilly a day and no hope of life?'

Devlin moved away, unable to bear the words he was hearing. His polished brogue touched the dry earth, stirring the weeds in the summer cracks of the graveyard path. For a lifetime he had existed on the brink of this chasm, terrified of contemplating its depth but hanging with tenuous hope to the Sir's coattails. The strength of the gentry is omnipotent, his heart used to tell him; trust the good fortune of a benevolent landlord. But now trust and dreams were shattered. Omnipotence was a misty myth and the edge of the chasm was not a place for clinging passively, but a battlefield.

But maybe that lesson came too late.

CHAPTER TWENTY

'I'll tell father.'

'Tell him what?'

'That you have been running about like a French dancing girl with a farmer, sneaking out even after nightfall, gambolling in Lord knows what devilry.'

Donna reined in her horse and gazed down, irritated. Letitia, walking by her sister's mount down the avenue, looked positively delighted, peering narrow-eyed from under her guipure-laced parasol. There was no wind and the day was stiflingly airless, laced with a heady turf smell and something else — a rank still odour like putrefaction.

'I have not long,' Donna insisted. 'I have been four days inside and I need the air. Make your remarks and be done with it.'

'Papa allows you your freedoms again. It seems you employ the devices of trickery I taught you to great ends.'

'Don't speak in riddles. I enjoy the freedoms you enjoy.'

'Ah, but it seems I am not belle of the household as you have become.'

'You mean, for looking after the child Serle?' Donna shrugged. 'Such task is a pleasure to me, and the child deserves some warmth and love after so tragic an entry to the world.' Donna's mind ran back over the distressing account given by Nurse of Alexandrine's malady. The full truths, she knew, were withheld from her, but the fact remained that papa had produced his professed son, and humanity called for love and attention.

'Can it be that you lavish care on the child with one eye cocked to your precious inheritance?'

'What do you speak of?'

'Drumloch! Isn't it true that you love this terrible ground with such devotion? That's how it seems to me. And I've seen you chatter and wave to the farm people, don't deny it – not to mention this escapade with Mister Devlin.' The words tumbled from her, alive with emotion. 'I wonder how papa might respond if he heard his prodigal daughter had turned back to her wild ways.'

'Nonsense.'

'You tailor your life to suit your fun, now. Don't you? What does this Irish rogue do for you? Tell me – how special is he that you invent games to keep him by your side?'

All along an inner voice told her she must not trust confidences to Letty. Her sister still boasted that hard, almost callous capacity for selfishness – and dangerous outspokenness. Donna felt herself burn – a combination of fear and indignation – but forced cool aspect. When she spoke again she did so casually, without calculated intention to wound, but her remark riveted Letitia. 'Can it be that the fantasies in your head about Colum Devlin spring from jealousy, that you hunger for him yourself?'

Letitia's fine teeth showed in a grimace. 'What *I* hunger for, dear sister, I get. I do not need fantasies of any sort.' She prodded Donna's leg. 'But you have not explained. How can you defend night-time dallying with an Irish farmer?'

'I should say, were I challenged, that I followed good example. I saw my own sister dally with Rob Devlin. Saw them embrace and kiss and suspect they did much more – in the coach house this last week.'

Letitia's parasol slipped from her shoulder and she became agitated and white-faced. 'You . . . you spied on me! What insolence. And anyway, Robert Devlin is a gent in his right, an esteemed adviser to the household, an educated lad –'

'No need to defend yourself to me, Letty. I do not covet your gentleman.'

'Which implies I covet yours?' Letitia was furious. 'I

have a mind to tell papa of your secrecy, whichever way. It is quite wrong, this dalliance, I am sure. *I* can defend myself about Robert – '

'And about Adam Rossitor?'

Letitia was silenced.

Donna smiled despite herself. 'For I saw you too with him, this Feast. I saw him kiss you at Estelle's and you surrender indecently. Should *I* reveal that to papa?'

'Beast! Timid, cunning beast. You play a high and mighty role, and disdain me for listening at keyholes and walking with gentlemen. Yet you appear to play more sordid tricks yourself.' She sneered. 'Quiet, passive little Donna, honesty incarnate. If only it were known! I have a mind to brave you out and tell anyway.'

'Do so and I will speak of the lust which so enthralls you.'

'Demon!' Letitia had closed her parasol. Now she drew it back and jabbed it with all force into Donna's horse's flank. The animal reared in fright, then sped forward into a wild gallop. Donna kept her balance only because the rein had been looped tight about her wrist. A practised horsewoman, she lay swiftly forward and relaxed her torso against the horse's neck. Senseless to pull away, she knew; one must allow its hysterical charge, then soothe it and gradually lug back.

The horse ran on, its pounding hooves whipping sprays of stones that bounced above croup and hips, raining over her. She held tight, then glanced forward in panic. They were making for uneven ground – the pitted, rock-flecked meadow that circled the fir forest. At gallop, the terrain would be deadly. Without control, the horse would surely damage an ankle and tumble. If it did, at this speed, she was dead. Straining forward, she stretched above the poll and grabbed the forelock. Her fingers barely reached and her body was taut, stretched so far that her buttocks had slid off the saddle. The ground around was rocky now. In two minutes she would be amid the cluttered earth. She pulled the forelock and twisted the rein. The mare jerked its head back but did not slow its run. Donna felt her bottom slide off the horse's middle. She clung tighter, arms circling the

190

neck, quitting the forelock. Her body started bouncing out of the saddle and darting agony knifed her hips. She was lost, she was gone, the horse was running faster, wilder . . .

She closed her eyes to wait her fate, then heard a rapid noise beside her – a fast staccato keeping time with the clamour of her mare. She glanced to her right. Incredibly, blessedly, there was another horse – a rider racing beside her, inches behind, rushing to assist, to catch the mare. Donna had a brief impression of a young man, ginger-haired and large in frame. She saw his left arm stretch out, fingers reaching for her harness. She closed her eyes again. The rocking and bouncing was unbearable and her body was half-off the mare. Scorching pain gripped her spine and her knees grazed the horse that ran beside her.

The mare shot an ear-rending whinny, then pulled abruptly to a stop. Donna lurched forward, lost the rein, and crashed to the ground in an undignified heap. The earth was mire and her knees and hands sank quickly. In a daze, she felt hands clasp her round the middle and bear her upright. As if she weighed no more than a feather, he lifted her high and sat her on the mare again. Then he crouched quickly to examine the animal's legs and fetlock joints.

'All right here,' he said. 'Lucky. That could have been real trouble.' He mounted, pulling her rein to draw her away from the marshy ground. She did not recognise him and her mind raced to think who he might be. His clothes were excellent – foreign, too ostentatious, but of fine lustrous cloth. He wore new riding boots and carried what looked like a shop-new crop. The dazzling-blond hair and limpid eyes made her think suddenly of an old copper wolfhound she had once befriended at school. This man had that sort of face: trusting, large-eyed, eager to please. As they gained better ground he turned to her.

'Do you always ride like Mercury?'

She laughed, blushing, and gave a swift, vague account of herself. The young man took off his riding cap and bowed. 'Paul Cabbot, at your service. I owe you congratulations and you owe me thanks.' His smile was beguilingly huge.

Her composure settling, she said, 'Should I know you, Mister Cabbot? A resident locally perhaps?'

'Indeed, no. I mean, not till now – though you may see a mite more of me in the future. I am American, from New York. My dear mamma has long sought some suitable property in these parts.' His expression became mildly glum, as though the very notion troubled him. 'Twice before we have, as a family – mamma, sister and I – visited these parts. Indeed, mamma was guest at your Drumloch not many years ago.' He grinned gallantly. 'I expect you were too small a child to recall Josephine Cabbot and her quest for a good Irish home?'

Donna bent her gaze from his. 'You still seek a property.'

'We have purchased. Fork Estate.'

Donna looked up sharply. Since papa's row with the Stephenses no mention of the Squire, his family or fate had been aired within Drumloch. Since then she had not seen William, nor any of the clan. Intrigued, she said, 'I understood the Squire enjoyed his lands and the climate here.'

'Financial troubles,' Cabbot confided, stooping forward as though cautious of curious birds. 'Mamma saw good prospects for the lands.'

'You will live here?'

'No, no. I doubt that. There is much reconstruction and reorganising to do. Mamma will engage in that, knowing her, over a period of some years. For now it will be a rest home, a pleasant peaceful estate away from the business worlds of New York or London.' He became quite serious. 'As many will tell you, Ireland is a good investment now – if the signs are right. Property is cheaper than anywhere in these islands and, they say, rent lands are at a premium with so large a population.' He looked over the country-side, unconvinced by his own words. 'The tranquillity will please mother in her retirement years. No cabs and rail-ways and bustling crowds.'

She wondered how old he was: thirty, forty – older still?

The scrubbed pink face was ageless. 'Tell me,' he asked. 'Is this a permanent home for you?'

'We have property in London.'

'Of course.' The gaze was demanding. 'Then you anticipate further travel? You may not be here through the next weeks?'

Donna hoped her nerviness gave nothing away. She focussed on the backs of her hands and strove to control the boom of her heart. 'Papa envisages our presence here for a time yet, I believe.' The sound of hooves intruded – thankfully – and Donna swivelled to see Brenda riding, her posture in the saddle indicating frantic alarm. Donna waved to her, signalling she was well. She turned back to Cabbot. 'My maid,' she said. 'I had better ride. I am for an appointment.'

Cabbot bowed again. 'At least I shall be your neighbour then for some weeks, while mamma lingers. No doubt we will call upon you before our return to New York.'

'I'm sure I shall look forward to that. And thank you again. You saved broken limbs.'

'Go carefully,' he advised. 'There is talk of some trouble afoot with the farmers.'

'Do not believe all you hear of them. The Irish – peasant and gentry – favour bardic legend. They are romancers.'

'Charming, I'm sure – especially coming from an Irish lady – ' He paused, 'of such beauty and grace.'

Stammering childishly Donna bade her saviour good-bye and rode to meet Brenda at the edge of the Doon Lawn. Having comforted and reassured her, they rode together round the forest path, then separated as agreed for Donna to proceed to a meeting with Colum.

The exciting developments within the household in the last weeks, with the introduction of the child, had occupied Donna's time and opportunities to escape to clandestine meetings were fewer. It had been ten whole days since she had ventured out and enjoyed Colum's company and the exchange of letters they shared did not fill that void. Now she rode with dizzy excitement flooding her head, her body hot in splendid anticipation. Today, she had told Colum in her note, she would change tactics and be bold. She would adopt a peasant guise and broadcloth cape and chance free movement among the plots. A confidence derived from papa's new ease with her gave encouragement, but she was still mindful of some risk – of the risk of Letty, if none other.

The further she advanced through the farmlands, the more it became apparent to her that something was amiss. It was harvest time, but the fields were almost unmanned and the oceans of greeny bubbles that were the ripe potatoes still draped the earth. In many areas it seemed as if the crops were half-pulled, then deserted, but as she looked more carefully she saw that vast tracts had not been touched, but that the potato plants were no longer vibrant green, and had faded in colour to a strange, burnished brown. She wondered at this, then supposed the raking sun had merely burnt the tall plants. In the pathways and yards there was much activity, and the cottage areas streamed with people scurrying about, carrying empty pails and spades and wearing jaded faces. But no one could be seen digging. Choruses of talk wafted out – Irish talk – cryptic and strange and somehow, today, disconcertingly loud. Crossing the granite prominence that gave onto the Devlin plots, Donna saw a broken line of police in the distance, marching through the fields, apparently interestedly inspecting the brown earth. Everywhere, as at all harvesttimes, there were donkey slide-cars but now they stood idly, the sun-washed animals chewing rye grass by the tracks' sides. Donna fancied she heard crying and wondered if it was a man's wail or a woman's; it was not the momentary weeping of a child.

She rode into Colum's yard and slid off her horse. The sun was past its zenith and, she guessed, it would be two o'clock by now. They had planned to meet on the high ground at half-past one, but as she had been delayed, she calculated he would ride home. Now, with the serene quiet here, she wondered was he still at the bogland, waiting. She filled her lungs and opened her mouth to shout for him, then the door swung open and he came towards her, dressed untidily in work shirt and breeches, his hair grimy and sweat-slicked.

'I am sorry if I left you waiting,' she began. 'Letitia and I . . .'

He hushed her and took her arm. 'Mother is poorly,' he said, 'and sleeping now. Let us leave her be. Dadda looks over her. Come.' With determined step he led her down the choked pathway to the back plots. It was here he laid his precious beds of special market potatoes, jealously protected because they were valued at five times the worth of ordinary lumpers and few took the time and patience to nurture them. They, she knew, along with the pigs and corn he kept, were the backbone of the Devlins' improved living standard. Donna looked towards the faraway bottom of the field and saw a solitary hunched figure at work. She recognised the wavy tresses of Colum's friend, Anderson. It surprised her to see him toiling with such industrious concentration on somebody else's land. With a widowed mother and a few sisters to keep, he would have labour enough on his own grounds. Somehow the forlorn sight of the lone worker depressed her. As she watched, unthinking, she held a gloved hand to her mouth, to mask it. The sickly-sweet smell of the air was all of a sudden unbearable.

'Anthony's wastin' his time,' Colum said without emotion. 'It'll be the same here as on Duff's.' He stooped and dug his fingers into the loose-packed earth, burrowing under the potato stalks, down to the tubers. She saw the plant leaves here were brown-edged too. Bewildered, she crouched beside him and helped to tear up the stalk. He laid it flat and cursed softly in Gaelic. ''Tis too much to believe,' he said. His fingers touched the yellow-brown potatoes and, before her eyes, the firm flesh became filthy, decayed pulp. Angrily Colum tossed the rot aside and drew her another plant. He explored it too and it turned, transformed by touch into vile, black-blotched paste.

'What is it?' Donna asked.

'It is death,' he said. 'Blight. Everywhere. Every farmer has combed through his crop and found it. Not one or two or three crops – *every one*. They say it's the same as far as

195

Ballinasloe, and beyond. Some even say it's across the country.'

'Where does it come from? How can it be stopped?'

'God knows, *mo chree*. Does it come from the ground, a seed of rot, the air? How can we cure it if we do not know.' He fell to his knees and gazed over the field. 'We have dug bits everywhere,' he said. 'Every plant is dead.' His fingers shook off the dirt that he had nursed and fed and dug and cherished. 'I have my few other crops, but what will the people do? Ireland is dying,' he muttered.

She put an arm across his shoulders, hugging his bulk in a consolatory way while not understanding the magnitude of his anguish. His arms returned the gesture and they held each other tight – disregarding the consequence of their boldness.

Words framed themselves in her brain, but the courage to speak them was gone: both had inescapable reasons for leaving, and their poverty was absolute.

The time to flee was now.

PART THREE:

AMERICAN ESCAPE

1845 – 1846

CHAPTER TWENTY-ONE

The panicked pronouncement of looming famine across Ireland had not yet been fully stated when Bouchard retraced his steps to Dublin with the determined intention of winning back Dermot Halifane's counsel. Mortimer's newest letter lent urgency to his quest. In it he stated his plans to seek a power of attorney, enabling him to recoup his 'investment' by forcing the sale of Bouchard's possessions. Bouchard knew he was on thin ice, that Mortimer could pipe whatever tune he chose. The only possible answer appeared to be in engaging Halifane's sympathies, for he had been the third party who had sat in on the loan discussions and had heard the spoken promises.

In a state of trembling nerves – fortified by drink alone – Bouchard sought Halifane in Dame Street, then at his rooms in Mountjoy Square. His man indicated that the attorney had departed to a meeting with Sir Davis Ross and a subsequent planned journey for tea to the vice-regal lodge in Phoenix Park. Not be deterred so easily, Bouchard resolved to ride to the Park. Heytesbury, the new viceroy, was unknown to him, but in years gone by he had often supped at the lodge and, to his present drunken reckoning, as a true old Tory, should find a measure of warm greeting there.

But persuading the guards at the gate was a task for Trojans.

Finally a brief note for Sir Davis was scribbled out and Bouchard was detained in the sentry outpost while a messenger ran. Minutes later the doors of the lodge were opened to him and, accompanied by a silent aide, he was led into a gilt-and-silk junior drawing-room and told to wait. Halifane entered in seconds, his gingery aspect decidedly pale. 'Sir Redmond,' he stuttered, 'may I say such incontinent behaviour rather embarrasses me. This is the viceroy's *home!*'

'Dammit, man, I have no time for niceties. Don't you know I was walking the vaunted corridors of power before you'd learned to scrawl your signature on a writ. Here –' He pushed Mortimer's missive into the other's hands. 'Your friend's blackmail attempts continue. I must hold him off. There is light on the horizon. I have succumbed to your advice. Mackie is arranging the sale of some of the river lands –'

Halifane was surprised. His anger stalled. 'Evictions?'

'Of course, must be borne.' Bouchard waved that aside. 'Point is, I shall have some money from that – to add to the surrender value on my shares.'

'I wish to hear no more of your shares scheming.' Halifane was adamant. He turned his back on Bouchard and crushed hands into his pockets. The back of his bristly neck, Bouchard saw, was salmon-pink, a sure sign of this man's ruffled calm. After a moment Halifane resumed, 'I am not decided whether I should any longer pledge association to you, sir. I admit my family's loyalty to the Bouchards has never wavered over countless years, but in turn the Bouchards have enhanced and supported us with their respected labours.'

'If you are implying –'

Halifane turned sharply. 'I only say that our association from now on would appear to be merely academic, rather than practical, since you have made it clear with this Mid-East nonsense and Samuel Mortimer that you no longer intend to accept the advice I give.'

'I . . . I have been bedevilled with problems of many sorts, you know.' Bouchard was conscious of the ingratiating sound of his own words and his ire rose. 'Dammit, you have eyes to see. Where once I would have disdained this tweeny's parlour, now I am forced to sit here, cap in hand, and deign to meetings with too-busy attorneys.'

Halifane sighed deeply and felt his fury die; for a

moment, gazing into Bouchard's eyes he saw profound, desperate sorrow and felt pity rise in him.

'What I require *you* to do now is stand behind me. Aid me. Meet your friend Mortimer and tell him – tell him he must bide his time and he will get his precious fortune back.'

'You could reconsider his demands, about Tipperary – ?'

'No. I may be down and trodden on, but I have dignity still. At least I can hold my head up when I enter these chambers. At least I can reflect on the honour of my political career and know that the devil Peel alone was responsible – '

Halifane's posture slumped and he flew up urgent hands, imploring quiet. Bouchard recoiled in shock, then the door behind him whispered open. He turned to the draught and looked twice before he believed his eyes. Prime Minister Peel walked in, his brilliant dark eyes flashing recognition and good-humour.

Bouchard shuffled awkwardly to his feet and the breezy mood induced by heavily consumed alcohol was suddenly gone. His head was clear but his heart fast-beating when he said, 'Good evening, Mister Peel. This is surprise to me, for I fancied I would not again set eyes upon you.'

'Pleasant surprise?' Peel asked.

'Pleasant for you, sir?'

The Prime Minister laughed and sat down before his former associate. From a distant chamber the drifting sound of warm laughter and bardic music reached. 'When I heard your name mentioned I thought I must come to see how my old acquaintance was.'

'And Sir Davis Ross chose not to accompany you?' Bouchard was looking with sarcasm from Halifane to Peel. When Peel declined retort, he went on, 'Am I so misinformed or is this a visit of secrecy?'

Peel nodded. 'Heytesbury bade me come, to see things and speak to resident friends for myself. He is alarmed by this new word of blight and intrigued by the split that is opening between O'Connell's Repealers and the Young Ireland people.'

'The blight is no more than farmers have lived with these fifteen years. There have been blights before.'

Peel frowned, interested. His pudgy fingers adjusted the silken stock at his throat and his manner became more relaxed. Halifane, unsettled by this weighty talk with its foreign nuances, melted into the background. 'You have knowledge of life *with* the people,' Peel went on. 'You have spent more than fishing seasons here. Tell me, in any way does your experience bear up what old de Grey believed – that the Catholics, as a body, are rigidly united against *all forms* of London rule?' A shadow passed his face. 'I see the need to win over their support, but inability to assess their purpose delays me.'

'My opinion is as it's always been: leave well alone. A system of life has survived well enough here for a hundred and fifty years, the Union has endured successfully. If there is rigid unity among rebel Catholic farmers, I have not witnessed it.'

'Could your opinion be old-fashioned, I wonder?'

'You would appear to have already decided it is. You have danced circles to placate the labouring classes, have you not? De Grey dismissed because he took a resolute attitude to the stirrings of rebellion. An increased grant of £17,000 for the Roman Catholic college at Maynooth. And now this bill through parliament to incorporate 'Queen's Colleges' in Galway and Cork and Belfast, allowing low-fee higher education for the masses.' Bouchard could not resist a chance to sneer. 'You have learned to eat your own words, Mister Peel. A time ago you were admonishing *me* for not voicing more opposition to O'Connell. Now you are eating out of his hand.'

'Not at all.' Peel was unruffled. 'I simply see the validity of *some* of O'Connell's views. But my resistance to Repeal stands on record. No. I abhor conflict, as any civilised man. And it seems to me I stand to gain more for our kingdom by appeasing the Catholic labouring classes.' He shifted momentarily in his chair as though a thought unnerved him. 'And anyway – I would rather hear O'Connell's political haranguing than face the likes of these Young

Irelanders who've sprung up from nowhere to preach Irish nationality and the spirit of Wolfe Tone.'

'I see. So your new-founded link with O'Connell is a counter-measure to save you from armed insurrection? That is your stratagem?'

'You think a general armed insurrection *could* come?' Peel was deadly serious but Bouchard laughed loud. He stood up and ambled round the room, shaking the lethargy of hard drinking from his stiff muscles.

'*I* think it not at all surprising that the most powerful minister must come rushing to Dublin like a worried fox if this is the game he has been indulging in! But why should I give benefit of my intelligence to Mister Peel?' Halifane coughed a warning but Bouchard swaggered on. 'Did I not say five years ago that a firm and decided attitude to the Irish question must be maintained? The Union laid down the laws. That is that. Ignore O'Connell, damn the man. Ignore these Young Irelanders, whoever they are! That is your problem, my friend. You appease O'Connell with Catholic concessions, then these young Irelanders demand refinements, more changes. Start changing the rule book and God knows where the final lines will be drawn.'

Peel stood and gathered his tails round him. Bouchard had become noisy and offensive and the Prime Minister had no intention of pandering to a fool. How wise he had been to take his friends' advice and see this old badger done down. It was easy to see how he had lost support in Kent and in the House: quite apart from these sordid tales of drunkenness and gambling, the man was the worst kind of old politician, an old-guard conservative, someone who wanted the world to stop still, a man without vision or perspective.

'You appear quite content with life in Ireland?' Peel said. 'Little confuses or alarms you?'

'Bah! Why should I be alarmed?'' Bouchard spread his hands innocently. 'I have an old estate and air to breathe. Mind, I have been denied a profession by my erstwhile friends and have discovered cancerous seeds sown among them.'

'You cannot refer to me, of course,' Peel grinned good-naturedly.

Bouchard stared at the Prime Minister boldly while Halifane shuffled his feet. There was silence now, disturbed only by the flap of the evening wind against the leaded panes and, distantly, conversational laughter. At length Bouchard said, 'You consider yourself friend to me still, do you?'

'Of course.'

'Then – lend me five thousand.'

Halifane choked and Peel's eyebrows curved up. Bouchard remained still, glaring at Peel with challenge. Then he burst into hearty laughter

'I perceive that honesty alarms my good Prime Minister! No, sir. I require nothing more of you, not even friendship. In return I offer you like quantities of – *nothing*. So if Mister Samuel Mortimer resides in your laughter chamber inside, or wherever, I suggest you bring back final word to him and to your Executive. Redmond Bouchard does not support a Conservative seat in Tipperary or anywhere else, and cannot be "bought".'

The Prime Minister sat heavily, shocked by insult, as Bouchard swayed towards the door. Halifane blushed furiously and turned away from his client, appalled. But Bouchard was not done yet. As he pulled open the doors he swivelled back to Peel. 'One trifle of advice I will allow you, sir. Perhaps the world is changing and in the years to come there will be no place for a traditionalist like me. But at least I take no part in the decline of things. Any contribution I make will be forced on me by others, by circumstances. But you, sir – you are *voluntarily* assisting this new world with your concessions and your policy-dodging.'

Peel struggled to regain composure.

Bouchard faced Halifane. 'Will you accompany me?'

The attorney shook his head with resolute ease. 'I feel there is little counsel I can now offer you, sir,' he said.

An extraordinary desolation clad the countryside that Bouchard and Rob watched from the windows of their carriage.

The September evenings were tranquil and vacant, beset by a calm unusual at harvest time. Few labourers walked abroad and the very air tasted damp and foul. Even the sky appeared different, a grey sun beaming dully from ashen horizons. Bouchard felt some awful sense of premonition.

'I would flee to England were there a sympathetic household to take me in, at this moment,' he confessed to Rob with naked candour.

By now Rob had a fair understanding of his master's dilemma and the worsening truth evoked deepening despair. Casually, speaking with forthright impropriety, he said, 'Perhaps one could impose on Sir Myles in Kent?'

Bouchard allowed the boldness. 'As a last resort, yes. But Sir Myles has confessed his own troubles to me. An encumbered estate and debts in taxes to satisfy, it seems. I really should not weigh upon him – ' He hesitated gravely, 'unless I must.' His eye turned away from the barren sights beyond the window. 'I want you to promise me, Rob, that your loyalty to Drumloch will not cease with my passing.'

Surprised, Rob muttered a response but the thought went through his head: *Drumloch must only be a stepping-stone to better things for me; it has already served purpose enough.* 'I obey all your wishes, sir,' he said.

'Good.' Bouchard's voice came from far off. 'You are man enough to take care of Serle and . . . and the girls.'

'I have . . .' Rob knew this chain of frank talk was unrolling too fast. 'I have great affection and admiration for Letitia. It would be a welcome honour to attend and provide for her.'

Bouchard's face creased unhappily. 'Beware of your position, Rob. I entrust their safe-keeping to you, nothing else.'

'N-no, sir. I merely mean, I like Miss Letitia greatly and hope you can see it in your heart to approve of that affection.'

Bouchard considered, then nodded. 'Yes, yes. You *should* like her. She should be dear as any sister to you, for you are as much a part of my house now.'

They returned to silent contemplation of the scenes outside. Rob tightened the travel rug around his knees and his mind wandered. Lord of the Manor! The day might well be soon. And what measures for advancement would he take when that heady day arrived? Sell out the estate and take residence near London? Or perhaps move north, where properties were grander and profits the better? A marriage to Letty would be prudent. Already he had discussed proper conversion to the established church and Bouchard had agreed its desirable value. The day of honour was coming, and Rob must be ably prepared. Obstacles must be minimised ...

Sleep overtook him, lulled by the beat of the team's feet and the rumble of the carriage wheels. He dreamed twisted dreams of grotesque, shapeless obstacles – unrecognisable images clove by one clear countenance: the face of foster-brother Colum.

CHAPTER TWENTY-TWO

For a month Colum was suspended in a fog between Donna's urgency and the wordless demands of his neighbours. Though he wanted to take her away, the blight seemed like a portent, a sign from God.

Panic slowly engulfed the valley – but that was a mere echo of the overwhelming shock felt in every corner of the land. The potato crop failure pervaded the country and everyone knew enormous poverty, deprivation and death would follow. Too many millions of small-holders depended on that solitary food. But the extent and effect of the failure gave little comfort to those, like Colum, whose wisdom gave them corn and pigs. The disease showed every sign that it was not to be of one season's duration. The farmers with corn might enjoy a winter's respite, but it would be bitter with the inevitability of approaching hunger.

Mackie's first eviction – a test case set apart from the rest – came on the last Friday in September. It almost seemed decreed by malice that the Duff household was the first out.

For weeks petition groups and deputations from clergy and farm folk had been exhorting Bouchard to retract his decision and cancel the evictions, but already the doomed lands had been roped off, with sale signs posted by Mackie. Even the brave plan advanced by Colum and Anthony Anderson fell upon deaf ears: they had offered, with the support of the few better-established farms, to submit to an increased rent and levy on goods sold. But, by implication, that had spelled out Bouchard's dire finances, and not surprisingly to some perhaps, reaction was negative.

The illnesses that held Kitty and Desmond Devlin in their grip grew worse, so bad that Colum feared neither would live to see the turn of the calendar, but still his preparations to flee stayed stagnant. Bemused and angered, Donna saw a new side to herself during this teetering unrest. The more Colum involved himself in his neighbours' troubles, the more she wanted his attention. His abstraction was a challenge to her resolve in some odd way, but on a prosaic level she understood it in terms of simple jealousy. On her now boldly frequent visits to the farm plots she saw how Colum admired Cara Duff, how that admiration was reciprocated. Cara, alone in her suffering now with a father jailed for four months, looked to Colum for help with house and farm and Colum acceded, lending his energies and communicating with her in a cryptic language of signs and smiles unreachable for Donna.

When on the morning of the eviction she stealthily crept from the manor and rode to the high ground to watch the proceedings, she saw Colum standing to the fore there, in turn awaiting the arrival of the police bailiff who was to assist Mackie in vacating the small premises. Crowds gathered flapping their arms to fight off the wintry chill and staring, bland-faced, at the victim cottage with its open doors and windows. Colum spotted her at the back of the crowd and elbowed excitedly to her. Taking her arm, he pulled her a distance away and said, 'I told you not to ride abroad anymore. Since this blight there have been dangerous nomads in the valley, people evicted from other lands who now have no hope of food – cut-throats who'd skin you with their fingernails 'cause you wear pretty frills.'

'It's three days since I saw you. I worried lest you'd forgotten me.'

'Donna.' He took both her arms and looked deep into her blue eyes. 'Understand what is happening here. Whatever division has stood between the Quality and we tenants has opened vastly and dangerously. A year ago my dadda would have said that this could never happen, and now it has – at the worst possible time.' He nodded down to the swirling crowd, now descending on the river farm as Mackie and three mounted police approached. 'Whilst a balance of respect or fear or whatever you call it existed between your father and my father and these folk, a peace of enduring strength was assured. That balance is gone – weakened by evictions, shattered by possible famine.'

'We must leave, Colum. What sense in involving ourselves any more? In England, or Belfast – '

'No.'

'What do you mean – no? Did you not promise me? Have you lost your warmth for me?'

He shook his head and screwed his eyes closed, as much to shut out the growing clamour from Cara's yard as to emphasise his feelings. 'No word I spoke to you was untrue. My warmth for you is as it was. But I cannot turn my back on my fellow folk.' He looked at her now with plaintive expression. 'I must admit the fears I've felt. Running away with you opens problems of religion – '

'We discussed all this,' she cut in angrily.

'I have prayed,' he said. 'For the right answers. In response I see this – famine and suffering.'

'You put superstition before love.'

Love. The word had never been spoken so brazenly before. He held her at arm's length, as though evaluating her expression, seeking remedy for his worries. The shameless clarity of her gaze won him instantly and, out of sight of the cottage, he pulled her behind a rock and embraced her. 'What foolishness do we follow?' he muttered.

'I ask no more from you than love,' she said, her voice deadly serious. 'If you cannot give me that, Colum, tell me now.'

He took her face into his hands and kissed her. 'I have a duty here. To my father and mother first, then to my neighbours. Without me Cara has no devoted friend. I have known her since we stood together no higher than a bramble-bush. When the hunger gets better –'

'No. That may never be.' Her eyes stung with tears. 'There might always be factors between us. If you want me prove it now, Colum. Who knows, in another week or a month papa might have me sold off to some new squireen –'

'I would save you from that.'

'No, prove it now. I am afraid for us. Everything seems to perish here at this time. Let us escape north while we can.'

The sounds of wrestling fury came up from the river farm and Colum peered anxiously down. The bailiff had Cara and her sticks of furniture out already and while she chased her few chickens round the yard, endeavouring to crate them, Mackie was nailing wooden laths across the closed doorway daubed with the black X of eviction. The farm folk booed and hissed, but the police-agents retorted with venom, shouting loud and brandishing their pistols. Even at this distance Colum could distinguish Cara's tear-streaked face and the surge of passions – resentment and pity – would hold no more.

He turned to beg Donna's understanding, but she was gone.

After the eviction tempest had blown itself out, Colum assisted Cara in transporting her belongings to his cottage, as agreed with Desmond. Here she would stay until she had reached a decision on her future. As the night drew in, bleak and windy, the young pair sat by the kitchen fire while Desmond Devlin sat in the bedroom by his wife, comforting her as the crisis of her illness began.

'I have cousins in Galway,' Cara told Colum.

'Galway has the hunger too.'

'To be sure, but for me at least there are friendly hearts there.'

'You can stay here as long as you like, *colleen*.'

'*Ara*, why would I bother now? The Sir's thrown us down to hell with all the rest. One place's good as another.'

'Supposin' the folk in Galway cannot keep you?'

'Isn't there a workhouse at Clifden, sure I'll be all right there.'

Colum imagined Cara's clean strong body amid the squalor of the workhouse he had once seen, near Banagher. After the Shannon's balmy air the noxious smells of human disease and rot might be nigh intolerable. But what real option did she have? With this creeping hunger who could support her for long? And what prospects would Swan have when he left jail to retrieve her? With his few possessions he might never realise enough money to make a fresh start in some other tenancy for them. In truth, Colum concluded miserably, she had but two choices: the workhouse or the unsavoury alternative of selling her body on the streets of Dublin town, a profession well known to attract scores of desitute country girls each year.

As if reading his mind, Cara hitched her petticoats and displayed a fine bare ankle. 'If all fails I may find admirers for my body.' She tossed her flame-red hair and cupped her ripely matured breasts. 'Many a lad's called me attractive, so there may be a penny in that, don't you think?'

Colum laughed with her, killing the earnestness of her words. He watched her and wondered at this morning's talk with Donna and its undertone of jealousy. Could he offer more than childhood affection to Cara Duff? – a respectable hand in marriage, a way out? But was there answer in that? His money might see them through a season or two here, but what if the crop disease persisted? And if he took her away, as he planned to do with Donna, would his affection sustain them, was it deep and true enough?

'What was that?' Cara startled, her head jerking up like a hunting animal's. 'I heard a sound – like a squawk of pain.'

'What? A banshee wind, no more.' Colum crossed himself.

Cara nodded sadly and her eyes drifted towards the bedroom door. 'Aye, a banshee.' But it had not sounded like a death demon. Her ears were good and her head was clear and that far-off sound was the din of an animal, a horse in tortuous pain.

Early on the morrow Paul Cabbot was announced at Drumloch.

It was Donna who received him, pale and languid and quite sickly-looking. After the initial shock of her appearance he regained his good spirits and professed himself charmed by so opportune and fortuitous a meeting. 'You may have heard,' he declared, 'these last weeks have seen quite major construction works at Fork. These alone have absorbed mamma and I, and prevented us from calling.'

'Really?' Donna spoke absently.

'So, at first opportunity, I thought I must ride to Drumloch – at mamma's behest – and invite you . . . and your kinfolk, of course, to accompany us on the Kilshowen Hunt this weekend.' Cabbot beamed with satisfaction.

'Invite *us*?' Donna felt almost annoyed: clearly American protocol and its Irish counterpart had their differences. 'Sir, the Hunt is very well known to us. On occasion in the past both my dear departed mamma and my papa mastered it. But for a time this household has had little association with it.'

Chastened, Cabbot struggled to explain himself. 'I mean no insult, my lady. But the nature of the Hunt has been outlined for me as a public event, a start-of-season run that quite happily accepts strangers like me. Lord Estelle masters it this season and has warmly invited myself and mamma to bring along whomsoever we would like to ride with us. Do not doubt I recognise your esteemed position in society here. What I simply ask is the grace of your company – *your* company, my lady – tomorrow.'

The tone of his purpose was clear but Donna did not blush. Papa had said nothing of it but she guessed he had not received direct invitation from Estelle. By now the friction between neighbouring landlords was clear, and she could see her father's standing in startling light. But how would *he* respond to this circuitous offering? Would it be easy-way-in for him, or insult? Without ulterior motive she said, 'I should dearly like to ride with the Hunt, but I fear extraneous events may not permit that.'

Cabbot feared she was side-stepping. He affected a hangdog expression and said, 'It would mean much to me to enjoy your companionship for one pleasant day, for in a week or two we sail back for New York.'

'You do not understand.' Donna stood and paced. 'Last night there was some . . . disturbance. Papa has had to ride for the police this morning.'

'Nothing dreadful, I hope?'

'The stables were attacked under cover of dark.' She bit on a handkerchief of fine lace. 'Our five horses were slaughtered – my beloved stallion Zephyr among them.' Her voice quivered towards tears.

Cabbot stumbled to his feet. 'My God! How outrageous. Villainy indeed. Who did it, do you know?' Before the words were spoken Cabbot sensed his answer. 'These so-called Ribbonmen?'

'How can one know? There is a hunger on the farms, brought down by blight. The people are desperate for sustenance, understandably. Papa has instigated a series of evictions in order to procure sale land – ' Donna related events simply, without adornment or critical comment. But the explanations left Cabbot no less appalled.

'Respectfully, my lady, one must take this dastardly event as a warning. No matter what you say about making concessions for the suffering poor, one must be on one's guard. My dear mamma – ' He sighed. 'She must be made aware of these things. I am afraid she can be dog stubborn at times and once her heart is set on a possession, it must be hers. But I will alert her to this reality. This tranquil fairyland she seeks may not so readily offer itself in Fork Estate.'

Donna swept the solitary tear from her eye, irritated by her moment of weakness. 'Let me not empurple your attitude to Ireland, sir. There are problems, to be sure. But there will be problems in heaven, I'll venture. When one lives here, one comes to understand.'

'You are brave. A rare trait in a lady.'

'Not brave. I merely have a true affection for Irish air. I think I was born with that in my blood.'

Cabbot watched her as she stood by the window gazing out towards the grey-brick stables. Would mamma like her? On one hand, he knew, she would heartily disapprove of so fragile and exquisitely pretty a creature; mamma liked canny women of notable wiles. But her Irishness should win the day.

Cabbot stood. 'I shall call again this afternoon to address myself to your father, and offer what help I can in the matter of horses and transport.' Donna did not turn from the window. 'Then I shall endeavour to persuade him to join us for the Hunt. Perhaps that happy distraction will free his concerns for a time.'

'Quite.' Donna was staring down to the yard before the stables and coach house. Colum had ridden up from the Doon and was conversing with Rob there, his posture animated and tense. Even at this distance her heart leapt at the very sight of him. Yesterday she had been wrong to speak to him with such grave fervour: his feelings for her were genuine and deep, conveyed in every gentle touch of his hand. She must not doubt him. And yet there lay this uncrossed ground between them, this unity of passions unreached. Why, when she sank submissively in his arms in the seclusion of night, did he not caress her in the secret ways Letty boasted of? Even Adam Rossitor had embraced Letty with greater intimacy: Donna had spied that herself. Small doubts wound up in her head and the temptation to leave the drawing-room and join him in the yard suddenly, painfully, faded. Momentary guilt came. Perhaps, in seeking unbridled passion, she was looking for too much. She recalled Letty's accusation: was she behaving like a French dancing girl, searching out a farm boy's favours? But if that were the root truth of it, she was merely following the call of her body, and there was honesty in it. No, there was no room for shame. She wanted Colum – heart and body – and must have him on those terms or not at all. Perfect love was not too much to ask.

In the coach yard Rob was bitterly argumentative. 'You come to offer aid, is it, when your friends have seen their destruction done?' He spat the words to his foster-brother with naked aggression.

Colum remained mounted and held his calm. 'I know nothing of this, Rob, but I understand your bitterness.' He could understand too how, in some circumspect way, Rob might feel responsibility: as recent chief of stables he had fed and cared for the slaughtered animals, and taken charge of their safety against rustlers and Ribbonmen.

'How can you hold your head high on this ground when I myself heard you speak in defence of these devils? No, I will not have it.' Arms akimbo, he inflated his chest and demanded, 'I decree who crosses these grounds now, and I will have no criminals. We seek no twisted help from the farm folk, so I will be pleased if you will take yourself away from here – instantly.'

Colum gritted his teeth for argument but the scuff of a boot on the cobbles halted him. Letitia approached, her wrap tightly about her against the blustery wet breeze. Rob's last words had been overheard and an ominous frown was aimed towards him. 'You come to offer service, Mister Devlin? I'm sure papa will be relieved to know there are still those among his tenants who regard him with such respect.'

Rob interjected, 'Mistress, my master made it clear that a careful guard was to be maintained in his absence. No longer is it prudent to allow casual treaspass along these lands.'

'I am aware of father's wishes,' Letitia blazed. 'I am not a child, sir. He spoke to me at length before departing for Banagher. Indeed, 'twas I who suggested the posting of signs warning off intruders.'

Rob reddened and bowed.

Letitia faced Colum again. 'Our distress can be imagined, I'm sure. Five beasts slain and the smeared marks of the Ribbonmen upon the walls.'

'You have my heartfelt sympathies, m'lady. No human being can wish to see the suffering or degradation of a fellow man or animal.' The severe undertone of that remark was not lost on Letty. She held Colum's eye defiantly but her fingers intertwined in agitation.

'Were these Drumloch tenants whose wrath was stirred by papa?'

Colum hesitated in answering: there was no truthful assured reply. 'I can speak only for myself, m'lady. I deplore mercilessly violent acts.'

'But you stand behind the aims of the Ribbonmen – aims that will bring about the total dissolution of social order.' Rob spoke in a savage burst.

'Please!' Letitia snapped. 'I have made myself clear. Papa would want a peaceful state of co-existence above anything, I'm certain, and Colum Devlin's journey here must therefore be welcomed. Your persistent foul manners serve no one.' Rob swayed before them, his lips trembling in anger. Letitia went on coolly, 'I will now ask you, Rob, to kindly leave me – as mistress of Drumloch – to discuss with this gent. Find some toil in the coach house, if you will.'

Colum slid off his horse and Rob stalked away, shaking in fury. 'Let me show you the horror of last night,' Letty resumed, smiling as though that "horror" were no more than a peep-show. She turned towards the old stable block and reached out to touch Colum's arm lightly. 'Should the sights overwhelm me, I must take your arm. Forgive, do.'

Colum looked into her face and saw obtrusive, unnerving friendliness. For an instant he felt like a worm caught in the beak of a crow.

CHAPTER TWENTY-THREE

Bouchard walked self-consciously into the warm, low-ceilinged room that was the Devlins' kitchen and nodded to the red-haired girl churning butter in the corner. Colum guided him across the dry-earth floor and rapped softly on the door to the larger bedroom. 'I am grateful,' Bouchard whispered to Colum, 'for this chance to speak privately with your father.' Colum tilted his head in courtesy and pushed in the door.

Devlin rose to his feet with effort and drew a finger to his grey lips for silence. On the bed beneath the window Kitty lay, her face immobile in slumber. The scent of death crowded the small room. 'Inside,' Devlin urged, and he pulled his master into an adjoining room of even smaller proportions. Some of Colum's clothes draped a wooden frame above the tumbledown bed and an ink sketch of the Shannon – not unlike Donna's fanciful work, Bouchard hastily realised – adorned the facing dobe-mud wall. Devlin drew two crude stools and said, '*Suig shios, anseo.* You are welcome in God's eyes.'

'I come in despair.'

Devlin watched his landlord's face carefully and saw the tell-tale signs of alcoholic indulgence and exhaustion – the rheumy eye, the patchy skin, the nervous shake. 'It saddens me,' he said, 'that hostile events bring you, and not a feeling of goodwill.'

'Goodwill goes unspoken,' Bouchard rushed. 'You know what our . . . friendship has been in the past.'

'That friendship seems long faded in time. It is many a year since you crossed my threshold.'

'Diverse events preoccupied me, as you know.' Bouchard was quiet for some minutes, gazing into his lap in the dimness of the room. Then he said, 'Your lad called upon us today, to express his abhorrence at this evil act of the Ribbonmen.' Devlin nodded. 'His openness makes it clear that what occurred was not an organised assault with the blessing of all tenants – '

'But he feels, as many do, that the evictions were callous.'

Bouchard lurched that aside. 'What worries me is that these devils have patently infiltrated our lands. I am mindful of the risk of allowing them a grip.' His eye found Devlin's. 'And so I appeal to you – as elder of the valley and respected source of wisdom. Assist me, please. Help me by making sure that what occurred does not happen again. Speak to your fellow farmers, caution them.'

'You went to the police, before you came to me.' Devlin threw the words out casually, inviting response. Bouchard had more motive in coming here than ordinary fear for his well-being. Most likely he was troubled by the effect the Ribbonmen's attention would have on the sale value of his newly annexed river plots. It was widely known that 'cursed' land found no purchasers.

'McClune plays his own game,' Bouchard replied. 'He promises vigilance, but speaks through a sneer.' He muttered, half under his breath, 'The man would rather me dead and gone.'

'You must see the calamity that has befallen our people. Hunger and eviction – '

'No less a threat rests on me,' Bouchard said. His twisted face relaxed. 'In confidence I speak, my friend. But what I say is true. My options were gone. In order to survive, I had to make lands available for sale. Believe me. It pains me to *have to* take the actions I am taking. But were I not to, I would jeopardise the future of the entire estate – not twenty families, but the whole lot.'

Devlin judged honesty in Bouchard's face. 'There would have been sounder ways of taking action. Engaging Nim Mackie was inviting hostility.'

Bouchard shook his head. 'There's no wisdom in discussing what has been. Mistakes may have been made, but they are dead and buried now. And I come to you entreating for a better, safer future.'

Devlin appeared undecided. He breathed quietly, watching the timbers of the roof.

'There are favours you owe me,' Bouchard urged. 'Incidents of the past.'

'Aye. You granted me a doctor for my wife in childbirth.' The smile died on his lips. 'Then you took Rob away – '

'To allow him an education and a good life.'

Devlin nodded. Bouchard could not interpret the strange irony in his host's expression. A surge of impatience hurried him on. 'For all our sakes, assist me. Gather the tenants about, address them. Tell them this villainy must never occur again, warn them. They will obey your voice before all others – we both know that.'

'But the threatening hunger they face banishes sense. They might not attend me when I have no reassurance to give.'

'But there are reassurances. All will be well if they bear up and tolerate. Relief Commissions are presently being appointed. Peel is promising cheap corn and scientific help to understand and kill this crop disease – ' Bouchard was straining in his seat, desperately trying to win agreement, to soften the look in Devlin's tired face. 'Both of us know the dangerous abyss that stands before us. We have lived through changes a-plenty these last sixty years. And both of us know the extent of your influence, should you deign to use it. You alone can halt a war on these lands.'

'No. Not alone, sir. *You* and I, perhaps. But not I alone.'

'Please, Devlin. Speak to them. That is all I ask.'

Colum pushed in the door and whispered urgently. 'Dadda – come now. Her fever gets worse.'

Devlin stood, alarmed, and Bouchard held his arm. 'I shall trust in you,' he persisted. 'Come to the manor, sup with me. Tell me the unrest is dying and all is well.'

'Hurry.' Colum's voice rippled from the shadows again.

Very gently Devlin shrugged off his landlord's grip and paced into the larger bedroom. Kitty had stirred to wakefulness but her eyes shone in a crazed heat and her breathing was fast. Devlin knelt by her as Colum left the room and Bouchard, on his way out, paused to look over the old farmer's shoulder. Kitty's unseeing eyes bore through his as they swept the darkened area.

'Desmond, *mo chree*, are you near?'

'By your side, woman.'

'I must make my peace.'

Bouchard gazed down on the woman and his eye flicked shut. Devlin was fumbling rosary beads into her hands but she resisted them, grasping his lean hands instead. As Bouchard moved to leave her gaze lit on him for a fraction and narrowed in recognition. '*Araghaidh leat*,' she muttered, showing signs of aggrieved agitation. 'Go, go and leave us in peace. My sins are done!'

Distressed, Devlin waved Bouchard hurriedly away. Then he crouched to hear the deathbed confessions of his wife. When Bouchard crossed the kitchen again Cara was sleeping in a chair by the heat of the evening fire, and Colum was absent.

The word of a meeting of subversives from far and near attracted Colum to the little whiskey-house beyond the valley boundary. Evening had fallen to rain-lashed night by the time he arrived but he found only a handful of dawdlers there, just one or two affording themselves the luxury of a dram. As he entered the conversation ceased entirely, then the farmers whispered their recognition and the talk resumed. At the serving counter Colum asked for a beer but the portly keeper shook his head. ' 'Tis the last of it I've handed out. Didn't McClune and his henchmen raid us this evenin' and locate a measure of illicit brew and a crate on unlicenced tobacco. All shipped off, be God, and me facin' the magistrates now.' The keeper sighed mournfully and invoked Divine assistance.

' 'Tis a sorry day,' Colum said.

' 'Tis war,' a voice at the bar murmured darkly. 'Mackie and McClune have hoisted their flag with the others. And Drumloch's tenants have pitched in with us. 'Tis time for open battle.' Colum looked among the crusty, weather-beaten faces and saw people from Major Middleton's land, long-suffering farmers. One or two grinned their delight at the prospect of so clear-cut a conflict.

Disheartened, Colum walked back out into the freezing night and focussed on the guiding lights of the farm cottages. Not fifteen paces from the whiskey-house a cheery voice called his name and tramping feet pounded from the darkness. He cupped his eyes and saw Teggie Kelly, a neighbour from Drumloch, with Anthony Anderson. The three stood back into the shelter of the lighted doorway and Colum swiftly recounted his purpose in coming.

'You missed the action then, it seems,' Teggie pointed out. 'For we arrived ourselves just in time to see the meeting breaking up. Black Hand O'Tracy was here, summoning friends of freedom to strike out against the Bouchard evictions and wreak new terror each night.'

'He found an ear, I'll wager.'

'McClune's boyos had just raided, it seemed,' Anderson expanded, 'so that helped the fervour. There was talk of lynching Bouchard himself, and of ravishing the girls. But finally they headed off in big numbers for Nim Mackie's – to try God knows what trick.'

Colum's boot crashed into the dirt. 'Our people must be careful. They must see that this trap of high emotions might lead them into worse trouble. Once the Ribbonmen devices come into play, McClune's people will never leave them alone.'

'You're right, Colum. The Ribbonmen are no answer. A more complete and lasting answer is needed – land reform, Repeal *and* a change of government will begin it.'

'What do you speak of, Anthony?'

'Co-ordinated rebellion, if needs be.'

There was sudden silence. The rain washed over them, blinding Colum's vision so that he could not explore his friend's expression. But the serious ring of Anderson's words persisted. 'I sympathise but O'Connell says force cannot be justified. Repeal will come. Justice will . . . evolve.'

'The Liberator is down.' Anderson plucked Colum's sleeve. 'Understand that. Repeal Year proved a waste of all our time. Now there is the threat of famine and Mister O'Connell is hiding his head in the sand, an old man too tired for fight. We will be left alone unless we unite and save ourselves and our friends. Our voices must be heard. We must have relief and Repeal. This is no religious war – it's a class war, a war of survival for the labouring people.'

'You have heard of John Mitchel, of the Young Irelanders?' Teggie asked.

'I have read their *Nation* news journal. Once. Protestants and Catholics, they are. John Mitchel stands among them.'

'An enlightened man, Colum. He speaks of truths beyond O'Connell's. He says reform must begin with Repeal, but – since tact has failed us – we must not exclude the choice of taking arms. Read.' Teggie reached under the skin cape and crushed a folded paper into Colum's hands. Colum tore it open:

> What are you doing to fight famine?
> Peel cannot help you. Most of the
> gentry will not. You must help yourself.
> This country needs the independent control that
> will come with Repeal. Lend us your voice. Help
> us to help you. Join together, tell neighbour and
> friend. Let us further O'Connell's work.
> Support the Young Irelanders.

'These are no rabble-rousing Ribbonmen,' Anderson insisted. 'They are educated men of principle who seek justice and a Dublin government. It is with great regret that they are drifting apart from O'Connell. They want what we all know we need – a unified Ireland of all creeds that governs itself. The need is desperate now. Peel's remote governing cannot perceive our troubles. We must have Home Rule now, before half of us is wiped out.' He paused. 'You must realise that another blighted season is a certainty. The rot is so widespread.'

Colum stared at the paper in his hands. Rain hammered the oily print till the words melted and dribbled. 'It is our hope,' Teggie went on, 'to speak to all the valley folk in turn and win their confidence and support. First of all we must persuade them that the Young Irelanders are a political force – not blood-hungry rebels – we must go further than O'Connell suggested to achieve our aims.'

'We have travelled north to meet with the organisation's leaders, Colum,' Anderson interjected excitedly. 'We did not meet Davis, their leader, as he is gravely ill. But we met with Dillon and Mitchel, his associates – fair-hearted men who can be trusted.' His eyes darted to Teggie, willing him to take up the story. Older, wiser, Teggie's harsh native talk could be more persuasive. Teggie immediately took it up: 'The Young Irelanders are politicians but constitutional wrangling may not be enough in this emergency, Colum. A rising must be a probability. They can be our inspiration, our guidance; but we must take our fate into our own hands.'

'You want to form a group among Drumloch's tenants?'

'And beyond,' Anderson said. 'Let the party and the cause be clearly seen. End this senseless villainy of the Ribbonmen. Stand to fight – if necessary – for Repeal. And famine relief.'

'I am ready and keen to fight for my neighbours, but I am opposed to unnecessary bloodshed.'

'And suffering?' Teggie added brightly. Colum nodded. 'Well,' Teggie rapped, 'look what suffering faces Duff, and twenty other families on our estate! See too that this is just a drop in the ocean against what suffering will be seen countrywide. No doubt some of the gentry will help our kind, but you know the majority will sacrifice us to save themselves.'

Grimly Colum nodded: he had heard much of Devlin's talk with Bouchard, understood its nuances.

'Come with us,' Anderson said. 'Let us devote ourselves to the cause of preparing for a day of unified uprising. Let us talk to the farm folk, find friends – '

'If you care for your land,' Teggie put in.

'I care for my land enough. And I care for my neighbours, and their plight. Do not think I oppose anything you've said.' He shrugged. 'All right. What if we banish the police and overthrow the Banagher garrison? What then?'

'Trust Mitchel and his friends – and the Liberator. The aims are the same.' Anderson prodded Colum's arm good-naturedly. 'We will not aspire to be the politicians. We must be the *muscle* of change alone. We must get behind good politicians of our choosing, and prepare to launch forth.'

The sound of a gun startled the night. Unseen birds cawed and winged and for a second even the rain drew its breath. The three men pricked their ears and heard distantly the hollow shouts of angered men.

'Ribbonmen tricks without direction,' Teggie mumbled.

'But what suffers now?' Anderson mused. He nudged Colum again. 'Well, what say you? You are not afraid to fight, but you hesitate still.'

'I am pledged to ... other matters just now.' He was thinking of Donna, of the tempting challenge of love.

'What issue can be more important than the call of one's country?'

CHAPTER TWENTY-FOUR

The close proximity of the arrival of two callers to the manor the following morning embarrassed Bouchard. Adam Rossitor, unheralded, arrived *en route* for Cork, professedly to examine some precious Russian icons by Novgorod artists which had found their way into someone's dowry. Despite the ever-present noble 'front', Bouchard now saw Adam as little more than an alley dealer – but still he was careful of his own image with the boy, wary lest the wrong aspect should filter back to Sir Myles and shatter whatever small confidence in Drumloch was left. This uneasy caution was not helped by Nim Mackie's loud-mouthed presence.

Renowned for the healthy power of his lungs, Mackie sat in the downstairs study and barked out his news in a stentorian drone that drove through the passages of the house. Bouchard repeatedly hushed him.

'I'll be askin' increase in pay, if conditions persist,' the hard-eyed Dubliner boomed. 'Last night me house was set upon by a gang of demons, carrying forks and clubs they were, and shoutin' for blood. All Drumloch's people.' He shook his dark hair unhappily. 'Weren't this way with Estelle's, nor anyone else I've served with. Seems to me these folk are barbarians.'

'I think it's not the folk, but the time this has occurred.'

'You implyin' the evictions was wrong?'

The strength of Mackie's face discouraged Bouchard's frank reaction. With a nervous grin he said, 'I'm just acknowledging that the crop disease has unbalanced the situation. I'm not surprised there has been some violence –'

'Some indeed,' Mackie intruded. 'I had to get a messenger to McClune, and he brought some soldiers from the garrison. They shot at the villains and scared 'em off. But they said they'd return, they'd get me.'

'I'm sure there'll be an end to these types of incidents,' Bouchard put in, stout-voiced. 'I have spoken to my friend Devlin, my old middleman, and I am confident of his intervention. This squall will pass.'

'Ne'er too soon, for I think it's done its damage in more ways than one.'

Bouchard's good eye narrowed to an icy slash. 'Our interested purchasers?'

With aplomb Mackie spread a sheet of scribbled paper before him and consulted names and numbers. 'The cattle farmer from Birr ain't interested no more. Mister Cramer from Limerick has seen the ground and is worried about the placement of labourers' cottages. He spies the evictions and is worried the farmers may return to squat. Old Cashel Ormsby cannot be contacted –'

Bouchard felt dizzy. He splashed some whiskey into a glass at his elbow and drank. 'What about the forestry man, the fellow who offered four hundred for the entire river stretch?'

'Reduced to two-fifty.' Mackie enjoyed spilling out the bald facts. Best to face reality, he mused. Sir Redmond's game was clear to be seen now. The man hadn't two brass farthings to rub together and Nim Mackie was not about to risk his neck indefinitely waving a flag for that grade of reward.

'We must advertise more widely,' Bouchard insisted. 'Post more bills, let neighbouring gentry know. The river lands are fertile and promising –'

'Not in blight, they're not.'

Bouchard climbed to his feet and terminated the interview before the storm of his wrath took control.

While Bouchard spoke with Mackie, Letty entertained Adam in the main drawing-room and endeavoured to override the buzz of alarmed talk. His expressed expertise and trade in precious works of art inceasingly interested her. In recent days she had given much thought to the negative aspects of her positioin within new Drumloch. An inheritance of value could clearly no longer be hoped for: papa's troubles were too evident. And the canny ingenuity that lurked within ingenuous Donna gave cause for concern. Through care for the babe Donna, overnight, had mastered the art of winning papa. Letty's prime position had slipped and, remembering the William deal, she was worried that she might now become the expendable one. But Letty was no longer prepared to turn her fate confidently over to her father. Rumours of William's collapse and ruin had come to her and the realities of papa's misjudgements were apparent. God knows what Donna's quiet plans were, but she would not sit back forever and grin to bear the worst of it. She would find her own way out, a way she enjoyed.

When Adam had rambled on for all of ten minutes, relating his manifold successes with princesses and parvenues, he came to sit by her and tried his luck immediately, palpating her bosom with passion. She had allowed that caress too easily at Feast and now shrugged his hand away. It was not that he was unattractive – with his oiled black hair and deep-blue eyes any woman might be excused for swooning – but Letty saw herself in love-play as aggressor, or at least equal aggressor. And free passion was not of her choosing today. 'There are codes, sir,' she hissed. 'This is improper in my father's home.'

Shocked by her new chilliness he drew back. 'I-I apologise for misinterpreting signs of affection.' He stammered a giggle. 'I thought you . . . found me attractive?'

'I do.'

That little encouragement was all he needed. He pressed on her again, drunk with desire. 'Come, you have given me your lips before. Do not be so unkind –'

'You have entertained the notion of marriage in your varied and exciting life?'

He released her to examine her expression. 'N-not much. A young businessman with far-flung commitments may see few great advantages in wedlock.' He qualified: 'When so engaged in the success of his career.'

'How strange the impulses that make women so different from men.'

'You cherish the idea of marriage?'

'I save myself for it. For the right man.' She clapped her hands and threw back her head as though enraptured by the thought. The gesture caused her bosom to thrust upwards, straining the little silk buttons of her bodice. Adam held himself from rushing forward again.

'You seek a gent with money and standing?' he said. 'The likes of which you would not so easily find around here?'

'Precisely. But a gentleman whose devotion is beyond question.'

'Of course, of course. Love means much.' He leaned against her and ran an arm around her shoulder. The fingers brushed her breast with deliberation and his breathing came in short snorts. She could tell he was excited. The touch of her body at Feast had served as an appetiser, a promise of the paradise he sought. Inwardly she grinned. She would not make such easy game for any man. *Her* desires may be fulfilled at the drop of a hat, but she wasn't in the market to hand out favours. Very calmly she pushed off Adam's hand.

'You look upon me as a remote friend, no more?' he questioned. She did not answer. 'Nothing could be farther from the truth, for I think of you always when we are apart. Indeed –' He paused to seek her eye. 'Only the prospect of meeting with you again drew me here.'

'The story of the icons is untrue?'

'No, not at all. I shall make my tidy fortune from those trinkets. But I came primarily to see your splendid face – and give you this.' He burrowed into his jacket and took out a small flat disc wrapped in satin. Eagerly she unfolded it and found a pretty coloured replica of a Russian mosaic, circled in gold.

'It is beautiful,' she said. 'And must have cost quite a penny.'

His fingers stirred the looped rings of her dark hair. 'Money means nothing when it sits by true beauty.' He craned down and twisted her face so that their mouths met in a long, deep kiss. Through the embrace Letitia's thoughts ran sharp as sunlight. Was she reading the signs right? A gift of value and responsive talk of wedlock. She must be careful of her reactions. If he was truly interested she must evaluate him anew. Perhaps he *was* wealthy, and really in love with her. Letty felt her own excitement surge. What escape, if all proved well!

He was kissing her hair, muttering endearments, but she pushed him away to say, 'Why not stay beyond tomorrow, Adam? If your treasures in Cork can wait another day there is the Kilshowen Hunt on Saturday and papa is quite pleased to allow us ride.'

'I'm unsure whether my time –'

'You could wine and dine and get to know papa and . . . get to know *me* better.'

'The pressure of time presents a problem just this week.'

She shifted in the cushions, turning her body towards

him so that one knee propped high, drawing the foot off the floor. He watched the movement unthinkingly, his eyes savouring the glimpse of fine inner petticoats and delicate ankle. Resolve snapped and he threw out a hand and touched her calf. She slumped back luxuriously, her eyes swimming. The invitation was in the expression. Adam slid his hand deep under her skirts and found the damp flesh of her thighs. Just as his blood started to boil her eyes flicked wide and she said, quite coolly, 'I'm certain one week-end would not cost you your fortune.'

'I . . . I could travel tonight,' he stuttered, sweating, 'and return for Saturday. It would mean going at all speed. But -'

'Why not?' She jerked up suddenly, whipping the prize away from his hungry grasp. Her dainty hands tapped her ringlets into place and she crossed to the gilt mirror above the fireplace to adjust her bodice frill. To his eye she appeared composed and collected but her bearing hid a quivering heart. The passion he had fired in her blazed through her veins and begged for release. But she could not sway, not at this early stage. He must learn to want her more, obey the rules she ordained.

She sucked air and turned back to him with a loving smile. 'I hear Mister Mackie departing,' she said. 'You may tell papa straight away that your route home will take you to us again on Friday night. I shall suggest the Hunt.

He nodded agreement and looked her over with eyes of desperate longing.

Colum's defences rose the moment he saw Letitia's distant figure bob through the blackberry bramble path and angle towards him. It was late on the short afternoon and his toil was taking him to the Shannon's banks, to fetch the night's water.

Her cape snug about her, she called from afar and when he played at ignoring her she shouted louder and ran.

'It's unwise to be out at dark,' Colum told her as she caught up with him.

She pointed back to the grey mountain that was Drumloch manor, peeping through the tangle of bare, dying trees. 'You forget the boundaries,' she said. 'This lies within the manor grounds and it is you who trespasses.'

'You have heard of the Ribbonmen? Their sense of honour may leave something to be desired.'

The bleak cold of his humour doused her spirits. 'Life must go on,' she said. 'Grief must be buried from day to day. But do I perceive stubborn sorrow in you today?'

'My mamma has passed on, God rest her.'

'Oh – I am sorry.'

'You couldn't have known.' He shrugged off his morose expression. ' 'Tis as well. Her illness lasted too long. My earnest prayer is that dadda's time will be soon. He has no wish to endure her suffering, and his heart is weak.'

They came to the grassy slope of the river bank and Colum separated the four pails he carried and crouched to fill them. Letty sat alongside him, her knees drawn to her chin, and listened to the gentle splashing water. The wind was heavy with rain. 'You told me yesterday that the Ribbonmen would find no great sympathy on Drumloch's plots,' she said. 'Yet by all accounts the Drumloch folk were abroad last night again, hounding Mister Mackie's.'

'I am proved wrong, then.' He sighed, scooping water. 'It goes to show there can be no certainty about anything any more. This looming hunger draws a blanket over christian principles.' He was silent for a minute as he pulled the last pail. 'There will be no proper peace until the question mark that hangs over the estate fades.'

'What question mark?'

'Your papa's future.' He avoided her gaze. 'The truth of his situation frightens those who know. Some say the evicted ones will be better off leaving.'

'You think *I* would be better off leaving here?'

The allusion to stealthy departure horrified Colum. He set down the last bucket busily, his face turned from Letitia's lest his secret be seen. ' 'Tis never fortunate to live on famine-scarred land.'

'How prettily you speak, Colum.' He glanced to her, intrigued by her sudden mocking tone, and she patted the dry earth beside her. 'Sit by me a minute, and tell me more.'

He had taken his place close by her before that alert wariness stole over him again.

'I envy Donna her ready friendship with you,' she said. 'For it must allow her an insight to the farmers' lives, and their thinking.'

'Miss Donna – like yourself – had the bright vision of an educated woman. She perceives the situation for herself and learns the history of it from books.'

'Yes, I have seen her with volumes from papa's library – great weighty tomes about the rebellion of '98 and Wolfe Tone, the hero-rebel of the Irish.' She giggled. 'I confess I know little of such wars. My education was markedly that of an English lady.'

'You care for Ireland, though?'

'I care for a good home, indeed. Ireland, England – what is the difference? I seem not to have the strangling roots that Donna boasts.' Colum did not speak and she eyed him curiously, her mind drifting. He stared back but could not fathom her brain, could not guess that those spiralling thoughts were laced with a powerful hunger that had been sparked earlier by the battle of wiles with Adam Rossitor. Had Rob been present in the house, Letty knew, she would have visited his quarters and devoured him as surely as a fish takes its bait. But he had been absent all day, on errands for papa, and she had had to content herself with her memories of his brutal, sweet caress and wild fantasies of an unshaped future.

Now she watched Colum, her gaze probing muscle and bone, and wondered how satisfying an embrace he could offer. What fun did he give stern Donna? Her hunger took firm form and a voice inside pleaded Colum's caress. And why not? With a farm boy one could dispel one's frustration and forget it ever happened; there could be no commitments, no promise.

Letitia glided a hand over Colum's shoulder and threw herself suddenly on him. Before he had time to evade, her lips were heavily on his and her tongue had his mouth open. He twisted to heave her off but her full weight was on him and his shoulders were pinned down. 'Be easy,' she hissed, tearing her head back to watch his eyes. 'Or do I repel you so dreadfully that you cannot withstand an innocent kiss?'

He lay still and felt her moist short breathing on his cheek. 'You do not repel me, m'lady. But I have no wish to behave ungraciously.'

'You insult me by inert response.'

'Forgive me, then.'

With teasing care Letitia began a slow-motion movement of her right knee, describing long strokes across Colum's middle, kneading his groin. Bit by bit she felt him react, stiffening. 'I am privy to a secret that could destroy the high repute of the Devlins.'

'What secret, mistress?'

'Your love affair with Donna.' Letitia's hand followed the movement of her knee and she found Colum's hardness and fingered him. 'You know what fate befell her when papa heard of her dalliance before? He whipped her – repeatedly.' She sucked Colum's ear. 'Imagine what fury she would command now, were I to tell of midnight escapades.'

Scared, he obediently looped his arms about her back. Already sensing the answer he asked, 'What must I do to persuade you to keep these secrets?'

'Touch me.'

His fingers trembling, he reached for her petticoats and bundled them. He had just began exploring when her hand roughly freed him from his breeches and plucked him under her skirts. The sensations were frantic, confused, and he felt nothing on entering her – none of her warmth or grip or movement. Instead her teeth bit deep into the skin of his neck and a pulse of violent tension pumped hard in his belly.

In the hazy frenzy of their labours neither stirred to see the solitary horseman who rode by on the higher slope, almost masked from them by a thin drape of bushes. But Rob reined in the horses he was transporting from Fork for a moment and took a second look to make sure his eyes were not deceiving him. Then, rather than face his horror, he spurred his mount and rode on.

CHAPTER TWENTY-FIVE

Shrewd minds among the Kilshowen Hunt knew it was too late for the ploy Bouchard was trying. Thanks to Stephens's demise word of his critical financial state was out, and rumours of gambling and debauchery (with a child from the blue and no wife) were rife. Not even the flaring violence on his plots evoked sympathy. Neighbours like Middleton remembered too well his former intransigence and reckoned he deserved all that came his way now.

But Bouchard, with an energy uncommon for his age, was struggling still. For him hope rested in retaining status and braving the storm. For now, Mortimer was laying low. The bricks and mortar of the manor were still his; and he possessed a fitting heir to hold the dynasty. The main thing was to regain friendship, rebuild trust; and keep a fast eye out for the saving deal.

That optimism perished in the freezing winter morning's air of Estelle's forecourt. The excuse of partnership with the visiting Cabbots had seemed so practical, but their party found little more than Estelle's blatant embarrassment to greet them. Donna and Letty were appalled, but Bouchard seemed mollified by a string of scant passing conversations with unknown gentry. With grand gestures he introduced his American friends but Donna watched and perceived the thinness of the veneer: in truth papa was outraged by the hardiness of growing opposition. As the master assembled the hounds and port was carried out by industrious footmen to help warm the riders Paul Cabbot leaned to Donna and observed, 'Seems our party is well matched. Only myself, mamma, Mister Rossitor and your family group appear true strangers here.'

'How unkind. These are our close neighbours.'

'I mean no insult.' Cabbot touched his forehead apologetically but looked no less serious. Josephine Cabbot came over on foot. The unctuous, humourless smile radiated to Donna. 'Paul, I'm in no mood for so cold a ride.' She jabbed a laced hand back to the conservatory outhouse that had been set aside for indoor celebration throughout the day, brightly festooned with bunting. 'That idiot daughter of mine knew what she was doing when she cried off ill again. This wind would fair skin cats.'

'Poor mamma.'

Bouchard led his borrowed mount across the cobbles, his saggy face like a sad bulldog's. Hearing Mrs Cabbot's intentions he prodded Donna's leg. 'Well, m'dear – let you suffer no lack of good company. Come down, Donna. Sit a time with dear Mrs Cabbot and entertain her.'

Donna dismounted almost gratefully. At this ungodly hour and with so fierce a breeze howling there were tasks less punishing than chasing an unfortunate fox.

'I will join you,' Cabbot offered quickly, stepping out of his saddle before anyone could object. Bouchard moved to intervene, to beg the American's company for the ride, but just then the marshalling horn sounded and the riders rushed for their horses. Adam Rossitor sidled over and held Bouchard's mount steady. 'All ready, sir?' he challenged, and Bouchard wearily took the saddle. Letitia, who had been toasting her hands on the warm brick wrapped in her muff, handed down the garment to Donna and whispered, 'All luck with your beau, sister. He seems a mite more worthy than Colum Devlin.'

'And yours more than Rob,' Donna could not resist.

Then the tally-ho went up and the ranks of horses broke into trot. Cabbot edged Donna out of the team's path and waved gaily in reply to Letitia. They watched till the last huntsman vanished round the forest turn and the yapping of the hounds died, then marched into the welcoming heat of the conservatory.

A breakfast party of mostly women, with some aged and infirm old gents, was under way. Donna took comfort in the fact that many were once-a-year acquaintances and the mood of chatter was no more than stiffly polite. She would, at least, be spared unwilling and more than likely sardonic conversations with Estelle's and Middleton's clans.

But the talk that ensued was no less exhausting. Josephine Cabbot had the brain of fox and the eye of a snake and her daughter Emma boasted like qualities of nimble-mindedness and taciturnity. For two hours or more their glib questions flowed, probing and prodding Drumloch's life style and history, and Donna felt as though she were some senseless circus creature being worked through its paces. When finally Cabbot eased her from their company Donna's good humour had worn thin and her patience was short. Her cheeks were sore from framing that artificial answering smile and suddenly she wanted to be rid of the elegant flower-hung cavern with its elegant unreal people. She thought of Colum and the opportunity the Hunt afforded her to seek him out. For days her mind had been full of him, but the arrow of confusion and jealousy that had split her heart and caused discord was back. Why in the time since their talk above the Duffs had he not found means to smuggle a note to her, or seek a meeting? What more pressing matters absorbed him? Donna recalled Cara, the attractively well-built girl with those wild Irish eyes, and was filled with a sudden restless desire to find him and plead for him, and stake her claim.

Paul Cabbot translated her sombre stare wrongly. 'Don't feel intimidated by the obvious connivance of mamma and Emma,' he offered as they walked down flagged corridors through the winter flowers. 'They simply have my best interests at heart.'

Wary, Donna smiled. 'I found them quite charming.'

'Excellent.' Cabbot was seriously pleased. After a profound silence he said, 'It seems sad that our families could not get to know each other sooner. In a week I will be gone. The demands of work in England and New York summon us – mamma and I.'

'Oh.' Donna tried to infuse warmth and concern, and Cabbot grasped for it.

'Don't feel you are being abandoned here alone,' he said. 'The events of the last weeks haven't scared us off. In due course mamma and I will be back, that's for sure.' He snorted a laugh. 'Mamma, I think, will never retire, though she pledges to week after week. Seems to me Ireland will become an annual retreat for her – and for us.'

His piercing gaze sought something from Donna that she could not give. She kept her eyes from him and said, 'I am glad you are not discouraged by what you've witnessed and heard of. The countenance of life here is not pretty just now. But it will not always be like this.'

'People are saying there will be full famine and economic ruin, or a rebellion. Those choices are bleak.'

'If the English government believe in the sanctity of the Union let them take total responsibility for the fate of the working classes now.'

Surprised, Cabbot recoiled slightly. He frowned to Donna. 'You speak like a supporter of this O'Connell. I detect asperity in your voice.'

'You are shocked?'

'N-no. It's just strange to hear such words from a daughter of the gentry – a very young lady at that.'

'I have read much. And my blood is Irish, remember.'

'And you have young Irish friends?'

The measured exactness of his speech made Donna shrink back. Blood rushed to her face. She looked for words that might divert this talk but Cabbot resumed quickly:

'I saw you walking together – that young farm lad and yourself – up on the bog land. I suspect friendship with him allows you insight to the life on the land?'

'He has taught me much.'

'That a famine or rebellion faces Ireland?'

'One need just look to see that.'

Cabbot stopped suddenly before her. Her eyes fell on the bubble of diamonds in his cravat. 'Why, may I ask, do you linger in Ireland when you admit openly that prospects are bad? Do you enjoy courting uncertainty and danger so much? Or is this a dislike of simple conformity – not unknown, I'm sure, in independent-minded young ladies?'

She felt herself colour. He was beginning to sound like his mother: brazen and demanding. 'I have no fondness for danger, sir. But neither do I see sense in turning one's back to the future. I am Irish and Ireland faces change. Why should I wish – ' She almost choked on her own words, 'to flee? No matter what happens I should be attracted back here, to my home, my heritage. And so I wish to remain in Ireland and see what fate brings.'

'Elegantly spoken.' He excused himself to light a cigar and announced from behind a screen of blue smoke: 'Then I should not embarrass myself by suggesting, with all respect, that you accompany me – to New York?'

She had known it was coming: nothing in his overt behaviour had given him away, but Josephine and Emma had, with their wily intrigue and blunt questioning. Now, the intention expressed, Donna was surprised to feel flattered and charmed. Cabbot had money and style, and the grace of good manners; a life with him would be easy, undemanding perhaps, and would afford escape from papa and the dark maybes that clouded the future.

'I am unready for marriage.'

'I did not suggest that – yet. A visit to New York, with Emma as chaperon and friend – I could think of nothing more pleasant for a lady of your position.'

'A gallant offer.'

'It comes with sincerity, believe me. I would be honoured if you would consider my offer carefully.'

'I – I am promised to another.' She bit her lip. She had given way to her innermost thoughts, and said too much too soon.

Cabbot's brows curled upwards but he shook his head. 'A local boy, by any chance? Come, Donna, I will not believe that. You have rank and class to remember – and you are a wise girl.'

She stammered. 'Please ignore me.' Her hand touched her forehead. 'The cold has eaten to my marrow. I have quite a headache and would rather lie awhile.'

He took her arm with concern and guided her towards

the door. 'Shall I accompany you home, or will you repose here?'

'Home, please. I can manage the ride alone.'

'No. No, please. Allow me.'

Cabbot would not be dissuaded. Taking leave of his kin and Lady Estelle he assisted Donna to the loaned horse and rode back to the manor by her side. Pearson offered warming drinks in the Great Hall but Donna insisted on repairing to bed. At the foot of the great stairway he kissed her hands boldly. 'Your father has requested my company for a drink on Sunday, so I may see you again. Perhaps by then you will have reconsidered my offer.'

'Perhaps.'

Her perfume exicted him till his very heart throbbed in pain. Her final word was warm but her eyes remained chilly and distant. Here is a statue goddess, he thought, that one may forever enjoy but never possess. He released her hands regretfully. In a few days he would be aboard the *Western Star*, churning through the blue of the Atlantic. Perhaps by then this desire that had so swamped him these last weeks would quieten. In truth, perhaps, she was not right for him.

The Hunt was intercepted and stopped on the fringe of Drumloch's territories by an armed mounted party led by sub-inspector McClune.

Letitia and Bouchard were among the fore group first halted by McClune's men. ' 'Tis unwise to progress any farther,' a young police-agent called out. 'We're turning back travellers till the police are done with their inquiries.'

McClune galloped up. The wry humour so often seen was absent and some wraith of defeat or misery haunted his gaze. 'No hunt,' he ordered. 'For everyone's good.'

'Meaning?' Bouchard cried.

'Meaning I aim to take no responsibility for lots of lone women riding through silent copses this day. And you may only hinder police work, in any case.'

'What trouble has broken?' Cold fingers drummed up Bouchard's spine, anticipating.

'Mackie's dead. Found this morn'. Trussed like a chicken and beaten to death.'

'My God!' Letitia shrilled and Adam Rossitor moved to comfort her. Fellow huntsfolk were cantering up and shocked voices rippled about, relaying McClune's news.

'Where?' Bouchard asked. 'Where did it happen?'

'Found along here,' McClune said. 'Edge of your lands. Leaves no doubt.' He grimaced, containing his own bitterness. 'Mackie was friend to me, Sir Redmond. We have had our failures in inquiry in the past, but I am not about to let this one pass. This will be a full-fledge murder hunt and a villain will be found. I've bided time enough. With your permission I will now begin house-to-house investigations on Drumloch lands.'

There was little choice. Bouchard remembered his evening talk with Devlin, heard again the voice of his own pleas. Devlin alone could establish calm, and Devlin had chosen not to try. He recalled his last sight of the old middleman, stooped above his wife's bed. Kitty's weak stare burned through his brain. Bouchard shook his head softly. He had known from that moment, *known* Desmond Devlin would not save him.

'Tread easily, McClune. Let it not be a witch hunt.' But the time for pleading and begging was over.

CHAPTER TWENTY-SIX

The winy odour of laudanum flared Donna's nostrils as she peered through the murk of the cottage kitchen and sought Colum. Her ruse with Cabbot had succeeded well and she had ridden down to the farm plots as soon as he was safely gone. But the sights she had seen had her on edge. At the crossroads she had encountered a group of police-agents interrogating some old fisherwomen, and there had been police-agents – and garrison troops, she thought – combing the distant hill side. Whatever their cause, their presence unsettled her and she judged it wise not to linger too long among the farms. But, to her chagrin, Colum was not to be found toiling in his fields, nor had he answered her cooing call.

She chanced another step or two into the velvet shadows and suddenly a hoarse voice croaked, 'Come in, and *failte*.'

Donna swung back, but the humoured tone of the old voice checked her:

'I hear the footfall of a *colleen-uasail*. You are welcome here.' There followed a dry laugh. 'Come, into the wee bedroom.'

Curiosity drew her towards the inner room. She pushed in the thin doorway and found Desmond Devlin lying abed, a single insufficient sheet drawn to his chin. 'Colleen, indeed,' he murmured. 'Daughter of the manor.'

'You recognise me, remember me?'

His small head shook. 'Sight is denied me now. But I heard your call, and the whisper of your breath. And now I scent your lotion.'

She held a hand to her mouth, stricken. He knew her call. What else did he know? Had Colum suffered for it? 'I come a friend,' she muttered.

'Take no step closer,' Devlin cautioned, holding a hand aloft. 'You must understand that these lands are no longer safe for a lady – for anyone. I speak not of war, but of fever.'

'I fear no fever.'

'But it is rampant, my child. The homeless are burning their dead in the roads. Bodies are being left, deserted to decay as they will. The hungry are already dying. Mine own dear wife was laid to rest last night, lest the disease grow out of her.'

Donna closed her eyes and the room swayed about her. 'Speak no more,' she pleaded.

'It pains you?'

'This is my land. Suffering pains me. In an enlightened christian world this horror should not happen.'

'It grows from a division of classes that will not survive

239

beyond many years.'

The dry rasp of Devlin's breathing grew thick and fast. He clutched his throat and his eyes closed. Alarmed, Donna moved to leave but he heard her step.

'Wait,' he whispered. 'I have a penance to make.' She stalled while he struggled up in the bed and regulated his breath. 'Allow my impertinence when I speak. Neither age nor wisdom makes way for propriety. Tell me, you hold affection for Colum?' She nodded, forgetting his blindness, but it seemed to satisfy him. 'I sense from his talk that he holds equal riches for you. But you must be aware of the barrier that lies before you.'

'Education and religion are mere furnishings of life.'

'Ha! Child of wisdom. Maybe, maybe. But I speak of a complexity beyond such things – the interwoven complexity of your different backgrounds and heritage. More than education, more than religion.'

'We are of similar blood. Irish blood.'

'You speak from the heart, not the head.'

'Colum will take me away.' Donna was astonished at the calm of her own words.

Devlin stirred anew and his face contracted in agony a moment. 'Will that please you, my lady? – a life in the clouds?' Before Donna replied he went on, 'My penance is twofold: a blessing and a warning. Firstly, I bless your love, if love it is, with Colum. I do so from the crow's nest of a death bed. All my life I strove for a better farm, a good standing in my society, all the temporal fruits of a hard-working life. Within my society I achieved all I set out for. I became middleman, most respected tenant, a successful farmer. All the things Colum inherits and drives himself on for. But now I look back, and I wonder at love.' He laughed, and brushed a hand across his eyes as though to hide a lapse of courage. 'I regret the lack of love in my life. Not that I lived without it – no. But its moments were too sparse and few and too frequently expressed.' He tilted towards her. 'I have learnt that lesson, and so I bequeath you love. Its problems and sins are your own, but you must be true to yourself – and fill your heart's needs.'

240

'A blessing and a warning?'

'Colum has been more a son to me than a foster-child. He is a lad of great strength and wisdom – but he is restless. All Rob's traits of self-promotion are quite foreign to him but they have sparked resentment and strange wayward impulses that even I could not fathom. I am a peace-loving man, but deep in Colum there is a fury that has grown over the years. Indiscriminate violence such as the Ribbonmen wreak finds no support from him, but since he was a boy there have been these stirrings of bitterness. The future of peace here is unstable now, and I worry for him. If you are to find enduring love you will need a man who is at rest with himself.'

The curtain that hung inside the door pulled back and Rob came in, looking out of place in the dank cottage. Bare pleasure shone on his face as his eyes set on Donna. Her flesh crawled and she hugged her cape about herself. 'I-I wondered why you did not join the Hunt,' she said.

'Came to pay my respects, and see dadda through the day.'

That had surprised her when she had first heard it, and she did not fully understand his reasons why it would be unbearable to ride cheerily with Letty today. She faced Devlin again, self-conscious. 'I really had better not delay longer,' she said. 'But I am glad I came a-calling. Papa will be pleased I spoke to you.'

'Yes, yes.' Devlin seemed near to sleep. He waved a hand. 'Bless you for coming by and for the words of comfort you have given me. And tell your papa – tell him *I am sorry*.'

Donna nodded, perplexed, and walked out of the airless room before Rob. In a fluid movement he swept out a wickerwork chair and guided her to the warm corner by the smouldering turf fire. 'I merely stopped by,' she mumbled, uneasy. 'I cannot dawdle.' But he would not let her flee so swiftly. He prodded her into the chair and raked the embers beneath the flaky turf. There was home-brewed whiskey on the dresser and, without asking her, he poured two healthy measures and softened them with water.

Donna felt hemmed in and had to force herself to smile politely.

Piled mountains of last year's potatoes filled the corners of the kitchen and a confusion of smells – vegetable rot, sweat, milk and straw – assailed her nostrils. Rob observed her gaze drifting about the room and said, 'Depressing, isn't it, all this clutter and cold?'

Without thinking she replied, 'Not at all. One must live. And at least what is here is all Colum's. He owes nothing to any man.' Rather than face Rob's lop-sided grin she stood with her untouched drink and ambled about.

'What good are ashes to anyone?'

'Drumloch provides more lasting treasures?'

'That is no question, my lady.'

'It seems, Rob, you are mesmerised by the gloss of rogue jewels.'

A foot scraped the ground and she swivelled to see him standing almost upon her. He stared into her troubled eyes. 'And it seems, mistress, that you are taken by the touch of rogue love.' When she did not respond his gaze grew sweet and he said softly, 'Why do you always speak to me in a tone of steel? We reside under the same roof and eat from the same kitchen. Yet you scarcely converse with me and refuse my good cheer.'

'I am courteous to you, I trust?'

'We should be friendly.'

'You have Letty's friendship. Isn't that sufficient for your needs?' Her voice was still casual, not mocking, when she addded, 'Or is it that you see an end to your games now that her association with Adam has begun.'

'Association?' Rob's tufty brows joined in frown.

'Of course you know what I speak of. You have seen for yourself. Did she not invite him back from Cork to stay?'

'I fancy you misjudge,' he said. 'You know nothing of my relations with Letty – '

Donna gave a short laugh. 'I think you should open your eyes, Rob. Letty has desires, but she has ambitions too. Adam Rossitor and she have a trifle more in common than you and she – and that appeals vastly to dear Letitia.'

'If you hint at position and money, I can give her that.'

'You? I'm afraid you have over-stepped yourself, Rob. Your privilege in the manor only extends as far as papa deems. You will always be what he wishes you to be and no more – a companion who will not judge him a drunken bankrupt, a temporary son-substitute. But now there is baby Serle and the land war threatens to turn him out. So, were I you, I would not be accounting for future pleasures at the manor – nor dreaming for wealth.'

'You play at making fun of me.'

'I do no such. It matters not one whit to me how you believe and behave.'

'Good.' He pushed her backwards and her body crashed against the mud wall. With a swift step he covered her with his body, pinning her there.

'How dare you! I will scream.'

'You will not.' His hand closed around her cheeks and squeezed until tears welled in her eyes. 'You misunderstand my role,' he said with venom. 'Your father needs me and trusts me. And Letitia enjoys me as a passionate lover. I am not servant to them, or to you any more. I am equal. I can be what your precious Colum can never be – as acceptable as any nobleman. And yet *you* disdain *me*, while you play around with such a devil. You are nothing but a slut.' His free hand descended to tear up her dress but she flexed her legs together.

'Release me, or I will tell father of this assault.'

Rob held her fast, his brain spinning. What could he say that would knife deeply into her? 'If you only knew what fun Colum makes of you,' he muttered wildly.

'I will not listen.' Tears spilled from her eyes. He *had* her. She was trembling in his grip, terrified at the prospect of piercing truths. That was it! He could play them both like fish. Set seeds of doubt in her, and in his foster-brother. Then perhaps some subtle words to Bouchard, advising separation . . .

'You come here licking at Colum's boots, but he is away in Galway with Cara Duff, his true heart's love.'

She flung out her arms and pushed him off. He stood

back, both staring each other like enraged animals. 'I know that to be false,' she spat.

'How? Old dadda tell you? Well, what would he know in his senility?' Rob stood back and waved a graceful hand towards the bedroom door. 'But if you doubt that he has jaunted off to Galway with her, why not ask him?'

'You are a fool, Rob, if you think jealousy will part us, or change me in any way.'

He smiled, gratified by the uncertainty that he heard behind those words. For a start, that was enough. A small measure of repayment that could be multiplied upon in the days to come.

Unable to bear the sneer on his face and the tangle of emotions in her breast Donna ran from the cottage.

Drumloch's mail two mornings later brought two interesting communications. One, from Dublin, contained only five or six badly-written lines and announced the death of Alexandrine. It was signed, *Yours in duty, Miss Griselda Fitzsimmons, maid to Lady Bouchard*. Bouchard, mellowed by brandy, mulled over it, then decided there was nothing to gain by acknowledging, nor going to Dublin to claim the corpse. Coming famine, it was known, had the city over-filled with vagrants. Every day more nameless, homeless corpses were uncovered. Mindful of the danger of plague, the city administrators threw the remains into paupers' graves. Such a fate would befall Alexandrine. Bouchard almost smiled at so fitting an end to a lowly French dancing girl. Then he bluntly turned his mind away from her, tossing the maid's note into the fire.

The second letter proved less easy to dismiss. Samuel Mortimer, writing from Lurgan, was extending one last chance. Though it was clear to everyone that the agricultural prospects for the south were not good, Mortimer might – just might – be interested in coming to terms with Bouchard on a settlement deal by which certain of Drumloch's lands (suitable for construction upon) would be 'sold' to him. This in effect would discharge the investment loan. Mortimer felt such an offer was fair, and gave ten days for a decision.

Disgusted, Bouchard tore the letter to shreds the moment he read the last line. Mortimer's tack was obvious: he wanted a foot in the south, pure and simple. If a parliament seat was too ambitious for openers, then the building of factory-mills might serve just as well. Bouchard was maddened, but this time reason made him pause to run the issue through in his mind again. Ostracised by his neighbours and cursed by violence on his lands what chances had he to rebuild wealth for Serle? Money may well breed money, but he had not a penny to gamble. The last resort was the girls. It was important that they found good, well-placed suitors soon. Cabbot, if he showed an interest, should be encouraged. He was of the right sort. Adam Rossitor, on the other hand, was a dud. Neither girl must lend him their arm. Someone more suitable could be found for Letty he was sure. Unresponsive, submissive Donna he had avoided. For now she suited his book, tending the infant well when old Nurse's arthritis put her out of the game. But – wise of women – he knew he could entrust his future security to neither girl. Though it appalled and disgraced him he was forced to consider Mortimer's offer in earnest. Perhaps the five hundred acres of unsaleable river lands might suffice? But its value was six hundred or six-fifty at most. He would have to evict more tenants, make more room, find more land to offer. And where would that lead? More strife with the farmers? And not alone that. Who could say whether, once the principle of concessions was established, Mortimer would stop there. Maybe, as Alexandrine had said from the first, *he coveted Drumloch*. Why not? He had coveted everything else: political life, friendships, even Bouchard's wife.

In bitter despair Bouchard glanced across the library to see his reflection in the polished brass canopy over the fireplace. The image shocked him: he saw himself, large-framed but without substance of flesh or muscle, hollow of cheek, white-haired, one eye hideously black-patched. A man aged before his time. His eye drifted the room. All the fine art pieces were gone, the best hangings and carpets quietly auctioned to pay Meehan and Kiely's. All that remained were books, cheap paintings and a few crates of poor Medoc in the cellar. The struggle to resist scandal was no longer viable: fact was, people knew. Even stolid, brainless Adam Rossitor had seen the decline, and his parting comments this very morning had been charged with open, awful lament. Word was out. There was no sense now in playing charades. It was simple survival.

'May I speak with you, sir?'

Bouchard twisted in his chair. Rob stood inside the door, thumbs laced in his waistcoat pockets and expression polite but arch. Lately the boy was fond of private conversation – but Bouchard's mood had no time for him today. He scrambled up from his chair and spoke firmly. 'I am bound for the boy Serle. What do you want?'

'I have been awaiting proper opportunity to discuss some intimate events of the house with you. While Adam Rossitor was here it seemed inconvenient.'

'And?'

'Well, sir, I have become concerned about the relationship between Miss Donna and my foster-brother, Colum.'

Bouchard sat again. 'I am not sure I know what you mean by "relationship", Rob?'

'Secret trysts, intimate correspondence, frequent meetings while out walking.' Rob was building on the scraps Letitia had sifted to him over the weeks.

'By God!' Bouchard spoke in a savage whisper. 'You confronted her with this, did you? Well, out with it!'

'Yes, sir. I did.' Rob lowered his head. 'But as you have confided to me – she is a stubborn and self-willed lady. When I spoke to her she . . . she told me the association was none of my concern and that, should I proceed to inform *you*, she would repay me by declaring that . . . that *I* had dallied with Letty.'

'This roguery behind my back, is it? How sweet she has been to my face, how full of pride and praise. I always knew the girl was a rat, like her good mother. What more scandal does she wish to bring down on me?' He whacked a fist into the arm of his chair and rose up.

'I would suggest, sir, if you moved her temporarily abroad –'

The glint of savagery in Bouchard's eye flashed to Rob. 'Whilst I admire and appreciate your help, Rob, I do not require your interference.'

Rob was winded. He began muttering in objection, assuring his good intention. 'Please, sir. It is for the good of Drumloch only that I draw your attention to this development. I ask nothing but your thanks . . .'

'My thanks? Rob, remember that you are my secretary. A servant of the manor whose *duty* is to advise and assist – to a proper point. After that, I make my own decisions. Now, I have heard all I wish to hear. You may go.'

Head hung, but red to the roots of his hair, Rob marched out. Bouchard pounded out of the room and upstairs. The soft crying of the child Serle attracted him to the nursery and he bumped past the wet nurse and pulled the baby from his cradle. He soothed Serle, whispering, 'I have learned my lesson, child of mine. No other woman will ever contribute a slight against the Bouchard name. I promise you that, as long as I live.' He set the baby down and swept out to the landing again.

He walked in a fluster, not pausing to knock as he moved into Donna's boudoir.

The room was dim, the drapes drawn against winter sunshine, but he could hear a movement from the dressing-room. Standing swaying in the middle of the carpet he boomed out, 'My girl, your play-acting is over!' He tore the belt off his trousers and smoothed the studded leather. 'I will whip you to pulp before I see disobedience again. You are clever, but not clever enough for me. I now understand your subtle change of behaviour these last few months. I will stop whatever nonsense goes on in your sister's head about this fool Rossitor, but at least she has the good grace to toy with a man of breeding! Your behaviour is ungodly and besmears *my* name. . . !'

He stopped, aware of the silence and the one faint, grating sound. He walked towards the dressing-room and pushed the door in. What he saw made him stiffen and withdraw.

Donna lay on the couch, clad in stays and shift as if her

247

morning dressing had been interrupted, gazing with motionless eyes at the ceiling. For a second Bouchard fancied she was dead, then he saw the cause of the creeping noise: while her body lay immobile, her fingers opened and contracted rapidly, scratching the sides of the couch. He craned above her, sobering quickly. Her skin was purple-spotted and her breathing unstable. He reached to feel her forehead, but froze in mid air. Even poised inches from her flesh, the radiating intensity of heat could be felt.

He turned and ran for help, understanding. Typhus, the farmers' famine disease, had found its way into the manor.

CHAPTER TWENTY-SEVEN

It was mid afternoon before Rob succeeded in locating Dr Appleby. Delayed in his search by the sudden thick fall of December snow, he had been led on a chase around the district, repeatedly missing the physician by minutes from house to house. Calling to Fork, where Appleby had been tending Emma's seasonal chill, Cabbot reacted to the news with extreme distress. Immediately joining Rob, he made tracks for Drumloch. Addressing himself to Bouchard he apologising for his forthright behaviour, explaining that he had some experience of the illness, having nursed a brother through a fatal bout. He insisted that the first measure must be isolation, and took it on himself to vacate the entire upper storey of the house and make ready for the doctor. When Appleby arrived Cabbot and Bouchard sat together in the library, Bouchard withdrawn and restless. 'I cannot believe it,' he muttered again and again. 'Why did it have to happen on these lands? Why?'

At length Appleby reappeared and Cabbot and Bouchard joined him for a quiet talk. The doctor felt quite helpless: the malady was beyond question typhus, a highly infectious disease currently being reported on a country-wide scale, the result of dead crops and destitute living. Appleby was uncertain whether Donna's case was sanable, but advised a course of continued isolation, pain-killing medication and as much cold drink as she could bear.

'What about the child, my God!' Bouchard said, un-nerved. 'What guarantee of his safety do I have?'

The bony-faced young doctor shrugged. 'What can I say, Sir? I can promise nothing. Obviously the farther away you can keep the lad – and the rest of the household – the better. A Dublin sanatorium might be worth considering –'

Aye, Bouchard thought, but a Dublin sanatorium costs money, and I have none.

Cabbot took the physician aside while Bouchard conveyed the sorry word to Letty. Then, as Appleby left, Cabbot requested permission and made his way up to Donna's bedroom.

He found her more composed, breathing evenly under Appleby's pain-killing potion, but her eyes were lost, faraway. He sat a small distance from the bed and spoke her name again and again until, in the flicker of her long lashes, he knew she attended.

'My dear, rest easy. This fever will not last long. Some few days at most. You will be well. But I need you to listen. Listen carefully.' He awaited her response and saw the gentle nod of her blonde head. 'Doctor Appleby advises quarantine of sorts. You must be carefully ministered to, but kept apart from your fellows. Drumloch provides no amenity for that. And the situation here is too remote from assured medical aid. Do you understand?' He watched, and she nodded again. 'What I wish to suggest may seem extreme, but it is well-advised. Mamma and I are ready to set off for New York. Our intention is to land home by Christmas and our route will be via Dublin, then Bristol where we have some business matters to attend, then aboard ship at Southampton. I would like to have you accompany us – to Dublin, to start with, where you can

249

endure the crisis of your illness in a good sanatorium. In a week or so you should be fit enough to move, and you may come to Bournemouth in South England, where they say the climate for cure excels all others.' He paused gravely. 'I should know. I nursed a dear brother there for two sad weeks.' There was a moment of quiet, then he urged, 'Come, Donna, give your blessing. Allow me to take matters in hand. I will look after you, I will see you well again.'

In her fever Donna saw mists and demons and darkness, but Cabbot's words formed a solid oasis of reason. Colum's image loomed in the mists and that alone drew her away from Cabbot. She had pledged to him . . . And yet there was a contradiction in her brain. They had exchanged promises, but he had waived his: she had ascertained that what Rob claimed was true; Colum had departed for Galway with Cara Duff. That bitter truth made no sense beyond the guessed at bond of affection between Cara and Colum. Maybe *all* Rob threw derisively out was true after all: maybe Cara and Colum were lovers. Maybe he cared for her not at all, and his promises had been simple Irish whim . . . In her delirium she shoved matters of love out of her brain restlessly.

'Will you come, will you come, will you come . . .?' Cabbot's words were rebounding, exploding inside her. She closed her eyes but his face manifested itself in her brain. A warm and affectionate face, a face she quite admired.

'Will you come, will you come . . . ?' Why not? Accept the chance to live, to escape. That was all she wanted, to escape papa's idiocy and his beatings, to get a chance to grow up, to be herself. And Cabbot was offering the means.

But was that *all*?

'Will you come?'

Colum was gone, with Cara.

She reached out a hand, aware of her movement but unsure of its direction. What she meant was 'Yes', yes, I will come. Yes, I want to live and find my freedom and be happy.

The tight grip of Cabbot's hand registered in her head and the words that choked her throat became the whirring drone of a million bees on the Doon, their clamour deafening her ears and confusing her mind until a bottomless abyss opened to swallow her and salvation in silence came.

'Sir Redmond has decided to close up the house and leave. His concern for the child is so great.'

Rob spoke with satisfaction, watching Letty sit by the high arched window of the drawing-room that looked out to a land drowned in snow. He was aware of a sense of mounting glee, fortified by the obvious distress and fear visible in Letty's poise. It was good to see smooth Letty ruffled, good to see her suffer doubt.

'It pleases you that we return to England,' she said, abstracted. 'You are away from reminders of your past, of this hell-place.'

'I'm sure your pleasure equals mine. I know you have no love for Ireland.'

She glanced swiftly to him, appraising him anew, detecting some sour inflexion. 'I am not sure I am any happier to flee to England with papa than I would be staying here. Papa has a curse of misery on him. I begin to wonder where these disasters end.' She sought something to unsettle Rob, so challengingly direct was his stare. 'I must set my mind to a course that separates my fate from his.'

He flopped down opposite her. 'What you require is a gentleman of ambition and capability. Someone who will take you to the stars.' He was cold-voiced.

'I know. I intend to find one very, very soon.'

'You do not make me jealous, Letty.'

She pulled herself upright and frowned. 'I do not *seek* to make you jealous, sir. I state simple truth.'

He came and sat by her, grinning. 'Someone like Rossitor could never appease you, Letty. Your demands are too great. You need a special sort of husband, a man who has some of the blood of the beast in him.' He darted to kiss her but she evaded.

'A husband?' she chortled. 'Do you think – !?' She pulled

251

her skirts about herself and shook her head smilingly. 'I'm afraid, Rob, you have forgotten your station once again.'

'Did you not swear I gave you pleasure you had never known?' He leaned to kiss her ear.

'I do not wish to speak of such things in my drawing-room, in a house of sorrow.'

'Come, Letty, such affairs are your life's blood.'

'Insult!'

'How? Is it too absolutely true for you?' She tore away but he held her, reciting the phrases he had mulled on and rehearsed over many days. 'Do not play at innocence. Your desires are known to me now. You are a woman of wild passions, enthralled by delights of the flesh. And I can satisfy you in that like no other man.'

'What nonsense you speak.'

'You forget so soon the demands of your hunger . . . the hunger that brought you to my bed and to Colum's embrace?' He resisted her attempt to break away. Eyes unseeing, he rattled on bitterly, withholding the raw aspect of his jealousy: 'No, Letty – you and I are of a type. We both hunger, and face our ambitions with a rigid determination. We both go out and get what we want. Don't you see? We both of us can satisfy the other's needs. I can give you a gentleman's manners with the passions of a peasant. You can give me this – ' His eyes ran around the once-grand room.

'You are mad, sir. Are you seriously proposing some . . . some permanent arrangement?' She grunted a humourless laugh. '*You* and I? That's preposterous. *You*, my servant?'

Indignation burned in Rob. 'Mistress, you were pleased enough to accept my kiss on too many occasions.'

She became deathly pale. 'Silence, *liar*. Speak that accusation once again and I shall have you flung out of this household.'

Stunned, he found his feet. 'Are you trying to say – ?'

'Trying nothing, my man.' Letty was no longer speaking in a subdued careful whisper. 'It seems some insanity has stolen upon you, maybe a touch of this fever. Never dare again address me with such familiar ease. Talk of marriage!

252

I have never heard such madness.'

He suddenly saw her pitch: the chilly manipulation of his passions to suit her whim. He saw, but rejected the vision. 'You must understand how I feel – ' he began, moving anxiously forward to take her arms. The door opening beside him interrupted his movement. Letty stood back and Bouchard strolled in, face grim and jaded, arms hanging in dejection. He flopped onto the window seat and ordered Rob to open the casement for air.

'But, sir, the drifts of snow – ?'

'Open, open.' Bouchard fanned himself with an open hand. Letty looked closely and saw driblets of sweat on her father's face. 'Sooner the better we get clear of this plagued land,' he said. 'I feel fever in every breath I draw. The child, the child must be kept well.'

'Are you all right, father?'

'Well enough. Just exhausted. It will pass.' He glanced to Rob, then keenly to Letitia. The stiffness of their respective demeanours made him suspicious and both blushed, guessing. 'Let us have good spirit and family unity at this dark time,' he said. 'We have had adversity enough. Rob – have you alerted the staff to prepare closing the house?'

'No, sir.'

'Do so now. Then ride to Cabbot and sort out our carriage for the journey to Dublin. Perhaps he will want to travel with us, perhaps not. No matter. But get these things done.'

'Sir.' Rob bowed and stalked out, avoiding Letty's freezing gaze. Anger swirled within him but the prospect of one other hatching plan – quite removed from Letty – gave some comfort, venting the painful frustration he felt. He refocussed his thoughts. The next turn of the screw for Colum would be effected with intensified resentment and rage. It might cost his foster-brother rather more than just the love of a lady.

The *fiabhras dubh*, called by Englishmen 'the purple death', had County Galway in its grip. Having delivered to the safety of her relations near Cleggan on the wild Atlantic seaboard, Colum turned back through a wilderness suddenly infested with human disease. White flags at crossroads and on cottage gateposts signalled areas of danger but those banks, it seemed, had already burst. In three days of travelling Colum encountered many thousand homeless gypsies, desperate and reckless for food; almost half of them were fevered. Already by the roadsides the pagan pyres of rushed funeral were in evidence and here and there abandoned corpses lay, festering in the sleet and snow. The only well-fed bodies Colum crossed were the troops, out in numbers everywhere, nervously attempting to marshall crowds and control the spread of disease. But even these young men looked weakened, beleaguered by the insidious, inexorable advance of death.

A week ago he had been glad to get away – to have time to ponder Letitia's trickery and Donna's demands and the estate's future – but now, as the grey and white tracts of Tipperary opened up, he found unbounded joy in home-coming. Here the ravages of disease were not as marked, the snows not as cold, the starving numbers fewer. At times as his path dipped into a quiet dell or crossed the broad desolation of a bog with no man in sight it was almost possible to believe that nothing had changed, that life outside rode buoyantly on and all was well. At such moments it was possible to forget what catalytic events had taken him on an errand of help and mercy to Cleggan, where Cara Duff rolled the dice on workhouse, prostitution, sustenance or death. But such forgetfulness would not hold for long. Round the next corner there was always a face of despair, a beggar by the roadside, to call one back to reality.

As night fell and the lights of Fork and Drumloch sparked out in the distance he found his mind latching pleasantly to Donna. After days when all questions seemed resolved with dejection, the thought of her gave a shelter for his spirit. Running away would provide no answer, he now knew. There were commitments here first, commitments to Anderson, to the future – and he must make

Donna understand them.

A hundred yards along the river track the black bulk of his cottage stood out against the fields of snow. Night was down and the east wind carried spiky ice. From the distance Colum could see movement in Drumloch's forecourt and against the yellow square of the front doors he thought he discerned Rob's figure. He frowned. It struck him that the only lamps burning seemed to be in the Great Hall. The house looked forlorn, empty.

His attention came back to his own homestead. No candle lit a window here either and, with sinking heart, he reined in and hurriedly entered.

Desmond Devlin lay peacefully in the frozen dark and Colum held his candle high and looked unastonishedly at the face of death. Then he slumped to his knees and began a silent prayer. Afterwards he prepared the body for shroud, functioning in a tired dream, unaware of his hunger or exhaustion or the biting cold. It pleased him that in death his foster-father appeared tranquil. There were no marks of sweat on the face, no signs of a final agony. Colum concluded his task, slipping a crucifix into the gnarled hands, and gazed down at the infinitely still sight. No wind stirred the blanket, nothing flickered or moved. There was just silence.

Silence!

Suddenly his spine crawled. He shivered, aware of some close danger. His ears pricked. There *was* silence – full, deafening silence. Not only inside, but outside too. Gone were the animal sounds, the never-ending babble of farm-yard life.

In fright he ran out.

He rounded the cottage and leapt the pen fence. The moon broke the snow clouds and the sharp-reflecting rime everywhere made the world pearly-bright. He could see clearly. Anger burst within him and he screamed aloud. The rear fencing had been battered down. His entire colony – pigs, chickens and horses – was gone. Stolen. Pirated in the night.

The nearby river farms vacated by eviction were useless,

but he made for the higher plots with all speed. The first door he hammered on was Teggie Kelly's and the old farmer brought him in and rushed a mug of reviving poteen into his hand. Colum gasped out his story, concluding, 'At any time during the evening, did you hear or see anything – anything at all suspicious?'

Teggie tilted the scrap of curtain on his kitchen window and looked down towards the river cottages. He shook his head. 'We're a distance away here, an' the sounds of the river rare come up to us.' He confirmed with his wife and sons. 'There was nothin' that alerted us tonight.'

'How could I have been so foolish – to leave for so many days, with just dadda, dying, and the goodwill of my neighbours?'

' 'Tis wild strange,' Teggie observed. 'Since McClune started whippin' up such fear and fury seeking out a scapegoat for the Mackie murder no one's had the crazy sense to venture out after dark. I'm thinking, Colum, whoever pirated your stock was more a madman than a villain.'

'A passing gypsy?'

Teggie shook his head and quaffed his brew. 'Not while McClune and the troops stalk. I haven't seen an unknown face here in five days – '

Teggie's wife stepped forward to refill Colum's cup. 'There was *someone* at the cottage,' she said casually. 'Earlier, durin' the blizzard fall. I was runnin' the chickens in meself and saw him mount in your yard. By hisself, I think.'

'Who? Did you see?'

' 'Course. 'Twas Rob.'

With no reply from the servants' bell Colum ran to the entrance colonnade of the manor house. The arctic wind was wild and a cruel storm was stirring, the ceiling of cloud so low one could almost reach to touch it. After a minute the great door swung open and Rob stood, a squire to the spurs on his polished boots, beaming out. A light flicked and died in his eye as he recognised his foster-brother under the snow cape. 'Brother Colum,' he exclaimed dully, lowering his lamp but offering no admission. 'What brings you abroad on so inclement a night?'

'I tried the servants' quarters. May I enter?'

Reluctantly Rob swept the door wide and Colum stepped out of the elements. The Great Hall stood in sinister shadow, a solitary candelabra tossing wings of light across the floor, invisible objects sighing and creaking in the gloom. Rob made no gesture of welcome. He set the lamp down and held Colum at the Hall's fringe. Unspoken antagonism reverberated but Colum was preoccupied. 'Dadda's dead,' he blurted.

'Bless his memory.' Rob crossed himself indifferently.

'You didn't know?'

Rob faltered – his mood suddenly uncertain. 'Why, how would I?'

'You were at the cottage this afternoon. Teggie's wife saw you. I was away. When I returned I found my herd's been stolen.'

'Stolen!' Rob affected distress. He sat heavily, his fingers toying the brass grip of the lamp. 'Everything? What will you do?'

'When you were there did you see anyone, observe any unusual signs – ?'

'No, no I am sure I didn't. I-I merely stopped by a moment to look to dadda. When I was there he was all right.' Rob's voice was convincingly loud. Colum crumpled, slouching miserably against the wall before him. Rob offered no chair.

'I cannot imagine the rascal who'd inflict such a blow – everything, even my chickens. My food securities for the winter, gone. The fruits of years of my labours, and dadda's before me.'

Rob made appropriate noises of sympathy. 'The Lord works in strange ways.' He paused. 'But what will you do, Colum? Ask McClune's help?'

Colum reflected. Deep in his brain the sole candidate for suspicion of the crime was McClune himself. He had motive enough, in his hatred of the Devlins and search for a convenient whipping-boy. But surely the sub-inspector would have been rather less subtle? 'Do you think I'd get a fair ear? With all the malice the farmers have seen this last week?' He shook his long brown hair. 'No. Unless I can myself make some lead and discover their whereabouts, I am gone. What crops can I grow through this fierce winter? And none of my friends can cope with another mouth to feed. I shall impose on no man, but I cannot become a drifting beggar in Tipperary – '

'Without a cushion of money where can you go in this diseased land?'

Colum had not the time yet to debate that. Most of his money was tied up in his good horses and the pigs. That source removed, how far would his few shillings take him? He thought about Donna, and a glimmer of sunshine brightened him. Maybe the omens were changing. This was a sign that he should leave with her. Contemplation of rebellion was suddenly futile in so gravely stricken a land. 'It's too early to think,' he muttered. 'Obviously the value of my herd is my fortune. At dawn I must set out and begin a search – '

'I would join you, were I not bound for Dublin in wake of Sir.'

Colum was aware all of a sudden of the depthless quiet of the great house, and recalled its dark aspect from afar. 'Where is everyone – servants and master?'

'Gone, bound for England.' He said nothing of the typhus; it worked well for him that Bouchard wanted to suppress word of the malady within his household, that the servants who had been dismissed had been denied the facts.

'Why?'

'Why not?' Rob shrugged, frowning. 'I do not question Sir Redmond's far-reaching plans for his household. Affairs of business, no doubt, engage him.'

'Donna – ?'

'Miss Donna was ill. Oh, nothing at all serious, of course.' Rob was enjoying his little game. 'She considered staying but . . . but then decided to accept Mr Cabbot's proposal.'

'What proposal?' Colum's words rasped.

Rob assumed his imperious look. 'I do not pry, Colum. I merely had conversational knowledge of her *affaire* with Mr Cabbot and their agreement to travel together.' He raised his black brows. 'To America, I shouldn't wonder.'

Devastated, Colum felt the great room drift around him. It was incredible, untrue. She could have known this newcomer Cabbot only two or three weeks, no more. And what of her talk of sacred love? Details of his last talks with her came to mind: her insistence on early departure, her criticism of his tardy moves. That last day she had run away from him. Why had he not pursued her? Cara's misery had distracted him, and Donna had found solace with Cabbot, and grown tired. Maybe there was more. Maybe Letitia had revealed a twisted truth about her abject trickery . . . He hung his head and cursed softly to himself. He could blame only himself. His foolishness had lost her.

Rob blew the cold from his hands and watched his foster-brother with pleasant victory beating in his breast. The story of Donna's departure was a final nail – seemingly every bit as accurately-placed and painful as he had hoped. No matter if the disease eventually took her, *this* simple deceit afflicted Colum's vanity at the best, most vulnerable time. Without money, or herd, or living farm he might never *survive* to discover the truth anyway. Rob mulled over the thieving of the herd – a straightforward matter, with Tom Og's aid, of drowning the chickens in the Shannon and running the pigs and horses across on the flat-boat for quick sale to the tinkers of Galway – and the revived memories brought no shame. Colum had earned nemesis.

' 'Tis late,' Rob said, rising to pull open the front door. 'I will stay for dadda's burial, but I must not tarry in joining good Sir Redmond.' He patted Colum's wet shoulder. 'Let me bid you goodnight, brother.'

CHAPTER TWENTY-EIGHT

The air Donna breathed was not Irish air.

She opened her eyes and took in a neat room that reminded her of a blue bubble – blue silken drapes, blue plain wall-coverings, and gay pieces of bleached Norwegian wood furniture. Little disjointed memories trickled through her consciousness: vile medicines, Appleby, a lone coach ride to Dublin, then a room in a peaceful cave that she knew was a sanatorium. And after that? She strove to arrange her thoughts but the aftermath of Dublin was just a blur.

Disoriented, Donna crawled up in bed and regarded her surroundings with a keen awareness. There was a window and, beyond, the pulse of the sea. There was salt in the air. The creaking sound of her bed alerted an attendant, a lanky girl dressed in unbecoming ochre whom, at first, she did not recognise.

'Lord, you look a sad sight,' the girl said, plumping the pillows. 'Any conversation today?'

The girl stood back, viewed Donna afresh and realised with a start she was fully awake and coherent. She sat abruptly and felt her patient's forehead. 'Ah, your heat drops at last. How do you feel?'

'Sore. And hungry.'

'Hungry! That's the Lord's good way of telling you your life belongs to you again.' She looked relieved. 'I am so glad. For more than a week you lay in the fever hospital, and the doctors were quite at a loss. The progress of your illness was stop-start all the time.' She frowned. 'Do you recall events? All these days of people trying to communicate with you – ?'

'Where am I?'

'Bournemouth.' That seemed inadequate return for the patient's curiosity. 'In England.'

Floodgates of memory opened. Bournemouth, beside Southampton. Paul Cabbot's professed route of departure for America. His caring offer of aid, and all the sense it made. Donna looked again at the girl. Why of course – Emma Cabbot. She felt a stampede of terror in her chest. Colum flashed through her thoughts, but she pulled down quick defensive shutters. 'Can you bring me something to sip, Emma?' she whispered. 'I do feel dry.'

'You remember me!' Emma Cabbot was pleased. 'Paul will be delighted! Hold tight, m'dear, and I'll fetch you the King's medicine.'

When Emma had gone Donna felt herself float into a shallow dream, but when the discomposing images faded and the blue room returned, so too had her control. She lay easy and felt the blood run warm and true in her veins. The tenuous grip on life seemed surer and a confident optimism elated her. When she again opened her eyes Letitia was standing before her dressed in ice-white lace, like a glittering hallucination. Excited, Donna stretched an arm. 'Letty – where is papa, what has happened? Tell me.'

Rather stiffly Letitia walked forward to take her sister's hand. Donna noted Letty's winter cape, its wings slung back over her shoulders.

'You have had typhus,' Letty said. 'Everyone has been quite concerned. But in the last days your fever has fallen. The Bournemouth doctor said it all depended on whether your strength improved or declined these next few days.' Letty kissed her sister's hand quickly. 'I am glad you rally so well.'

'Papa – ?'

Letty's eyes were huge, fretful. 'After the agreement on your nursing, papa decided to repair to Sir Myles's house for a time, and he closed Drumloch and discharged staff.'

'Staff gone? But that means – ?'

'I am unsure what it means for Drumloch. Somehow I think papa's immediate inclination to return will be slight.

261

Not after the illness in the house, and with young Serle to think about.' Letty pressed Donna's hand to reassure. 'But do not flap for your Ireland. There is always Fork.'

Ignoring this sly reference, Donna pursued, 'Does papa still reside in Kent, while I'm here with the Cabbots?'

'Paul's mother sailed for America yesterday, leaving Emma to look after you. Paul insisted on staying by your side.' Letty paused and her eyes sidled off. 'Papa is still with Sir Myles, and he is ill, I'm afraid.'

'How ill?'

'I do not yet know. But he has been confined for the moment, and is bearing up well.' Letitia showed no immediate alarm. Instead she shuffled skittishly, her face pinched in a restive nervous pallor as though some personal burden weighed on her mind.

'You are dressed for journey,' Donna observed, 'Are you visiting from Kent, or staying here?'

For a moment Letty said nothing. Her cheeks tinged bright and she drew her hands into her lap and fidgeted. 'I should not burden you when your convalescence begins, sister, but . . . I am afraid.'

'Why? Speak what is on your mind, Letty, for I perceive your excitement.'

'I should be wary of what I say, but I cannot believe you would go against me.'

'In what matters? Tell.'

'Adam Rossitor accompanies me this moment, and we have come from Kent under guise of visiting you – but we are bound for another country. We are running away together, Donna, and intend a secret wedding as soon as possible.'

Donna shook her tired head to make sure her ears had not deceived her. 'Why a *secret* marriage with Adam? I don't understand.'

'Many of the answers to that will be inside your head already, Donna. The indications of the last months have painfully shown papa's dilemma. He himself took me aside three weeks ago and explained the pressing necessity of a convenient arranged match. Drumloch's peace and future is shattered and he has no recourse to London or Dublin any more. He needs big money quickly.'

'And Adam has none?'

Letitia's full mouth pouted. 'That is what papa claims, but I suspect it to be false. Adam has money enough for me and he's proved it with the splendid gifts he's presented me with. No. The crux is that papa is in debt for thousands and seeks a suitor from heaven. Remember dear Samuel Mortimer, our step-uncle from Lurgan? – he bears the strain of some *enormous* debt owed by papa. I know. I spied on some mail papa had abandoned in the fireplace. The situation is that serious – But I have the chance of Adam and I'm not about to risk it to serve father.'

'You love him so dearly?' Donna was aware of sarcasm in her own voice. Letty's gaze drifted.

'I have many reasons for accepting his offer of matrimony.' Momentarily she looked stricken and feverish. 'Not least of which concerns a . . . a confession papa made to me in his illness.'

'What confession?'

Letty became agitated, shifting in her chair. 'Nothing that matters to you, I'm sure, sister. But it grieves me to even think of it.' She fanned herself with a hand. 'I cannot discuss it, pray, let the business lie.'

Suspecting some strange guilt Donna said, 'Then it is more than a quest for love, this flight? Could it be that you are fleeing some truth? – or fleeing from yourself?'

Letty forced a cool smile. 'Nonsense. I have the offer of a gentleman's hand, and the chance of peaceful love.'

'Papa will pursue you.'

'I think not. Not while his illness lays him low.'

'Then Rob Devlin will.' Bitterness was infused in those words, and their direction was deadly. Seething Letty exploded.

'What claim can he have to me? He, a mere peasant! Follow me! He would have no right.'

'Rob has spread his wings under papa's guidance. He sees himself as peasant no more. And perhaps your willingness has encouraged him more than you think.'

'Dear sister, I think you confuse again your artistic fantasy with real life. Perhaps your own nonsense with Colum Devlin makes you woolly-headed.'

'Is it so easy to turn on – and off, to manipulate affections to suit your mood?' Donna sighed tiredly. 'I know that has been your belief, but I can no longer hold it to be true. In all human relationships there are two sides to be honoured, Letty. There are dues to pay all along. Nothing comes so easily that it can be dismissed with the click of your fingers.'

A kind of fear haunted Letty's eyes. 'Perhaps, sister, you have encouraged Colum so much yourself that now you fear *his* pursuit? Perhaps you speak your own fears?'

Donna smiled. 'No, I have nothing to fear in that way.'

The smugness seemed to rile Letty. She toyed with her rusty-coloured hair. 'You are better off with Paul Cabbot in any case, I'm sure. Colum would have disappointed you.'

'What do you mean?'

'Nothing.' Letty's pallor warmed to a contented lustrous pink.

Donna wanted to pursue question but weakness overcame her and she sank back in exhaustion. Letty's news had drained her and she was trembling again as in fever. But Letty had regained herself: the edgy ferment had retreated and she was once again collected and serene.

'Do not resent me too much,' Letitia said as she stood to shake down her cape. 'Some day you may thank me, for in absconding I am surely dispossessing myself. Who knows? – after Serle precious Drumloch may be yours.'

Donna knew her sister was mocking her. *Precious Drumloch*, Letty was thinking: *rubble, war and disease*.

Approaching footsteps could be heard, climbing the stairs not far off. Letty gripped Donna's hand. 'It relieves me to see that you are getting better as I depart, sister.' Her lips touched Donna's hand again. 'Will you wish me luck?'

'Of course.' Sleep made Donna's eyelids heavy. 'Although I doubt you need luck, Letty. As you once told me yourself: everything you seek, you get. How blessed you have been. How I envy you this moment.'

Emma came into the room with a tray. To Letitia she

said, 'Your, er, gent awaits you. He seems a trifle impatient.' Letitia nodded and took her leave without another word or a backward glance.

A mirror and comb were set upon the tray but Donna's sudden hunger made her leave them aside and tackle the food. After a few mouthfulls she was sated, her energies gone. Almost carelessly she took up the mirror. The ravaged face that gazed back at her set her heart racing. Her blonde curls were matted with sweat, her eyes sunken, and she seemed to have lost four stone in weight.

She dropped the mirror and gave way to pent-up tears.

Cabbot came a half-hour later. Emma led him in, but he dismissed her forcefully and sat by the bed, his obvious relief reflecting his sister's. Donna mumbled out her gratitude, apologetic for the worry and inconvenience she had caused.

'What matters is that you are getting well again. You rallied yesterday and the prognosis then was good. What will the doctor say when he sees you now?! I am quite delighted.' He clucked his tongue. 'I was in fear for days that my decision to take you from Dublin was wrong. But what I have heard since of Ireland appalls me. The purple death grows everywhere, claiming lives all the time. With this new practice of families deserting their dead by the open roadside to avoid the price of christian burials the disease is helped along. Ireland is no longer safe for any living thing.'

'Someday soon all will be well again.'

He sighed, unconvinced. 'Dear mamma was frightened a lot. She curses the day she bought Fork, for she never guessed the Emerald Isle could be like this.'

'You should have accompanied her back to New York. I am so sorry I delayed you here.'

Cabbot took the brazen step of shifting closer to her at the bed's edge and looping a casual arm about her shoulders. With sincerity he said, 'My dear, the affairs of business come second to the health of a sweet friend. I cannot express my joy at being by your side throughout this trying time.' He kissed her hair uncertainly but the gesture somehow only irritated her. 'Permit me now to advance another bold suggestion – already blessed by your poor father, I'm glad to say. Now that this breakthrough has been made, we must capitalise upon it. Bournemouth's air is good, but Newark's is better.'

'Newark?'

'In New Jersey. We have a small home there. The weather is temperate and the air soft even when it snows. It would be perfect for you. Emma could . . .' He rattled urgently on, face animated and eager, and Donna lay still and realised what path he was paving for her. She appraised him again, eyeing the ageless face, recalling the generosity of his manner. Papa might indeed approve of him as suitor, but if it came to that she would fight to obstruct a 'deal'. Why? She reflected. It wasn't that her hatred was so deep that she wished to deny him a home and a living, but the call of honour was the louder: a 'deal' with Cabbot must be based on true affection alone. Inwardly she frowned. Affection? Why not love? Why was it impossible to consider Paul Cabbot and the ideal of love together?

He was squeezing her hand with passion now and his vigour alarmed her. 'I am not an unreasonable man, and not unattractive, I believe. So I entreat you. Please say yes –'

'Paul.' The gunshot word silenced him. 'Were I to accept your kindness again I would be lighting the bush that begins the forest fire –'

'But, no. My intentions are innocent and honourable –'

'Hush. Hear me out. I am grateful for all you have done, and all you wish to do. But it would be deceit to agree to go to America and press upon your kindness.'

'Why?' he said bitterly. 'Because you feel promised to another?'

'Maybe. There is confusion in me. Affairs of the heart have not been resolved and I live with monstrous doubts about things unsaid, things undone.'

He sensed her meaning. His curiosity and interest in her in Ireland had ascertained bewildering facts, but the servants' hearsay about her association with that farm lad had

266

seemed almost unbelievable: nonetheless, at the Hunt she herself had intimated . . . He pushed aside seeds of doubt. 'With time such matters will resolve themselves. Give time –'

'No. I speak of a question too fragile yet too great to be chanced to time. You cannot know, Paul. It inhabits all my sleeping hours. In my fever I lived this business out again and again.'

He soothed her. 'Do not distress yourself, dearest.' The frantic search for winning words was apparent in his sullen face. 'What can I say? If you will allow me, I would like to assist you to resolve this doubt in your heart. I am devoted to your well-being, Donna. I will do whatever you wish –'

'I must return.'

Cabbot sighed. 'Donna, there are aspects you must remember before any rash step is taken. I know there are blinding passions which can, from time to time, touch everyone's life. But one must be sensible. Any possible commitment to a future life in Ireland would be reckless and unwise in the extreme.' He shrugged. 'I could perhaps see a certain sense in allowing the *expression* of your passion with some remote Irish lad – sometimes hunger must be satisfied – but any consideration of a settled or permanent association in Ireland –'

Donna's temper blazed. 'Expression of passion! Good Lord! Am I alone in thinking of love in terms of a deep and honourable bond? Do selfish passions rule everyone else?'

'Please! I am merely trying to underline the senselessness of a return trip to Ireland and any possible consideration of residing again there. All I want is to make sure you recover well – and stay happy. Your happiness means much to me.'

The rage died. How was it possible to argue with this sombre, earnest man? Donna felt for his hand again. 'Forgive me. I am grateful in my heart for your warmth. But I know what duty calls me. I know when I am fully well again I must return to Ireland. If only to allow myself the chance to leave of free will, and not in a fever state.'

'It will be dangerous. Bandits and rovers roam the

countryside and the purple death is rife.' He paused. 'But if you wish, *I* could take you –'

'No, it would be unkind to you –'

He would not listen to her objection. 'You need make no pledge to me. I can accompany you and at least assure your safe passage. It would be all quite decent, and anyway I suppose there are affairs at Fork that were too hurriedly wrapped up. Then, when you have those answers you seek, you may again reconsider Newark.'

It was too good an offer. Donna felt her exhaustion fade and she pressed his hands excitedly. 'That is a crazy generosity, Paul.'

'Decide that for yourself. I think I stand to gain much. In a week or so you may judge Ireland in a different light, when you see all that has changed. And you may judge me in a different light. His expression was full of appeal. 'But be certain, Donna, for the risks of travel are real. Does this confusion in your mind *demand* answer?'

'Yes.'

Nodding resignation, Cabbot stood. What kind of passion of the heart was this that made Donna quite insensible to sound reasoning and the colossal threat of personal danger?

He kissed her forehead, thinking of her lips. Mamma approved and Emma approved – but was money and charm and kindness enough to win her? Back in New York mamma would be expecting his return with a prospective bride, he was sure. A well-bred Irish lady to yield fine sons and court the vitally influential Irish community – what more could the prospering, expanding aristocracy of Cabbot Industries want? The thought was paradisical, delicious. But good sense told Cabbot to try to suppress optimism. Donna Bouchard was a brave, self-willed lady, inspired by ideals quite foreign to him.

CHAPTER TWENTY-NINE

From Bournemouth Letty and Adam Rossitor wound their way to Dover. Their elopement plan was a sketchy medley of intuited moves and common sense caution and escape from Dover offered safest anonymity because of Adam's good friendships there. The Dover mail set them down at the Royal George, a rambling Tudor inn carved into the cliffs high above the bay, its proprietor an old drinking acquaintance of Adam's, and from here they hurriedly plotted their departure for France. Another friend, a crusty-voiced Breton called de Berac who assisted the harbour-master, visited and contributed suggestions for easy secret passages on traders well known to him. Adam paid the sly-eyed Frenchman a sovereign and a secure promise of placement was made. Within twenty-four hours, de Berac assured, the right trader would be found and a messenger would alert them at the inn. When de Berac had departed the tension and fatigue Letty felt since leaving Pegwell vanished. An entirely new life was opening to her and nothing – not even the odd implications of Adam's ready associations with such piratical folk – could dismay her.

'We are bound for such happiness,' she told him as they sat in their room and toasted each other with crude port. 'I prophesy sublime success in Paris. Monsieur et Madame Rossitor, dealers in fine art, with a château in the forest of St-Germain and a petite maison in the glamorous Rue Fortunée! What bliss it will be!'

Adam, tussling to take her in his arms, drew back. 'Do not be hasty in expecting *great* fortune, my dear. Did you not attend de Berac when he spoke of the changing face of

Paris? He described it as a political volcano. Even the Garde Nationale are calling '*Vive la réforme!*' and the lesser bourgeoisie are threatening their bourgeois regime – '

'I seek no lesson in politics, Adam. Such matters are no concern of ours. I agreed to flee to France with you to enjoy an atmosphere of liberality and love – and find a path to fortune. Those are the very words *you* used.'

'Of course.' He kissed her, wishing he had never spoken. 'And so it shall be. If I have nothing else to offer, I have enthusiasm.'

Some cadence in that speech doused Letty's spirits a moment but her wariness was drowned under his amorous assault. His body covered hers and his hands ran over her in sinuous, sensuous circles. Her mood was suddenly not right. She wrestled from under him and gathered her skirts tightly. 'No, Adam. You must allow us the dignity of a proper ceremony in France, then you will get what you so passionately seek.'

His fervent kisses continued and he caressed her with rapacious hands. 'But have I not the right now? I have made my promise to you, and seen it through. I have taken you away and will give you marriage – '

'And a life of luxury and peace?'

'As far as I can.' His confidence faltered but he struggled with intent. 'Please, Letty, you have twisted and tortured me enough. Now allow me – '

'Paris is just round the corner, my love.' She wriggled away from him and escaped.

'You do so tease,' he complained. 'Not since that glorious Feast have I been graced with your willing love.'

There was nothing but a smile in Letty's heart. Poor, panicked Adam – so seeking a gift long lost. It came to her suddenly as she watched him squirming on the settee, that all his boasted escapades had been lies. In love-making she would have to teach him much, she guessed.

They dined that night in their room and slept in separate sections of the U-shaped attic. As dawn broke an urgent hammering on the door awoke them and an urchin messenger delivered a note from de Berac, summoning Adam. There was the immediate possibility of a ship, but a fee to the captain must be agreed if anonymous journey was to be guaranteed. Adam dressed quickly and left with the boy, promising a fast arrangement.

The biting winter winds off the Channel chased Letty back to the snug hollow of her bed. Sleep found her in minutes but her dreams were dashed and silenced by a sudden ferocious constriction about the throat. So tight was the grip that, when she opened her eyes, a cloak of red darkness blinded her. A loud carillon thundered inside her and unconsciousness came in waves of dizziness. She thought she was dying, then focus came to her eyes and she found herself staring at Rob.

'Release . . . me!' she gagged.

'*Why*?' he said, glowering with sadistic glee. 'Why should I spare your life when you chose to damn mine?'

She scambled up in the bed and began to fight, her body heaving like a rag-doll at the end of his powerful arm. All the time he grinned wide, his fine teeth clamped together in a sneer. She ground on, then he flew his free hand up and crashed her full in the face. She collapsed in the pillows, her screams dead in her throat.

Whimpering, Letty curled her hands over her face to protect from further attack but his rage seemed spent and he sat on the deep bed and hung his head. 'H-how did you find us?' she stammered. 'Is papa – ?'

'I come charged on my own account,' Rob spat. 'And I found your game by trailing you from Bournemouth. Then I bided my time.'

'For what purpose?' She still cowered from him, unsure.

Rob was pensive. He had slept rough, she perceived, noting the glistening varnish of morning frost on his coat. 'You have an evil cunning mind, Letty. You take advantage of your papa's indisposition to make more fun for yourself. Are the simple devices you employed with my foster-brother not thrilling enough? Do you seek outrage as well from time to time?' He shrugged in amazement.

'You think your father will not find out about this? What makes you believe he will treat you any differently from Donna, whose madness earned the whip?'

Courage came back to Letty with the quieting, even beat of her heart. Still wary of Rob's intensity she eyed the cheeseboard of last night's supper on the bed-stand; a short-blade knife lay amid the crumbs, only a hand's-reach away. 'You seem to misjudge my actions,' she told him. 'Whether I utilise the sad fact of papa's illness to my own ends or not is solely my concern, but I am engaged in no "game". I am to wed Adam Rossitor.'

Rob's head flashed round and he gaped, slack-jawed. 'You cannot be in your right senses. Wed Rossitor – the penniless fool!'

'It is none of your business.'

He leaned towards her again and she moved closer an inch to the cheese-knife. 'Your papa disapproves of Adam Rossitor and I am your papa's agent. He will thank me indeed when I bring you back to Pegwell, having scouted this insanity.'

'I will not go back. You cannot make me.'

The fire of his eyes became soft. 'You can't destroy your life by absconding with this uncertain cad, Letty. Don't you see your name and reputation will be sullied forever, and no respectable gent will host you in his house again?'

Impatient aggravation burst in her. 'Don't *you* see? Drumloch is gone, papa is finished. By sticking at his side my reputation is sullied forever.'

'No.' A misty curtain veiled Rob's eyes. 'You are wrong. This is a temporary set-back.' He took her right hand fiercely. 'You must have faith in the future. Things will be better. Your papa will guide himself out of this murk and you and I will be wed and, in time, take the legacy of London and Ireland.'

Letty's hands covered her ears. 'You are talking fanciful nonsense, Rob, and I will not listen. Get it into your head: I want no part of you. My heart is with Adam and I am bound to wed him.'

He tore her hands down. 'Often enough in this past year

you have wanted a part of me. I gave you all the gifts you sought then – and now I want my returns. Don't deny me, Letty, because I have lost the mood for arguing. My determination matches yours. I have your father's ear and his respect. I will take you home and say nothing of this flight of yours if you so desire. If not I will take you home anyway and play it *my way*: your father will be grateful for my diligence and will be pleased to repay me a favour. As time goes by he will become more accustomed to a betrothal.'

'You don't know what you say,' Letty hissed. 'I will not hear it!'

Rob threw Letty her petticoats and skirt. 'Be silenced now, and prepare yourself for travel.'

His back was to the attic door but by the shocked expression that swept Letty's face he knew someone had slunk in behind him. He swivelled and saw Adam Rossitor in the doorway, riveted in fright.

'Gad, man,' Adam stumbled. 'What place have you in a lady's boudoir!'

'Mister Rossitor, you must ask yourself that question. I come to take my lady back to her father's side. Her fun with you is finished. She will be happy to accompany me.'

Adam looked to Letty and she signalled her unwillingness. He drummed up indignant anger. 'Servant, do not dare to impose on myself or this lady. Get yourself out of here before I call my friend the proprietor and have you arrested for trespass.'

Rob stood all of six inches taller than Adam and his bulging muscular frame dwarfed the other's, but Adam was not to be intimidated. When Rob did not move he prodded out an arm and rushed him aside. He had taken not two steps past Rob when a crushing blow cannoned into his back. Holding his balance he turned, just in time to duck a second pile-driving blow. Rob leapt on him and dragged him down. They collapsed in a struggling heap on the bed, wordless in their fight but groaning like wounded bulls. Letty bit her knuckles in terror, reeling across the room.

In a minute of furious violence Rob gained the upper

hand and pinned his opponent flat but Adam was practised at ungentlemanly tricks of combat. With force he jerked a knee into the fork of Rob's legs, throwing his weight forward at the same time. Rob rolled off, grunting agony, and Adam sprang on him. 'Consider yourself fortunate,' he said, gasping his victory. 'I have a mind to pay my friend a shilling or two and have you handed to the police and thrown into jail.' He jabbed his thumb into the pumping artery on Rob's neck and trapped the flailing arms beneath his knees. 'But I don't think you are worthy of the Queen's prisons. However, I will not permit insult to my future wife – so I will ask you to retract your remark about "her fun" with me.'

'Never,' Rob whispered, choking for breath. 'She deceives you, my friend. Fun is all she cares about. Ask her about her frolics with others – like my own foster-brother.'

'You try to raise my ire and distract me, eh?' Adam screwed his grip on Rob's throat tighter. 'Well, you fail. The bond between Miss Letitia and me will not be loosened. So you can bring word back to your master or whoever else you like – nothing and no one will stop this association. Letty and I will wed –'

Adam got no further. One of Rob's hands had crept free of the pressure of Adam's knee and slid away in a blur of movement. Now it sped back and pommelled Adam's side. Letty observed no detail of the attack, merely heard Adam silence suddenly and saw Rob's balled fist beating his opponent's hip relentlessly. Hours passed, it seemed, before she recognised the cheese-knife clasped in Rob's hand and saw the thick splashes of purple blood. She went to scream but Rob twisted from under his fallen victim and was upon her in a split second. She swooned in faint but he bore her up, one blood-stained hand round her waist, the other masking her mouth. 'Be quiet,' he entreated. 'Or you'll suffer too.' He held her till her breathing levelled itself, then released her.

The savaged body of Adam Rossitor lay in a knotted heap, emptying itself of lifeblood. 'You villain,' Letty gasped. 'You will hang for this.'

'Self-defence. He was throttling me. In another minute I was dead.'

'Liar. You acted in jealousy, in spite. God will not forgive you!'

She wept, but he grabbed her fiercely and shook her till, in dumb awe, she listened to him. 'I am afraid of nothing – neither man nor God. This act proves my devoted love for you. Let it be a warning. No man will stand between us. You and I will return to Pegwell and address your father. With his blessing we will wed –'

'Rob, that can never be. Never!' She pushed him off in disgust.

The cheese-knife still protruded from Adam's torso and he whipped it out and poked it towards her. 'I am tired of your canny playing, Letty.'

'A wedding can never be because you and I are related by blood. You are *my half-brother*!' Letty cried out the words, tears flooding after them.

Rob stood, swaying dizzily. The knife fell from his limp grip and clattered onto the bare boards. 'What devilry do you attempt?'

'It's the truth. It sickens my stomach to think of it.' He moved forward with arms outstretched but she halted him. 'I cannot bear to feel your touch! My half-brother!' Her crazed eyes held his stare. 'It is true. When papa fell into the first fever of his illness on the train from Chester to London he revealed to me. At first I made no sense of it, then the pieces fitted together and I realised he was ranting a confession from the soul to me, confused in his sickness. When Desmond Devlin was middleman and his wife visited the manor house with rents, papa . . . on one occasion made love to her. An agreed deal, it was, giving her the money she wanted to expand some crop or other. That was their understanding – and from it you were born. Kitty Devlin knew from the beginning whose child it was.'

Rob's knees seem to liquefy and he sank onto the bed. Son of Sir Redmond Bouchard! The irony of it – the miserable, filthy, unjust irony of it! Years of striving, years of painfully hopeless ambition. The struggle to be respectable, a part of the landed gentry – when all the while the blue blood of honour ran in his veins. He rubbed the blinding sweat off his face and said, 'Then I am, more than I could have hoped, a son of Drumloch.'

Letty shook her head. Through her bitter tears she grinned. 'That is all that matters to you, is it not? – a well-set place in the drawing-room? How I despise you, Rob.'

He hadn't heard her. The memories of many years were marching through his head and wondrous questions suddenly posed their answers. The mystery of his adoption to the household, of Bouchard's spontaneous trust, all were instantly unravelled. But at their heels the answered mysteries carried sinister shadows.

'You cannot yet see, can you?' Letty chided. 'You sit with triumphal smile upon your horrid face and disregard the implications. Yes, you are more a son of Drumloch than you could ever have hoped, but look again at what Drumloch now is: a derelict in a wilderness, despised by the farm folk and disdained by the gentry. And realise this too: this truth of your origin that I reveal to you can never be admitted to. Papa will never want it to be known and, no matter how hard you may try to press its knowledge and gain yourself a better standing, *who would believe you*?' She chuckled drily. 'No, Rob, that sorry truth will serve you in only one way: it will be forever a tantalising reminder of what *almost was* for you.'

Rob was in trance for many minutes, then he stood shakily and took her arm. 'We must go back – together. You and I –'

'Force me if you will. But I must warn you. The first chance I get I will report this foul murder – to papa as well as everyone else. You will hang for this brutal act.'

'You could not incriminate me, your brother in blood – ?'

A panic surged within him and he felt trapped by his own emotions and deeds. Suddenly the visions of Pegwell, ailing Bouchard, and a criminal inquiry were daunting; and Ireland offered no welcoming alternative, with a famine and his foster-brother's inevitable enmity. A voice inside him whispered: *Go, get out, flee*: you have tried every corner of this pitch and now there is nothing left to game on or explore. *Flee*.

He backed nervously away from Letitia until the door-knob bumped his spine. Then his calm deserted him and he turned and dashed for escape.

CHAPTER THIRTY

' . . . And so, aware of the incriminating nature of my position and terrified of possible scandal, I realised I could not face papa and I thought of you.' Letty affected childlike unashamed flattery. 'Mamma had spoken of you as a supremely generous benefactor.' She looked away from Mortimer's direct gaze. 'And I personally recalled you as a man of great wit and kindness.'

Samuel Mortimer strove not to reveal the shock he felt at this visitation. Sir David Villers, respected politician and Mortimer's champion with the London Tories, had come to stay the weekend at Meadow Hill and was presently en-sconced in the next-door drawing-room. What he would make of this astounding tale of jealousy, elopement and murder! Mortimer shuddered to think. But even as his horror waned with Letty's story another parallel train of reasoning – cool and detached – rattled in his brain. All those months ago Alexandrine had served herself to him in just such a fashion – troubled and begging for aid; then he had been ill-prepared and had misused his advantage. And now history was repeating itself. Beautiful Letty, a despe-rate – and ravishing – twenty-one year-old , was in a hole, prepared it seemed to concede dignity in order to gnaw a way out.

'Your papa, I've been informed, is quite ill in Kent. Did you not feel the summons of blood? The need to return? I cannot imagine he would have been fit and keen enough to cause much trouble.'

'You do not know papa, sir. His resolve can be matched nowhere. I don't doubt he will be well soon.' She shook her head. 'But that fear of his punishment is secondary. There are more obviously vital considerations. Firstly, in facing him I must accept that the dreadful events of the Royal George would be reported to the authorities and investigated.' Letty had detailed nothing of her blood link with Rob, or her earlier dalliance with him; but the memory made her flush wildly as she spoke. 'I would face suspicion of murder, since this villain Rob has fled. And, as well – what future lies before me with papa? He has made it clear that, in his strained financial position, a swift arranged marriage is a necessity.'

'You resist that?'

'The notion of marriage quite . . . . agrees with me.' She dabbed her lace handkerchief to a tearful eye. 'But affection comes before money, no matter what papa says.'

'Of course.' Mortimer crossed to Letty's chair and patted her gently on the shoulder. 'Please, no more weeping. You have taken your courage in both hands and journeyed far to Meadow Hill. The least I can provide is a sympathetic refuge. Do not fear. I am not about to throw you back into Bouchard's lap.'

'You are too kind, sir.' Letty blew her nose and regained herself. She watched Mortimer pace across the carpet and pour her some wine. Her mind was racing. Meadow Hill surprised her. The house, though pleasant, was no great mansion, the staff small, the furnishings plain and unremarkable. From this tiny reading-room the mullioned window opened towards an ugly black-brick factory-mill, one of Mortimer's two. Somehow Letty had envisaged different manifestations of success and wealth: liveried servants, ornamental gold throughout a sprawling, exotic manor house. She narrowed her eyes and examined Mortimer's garb: the frock coat was crumpled and old, its hem frayed here and there, and the boots were none too grand. Perhaps his reputed wealth was not so great after all; or maybe the trappings of success in the industrial north were of a different type. She shrugged to herself. What mattered now was that she was safe and the horror of Dover was receding. She did not think of Adam's demise, or of the fact that, by now, the balloon would have well and truly gone up: the police would be searching for Rob – and for her, no doubt – and the knowledge of her flight would have dawned on Pegwell, verified by Donna. Her concentration instead was absorbed with the business of winning Samuel Mortimer's help.

'You are a resourceful lady,' Mortimer said as he pressed a glass into her hands. 'Others would be quite insensible as a result of the terror they had been exposed to. I admire that trait. A wily woman is an asset.'

'You have a lady-wife yourself, sir?'

'Er – no.' Mortimer turned his back to her and peered through the drizzle down towards his factory. 'I am a rather lonely widower, m'dear – ' He swivelled back to smile. 'So your lovely presence is doubly welcome in Meadow. I not only lack a wife, but a family too. My only son, Nick, died this Christmas, stricken in an accident on the games field.'

'How horrible!' Letty dropped her head in respect.

Mortimer watched her fine manners appreciatively. How easy it might be to manipulate her, he was thinking – so young and pliant a personality. And, after the shock of it, how timely her arrival was! He sat in his wing-back desk chair and mulled over recent events. Labour problems and government pressures were rapidly making his mills impracticable concerns and overheads were eating into his not too great personal fortune. Politically he had advanced little – largely because of the shift of party loyalties which had latterly brought about Peel's resignation and shaky reinstatement. In that sphere the writing was on the wall: Peel's moderate attitude towards the Irish was no longer worthy of support. But there were other big cogs in the Tory wheel and the best offer of improvement was still the procuring of a 'dead borough' like the north Tipperary domain of which Drumloch and its neighbours were so major a part. Eighteen months ago the attraction of Drumloch had been little more than as a source of quick profit-through-investment coupled with the shapeless benefits of association with a longtime respected Tory family. But now the attractions were great and clear-cut. Possessing Drumloch could work in two ways for him: he could sell out and transfer his factory concerns at negligible cost (and with the extent of the estate, the navigable waters of the Shannon and the ideal topography he could ask for no more suitable factory site), *and* he could secure an admirable 'strong house', a base within his intended borough with all the noble connections to a traditional Tory family. The simple truth was that Mortimer now wanted the estate – and he was being spurred on by the likes of Sir David Villers and Peel's obvious successors who so desperately wanted to employ all devices that might restore proper Tory power.

The desirability of Letty was immediately apparent. If, as she had admitted, Bouchard needed her for the financial boost of a suitable wedding arrangement, he might easily woo her into his own household and use her as a bargaining card. On the other hand of course there was the possible prospect of Bouchard's death – in which event the situation might be simpler, but might just as well grow more difficult! No, Mortimer decided. He must leave nothing more to chance. He must think shrewdly and play his cards right this time. His very bones told him that Letty was an offered treasure, and he must not miscalculate her value.

'You may as well know that there is little love lost between your father and myself,' he told her. 'But I may suppose you had already some inkling of that?'

'He could not repay a debt to you?' Letty muttered, blinking innocence and non-understanding.

'Please,' Mortimer urged, 'do not think I bring up these affairs to embarrass you or disparage your father. No. It's just that, were I to help you – take you under my wing – you must be aware that you risk estranging your father fully and finally. You are quite correct about this debt problem, and my polite requests to make some easy settlement have been met with nothing other than violent aggression from your father.'

'He is a stubborn and hard-hearted man in some things.'

'Aye. Used to seeing things his way and no other.'

Mortimer blew his cheeks out tiredly. 'What of your sister Donna? You mentioned she's in Bournemouth, quite ill?'

'An American called Cabbot – a new neighbour at Drumloch and quite a comfortable gent, I should guess – is tending her generously.'

'A worthy suitor for Donna?'

'It is hard to say. Donna is whimsical. And takes after papa in stubbornness – '

My main obstacle, Mortimer was thinking. He recalled her: an odd, moody girl with icy eyes and exact beauty, her poise and well-proportioned limbs reminiscent of some fine thoroughbred animal's. 'What illness, may I ask?'

'Typhus.'

'I see. Poor child.' That was encouraging.

A soft knock sounded and a tall attractive girl with flashing dark eyes whom Letty assumed was housekeeper (though her style and age made her unlikely candidate) entered. 'Sir David would like to enjoy a short constitutional now that the rain is passing,' she announced, 'and begs your permission.'

Letty observed the proud relaxed girl and found herself covetously evaluating her engaging masterful approach. When Mortimer strolled across to whisper to this Miss Prendergast Letty noticed he spoke with courtesy and warmth. She seemed more than a casual paid help and Letty suspected she was of family staff and had grown up in service, becoming more a 'daughter' of the house.

When Miss Prendergast was gone Mortimer poured more wine for Letty and declared, 'I am to take it, then, that having given profound consideration to your situation you wish some sort of longterm sanctuary here?'

Letty blushed. 'I would not impose on you so greatly, sir. But until I recover – '

'And you know and understand precisely the situation with your papa and me?'

She nodded, but uncertainly – unsure for a moment of the grim inflexion. He took her hand in his and she stared down at the pattern of thick wrinkles in his aged flesh. He is old and I am safe with him, she thought. He is charmed by a young female's pleading interest and he will bend any way to aid me. And, no matter what the outward signs, he does have money. Alexandrine swore that. After uncertainty, self-satisfaction stole over Letty. The shock of Adam had not weakened her, and the fighting move she had made now placed her in a new intriguing position. Mortimer was acting great grace, but underneath it he was drooling over her. She tuned back to his words.

'. . . I think we can disregard this Rob for now and just wait to see what occurs. Dover is a long way away and, who knows, some vagrant bandit could earn himself the blame? This affair might dispel quite harmlessly. Now!' He clapped his hands, gratified and decided. 'You have little baggage and not much by way of apparel, I suspect. But Miss Prendergast can fix up something there. I have already instructed her to prepare a room –'

'You are most generous, sir.'

'Call me uncle.'

She hid her face behind her glass. 'Respectfully, I'd rather not. You seem far too distant an uncle to merit the title.'

He rose and stood behind her chair, pressing her hands. She could see her brazen openness unmanned him. 'You are quite right, I'm sure. Call me Samuel, then.'

'Samuel.'

'This new friendship will please us both,' he said. 'You know where I stand, and I know your situation'

His knuckles accidentally prodded the supple sponge of her breast. She did not jerk away but squeezed his hand thankfully. The gesture pressured him further into her softness. He reflected swiftly: she is experienced and tough and she has herself chosen the devices by which to wriggle free of this trouble and re-establish some form of good life; I am not seducing an innocent virgin; nothing I could say or do could corrupt her; she knows the rules.

He crossed to the bell-pull. 'And now I am sure you would like to bathe and unwind after your exhausting journey. Perhaps later you will join myself and my guest, Sir David Villers, for a good dinner? He will be delighted to meet my *young* old friend.'

'How will I ever repay you?' Letty asked.

Mortimer merely smiled.

CHAPTER THIRTY-ONE

No news of Letty's adventures or papa's progress filtered back to recuperating Donna in Bournemouth. Paul Cabbot had taken her convalescence firmly in hand and a strict policy of good cheer and prudent isolation was maintained.

In this climate Donna thrived and, before the spring sun grew hot and high in the sky, her strength had returned sufficiently to allow active planning of the return trip to Tipperary. Cabbot did not cease in his subtle efforts to dissuade her project, but her resolution was rigid and as soon as the doctors deemed her well enough they set out. Delicate-natured Emma quailed at the prospect of exposure to infection again and cried off, but Donna was secretly delighted and contented herself with the personal companionship of a hired maid.

The decay across Ireland was of tragic proportions. The potato planting season was about to begin and as they drove through the checkerboard countryside they saw the tattered groups of diggers everywhere, but already their numbers were vastly reduced and their labours were listless and without care. The earth shimmered oily and fresh under the sun, but no one trusted it. Peel's scientific commissions, set up to point the way to immediate relief, had produced bulky crops of negative answers. Contributive factors – like the lack of fertilizers and overwork of plots – were established, but the mystery of the blight remained. The farmers for their part were not keen to listen to textbook mumbo-jumbo and reacted more favourably to the government's practical measures – like the setting up of occasional depots to feed soup to the starving. But no such stop-gap device could stave the problem for long. The fact was that while politicians in Westminster argued and commissions inquired, thousands upon thousands were dying. Those who had previously lived on the borderline had sunk into oblivion during this one harsh winter; and now, with their better reserves of corn and chickens running low, a half-million others waited to follow them.

Disease too waxed strong. From their carriage windows they saw the signs – the dangerous bodies abandoned on prominent rocks, with their beads and crosses and their parched skin; the cottages with their warning flags; the busy hearses in every tiny town. And they saw droves of beggars never before encountered – scant-dressed, purple-skinned entities, their arms endlessly outstretched, gabbling in sweet, sad Gaelic.

'Mamma has written to announce her imminent sale of Fork,' Cabbot told Donna as they drove through Birr and took the western road. 'She quite surprised me, especially since so much reconstruction work went into it. She's sold it to Estelle, I believe, for something like one third her purchase price. I must reprimand her when we return. Her business acumen fades with age. This rot can't get much worse, we all know. I told her not to act when the market was so obviously on the floor.'

The chilly pragmatism appalled Donna and she bundled herself up by the open window, one hand covering her mouth and nose from the piercing miasma that rode the earth, the other holding her wrap tight to ward off the dry breeze. 'So Ireland is over for you?'

Wary of slanting the odds against himself Cabbot sighed, 'In this life one can never be *sure* of anything. The time for a Cabbot investment in Ireland was wrong, that is all.'

'You do so speak like a shop-keeper at times, Paul.'

'I'm sorry if I do.'

The timidity of his manner annoyed her as much as the words he had spoken but she reckoned the blame on herself: for weeks she had longed for these hours and now she was traversing the green fields of Erin and the hope that had lived in her was turning to bitter ice. The nearer she came to Drumloch the harder it was to conjure Colum's face.

They stayed at Fork, a haven in a sea of troubles amply run by slick Dublin staff, and Donna announced her intention to ride to Drumloch during breakfast on their first day.

'This is the farm lad Devlin you wish to converse with?' Cabbot questioned.

Donna averted her eyes. In a gruff tone she said, 'Paul, please remember that you chose to offer your company on this trip. I outlined my intentions clearly. If you intend to hinder my freedom I must ask that my bags be packed –'

Cabbot stammered placating assurances and clicked his fingers.

'Saddle two good horses,' he ordered his butler. 'My guest and I will be riding this noon.'

They rode out together, Donna muffled against the germs of recurring disease, and crossed the hill that gave onto Drumloch's valley. The sky was slate grey and the wind high but the sun was generously warm and its vibrant light made the grass emerald green. The valley unrolled before them like a Persian tapestry of intricate design, black paths winding through grey plots dotting weedy fields, all encircled by an arena of spectacular green. Away to the west sat Drumloch manor house and Donna's heart sank to her boots as its wan, spent visage took her eye. Even at this distance she could see a window pane or two shattered and the diseased ivy that had adorned the colonnades adrift in the breeze. From the crest of the hill she could see too the Doon and its Holy Well, and her spirits lifted.

'You are smiling contentedly,' Cabbot observed. 'Why?'

She shook away the moment. 'What's it the French say, my step-mamma had a way of expressing it? – *Mal du pays*. Nostalgia.'

Cabbot watched her expression as she regarded the land and the river and the scattered specks of workers in the plots and he marvelled at the transformation. Since Holyhead she had been grim and brooding, now unbridled happiness radiated. 'You are safe to ride on, I'm sure,' he

285

suggested, unwilling to challenge this joyous moment. 'I shall await you here, by the sheep shed.' He dismounted to rope his horse and she just smiled, nodded and spurred on.

Down the river track she went, round the high rock crop, and onto the plots. Drumloch's shadow crossed her path but her eyes were fixed beyond, latched to the solitary whitewash cottage perched near the river bank, surrounded by the greystone wall she knew so well. At last Colum was back in her head, a burning vital memory that yearned and begged for her arms with a passion that matched hers. How could she have stayed away from him for so long? Every week, every day, every hour was a burden – yet his memory had helped her, beckoning when death threatened, luring her back. She owed her life to him, as surely as she owed to Cabbot or her doctors. She thought about redhead Cara, but dismissed the doubting moment. Colum cared for her, he had sworn that more than once. He had promised to stick by her, to save her from misery and give her freedom and love. And, when the shackles of illness and papa and Cabbot were off, how she wanted his embrace. What Rob said could not be true. If he had gone to Galway with Cara he must have good, true reason; and he must have returned. He would not, she was sure, leave his father alone to a deathbed. . .

While she approached the cottage the confident sense of his presence grew but as she slid off her horse in the yard she froze.

There was absolute calm.

No winter smoke curled from the chimney, no animal cries stirred the air. She moved closer and started when she saw that the place looked as though it had been ransacked. The windows were glassless and the kitchen door battered off its hinges. Trembling, she stepped inside. The atmosphere was dead and filthy, the interior illuminated by a single shaft of drilling sunlight through the bedroom window. All the furniture was gone, all the books – everything. In Colum's small room a white faded square on the wall showed where once her ink sketch had hung. Gasping for breath she ran outside. Mystified and afraid she walked through the sun-baked troughs of the Irish Apple field, the nurled brown stones prodding the soles of her feet, twisting her ankle and rasping drily against each other. There seemed to be no soft earth, just mud-coloured pebbles and grit covering a soil as tough as granite. Donna moved up the hill with purpose, scrambling through a winter-bare hedge and crossing to the high path. In the next field, just as she hoped, she saw an idle group of diggers. As she approached Anthony Anderson recognised her and broke away to greet her. Teggie Kelly, whose field it was, waved a fond hand. After Colum's bleak plot this land was cushiony soft underfoot, turned and ready for seed.

' 'Tis a welcome sight you make, Miss. We wondered what had become of the Sir's household with so sudden a departure. Rumours have been runnin' like a spring stream.'

'All is well.' She beamed a smile. She was glad it was Anderson she had encountered first; the childlike warmth of the man always won her. 'My visit may be short,' she expanded. 'But I'm saddened already to see . . . Mister Devlin has died?'

'He did, God rest his soul. Many months ago, I'm sorry to say.' Anderson regarded her with a trace of a knowing smile. *He understands*, she thought quickly and nervous embarrassment took her.

Anderson lowered his head to spare her blushes.

'Colum chose to reside here no longer?'

Anderson's shoulders heaved in a despairing shrug. 'He moved off without much to say to anyone.'

A stab of unbearable grief split Donna's heart. She had been wrong, then. Cara *had* lured him away. 'I-I am surprised,' she muttered. 'He spoke nothing to me, to anyone I'm sure.'

'You must see he had nothing left here. His family were gone and the Devlin ties to the manor house were broken fully. Then his animals were taken, stolen by some cowardly thief – '

'I had no idea!'

'What choice had he? He had to go to find some reward-

287

ing labour in order to eat, to live.' Anderson's brogue thumped the dirt. 'He had little faith left in this, and refused to burden his neighbours with the problem of support. I suppose all he wanted was to get away and rebuild some worthwhile life.'

Donna could think of nothing other than Cara's hand snugly in Colum's. The logic was apparent: Cara was of his kind, she had known the land and understood the problems; she had offered immediate comfort and understanding when Donna's position within the manor distanced her from events of farm life. And how could she blame him for turning away from a pledge to her? She had argued with him, badgered him selfishly, played a haughty game. And in the end her tactics lost him.

'I am sorry for you,' Anderson said, and she recoiled in amazement.

'So true a friendshp should not have ended like this.'

'It was inevitable, I suppose.'

'No.' His tone was sincere. 'Just untimely. In another place at another time – ' He sighed and spread his hands. 'What message can I give him if he comes back?'

'You think he may?'

'Not unless the ground heals, and that may be a long time yet. He will not live a beggar here.'

Her vapid eyes were frosty. 'Then it does not matter.'

She walked away from Anderson and watched the river birds wheeling angrily in the sky, desperate for food as she was for the irretrievable past. Finding her horse and riding past the manor house she suddenly could not bear to look on it or listen to its memories. She cried without tears and wanted to be alone no longer. Her illness, it seemed, had been the dividing line between wild, intoxicating youth and sober maturity, and this very earth marked the spot, a monument to past happenings. She was relieved to find Cabbot awaiting her, his smooth ageless face pinched in anticipation. He made no effort to press reaction, but mounted quietly beside her and carefully adjusted the folds of her cape. At length he said, 'I hope in some way your confusion is eased.'

She said nothing for a long time and they began a gentle trot homewards. As Fork's high chimneys slunk into view she started, 'Newark's air is agreeable, you say?'

He tugged at the bridle of her horse and slowed her. His face lit in delight. 'You will not regret this – if you mean what I think you mean. I swear to you, I will make you happier than you could ever be in Ireland. I have wealth and sound standing and Cabbot Industries has a tremendous future ahead. Mamma, Emma and you will be excellent friends –'

She frowned. 'Very well, Paul. You have persuaded me. I will accompany you to Newark, and wherever else you wish. But I must qualify my agreement. I have no great desire for the riches or comforts your wealth can no doubt give, but I want my freedoms.'

'What sort of freedoms?' Cabbot was nonplussed.

Donna pulled back the hood of her cape and bathed her face in the watery sunshine. 'Freedom to be myself, to love Ireland if I wish to do so and travel when I want.' She met his gaze again. 'Do not doubt that I will become friends with your mamma, but she is a self-possessed and strong-minded woman – as, in ways, am I.'

Appeased, he nodded quite happily. The excitement that billowed within could scarcely be contained but he said coolly, 'Do you wish to talk about your Irish friend, to tell me anything?'

'No,' she smiled. 'It is done and over. I wish to talk about America.'

Those jaunty words neither warmed her smile nor chipped the ice that froze her heart.

Defeated by the irrevocable signs of total famine and with a life's-savings purse of a few miserable pounds, Colum had chosen the course followed by thousands: he made for Liverpool.

His efforts to trace the pirated herd had come to nothing: sub-inspector McClune, still seeking a scapegoat for the Mackie murder, had shunned assistance and laughed in his face; and the primitive recourse of following animal tracks

289

proved useless with so huge and uncontrollable a traffic in nomads. It had taken a week or two but the insidious truth had hit home: with nothing but small stocks of corn left, survival through the winter would be a mean, soulless battle. He was beaten. And so he had reviewed his prospects in travel: the west offered only the workhouse, Dublin was overfull. The city of Liverpool beckoned. Just 140 miles across the Irish Sea, its wealth and size were legendary. Even on Drumloch's plots the stories of proud Liverpool were recounted. Many families boasted relatives who had trekked in search of foreign fortunes and got no farther than there. For the discerning the myths were sweet but the facts equally enthralling: Liverpool was second only in size to London and three times the size of New York; it blared its success through no less than *ten* city newspapers, and had a merchant community the wealth of which was matched nowhere in the kingdom.

At first Colum saw the signs of opulent promise. After the grey air of Ireland it was hard not be impressed by the trim elegant streets with their glossy Venetian doorways, the Doric-pillared warehouses, the bustle of dandys and pretty-dressed trulls. In contrast to shocked, stagnant Dublin, Liverpool swelled and rattled with growth. Although it was packed with hordes of fleeing Irish, thousands en route for America but just as many lost and loose in the backstreets, Colum found little difficulty in procuring work – first as shovel-man on the massive new law courts of St George's Hall, then as tout for Tapscotts the emigrant-brokers. His youth, strength and intelligence rendered him a desirable employee, and his facility with the Gaelic tongue helped at Tapscotts. Colum was pleased and relieved to find good work so quickly. The weeks of despondent search and journeying had not freed him of the guilt and sorrow he felt in losing his farm and Donna, but in hard toil he could drown his emotions and forget.

As tout or man-catcher for Tapscotts he earned his fees by persuading emigrants off the Irish mail boat that their fortunes lay in the New World of America. For £3 10s he could offer them Tapscotts' blessing and a ticket for a west-bound packet, an assured path to a limitlessly better life, according to the broker's manifesto. For a time he worked assiduously and successfully, but gradual disillusionment set in. Suddenly the veneer of Liverpool was as thin as the paper on which Tapscotts' manifesto was printed. A less shining picture emerged: Liverpool, once famous for slave-trading and privateering, still had its tricks; the popular packets he promoted were insanitary and unsafe and the promise of America untrue; the American government really wanted to stem the flow of human derelicts from strife-torn Ireland, and the workhouses there were just as full and lowly as any in Galway. And, too, the more Colum roamed the backstreets of Liverpool, the rawer and sadder the face of the city became. Though untouched by blight and its problems, the ordinary residents of cottages and garrets knew just as well the scourge of hunger.

On point of debating a decision to leave, Colum's diligence at the docks won him transfer to the sought-after respectable post of clerical assistant in the broker's dockside office. With a stable wage guaranteed and two shillings a month extra in his pay packet he succumbed, sweeping from his mind as best he could filtering stories of the sea disasters where unfit brigs brought scores of hopeful emigrants to their deaths, and all the concurrent doubts.

But it was a frail inner peace, and a crossroads decision for the future could not be far away.

In the early spring evenings when his eleven-hour shift was finished he took to walking the docks and piers, meditating on the avenues that lay before him as he watched the great ships from all over the world. There was comfort somehow in the farewell blast of a foghorn or the crack of rigging as mainsails took the breeze. Colum sensed what this meant, sensed the call of home. As he toiled on and saved his shillings the dreams firmed into plans. Bitterness replaced guilt and he resented his exile more and more. Suspicions of McClune's involvement in the herd theft were revived, as were the abandoned proposals to join with Anderson in preparing a path for co-ordinated rebellion. The Young Irelanders' advances had been small because of the distraction of famine – but that was the very reason why he should no longer tolerate exile. Strength of purpose was lost because of upheavals in Irish farming society, but a line of fight must be held somewhere. Otherwise the upshot of the famine would be even greater power for the gentry. Now Colum came and sat by the wharf's edge and contemplated a return – to re-establish the farm that was rightly his, and to help the rebels . . .

Inevitably his thoughts sailed on to Drumloch and the radiant memory of Donna. How different life could have been. Had his courage been high enough . . . But was that true? Escape with her would not have freed him from his love of farming life, nor of the tortured sights of injustice that so challenged him.

Restless in his memories, Colum stood and sauntered into the teeming crowds that choked the main wharfs. Several ships had recently docked and the hustle and fuss of unloading rumbled at a cracking pace. The evening was alive with the cheers of passengers and the shouted commands of longshoremen.

Nearing the Cunard pier the crush became so tangled that, in order to cross the quay, Colum and others were forced to ascend a fire-escape platform that straddled the Cunard warehouse. Halfway across the iron walkway, his head still full of Drumloch, he stopped dead and gazed down into the crowd with steely intent.

'Move yerself on,' a navvy lurched, crushing an elbow into Colum's back. 'Can't you do yer gawkin' elsewhere!'

Colum didn't move. A private carriage had pulled up before the last gangway to a giant Cunard steamer that was readying itself for departure. The passengers that eddied about here were first-class types, draped in fur and finery, so unlike those normally dealt with by Colum. Wharf loaders were moving baggage from the late carriage and three people were stepping down. One, like an exquisite dove among crows, was Donna Bouchard. Colum's pulse raced and his hands on the iron rail were damp. The immediate instinct was to call to her, to open his lungs and his arms and run to her, and enfold her with love. But he held back and frowned as he saw the fair-haired American from Fork, together with his lanky, unpretty sister. Cabbot walked forward to take Donna's arm and Colum watched as she gracefully obeyed the American's directions. The struggle to refrain from shouting out was almost too much, but already the travel party had begun to ascend the gangway.

A steamer from the Collins line passing hooted a salute to its Cunard rival and the passengers aboard ran to the far deck to answer in cheer. Colum waited. Donna emerged on the near deck at last, at eye level to the warehouse fire escape. Nothing but vacant space stood between them and he could distinguish every soft line of her lovely face. If she looked in a horizontal plane, he observed, their eyes would meet.

He blasted the thought away: what right had he to this terrible yearning? She had offered herself those months ago and he had refused. And Rob had spoken the truth, she had chosen the safe escape of a wealthy American instead.

Through the din of the crowd the clatter of the gangway stays rang out as the dock labourers prepared the Cunarder for departure. The Collins ship was blaring again and the Cunard decks were in turmoil. Cabbot's sister had disappeared to join the cheering and Cabbot had Donna's arm.

The great steamship belched smoke and shrilled its whistle.

The dock foreman shouted, 'Stand clear!' and freed the final stay.

Donna was turning to sidle off the foredeck with Cabbot. Her eyes scanned the dock swiftly, drifting unseeing through Colum's for one split-second. Cabbot's arm was round her waist and his smiling face was whispering in her ear. Donna laughed, and Colum waved farewell.

PART FOUR:
HOME
1846 – 1848

CHAPTER THIRTY-TWO

Bouchard's retreat from grievously debilitating illness – finally diagnosed as liver disease incurred by excesses in alcohol – was a slow business, occupying as it did the remainder of the winter and the first months of spring. Pegwell Hall was his haven – a quiet limbo in a forgotten corner of England, remote from the ravages of the world. Here he lay abed for weeks and weeks, always comatose, often incoherent, enmeshed in a mortal struggle, with just the drifting faces of Sir Myles, and a nursemaid, and a bald doctor, to punctuate the despair of his inner thoughts. For a long time he sensed he was vacillating on the edge of death, that it would take little to push him over. Sir Myles did not sense this, but knew it to be true, and it was for that reason he revealed nothing of the astonishing Dover escapade – not of Adam's letter of explanation and farewell from the Royal George, nor of the subsequent tragic news of his death and the girl's disappearance. Appalled but not surprised by Adam's behaviour – for he knew his son to be a penniless madcap full of improbable greedy dreams – Sir Myles had not been comforted by the police deductions. It seemed to them that the couple at the George had been victims of vicious robbers who, on finding no money, had savaged the man and abducted the girl.

When finally in late spring Bouchard was well enough to hear out the story his response was calm, tempered perhaps by the sedative recently administered. His immediate concern had been all for Donna, and he had requested writing paper and drafted some hurried letters to Bournemouth.

Bouchard's improved health had not come a minute too soon. Only a week after he had left his bed Sir Myles confronted him in the rhododendron garden behind the house, expression heavy with remorse. Bouchard was relaxing in the soft seaside sun, the baby Serle on his lap.

'It grieves me greatly to have to tell you this, Redmond – but I am glad at least you are up and on your feet again. It would distress me, knowing your position, to see you thrown out with no secure home to go to.'

He pushed a rolled document into Bouchard's hand. Bouchard read the enfacement: *Evacuation of premises: Bailiff's Final Notice.*

'Pegwell?'

'To be vacated by Thursday,' Sir Myles nodded. 'Power of attorney went to my major creditor after a court wrangle. I had no say in the matter.'

'My dear chap – ' Bouchard was at a loss for words. He sat silent beside his friend for many minutes. 'How will it leave you, when all debts are satisfied?'

'A few hundred possibly, no more.' Sir Myles croaked a laugh. 'Can it be that we old Tories hold the monopoly on intemperate living – ?'

'And bad luck?' Bouchard grinned humourlessly and rocked the child. 'Worry not for me. I'm in fine fettle now and the air here's done me so much good.'

'I am repairing to Argyll, on blessed invitation of an old cousin. But I can see you right to a good residence in the village of Kingston-upon-Thames, if you'd care. It's a gamekeeper's lodge only, on the estate of Lord Markham. He's a Whig but a swell chap and it would suit you with the babe for now – and allow you access to London.'

Bouchard cocked an eyebrow, questioning. 'I'd be better off in wretched Tipperary than in London, you know – though Kingston will do me very well, thank you.'

'Are you sure? You have yourself confessed to me that your options of choice are gone, what with this worsening famine and land unrest. All else having failed, might it not be a good time to go back to the old party and plead some aid? You cannot have become *such* a villain in their eyes that you have access to no friendships now. Even a token alignment *with Peel* would help, affording you more

Society openings –'

'No. I shall not trouble you with the biteens of the story, Myles, but mark me, I stand to gain nothing with Peel. I've hoisted my flag and he'll never bow to that.'

'So what future lies ahead?' Sir Myles was watching the child stir to wakefulness in Bouchard's grip.

'There is steam in the engine yet. I still own the four walls of Drumloch and, regardless of its current market problem, more than a thousand acres of Ireland. And I have Donna –'

Bouchard slouched back in his seat and reflected: destruction had slunk near but he had side-stepped once again; the fates were against him but providence on his side; Mortimer had obviously been silenced by Peel's parliamentary defeat and by the famine curse on southern lands, so that noose was loosened; Letty was gone, but Donna was satisfactorily playing into Cabbot's pocket. Against all the odds, he guessed, *she* would be the one whose fortunes relieved him. What twist of fate! Bitter, awkward Donna – the sullen minx who so reminded him of Janet.

Bouchard smiled in the unwavering Kent sunshine. Life really was full of surprises.

Just three weeks later, not a day settled into his new temporary abode in Kingston village, two devastating surprises befell.

In a letter postmarked Liverpool and redirected from Pegwell Cabbot curtly and politely replied to Bouchard's recent communication. He expressed his joy at the reported recovery and stated that, as agreed, he was now accompanying Donna to America where, it was hoped, their relationship would blossom under mamma's guidance. Bouchard's request for money assistance was flatly ignored. An attached note from Donna hit target: whilst her fate and affections were in Paul Cabbot's hands and the likelihood of marriage had been mooted, she was adamant in her resolve to resist any 'arrangement'. If papa needed aid he must seek it elsewhere, but Donna was not about to allow avarice to thwart the course of honest affection.

The second letter forwarded by Pegwell's administrators bore a date mark six weeks old. It came from Mortimer and outlined Letitia's arrival and search for solace after the tragedy of Dover. Halfway down the first page the meaning and purpose of the approach was apparent: Mortimer possessed a saleable property of Bouchard's and reckoned it might be worth a deal. Lest Bouchard should think he could entice Letty away, it was made clear that Letty had grown very fond of Meadow Hill and its owner and emphatically refused any return to her father's side. Mortimer's tone was reasonable, almost friendly. He thought it unfair, he stated, that Sir Redmond should withhold settlement on his 'investment' any longer, but if the cash return was inconvenient, an exchange of property – Drumloch for a full discharge of the loan – would be acceptable. This really seemed mutually worthwhile to Mortimer! With prevailing conditions in the south Bouchard would be well shot of his troubled estate and a new plateau of friendship between both men would, Mortimer assured, allow Bouchard fresh purchase on former proud Tory associations.

A stifling sense of degradation sent Bouchard on a orgy of reckless drinking. Mortimer had him cornered. He had not the money to pursue Cabbot nor the prospect of any kind of permanent peace in Kingston. He had to act, and the direction of action was unavoidable. Mortimer must be tackled and beaten, and valuable Letty captured back.

Half-sobering after two full days of abandon, Bouchard decided the time was ripe for attack. Leaving Serle in the hands of his new nursemaid, a hard-nosed Cockney with the face of a goat and charm of an angel, Bouchard took the Chester train. It took him three days to get to Lurgan but none of the fury of his plan had diminished in that time.

Red-eyed, violent and unwell, he arrived at Meadow Hill on a wet Friday night, and stepped down from the cheap coach of a shoddy Lisburn fleet. The forecourt was dotted with carriages and mellow laughter whispered on the night breeze. The pillared front doors stood open, splaying yellow carpets of light out over the gravel and it became obvious that a ball was about to commence. Bouchard brushed past the servant at the door and grabbed a young serving-maid in the dining room. 'Where is your master?' he demanded, and the girl cowered and stumbled an answer.

Satisfied, he ran upstairs. The old house was full of movement and sound and no one took particular notice of him in spite of the fact that his tired clothes were crumpled and wet-streaked. In the upstairs corridor he tried some rooms unsuccessfully, then he stomped into the small north-facing wing. The first door he chanced yielded and he found himself staring into a spacious drawing-room, in the centre of which Mortimer stood, his long arms hooked about Letitia's neck, securing her necklace. Bouchard stepped inside quickly and slammed the door. As he backed to it he felt his palm cup a key in the lock and he twisted it. His heart pounded in his chest.

'My God, sir – an outrage!' He spoke with menacing slowness, his finger pointed accusingly. 'Unhand my daughter and pray recall that she is your niece before you molest her farther!'

His hawk face became florid but otherwise remaining composed, Mortimer replied, 'I detect instantly that you are drunk! How dare you burst in here?' His voice dropped to measured coolness. 'You forget that dear Letty and I share no blood bond, and I am not truly her uncle.' Mortimer retained his close familiar posture alongside Letty, underlining his claim. 'And may I say now that I do not intend to listen to sanctimonious hot air from one whose sense of propriety leaves so much to be desired.'

Letty's face was white in fear and she took a step away from Mortimer's arms. Her knees were quite weak. The last person she had ever expected to see at Meadow was papa. How could he have found out she was here? Unless Samuel . . .? She discarded the notion before it was formed in her head. In their weeks of growing friendship the candid confidences Mortimer entrusted to her proved beyond doubt his ingenuous scrupulousness.

'*You* speak of propriety,' Bouchard grunted. 'You who abduct my daughter and use her as a piece in your chess game!' He took a step towards Letty and addressed her: 'You know what his ploy is? To bargain your freedom against my manor – the property he so hungrily wants, to feed on southern cheap labour and help his political greed.'

'Your daughter came here of her own will,' Mortimer said. He placed himself squarely between Letty and her father. 'The deceits you speak of are all in your drunken head.'

'Come, Letty!' Bouchard said. 'Get by me!'

'Sir, you do not yet understand. Letty chose to seek refuge here to avoid *your* games-playing. She had no wish to feel the power of your belt, nor had she desire to suffer some convenient forced marriage. After the horror of that unfortunate incident – '

'I will hear no more!' Bouchard's voice roared. His attention settled on Mortimer again and he balled a ham-like fist before him. 'Get this straight, Mortimer. No matter how you try to cajole me, Drumloch will never be yours. I would give you the blood from my veins before I would surrender that legacy. All right – you have my daughter under your roof and brainwashed now, but I will use my own tactics. I will fight you rather than bargain. But mark me, I will get her back, slut that she is.'

'How dare you insult her.'

'She is beyond insult. Like her stepmother she is no more than a trollop who seeks self-pleasure and to hell with all else.' Letty feigned a shocked scream and Mortimer lunged forward but was held by Bouchard's jutting fist. 'Have you revealed to her?' Bouchard sneered. 'Have you revealed how you seduced my own wife in order to purchase a foot in Drumloch? What sweet lies have you been telling her? Can it be that your secondary plan was to court and win her over, then hope to inherit a share in my property had I died in Kent? Was that it? Was that your smug insurance plan?'

Controlled, Mortimer sat and adjusted his stock pin. 'You still cannot believe that she came here of her own accord? A pity, for it is true. I have allowed her to choose what *she* wishes, Redmond. More than you have ever done. And now hear *me* out.' Mortimer's dark eyes engaged Bouchard's in a fierce gaze. 'A long time ago you came to me and sought something desperately. I obliged, and gave you what you wanted. Now the tables are turned. I seek Drumloch and I expect you to be a gentleman and accede to my wishes. You are down and out, Redmond, and must admit it. If you give me Drumloch I will pay you some worthwhile fee, and you will have the freedom of ready cash again.'

'I will not give up the manor.'

'Before long you may have to. If I do not get a power of attorney, then the planned Encumbered Estates Act which parliament has been toying with for so long, will do the job for me. Under the provisions of that act – and you and I know it will go through, from all accounts – any Irish estate in difficulty can be dissolved or annexed at the behest of the encumbrancer. All I need to do is sit back and await that day, Redmond.'

Bouchard saw the veracity of Mortimer's declaration. He searched for a resolute equal reply but found none.

'Come now,' Mortimer persisted agreeably. 'We are intelligent men, both with our vested interests in different areas. I will be pleased to give you what you came here for, to do what *you* want. Please grant me the same generosity.'

'Never.'

Mortimer considered Bouchard's red-faced rage and decided he was no longer perturbed or uneasy. 'You are stubborn, Redmond – and I could be equally stubborn about *very* delicate matters.' He hesitated to find a fondant of his liking on a salver. 'For example, my boy Serle.'

'*Your* boy?' Bouchard's voice cracked.

'Come, we both know the truth of that sorry occurrence.'

'She was *my* wife. You could have no possible claim to her – or to the child.'

'Oh but I could. You see – ' Mortimer chomped his sweetmeat carefully. 'I have letters. Many intimate letters. Graphic and frank in their content. They leave nothing to doubt.'

303

'The courts would never decide in your favour.'

'Wouldn't they? Ample evidence of my, er, association with dear Alexandrine. Then I will have obvious recourse to the fact that you are unfit to maintain the child, that even your daughter deserts you, that you are absolutely penniless.' He swallowed noisily. 'What, d'you think, the courts might say about that?'

'Have you no shred of decency in you?' Bouchard whispered, his brain suddenly foggy and confused. 'You used my wife, but discarded her and ignored her in her final hours of need –'

'I could afford no breath of scandal, could I? A man in my position, bound for political life. But that is neither here nor there. Fact is, it can easily be established that she dallied with me and we had a son. And *you* turned her out.'

'I have never heard such meanness or known such avarice.'

'What did Horace say? – *Virtus post nummos*. Cash before virtue. One must be a realist, Redmond. I am not being greedy. It is simply that there are things *I need*.' He smiled. 'I cannot see that that trait would be frowned on by you. You would agree with me that magnanimity merely reduces man, and one must fight to win.' He stood and approached Bouchard. He laid his hands on the other's shoulders. 'Now, what is it to be? Shall we sit in peace and draw up our exchange plan – or shall I summon my man to throw you out?'

Bouchard reeled: Mortimer's face swam before him. The row was over, the victory bell had sounded, it was no bone of contention any longer, it was *fait accompli*, Mortimer's win. Bouchard shuddered into life, his big hands gripping Mortimer's throat. 'You bastard,' he began. 'There is no way I can escape from you. Your purpose is to destroy me, to wipe out the Bouchard name. The manor will not be the end of it. You will whittle me down till there's nothing but my blasted soul left –' He stammered on, strengthening his grip little by little. Mortimer's knees gave and his vision darkened. His hands flailed ineffectually.

'Help – help me,' he spluttered, his voice no more than a

thin rasp.

Bouchard clenched his stubby fingers deeper into the jugular, intent on the final killing pressure. He shook Mortimer's big body with inhuman force, tossing it before him like a hound worrying a rat. Together they collapsed onto the ottoman by the window, Mortimer's breath and voice fully gone, his last surge of resisting energies fading. In the back of Bouchard's mind the sound of running footfalls and irate voices seeped through. The doorknob behind him was shaken and alarmed women were shouting out, calling their master's name. But he was too near to his goal to retreat. Mortimer lay under him, spent and immobile, his bare neck offered for that lethal conclusive squeeze. Bouchard gritted his teeth and flexed his fingers – but too late. A shower of brilliant stunning sparks burst inside his brain and he felt blood in his mouth. His grip on Mortimer was gone and, before he could gather his senses, he was flying bodily across the carpet.

It took many minutes to reassert. He rolled over and brushed the sticky warmth of running blood from the side of his head. His good eye opened to focus on Letty, poised over him, white-faced, with a brass fire-iron dangling from her hand.

'Devil,' he hissed. 'You strike your own father.' He shuffled weakly to his feet and lunged for her hand. 'It's over,' he grated. 'You will get your cloak now and accompany me – home.'

She raised the fire-iron as though to strike again. Mortimer stirred, crawling back from the borders of death, spitting his own blood. Just at that moment a pressure of weight was flung at the passage door and it cracked in. A knot of serving staff burst through, led by the elegant figure of Sir David Villers, a face well known to Bouchard, effigy of the front benchers of parliament, of a hundred disloyal friends.

Bouchard ignored them and stared at Letty. 'Your own father,' he urged. 'How can you dare raise your hand – ?'

Sir David came to her side immediately and eased the

iron from her grasp. His arm encircled her in comfort. 'I will not go with you, sir', she gasped, 'because I fear for your sanity. I have no wish to be returned to the uncertain ship that is your household, nor to leave myself at mercy of your beatings or your whim.' She dropped her eyes. 'I have no wish to face the past – and Mister Mortimer allows me pleasant security.'

While Bouchard steadied himself Sir David soothed Letty. Miss Prendergast and her assistants tended Mortimer, reviving him with strong spirit and smoke vapours.

'It would appear wise for you to make your departure,' Sir David said, twisting the sweeping curl of his white moustache and avoiding Bouchard's eye. 'Unless you'd care to stay for the police.'

'You do not understand – ' Bouchard begged. 'I can imagine Mortimer will spin some yarn, Sir David, but – '

'Please!' Sir David would hear no explanations. He patted Letty's shoulder and shot a disparaging side-glance to his former colleague. 'Do not degrade yourself any further, Bouchard. Such acts of wanton emotion find no place in a gentleman's world.'

'Allow me to explain – '

'I-I think you had better go,' Mortimer announced, pulling himself to his feet with Miss Prendergast's support. 'The facts have been spoken and you know where you stand.' He glanced round the gathered group, as if to make sure everyone was attending. 'I will not have a curmudgeon in my drawing-room, sir, and I do not wish to see your face or hear your name again until such time as your just debts are paid.'

Guests from the ball were gathering around the doorway and the murmur of appalled, delighted conversation ran. Bouchard looked at Letty and saw Janet, Donna and Alexandrine – the treachery of all women. Then his eye shifted through the crowd, recognising prominent personages, old acquaintances. Accusation was painted on every face. His nerve broke. He fled the room, a dirty, dishevelled pauper.

*

The final axe had not fallen.

In a trance of humiliated confusion and fevered sickness Bouchard made tracks for Kingston-upon-Thames. Mortimer had him over the barrel and the only choice now lay between Drumloch and indigence, or Serle and the pennies for survival. Either way, it seemed in his dejected state, the Bouchard ascendancy was doomed. Famine and the troubles of the south tormented his thoughts and, by the time he reached London, the last ditch decision of surrendering the manor was made. But Serle he would keep; Serle he would cherish and keep; to Serle he would give the legacy of lineage. Maybe, in twenty years, *his* efforts and fame would win back the honour of the Huguenot name...

Fate awaited with its cruellest twist: At Lord Markham's game lodge the Cockney nursemaid and Serle had vanished. It was, the police believed, another sorry case of child-theft, investigations of which usually produced a hundred-per-cent failure rate. The boy had gone to childless wealthy parents or to white-slavers, the police-inspector guessed, and the likelihood was that his identity would be lost forever.

CHAPTER THIRTY-THREE

'Your father is dead,' Samuel Mortimer told Letty bluntly.

'Lord.' She remained dry-eyed and upright, painstakingly sewing the edge of an embroidered kirtle in her cramped sitting-room that overlooked the depressing murk of factory smoke. She set down her needle and pushed the garment off her lap. 'A recurrence of his ailment?'

Mortimer waved a lengthy letter before her. 'Sadly, no.' He frowned. '*Sadly* because the circumstances were rather more distressing.'

'Speak, I am not afraid to hear.'

'This letter comes from the district coroner at Richmond. As you know I was endeavouring to secure my power of attorney and permission to sell – or rather, buy – Drumloch. Having difficulty in establishing contact with your father again my London solicitor opened up inquiries. It soon came out that when your father returned from Lurgan he found the child had been taken, abducted, by his nurse.' Mortimer lowered his head as a mark of necessary respect. 'It quite unbalanced him and – ' He trailed off.

'He took his own life?'

Mortimer nodded. 'In a Soho doss house. Four weeks ago yesterday. There was an inquiry, of course, and the coroner recorded death by suicide.'

'My God. The child?'

'Disappeared without trace. Such happenings are not unusual in the mire that is London today. Children vanish every week. Bouchard was foolish to entrust the boy's safety to one untried girl.'

'This is the saddest event I've heard of,' Letty said. She abandoned her sewing and crossed to the writing-desk perched under the high window. 'Donna must be informed. I shall write to her this evening.' She started rummaging amid books and notepaper. 'Where did I leave that note she sent from Newark in answer to my first letter?'

Mortimer regarded her with interest, intrigued by the unflustered ease of her response. As she sat by the desk he stood behind her and massaged her shoulders. His eyes wandered out to the hilly sweep of the factory and the faraway flax field. The smoke from the chimneys was thick and rich as ever but the turnover for today would not, he knew, be high. Once again – fifth time in two months – a renegade group disputing conditions and pay had fractured the labour force and caused a walkout. The situation was outrageous but firm control was becoming more and more difficult. Two new mills had opened near Lisburn – that was the bane – and unhappy but experienced labourers were being sifted away. By God, the changes Mortimer would introduce were he in a position of stronger power – on the

Olympian plateau of government *or* on the virgin plains of the south! A change of approach was vital if work forces were to be kept in control. He had said so a thousand times. He had said so to Cabinet people. How satisfying that some small indications of others listening to his call were forthcoming at last! How sensible he had been in putting money into the Tories and courting the likes of Villers and Cavendish and the others.

The scratch of Letty's quill intruded and he sat by her and said, 'My dear, we have spoken little of those shocking events of the night of the Maytime ball, and I have been careful of my words lest I recall the incidents and upset you further. But you must know from the claims made and from the hints I have given that Drumloch is, in truth, a desirable property for me at this time.'

Letty paused in her writing. 'Papa said some horrid things that night, but I have concluded that in his last months his mind was unsound. I have turned those incidents over and over in my head and added them to others – and I have glimpsed the truth. Papa had a crazed and reckless attitude to life, and sought only to satisfy his own gambling or whatever insanity he was involved in. I know. I overheard many conversations – innocently, I assure you. But the doubts were in my mind a year ago or more.' A blush of vivid pink highlighted each cheek. 'He treated mamma quite badly, I'd guess – '

'He alluded that night to my seduction of your dear mamma,' Mortimer rejoined. 'But I am afraid that was *far* from the truth. As you say, he spurned Alexandrine, and mistreated her.' He paused for emphasis. 'He was a very wayward man, a selfish man.'

'You need explain no more to me, Samuel. I lived long enough under his rule, feeling more and more that I was either to be abandoned to life in miserable Drumloch or sold off as some cheap concubine.'

That statement seemed to depress Mortimer's spirit. He grunted agreement and took Letty's hand. ' "Miserable" Drumloch depends very much on the quality of life within the household. Naturally with Redmond things must have been hard for you.' There was something on his mind, some declaration he wanted to make, but she could see the difficulty he was having finding words. He stood to pace and light a cigar. 'According to my solicitor and the coroner – who in turn has been in touch with Redmond's former man, Halifane – no will can be traced for your father. Two years ago, it seems, he scrapped the one lodged with Halifane and proposed another, but that never went to signature. Neither did the subsequent one. Redmond was quite casual about such matters during these last years.'

'Which means whatever stands in his estate is mine – and Donna's?'

'Precisely. But Donna, as confirmed by that note she sent, is quite comfortably engaged in America. So, to all purposes, Drumloch may be considered to be yours.'

'But papa's debts – ?'

Mortimer waved a hand, dismissing. 'I can look after that, worry not about trifling matters. The point is, it is yours.' He moved no closer to her but puffed heartily on his fine cigar. 'And therefore can be your dowry to me.'

'Dowry?' Letty jerked back in her chair and raised a hand to her bosom. 'Samuel – could this be a proposal of sorts?'

'I am not a fumbling fifteen-year-old, so I will not pretend to flush with embarrassment.' He smiled, confident that it mattered not a lot if this tack failed. If it succeeded, the ideal set-up for future plans was assured: fuss and disruption at Drumloch would be avoided and he would slip easily into an old Tory house in a promising borough; the romantic and carnal pleasures of so young and alluring a catch would be but a good bonus. But if she refused – as well she might: it was difficult to predict Letty's behaviour – all was not lost. With the help of Halifane and his own attorney the debt claim against Bouchard's estate should readily yield an opening to acquire the property.

'I have a mind to say "yes" without delay,' Letty said, reviewing the last weeks in a rush. 'I may not get a second chance.' The thoughts running through her head were bleak and savage: marriage to an old man would be easy and, by the odds, short. She would have with Mortimer the chance for plenty of rapturous flirtations outside their relationship, that could be judged already by the way he permitted the openly amorous attentions of the likes of Sir David. He had no great style, but he had money. And he had valuable political connections, worthy substitute perhaps for an abundance of Society friends. If she turned him down, what immediate courtship prospects had she? more: what prospects of a home?

'Well, do not leave me dangling like some fish!'

'I thought you had your answer! Yes, my dear – yes, I accept your too kind offer.'

He walked quietly to her and enfolded her in his arms. They kissed and she pulled away to say seriously, 'But can I give you enough, Samuel? A penniless girl with little experience of life.'

He sat her down and addressed her with earnestness. 'Your affection is all I want, my sweet child. And Drumloch. I have a building plan for that area which must get underway soon, to make the best of the summer and autumn weather for construction. I want to establish a Shannonside factory, and I may even convert the manor house. But, for now, we will move there and begin work. Drumloch will be our new base and our home – '

Her expression frosted. 'I shudder to think of Drumloch as home, Samuel. Not again. Not with the murders in its shadow and the purple death around every corner.'

'You exaggerate the reality, m'dear. This hunger that triggers devilry will be gone before the end of this season. You'll see. Another potato crop and all will be well. Please – ' He kissed her again, this time with a persuasive, pleading passion. After a second or two she forgot her reservations and allowed herself enjoy the touch. 'It will not be for long,' he swore. 'A season or two and my work will be done. Then we will take some pretty property in Dorset or Down, and resort to idyllic indolence.'

'But I do hate the boglands and the emptiness of the south. At least there is some pulse of life here, and Belfast is a stone's-throw away.'

'I shall afford you a honeymoon in Venice,' he cajoled.

She hesitated, then melted under his smile. 'You are a beast,' she said.

Mortimer laughed and took her in his arms. He reached down and crushed the letter she had been writing in his fist. 'Forget Donna for now – '

'No!' Letty simpered. 'I wish to play the braggart sister and reveal *all* my splendid fortune. She is not alone in finding a good companion.'

'Another time,' Mortimer insisted, kissing her cheek. 'For now let us celebrate our agreement in the privacy of a good inn. The Essex Café in Lurgan offers the finest cider ham in Ireland and the new season's prawns will be in. The proprietor is a friend of mine and will find us the best table. What say you?'

Drumloch was his.

Mortimer's carriage bumped over the last scrub-clad hill and the panorama of Lough Derg and its lowland banks opened to him. Through the misty haze of an early summer's day his eager eye immediately found the grey manor house, perched at the upper V of the valley, its shadow darkening the Shannon. Elation lifted him. Letty would follow in a week's time, but that thought did not preoccupy or distract him; nothing detracted from this satisfying moment – not the continual sights of death by the roadside, nor the circulating word of renewed blight in the early summer potato crops, nor the living face of destitution in idle farmers from Dernakesh to Drumloch.

Tom Porter, his manager from Lurgan, rode with him on his first trip south and surveyed the land with an expression of pure dejection. ' 'Twill be no easy haul, sir,' Porter said glum-voiced. For two hours at least he had listened to his master's ardent speculation about transferring his interests. 'A scientific examination of the soil will have t'be done before we can trust expansive layin' of flax. The weather here has a reputation for toughness unparalleled, as well.'

'Not flax, I think, Tom.' Mortimer's small eyes grew

large in eagerness. 'Brewing this time. Not relying on the vagaries of the weather but taking in our crop from outside – importing the hops and concentrating ourselves on the factory end of things.'

Tom Porter was not comforted. 'Leaves me a mite outa things then, sir. My craft is turnin' flax. Brewing is a specialist game.'

'Not at all, Tom. No more. Since the government took the heavy controls off hops and replaced the tax on beer with the malt tax clever men have been seeing openings for fortunes in producing beer. But it's being done on too small a scale.' Mortimer balled a fist and shook it before his manager. 'Streamlined factory work we have already seen is the way to fast yield and high profits. That's what we can bring to the midlands. What better place to operate a countrywide concern? We have the Shannon and the Canal within a pitch of us. The terrain is good for access roads. Limerick and Athlone are to north and south, both attracting major road and rail work which is laying the whole country open to us. And the workforce – look.' Mortimer flicked a hand towards the window. 'Thousands upon thousands, Tom, doing nothing except burdening their landlords and paying no rents. How many of them will jump for the chance of regular work? All of 'em! And the neighbouring gentry will thank me – by Jove, they'll thank me. I'll be offering industry and the prosperity it brings to this corner of the world.' He sank in his seat and watched the gateway of the manor house open up. 'Cheap labour, Tom, and an opportunity to earn money and distinction fast. Saviour of the West, they'll call me.' He laughed. 'By God, it could not have worked better for me. The timing is right. People will accredit me with single-handedly ending the famine, for as the blight fades Mortimer Breweries will come into thrusting power.'

'You'll want me to canvass a workforce for the construction?'

'Yes. And we'll follow the example set by those northern land owners who kindly arranged assisted packets to America for those tenant families who caused problems.

Anyone who opposes our developments will go. That's the choice for Drumloch's tenants. Construction work or a passage to America . . .' He grinned. 'In the nicest possible way, of course. Remember, we have the good of the community only at heart. We will want their votes, mind, in other fields. So that is our charter.'

'It might not be so easy. Industrial concerns and farm life do not much mix. There are traditions of hundreds of years in force.'

'Bah, these people are uneducated, ignorant peasants, Tom. People used to deprivation and hard life. They listen to the crack of a whip, believe me.' He winked. 'A Scots-born Englishman like yourself would never understand. But have confidence in my planning. A year's tough work, and we will have oru empire.'

CHAPTER THIRTY-FOUR

Newark, New Jersey filled Donna's heart with a tangle of emotions. On one hand it allowed her a new lease of life, banishing oppression and the everyday reminders of suffering; on the other it denied her some ambiguous ingredient that made Ireland dear.

Not ten miles west of lower Manhattan, its contrast to raucous, rambling New York was acute – and welcome. After the din and crush of Fifth Avenue and the tinsel brashness of Broadway the new city was a pastoral oasis, built without the confusing affectation of Greek and Georgian architecture. Its ranches and houses bluffed some Gothic grace but the predominant legacy was the whitewood simplicity of the Pesayak Towne settlers of two hundred years before.

The Cabbot base of Milford Ranch stood on the banks of the Passaic River in good view of the massive leather tanning factories commissioned and constructed twelve years before under Paul's control. They were, Donna was to discover, rather minor manifestations of the prowess of Cabbot Industries. Everywhere she journeyed, it seemed, Emma or Mamma Josephine was pointing out further Cabbot monuments – rail bridges, mills, theatre halls – and Donna was soon in little doubt that her guardian and friend stood to inherit a dominion of very real wealth and sway.

For the four months at Newark a week never passed at Milford Ranch where esteemed guests were not introduced to the household. The British Consul visited, an Indian potentate came to sup, lords, ladies and lieutenants trundled endlessly to the luxurious drawing-rooms. Paul Cabbot was absent on business often and Donna was left to Emma's verbose company but when he returned for his habitual weekend of entertaining he took special joy in boasting her presence to the stream of famed or influential Irish-Americans. They in turn were impressed by the arrival in their midst of a true-blood colleen with hair of corn gold and eyes as wild and lovely as the blue Tipperary sky. In a short time she won many hearts.

'These people are important to me – and to Cabbot Industries,' Paul explained to her. 'Some of them are closely involved with the famous Tammany Hall movement, an Irish community spearhead which virtually runs the city of New York and supports its own shadow government.' Donna's eyes widened in disbelief but Cabbot was serious. 'No other immigrant community is organised like the Irish – they look after their own militia and their own fire service even. And those few men you have met sit in controlling positions, heads of precincts and so-called District Leaders, and they decide which company executes which job, or whose tender goes through.'

'Amazing – and many seem to be ill-educated Irish land folk. How different their lot is from their fellows at home!'

Cabbot shrugged. 'Be not misled. These are survivors, the top of the pack of many, many hundreds of thousands who come here and work in piggeries and gutters. But if they do not have fortune, it is true that they have power – and all the indications are that that power faces no diminution.'

315

Donna was pensive. 'Perhaps this will be the new Ireland, the home of land workers and peasants displaced by greedy gentry.'

Cabbot saw his advantage. He took her hand and pressed it to his heart. 'You are right – New Ireland! And what more suitable home for you? A fresh and healthy new world without the threatening gloom of Tipperary . . .'

Those conversations, oft repeated, prepared Donna in some ways for Cabbot's suddenly determined romantic onslaught and the intervention of Mamma Josephine at Christmas. Still active in the business despite age and weakening eyesight, Josephine Cabbot divided her time principally between the family Fifth Avenue mansion and the company headquarters in Washington Square, viewing Milford as a holiday retreat only. As a consequence Donna saw little of her for weeks on end and the casual, distant flavour of their relationship did not much change. But, no matter how tenuous their association, Mamma Josephine's penchant for hard talking vented itself with its customary ease. The week before Christmas she arrived for the vacation, and wasted little time in cornering her guest and facing up to facts.

'I have been thinking, my dear,' she announced as she found Donna alone, 'that you and Paul must settle some arrangement for marriage soon.' When Donna frowned Josephine plunged on: 'Oh come now, you cannot have supposed anything other was on the cards. Paul has been slavering over you for six months. Since the day you two met he's been singing your praises, praying for my approval. And, having seen you among our kind and watched your manners, I think – yes! – yes, you'll do just fine.'

'I am glad my presence pleases you, Mamma Josephine, but – '

'But what!' Josephine was rattled. 'No buts, my dear. You are past twenty-one. You are a bright and intelligent girl. You must know what Paul has been thinking – damn his eyes if he hasn't already spilled it out!'

'Of course I know the affection he holds for me. And, indeed, I cherish him as a dear, dear friend.' She looked

316

away sheepishly. 'You must forgive my frankness – but I have no wish to be looked upon as some possession or artifact that an "arrangement" must be made for.' She paused to observe Josephine's reaction and saw bland apathy. 'At times in my life I have felt like a bartered bag of salt.'

Josephine reflected. 'You mean Coney Island?'

'What is Coney Island?'

'He hasn't told you? Coney's the Brooklyn island that is being planned out as a major holiday resort. Massive construction and as much as three million dollars will go into it. Paul is scouting for the right tender and wants to swing certain key people.'

'Irish people?' Donna was remembering their earlier talks and the myriad faces introduced to her at weekend parties.

'It's unreasonable to feel "used", my dear – if that's the word. No point in prating, but the fact is, Paul holds you in high regard and whether you assist with his Irish connections or not will not alter one iota. And a lady like you will acknowledge the importance of etiquette. You have been with us for many months. Your troublesome health is at last settled. You have met our acquaintances and grown to know our family. So the time is right. Decorum demands.'

The tone of the old woman's delivery was such that Donna could not help but laugh. How unlike Paul she was! Dear sensitive Paul would buckle at the knees under any like assault. But Donna remained quite cool-headed. 'Marriage is something Paul and I may well discuss,' she said. 'But I am a believer in following the truth of the heart. Social conventions never much impressed me.'

Challenged by a candour that matched her own, Josephine's stony stare seemed to crumble. 'Your life's your own,' she came back. 'But the world is not, regrettably, a continuous vacation place, a continuous Milford. Cabbot Industries roll on and Paul must get on with his career. This last year has seen him waste too much time on silly secular affairs.'

'I must speak to him soon, then – lest my presence here

encroaches on his work. I would not like to think, quite truly, that I provided a worrying distraction for him.'

At that Josephine thawed and moved to squeeze Donna's hand. Her leathery face split in a smile. 'You will learn, my dear, that Americans are the free talkers of the world. There is no substitute for crisp fact! Then, perhaps, you will look more kindly on an old bag like me.'

'True talking's a virtue,' Donna said sincerely.

A few days later, the day before Christmas Eve, Cabbot insisted on pursuing his subtler course by taking Donna to dinner at the palatial Astor House facing New York's City Hall, reputed to be the best-appointed and most expensive hotel in the world. Here he revived at last the subject of matrimony. 'It would seem the time is right,' he bungled out over the lemon mousse, 'for you have become very much a part of life here. You like it in Newark, you've said yourself, and you've seen that we are none of us craven varlets.'

Donna's eye tripped round the domed gold room with its marble floor, *recherché* carvings and elite diners. 'I can believe that. Cabbot Industries are grander than I ever imagined. The price of the meal I've just devoured would buy me garments galore for a year, I'd wager.'

'Or a trousseau.'

She set down her spoon and regarded him seriously. 'Have I proved myself so valuable to you in this Coney venture that you wish to fetter me now for further negotiations?'

He assumed a hurt frown. 'Donna, how can you say such things? Mamma has spoken to you?' She nodded. 'Coney is very much a pot of gold at the bottom of someone's rainbow, I'll agree. And I do want it for Cabbot Industries. But do not for a minute think that my interest in you exists or depends on that alone, on the assistance your presence might bring.' His plea was spoken cold-voiced and Donna was suddenly reminded of Josephine at her worst. How in her heart did she *know* he did not truly love her? What differed in the passion of his eyes from Colum's?

Colum.

The wandering thought, once in her head, conquered all else. Dear Colum, the soul of so many dreams. What had become of him this last year? Had he found full happiness in wedlock with Cara?. . . Every day, every night, she wondered . . .

'Donna . . . are you listening to me?'

She snapped back to her senses, to the genteel hum of Astor life. 'I'm sorry, Paul. I was thinking how uncertain of the prospect of marriage I have always been.'

His mouth drew down. 'But you accepted my offer of America. You must have known what was in my heart. Come, do not try to hide it.' His eyes became worried. 'Unless, of course, I have failed in making my devotion properly known?'

She took his hand. 'No, Paul. I could ask for no more in a friend than you have given. I owe my life to you.'

'Then marriage must follow.' He returned the pressure of her hand and lifted it to kiss it quickly. 'Forget Coney,' he muttered, 'forget baseless business reasons. I *want you*, Donna.'

But do you love me? she was thinking. Love, in the sense of a passion of the blood, of the soul and mind and senses. Do you lie awake at night and weep? Do you dream in fever and wake in sweat? She checked herself, feeling a strangled sob in her throat, confused. She tried to empty her brain, but found Colum's ghost too stubborn.

Cabbot called the waiter and ordered the finest champagne. He took masterful pride in announcing, 'It is Christmastime – a time of humanity and good deeds.' The champagne arrived and he swept the iced bottle from its bucket. 'And here is blessed French wine, the drink of sound business deals and of lovers.' He took her glass and poured a measure. 'My proposal of marriage is in that glass. I will say no more, for everything has been said.' He pushed the glass towards her. 'You may judge it as you like – desert it as it stands, or toast our future happiness.'

She hesitated, then cupped the glass and raised it to her lips.

Cabbot's eyes sparkled and he sighed. 'My darling, you

will never regret this moment. We need waste little time. Our engagement can be announced on Christmas morn and we can marry in late spring, as soon as the weather cheers up and you can step out in the prettiest lace.'

'No,' she said. 'Let us marry sooner. I want it to be a blustery dark grey day. Wind and rain. An Irish day.'

'My love, he acceded, and he held his glass aloft.

Immediately preparations for a March wedding – the nearest justifiably decent date – began. No one's enthusiasm could keep pace with Paul Cabbot's. A twelve hour day pursuing the fortunes of Cabbot Industries did not, apparently, sap all his energies and, like a birthday child, his unbounded jollity was showered upon everyone. He could not do enough to assist Donna's arrangements. The best milliners, dressmakers and shoe fitters in Manhattan were directed to Milford and Fifth, laden with design sketches and exquisite sample materials; Paul's favoured architect visited with plans for a modern marriage home; jewellery, perfume and intimate gifts flowed. Emma soared to a trying mood of sustained excitement and even Mamma Josephine allowed mellow moments, gracing Milford with more frequent visits and addressing Donna, with the atrocious American endearment of 'sweetheart'.

Though Donna was not kept closely informed of the trials and triumphs of Cabbot Industries, throughout February she became aware of a heightening of mood and expectation in the household which, on top of the marriage fuss, enkindled almost stupefying exhilaration. Some majestic deal was at hand, she sensed, and the Cabbots were steeling themselves in thrilled anticipation.

The week of the wedding the facts spilled out.

The first of March had been greeted with snow storms and Cabbot took Donna for a saunter by the frozen Passaic at noon. She had not expected him home from Manhattan that day but knew by his early and boisterous arrival that the occasion was one for celebration. The air was sharp despite a breaking sun, but bracing rather than bitter. Newark was alive with happy sounds: children skating on riverside pools; vendors over their braziers, stirring and scooping the hot potatoes; the creaking wheels of basinettes, as nursemaids took their charges for midday strolls. A richly happy day, Donna thought, a day for pleasant news and quiet emotions. She wondered what dramatic revelations Cabbot had to make and shied away from her own explosive news. The serenity of this day would not last long, she knew.

'Mamma brought me the news last night in Washington Square,' he told her. 'Our tender for Coney looked uncertain for a while, but a few weeks ago the word filtering back became à lot more positive.' He clapped his gloved hands. 'Yesterday the decision was given: the job will be ours.'

'I'm delighted for you.'

'It will be a vast project, if all indications bear up. Our basic construction work is merely a drop in the ocean, but once we have our foot in – well, it's a million dollar commission for Cabbot Industries.'

She felt there was more she should say, but words deserted her. Cabbot recognised no hesitancy and stopped before her. His cheeks were vivid red, whether from excitement or cold she could not tell. 'I am confident the announcement of our marriage helped the Coney deal. The Brooklyn borough manager I brought to the house liked you enormously.' He kissed her forehead. 'You presented the vital good impression at the right time, my darling. We *won.*'

'You deserve it, Paul. You work very hard, and toiled to win the friendship of those Irish-Americans.'

He pressed that aside. '*We* succeeded, that's the main thing. Mamma is ecstatic. But – ' He held her away from him and his tone became serious. 'The more important news is that this commission interferes a trifle with our wedding plan.' He looked properly ashamed. 'Urgent talks with the borough council must begin tomorrow. They will take some two weeks. It's damned inconvenient, Donna, but it really will encroach a little on our time. If you will permit, I will put back the ceremony till Tuesday week.' He hugged her. 'A liberty, I know,

321

but what's a week in a lifetime?'

'Paul, there's something I have to tell you.' She wedged her elbows between their bodies as he pulled her to him. It was ridiculous, unreasonable, she told herself, but she felt guilty for what she was about to say. He edged back, the hot steam of his breath clouding the area between them.

'Out with it, then. I do so hate to see a frown of such severity darken your pretty face.' He laughed without conviction.

'I must go back to Ireland.' Her eyes fell from his. 'As soon as possible.'

There was a soundless pause. The world held its breath. 'If you want a honeymoon in –'

'Not a honeymoon, Paul. I wish to return alone.' She glanced up to him, eyes fearful. 'And please do not plead to stop me. When I first agreed to come to Newark I did so on the sole basis of being allowed my freedoms. I told you I may want to return and you accepted that.'

The heat of his face faded and he stood back from her, pale and intense. 'Yes, but this was before marriage was settled on. You were weak and ill at the time –'

'No, Paul. Do not attempt to dissuade me. I know what I said and I want to go now.'

'You are chastising me for permitting business to intrude upon domestic affairs.'

'No, that is not true.'

'I don't believe you. Last week you joked about it and now –' He moved to enfold her again. His expression was troubled. 'Please, Donna. Realise that Coney –'

'It's nothing to do with Coney.' She turned away and moved down the path to the river's edge. He followed, bemused. 'I had a letter this morning. From Letitia. Its content shocked and annoyed me. In it she detailed papa's death –'

'You should have said.'

Donna shook her head, revealing no emotion. 'I was sorry for that, but I confess no torrent of sadness engulfed me. But the circumstances of his demise gave rise to events which I find unacceptable. You see, Letty's planned elopement having failed – as you know – she settled in with Samuel Mortimer, our mother's foster-brother, in Lurgan. Now it seems with papa's death and the tragic news that the child Serle has vanished, believed kidnapped by his nurse in London, Letty and Mortimer have taken residence in Drumloch.'

'I don't envy them – not with conditions on the land after another season's blight.'

'That's neither here nor there, Paul. But the point is, Letty is planning marriage to Mortimer and both are viewing Drumloch as a new home. Mortimer has transferred residence and begun a reconstruction programme that will mean redeveloping the manor lands for factories. In her note Letty says that work begins as soon as the wintry weather passes.'

Cabbot was clearly no more wise to Donna's reasons for departure. 'I should think quite a few beggars will be glad of the work in Drumloch factories.'

'What about the people whose lands will be swallowed up? – the farmers who have occupied those plots all these years? People whose fathers and grandfathers serve Drumloch. What say have they had in the matter? Are they agreeable to this radical change, or have they been evicted heartlessly like so many others before them?' She stared Cabbot with fierce eyes. 'Those are answers I must have, for I share the responsibility of Drumloch. Letty may think I am too far away to bother to interfere, but she reckons without my fondness for the estate. Whatever her interests there, I too have my rights to a portion of Drumloch. Mortimer cannot build without consulting me.'

Cabbot sighed and kicked the ground to stir life in his freezing feet. 'May I see this letter of your sister's?'

Donna blushed. 'I-I'm sorry, I discarded it.'

He eyed her with suspicion, then shrugged. 'All right. Buy Letty out.'

'Paul, you do not understand what I am saying. *I care* about that estate, about the people. If papa is gone, and Serle too, responsibility for its *future* falls equally to Letty and me. I will not give her a free hand to rule and raze the place.'

323

'Very well.' His ebullient humour had died completely and he spoke in a brutal tone that mimicked his mother. 'I will accompany you again and – '

'No. I am sorry, Paul, but I intend to be adamant about this. The row is mine and mine alone. The call to return is in my heart and I must honour it – alone. I have my maid and she is a mature and capable woman. I will look after myself well.'

'When will you return?' When she did not immediately answer he took her arm firmly. 'I must know, Donna, because I have mamma and all our weekend friends to face – '

'Your Irish-American people who find me so . . . impressive?'

'Don't be cruel. You know what I mean.'

'I will return . . . as soon as I satisfy myself that all is well at Drumloch. Letty and I will reach some agreement over the property, I'm sure.'

'It breaks my heart to hear all this, Donna. With just days till our marriage.'

'I'm sorry, Paul. But you would rather a contented bride by your side than one whose heart is heavy, I'm certain.' She touched his cheek a moment.

'Are you sure you have told me everything?'

'All that matters, believe me.'

'How I shall miss you.' He swung an arm around her waist. 'A part of my brain urges me to stop you, but another part recalls the pledges I made in Ireland.' He whistled a sigh. 'But how shall I survive without you?'

'You have all those important contracts and the Coney plans to occupy you,' she said without sarcasm. 'You will survive.'

It was dishonest, immoral, but he had to know.

At dead of night Cabbot used the housekeeper's key and entered Donna's dressing-room. He knew she kept notepaper and correspondence in her work reticule and sought that on the dresser. He found it and, under candlelight, checked its contents. Letty's long letter lay crumpled at the bottom. With care he spread it out, flattening the creases with his sleeve.

The gist was much as she had said – mainly about papa's death and Mortimer's building plans.

His intuition had been wrong then. Donna had spoken in truth. Her plans were well-founded, straightforward. A stab of remorse cut his thoughts and he went to crush the paper aside. As his fingers flexed his eye caught the penultimate paragraph. Through angry narrowed eyes he read:

. . . Even Yuletide merriment did not mollify me as I arrived from Lurgan and saw how dreadfully little Drumloch had changed. Ugh! You will never know! The water still freezes in the pipes at the smallest hint of soft frost and the farms are just as glum. Why, yesterday I even saw the grim familiar face of Colum Devlin, soulless and disinterested as ever, intent upon his toil . . .

Colum Devlin! How had he known? What factors hinted this? – Donna's wary gaze today? Or Donna's ever-wary gaze? Or, in truth, was it more? Was it the recurring dream that haunted his nights? – the memory of that day long ago on a wind-swept Irish hillside when he had seen them together, an uncouth farming gossoon and a wild Irish rose, as perfect a vision together as sea and sky.

Silently he screwed up the paper and rearranged her bag. Then, on light feet but with heavy heart, he left the dark room. Perhaps his doubts were premature, he told himself. That reference to the boy was oblique, might represent nothing. He was over-reacting, behaving like a juvenile. Over and over he told himself there was no cause for concern, that her marriage promise was made and that was that. Over and over, until reason muffled instinct.

CHAPTER THIRTY-FIVE

The four weeks of exhausting journey were for Donna an adventure that would lead her into the past. At the last minute Paul Cabbot had assailed her, plying censure and plea, and that had started the venture on a sour note, but by the time they found the high seas and an unseasonally fierce sun beat down on the steamer's decks, America was forgotten. The void was filled with intoxicating remembrances of Ireland, recollections of her first adult sights of the country, and of Colum. At Queenstown in the cove of Cork tropical sunshine welcomed her and the weariness of the sea trip receded. From the moment her shoe scraped the green spongy turf beyond the pier her heart was at peace and it was as if Newark had never existed. Here the world was full of brilliant light and black shadows, the wet smells of pine and peat, and the endless chatter of garrulous children. Instantly Donna was at home. Up till this moment she had always nervously felt herself an alien here, oppressed by papa's demands and by the strictures of her class; but far foreign travel and a near-fatal illness had matured her. Now she drove through the undulating hills relaxed and confident, and she waved to washerwomen and gave pennies to beggars without fear of reproof. Old Midgie her maid of four months, a self-possessed Bostonian spinster with a kindly soul, withheld comment, openly impressed by her lady's ease of manner in so bleak a landscape.

Ostlers and innkeepers between Cork and Tipperary enlightened her on events of the past year. The blight persisted, they explained, and famine swept the farming world. Decent-hearted gentry had themselves introduced local relief schemes, but it was no secret that thousands were dying every week and thousands more took the emigrant route. The pattern of rural life was broken, and Irish society would never be the same. 'Every week there is talk of a countrywide organised civil rebellion in planning,' a spirit vault owner in Limerick told Donna, 'but its impact now would be nothing. Already the emigrant-brokers have won half the supporters of rebellion to *their* cause, and the gentry have accustomed themselves to bickering and strife.' Knowledgeable of the split in O'Connell's ranks and the aims of the emergent force of Dillon, Mitchel and their new-founded Young Ireland 'Confederation', Donna pressed for information:

'Is there serious likelihood of armed revolt?'

'Judge by the counter measures the government is planning to take, Miss. A new Treason Felony Act is to be introduced, toughening penalties for those who lend a hand by taking up the gun. Deportation and hanging are the cards the government plays.' The old sage grinned. 'The high 'n mighty swear there can never be sufficient unity among farm folk for a successful rising – but the government fears speak for themselves.'

With that dark omen ringing in her ears Donna crossed into Tipperary and made for Drumloch. The last hours of travel were the longest but finally the boundary was passed and the familiar old plots unrolled, jaded and sad-looking, some ambitiously planted once again, others disused. Donna started forward in surprise when she saw the manor house ahead. Mortimer had wasted little time. Already a portion of the east wing was dismantled, the exposed broken rooms gaping to the sun. A scaffolding framed the incomplete work and a handful of busy labourers toiled, jeered from the ground by unhappy groups of their fellows. Even at this distance the dull staccato of axes and hammers was audible, chipping down the old stonework.

Donna's intentions had been quite different, but the aspect of the house shocked her and she craned out the window and ordered the driver to make for the forecourt at all speed.

An assortment of irate mongrel dogs ran down the manor house steps to greet the carriage, followed directly by old housekeeper and companion, Nurse Shine. Shuffling painfully on arthritic feet the old woman threw her hands to the sky in amazement. 'Be God, is this a vision or is it you? My little lass! *Is naire orm*! Shame on me indeed, for I didn't recognise those moonshine curls from the drawing-room window.' She embraced Donna warmly. 'Didn't I think, m'dear, I'd never live to see your pretty face agin. With your illness, and your old papa passing on – and the dear house closing down!'

Donna's eye ran over the house façade. 'Then Letty came to save the day?'

'Ain't that strange!' Nurse whispered. 'Not for me to pass judgement on my mistress, but I nigh could not believe that she'd take the hand of Samuel Mortimer. Quite improper, I thought of it at first – and her living under the same roof with him, as though they were proper wed.' She clucked noisily. 'And no wedding till May, I'll have you know.'

'Letty was always one for finding her own way of doing things.' Donna hugged Nurse swiftly and shrugged off a grim frown. 'Later I shall tell you all the adventures of this last year, Nursie – but now I must see Letty and this Mortimer. Are they about?'

'Without introduction you come?' Nurse shook her head. 'Whatever will Miss Letty say!'

They walked through the Great Hall, Donna feeling much the trespasser, and into the old library. Mortimer turned from the window where he had been surveying the groups of on-lookers ringing the scaffolds and supported himself with a firm grip on the back of a chair. He forced a dazzling embarrassed smile. 'My dear Donna! What a surprise. Letty gave me no hint – '

Donna explained herself in a few short sentences, outlining Letty's correspondence and her steam voyage. Mortimer made a great fuss of drawing her a chair and pouring his best port.

'Had we but known we could have readied a room and fixed a greeting party. Letty should have informed me of her communication to you.' His voice was grave. 'She never said a word.'

'Slipped her mind, no doubt.'

He handed her a drink and sat far away from her, perched at a table's edge. 'The last Letty said, she believed you and your Mister Cabbot had exchanged vows by now in New York. She was very happy for you, and said Cabbot was a fine, upstanding gent.'

'He is that.' Donna felt a fast pulse in her forehead; her blood was boiling and there were sentiments she must speak. Mortimer began gabbling, expressing sorrow for her father, but Donna cut in: 'Respectfully, sir, I must make issue straight away of your rebuilding plans here. I perceive some work has commenced already.'

'Indeed, indeed.' He became animated. 'I have sketched plans here I must show you. You will be very impressed. Drumloch's countenance will be revitalised. The lands will become bountiful once again and local folk will never have to worry about blight. There will be work in the factories –'

'Factories!' Donna breathed a short laugh. 'Now that I hear it from your own mouth I believe it!' She stood and set aside the almost-full glass. 'Mister Mortimer –'

'Call me uncle, pray do.'

'Are you aware that, after papa and in absence of Serle, both Letty and I equally inherit this estate? No will has been found, I know, but that is the way the law goes. Now, whilst I see the direction of your interests following a marriage to my sister, I must point out that nothing can be undertaken here without my agreement.'

Mortimer froze. He gazed into Donna's lovely face and saw all the grim determination of her father. The sequence of recent events had been so perfect, but he had never ceased to fear this moment. Donna all along had been the area of danger, the worrisome unknown quantity.

'I have no wish to enrage you, dear girl,' he laughed. 'By all means I am prepared to welcome your blessing – or pay you some agreed settlement, if that is your wish. Cash perhaps, or a share in my new concern –'

'Tell me, please, what advances you have already made?' The hard eyes gave warning of aggravation. 'Or would Letty prefer to talk?'

'This is principally *my* development,' Mortimer returned tartly. 'Letty can tell you no more than I can. What I project is a brewery complex designed to make the best use of these lands and the Shannon and the new Dublin to Limerick rail line. This house will become headquarters, with a new wing designed as business offices – '

'A task you have already started?'

'Yes. First things first. It seemed correct and I wish to avail of the fine weather. I am offering good employment to those redundant potato farmers who would otherwise starve. It's quite a relief for some poor souls, I'm sure. The labourers I have engaged this last month come from as far away as Lord Estelle's. They are families whose original livelihood would hold them no more. The gentry are delighted – '

'But there is resistance to your project from some farmers, I detect? Those groups outside – as I passed I heard them call abuse to the men on the scaffolding.'

'Some are unhappy, naturally.' Mortimer shrugged and spread innocent hands. 'They are dyed-in-the-wool farmers who claim they intend to transfer their tillage grounds to pasture or whatever. But you know the landed peasants as well as I do. That is fanciful talk. They are lazy, they will not strive to beat this hunger themselves. People like Middleton and Estelle are delighted for the changes I bring.'

'I can see how they might be.'

'And one must not be thwarted by those who disagree.' Mortimer was lost in his own enthusiasm now. 'The simplest and most efficient answer in that case is to get rid of them. Band them together and ship them out. Banish opposition and force a settled peace.'

'To where might one ship them, pray tell?'

'America. It's being done already up north by many land owners who cannot sustain no rents and constant death on

330

their plots. Simply herd the no-gooders together, charter a cheap packet, and rush them off!'

'I cannot see that farmers who want to work their plots here will too readily agree to join such a scheme.'

'The police will help,' Mortimer laughed. 'I've had old Inspector McClune to tea. He's indicated his absolute desire to assist my plan. A list is being drawn at present of all those unwilling to partake in the factory work which is scheduled for May.'

Before Donna could launch back at Mortimer Letty entered, gushing apology with thin feigned gaiety. 'How fat and smug you look, sister,' she cooed. 'But unchanged still. You still spring sly surprises, it seems.'

Donna returned an equal wry greeting, adding the concise story of her circumstances in Newark and the whim to voyage and concluding: 'But, having read your letter, I thought it essential to travel home now and put you in the picture. The fact is, Letty, I cherish my own plans for Drumloch, and therefore cannot extend permission for a projected factory.'

'*Permission*?' Letty blurted, red-faced. 'Dear sister, remember *my* position too. I can oppose you fairly, as this is as much mine.'

Mortimer jumped into the temporary breach. 'Let us avoid silly argument at all costs.' He turned to Donna with a careful expression of genial ease. 'Donna, you should know that *I* own perhaps an equal amount of this property. I have not clarified myself legally, but I know you are aware of the debt owed me by your father. So, in truth, part of this is mine – '

Letty rushed in: 'Anyway, I cannot imagine what plans for Ireland Donna might have. Didn't wise Cabbot sell out, and haven't you got all the comforts you may need in New York? From all I've heard the Cabbots want for nothing. So you have your glories.'

Donna rose to object but Mortimer intruded again. 'Please! Let us act sensibly. Donna – you have had a long, trying trip and are no doubt tired. Much has changed in Ireland since you have been here and if you knew the facts

331

your attitude might be different. And, as well, you have not even seen the drawings of my plans. Please. Allow yourself a little time with us. Listen to my manager's projections and mull over the facts.'

'A day or two will not alter my outlook. I feel a sense of responsibility to Drumloch estate and I must satisfy that.'

'Then I think you will realise the best way of doing just that is by changing the situation radically and abandoning the past.'

'I'm a believer in the past, sir. That might sound romantic and idealistic, but it's what I feel. The past is a part of the future. One must keep its lessons in mind all the time.'

'Allow a few days.'

'I *intend* to stay a while,' Donna replied brusquely, crossing to the door to summon her maid and luggage. 'In my heart this is home.'

A tangle of emotions choked Letty. The sight of Donna, full of rosy health and dressed like a queen, imperiously straddling two domains – the worlds of Drumloch and America – maddened her. She screwed her eyes shut. It was painful to think how things might have been different. If only papa had approved of Adam and permitted honourable wedlock; if only *she* had gamed for Cabbot . . . The trouble was, she confessed to herself, the hopelessness of papa's position had been recognised too late and she had wasted herself on frivolity with the likes of Rob. She had misjudged, and suffered for it. Now, back residing in miserable Drumloch these four months the full impact of miscalculation had flooded her being. Mortimer was decent and tolerable, but she was bright enough to see that his commitment here might mean residence for many, many years. She was also clever enough to realise she had no alternatives but to accept that. The hard truth was, in spite of the tribulations of Adam's and papa's death, she had advanced herself not one inch from the slimy turf of Tipperary. But Donna's gamble *had* proved good. And yet that was not enough for her. *What more did she want*? Letty cursed the day bold pride made her scribble that forbidden informative note to Newark.

The girls exchanged a menacing stare, then Letty gathered herself and rose. 'Well, let us hope the battle is over with soon. We would not want to obtrude on your wedding plans, Donna. I'm sure Mister Cabbot anxiously awaits your return.'

Dejected by her reception but unable to contain her impatience Donna insisted on riding out alone even though afternoon was fading to evening.

She made directly for the Devlins' river farm, but disappointment met her. Little had altered since that day, more than a year ago, when her quest had been frustrated by Anderson's story. The cottage still lay in sullen disrepair, the flags of its small yard darkened by thistly weeds. The only obvious change was that the windows had been shuttered and a rough boarded door locked into place. Donna's heart fell. In tremulous excitement she ran round the cottage and surveyed the potato plots. The evidence of cultivation was here all right, but subtle changes in the fencing and shape of the plots did nothing to allay fears. It appeared as if the nextdoor tenancy, formerly the Duffs', had been recently occupied and its plots worked as one with the Devlins'. Did that indicate the presence of some newcomer? Or was there still the chance . . . ?

She mounted and made for Teggie Kelly's farm. Finding no one about her immediate next thought was for Anthony Anderson. If anyone knew – and understood – Colum's situation, he would. Whipping her mount to a gallop she angled back to Drumloch, avoiding the river path on impulse and taking the circuitous road that would bring her round the front of the house and through the Doon Lawn. The sun had started its final descent. Silver-green grass and the steel of the Shannon reflected and splintered the glow, startling the eye with rainbow hues. But Donna rode unseeing, her feelings numb. A stark question loomed again and again: What sense had there been in pursuing the past? But reason and sense did not come into it. Over a year a storm of emotions had built up, and Letty's note had merely provided an outlet that forced new action.

The fir forest stood ahead and Donna had to choose a route around it. The shorter path would take her back to the river banks and keep her in sight of the manor house but suddenly she had no wish to look upon its shattered face any longer. She pulled the horse sharply northwards and turned for the forest shoulder and the barren desolation of the ancient ringfort. Her brain was set on Anderson but at the last minute as she passed the dip of ground that led to the Doon a voice of memory called her and she reined in. Her mind revived the events of distant times and a tear blurred her eye. Slowly she headed for the valley of the old fort. Night was coming down but here timeless daylight was trapped in a bubble. The ground soon became too soft under hoof and she dismounted to walk the last yards.

When she reached the slope of the fort her breath died in her throat and she faltered a step. She shook her head and blinked fast as though to dispel a dream. It was uncanny, incredible, but the past was truly alive and recalled happenings were unfolding anew. Colum was here, not a day older nor a speck different, sitting in deep contemplation on the swell of a cairn, his head resting on the heels of his hands.

She remained still for many minutes, wary of hallucination. Then her horse shuddered in chill and the vision at the cairn was alerted. He twisted to her, and his jaw fell slack. '*Dia liom*.' A hand flew protectively to his chest. He found his feet and moved towards her. 'Can it be you?'

''Tis me, unchanged,' she said and she walked down to meet him in the dell.

His eyes devoured her, disbelieving. Unchanged she was not. How plump and well she looked, he thought, fresh as dew, without a shade of pride or affectation. Good fortune had befallen her indeed, and he noted the golden torque that adorned her neck and the sapphires on her fingers that matched her deep blue eyes. Her lapis-lazuli brocade gown, under a miniver cape, set off an impression of queenly wealth. She looked mightily powerful, and yet she was shaking.

'I could scarce believe the word I heard, that you were

334

among these plots again,' she said.

'I am not long returned.' His mouth working busily but he seemed to find no more words. They stared each other, lost in recollection. Finally she said, 'This is still your haven for meditation?'

'Aye.' He pulled his eyes from hers to regard the ring of stones. 'I come here to remember, and it soothes me.' As though his knees would hold him no longer he flopped onto a jutting rock. 'I was grieved to hear of the Sir's death,' he said. ' 'Tis said the circumstances were tragic indeed.'

'And I was sorry to hear about your father's.'

He nodded. 'I heard you came to visit after he passed.' He paused to add, 'With Mister Cabbot. I was sorry to have missed you.'

She sat stiffly by him. Letty's Newark letter came to mind. There had been no mention of Colum's wife and that had somehow appeared significant four weeks ago. Letty was the sort who would note such things. Donna shook herself, appalled. What was she hoping? That Cara had fallen to the purple death? Dare she ask? 'No mention has been made of . . . your wife. Have you . . . wed yet?'

Momentary humour touched his eyes. 'No time for weddin' in Liverpool. One goes there to toil and earn a good purse.'

'You worked in Liverpool for a time? And what of Cara Duff?'

His brows curved up. 'What of her? She settled in Galway, and hoped to miss the workhouse.'

A pang of joy struck Donna and she took hold of Colum's hand suddenly. Alarm showed in his dark eyes. 'I sensed it in my bones,' she said. 'Why did I not listen? You did not wed Cara after all. You laboured for money and returned here to resume your farm and rebuild the herd that had been stolen?'

Puzzled, he pulled back from her but left his hand in hers. 'Wed Cara? Why should I do that? She was no more than dear friend to me and I tended her and took her to Cleggan when she desired to go.'

'Rob told me quite another story – and it seems I fed my

335

doubts on malicious untruths.' She reflected, gazing off. 'He was jealous of us then, frustrated that his affections for Letty found no equal return. He wanted to step between our friendship.'

A frown creased Colum's forehead. Donna's words unsettled him. After the incident of the pirated herd Rob had existed in a grey and mysterious shroud in his thoughts. The smallest grain of suspicion had been planted then, but had never been allowed take root. 'Is it true that you eagerly accompanied Mister Cabbot to foreign places? There was talk of the fever in the manor house, but no one knew for certain.'

'There was fever, and I was laid low for a time. But – yes, I did quite consentingly go away with Paul Cabbot.' A sob of emotion was audible. 'I did so for many reasons, not least of which being that I believed you gone and wed. Rob told me – '

'Rob took pleasure in informing *me* of *your* departure with Cabbot. He was eager to imply the nature of your bond of affection.' His bared teeth flashed in an expression that was quite brutal. 'It's an astounding thought, but I would not be surprised if – ' The words trailed. The most painstaking inquiries since his return had brought him no nearer to solving the herd mystery. Much as he would like to indict McClune and see him suffer for it, the evidence had not been borne up. But could it have been Rob after all? Here was proof of malicious spite. The motive? Colum recalled Letty's indecent blackmail on the river bank, and Donna's admission of Rob's involvement with her sister. Had Rob learnt of that incident? He spat. ''Tis no wonder my foster-brother's path keeps him far from Drumloch since the Sir's death.'

Donna told the story of Rob's Dover escapade and Colum sighed dismal resignation. 'He has purchased payment for his own sins, then,' he whispered. 'And the high life will slink further from his grasp.'

'You come back to work your farm alone, then?'

'That was one of my reasons. With what little I'd saved in Liverpool I intended to give myself a start, buy some sheep maybe and start over. But since Christmas circumstances have not been happy. Drumloch is in tatters. Many, many farms have been vacated, left to rot by emigrant farmers. Squatters are in here and there and plots have been re-drawn willy-nilly. All this has been crowned by the arrival of Samuel Mortimer with Letty.'

'I know his plans.'

'Aye, but do you know his ruthlessness? Sir Redmond was problem enough in his last years, but this man is a thousand times worse. For generations the Devlins have worked those river plots, but what's Mortimer's answer to my desire to continue that tradition? – transportation, by God!'

'You are among those who have objected to redevelopment?'

'That's a question you know you need not address to me. I see Mortimer's benevolent "front", I see his game. What he offers is not famine relief but a ticket to oppression far worse than the former landlord system.'

'How strong is the force of opposition here?'

He looked at her warily. 'Not as strong as it might be. The people are weakened by hunger. Mortimer is playing clever and winning much sympathy. But the old farmers see the truth and resist – though little good it will do them since they have no fixity of tenure.' He flexed his fists. 'If only a vision of today could have been known to Drumloch's farmers five years ago. We all spoke of O'Connell and reform, but how complacent we were. What was really done to help change? We should have banded together then and *forced* our voice to be heard –'

'Like the merciless Ribbonmen?'

He hesitated, his anger subdued. Her knowledge of the political scene was known to him and he detailed his support for the Young Irelanders' Confederation and for the concept of co-ordinated armed rebellion, concluding, 'The time for indiscriminate killing is done. I have no wish to start or see a tit-for-tat war with the likes of Mortimer, but a proper military engagement must come, and the peasants must wrest power from the authorities and

337

demand new government.'

Troubled, she said, 'Then you are here to fight, not to farm?'

'I love my land. That affection hasn't died.' Their eyes locked together and the moment was tense with a million unsaid questions. ''Tis reported Mortimer has full and complete ownership of Drumloch now, and back rents must go to him?'

'That's nonsense, Colum.' Donna recounted the facts of Mortimer's position, giving details of her talk with him. 'No matter how determined his game, I can be equally obstinate. No changes will be enforced while I have my own plans for Drumloch.'

His eyes lit. 'Then there is some hope for the honest farmers who wish to toil on?'

'It might prove difficult, but I will outdo him. Letty has no real fondness for the place and will be happy to go if he can be wedged out.'

'It would be a welcome twist were you to buy them out and preserve the manor as a holiday home for yourself and your wealthy husband.'

'I have no husband.'

His eyes flitted, full of hunger and heat. 'But, I assumed –'

'A wedding is planned, that is all.'

He turned away again. 'Cabbot will be good for you. He can offer you so fine a lifestyle.'

'Having agonised for too many nights, I know where my ambitions lie.' She won back his gaze and said seriously, 'Ireland is my home.'

''Tis teasing me, you are.'

Donna plucked her hand to his lips. The control she affected held no more. 'It relieves me to see you again, Colum. If only you knew the nights and days I wondered about you, hoped for your happiness. When I heard about the theft of your animals it fair distressed me, but by then my heart was well broken anyway. I believed courage and love had left you and you had taken Cara instead.'

He slipped his arms about her and pulled her softness to

him. The hood of her cape fell and his cheek was cushioned in golden hair. 'Mavourneen, I could never have left you. 'Twas you I thought had abandoned me. Had I known of your illness and your doubt I would have fled to your side and spat on propriety.'

She turned her mouth to his and he kissed her with infinite gentleness. A fraction of fear and guilt held her but the sweet pressure of his mouth crushed it. The presence of his being and the touch of his words filled her – but a vacancy, an urgent vital longing, opened up. Divining her thoughts, he pulled her to the ground, where the night shadows of the old stones were impenetrable. 'Indecision and folly lost you before,' he murmured, 'but this moment is a marriage for us.'

There was a maze of problems ahead for both, but she could think of none of them. The magic of his excitement fluttered into her. 'The legend of the Love Well proves true,' she whispered. He lay atop her and pulled open her bodice and the night breezes carried them away.

CHAPTER THIRTY-SIX

While Donna's struggle with Mortimer raged the quiet work of Anderson, Teggie Kelly and Colum hurried on. Though the rebellion movement was allegedly winning successes of support everywhere, progress for Anderson locally was slow. Bad communications hindered the aims but matters were made worse for his group by Samuel Mortimer's activities. Opinion seemed divided sharply between those, mainly newcomers to the valley, who backed the factory project and sought no trouble, and the others who favoured drastic direct action against the new lord of the manor, and no more. There was little interest in political grand plans.

A few days after Donna's arrival Anderson convened an

emergency meeting on the high bogland and produced, against Colum's and Teggie's wishes, a trump card designed to secure some definite support, if only from the one quarter: Black Hand O'Tracy himself had joined the underground planning for rebellion. Colum sat to the fore of a group of about forty farmers who listened attentively as Anderson and O'Tracy preached from a mound of cut turf. A sight they looked, he mused: Anderson fair and slight, a schoolteacher in looks and language; and Black Hand, built like the turf stack he stood upon, a shapeless giant with a face as characterful as a scarecrow's and lank black hair.

'Please believe Mortimer will not stop at cheap labour factories,' Anderson was entreating. 'Only yesterday he addressed me, seeing me perhaps less the enemy. He told me of his ambitions for parliament and the old Tories' promised support – and the aid of the local gentry guaranteed – for the next election.' He clenched a fist in an uncharacteristic gesture. 'We must recognise the deadly game! People like Mortimer are promising no better world for Ireland, just more exploitation. Conditions for tenants will become worse.'

'I lief uphold that,' Black Hand shouted, not to be outdone. 'People like Mortimer must be destroyed.'

A rumble of accord tripped through the crowd but Anderson was quick to caution. 'Wolfe Tone's ideals are tenable as ever. Casual violence cannot serve us now. We must form the type of close-knit team that other counties have formed. We must pull together and prepare for the call that will come soon – the call to rise up and tackle the garrison and the police and force reform.'

'Why not just kill Mortimer and be done with it?' a voice bellowed. An angry jeer soared from another part of the crowd.

'All right, good if Mortimer is beaten!' Anderson replied. 'But what of the others who suffer, the countless farmers all over the country who live under oppression? Come, I have pleaded these facts to you long enough and the grave situation I forecast has come to be. This may be our last hope. If Mortimer and McClune ship half of us out the spirit of defiance will be gone forever.'

'O'Connell said – ' another voice began.

'O'Connell is dead, and his wordy dreams came to nothing.'

Dead! The word rippled and rebounded. Farmers crossed themselves and others shook their heads, disbelieving.

' 'Tis true. Word came from Italy. His health was failing and he'd gone in pilgrimage, bound for the Holy City.' Anderson's tone became sweet. 'Let us not disgrace ourselves. The Liberator's tradition has been handed on to the Young Irelanders and thence to us. Their aims are the same and you know them to be valid.' He pointed towards Colum. 'Here by my side are men of unquestionable honour, men like Colum Devlin, ready and willing to take arms against the military. Yet to date we are only twenty here, where the group across the river in Galway numbers one hundred and sixty-two. And at Banagher there's an even bigger cell. Let us not be cowardly.'

'How will this call to rising come?' someone shouted.

'A command will come from Athlone. Our messenger will tell us what key centre to attack, whether barracks or police-station.'

'Strength!' Black Hand roared, powering a huge fist high above his head. 'Let's have no shirkers! Let every able-bodied man agree to fight!'

His demand was met with a broken cheer. A few unconvinced farmers began drifting away and the burly Ribbonman whispered to Anderson, 'We've done well. This'll sort the wheat from the chaff.' He moved to jump off the turf pile. 'Leave the next bit t'me. I'll pass among 'em and do a bit o' recruiting.'

Anderson followed Black Hand down and crouched on hunkers beside Colum. 'Unwise,' Colum said immediately. 'I didn't believe you'd done it till I saw the devil beside you with my own eyes.'

'You still despise the Ribbonmen?'

'I despise gratuitous murder, and that fellow's had a day or two of it in his time.'

341

Anderson sighed. 'Time has run out for us, Colum. If we are to contribute decently we must find aid now.'

'How soon?' Colum interpreted the seriousness of his friend's frown.

'Word is that the co-ordinated strike will begin on Saturday or Sunday. All over the country groups will kick out against police and military targets. Ours will most probably be McClune's police-station up river.'

'Saturday? So soon? Are you sure?'

'No, not certain. Our major problem all along has been communications. These few months since your return things have got much worse. Life and order are so disrupted by the famine. But this alert comes on excellent authority.'

Colum thought of Donna and considered the risks she might be exposed to were she to linger much longer in the manor house. In spite of assurances of a fair-and-square military engagement he knew there could be no way of estimating the shape of the coming fury. Anderson saw the worry etched in his friend's face. 'You will quietly forewarn your friend Donna?'

Colum looked into the sky and saw by the high sun that it was gone midday. 'She will be awaiting me at the farm,' he said. He struck out for the valley slope.

Donna had not yet come to the cottage but Mortimer was arriving as Colum walked up the river path. His northern manager and McClune accompanied him but he alone rode down the corn plot, his tall body rigid in the saddle. He consulted a paper in his bony hand.

'Devlin?'

' 'Tis right.'

The pebbly eyes crawled over Colum, full of suspicion and unease. 'Plot 22,' Mortimer observed. 'Land detailed for hops warehouse, for construction commencing June the first.' He did not blink from Colum's bitter stare. 'You must vacate this ground before the weekend and take your crops with you.'

'What crops would I have fit for pulling in May?' Colum threw a hand round the field.

Mortimer adjusted the soft tartan cap on his head. 'I am

no expert in crops, Mister Devlin. I merely wish to respect your rights.'

'Farmers have no rights.'

At the head of the field McClune was showing signs of interest, glowering towards Colum. Undeterred Colum said, 'I made my viewpoint clear to your man Porter and now I shall add to it. I have no wish to work in your factories and no intention of surrendering my land without a struggle. And I now know that you are in no legal position to enforce eviction because this property isn't yours.'

Stifling rage, Mortimer busied himself with the papers in his hands. Donna's friendships with valley folk were known to him but this consolidation was quite alarming. Perhaps he had been wrong in passively tolerating her. The hope had been to win her over, gain her friendship and purchase her blessing. But had that been over-ambitious? For a time things had seemed to improve, but these last days had been wordless stalemate. She would now not discuss his ventures and had summoned attorney Halifane from Dublin. She was a brittle, determined woman, but Mortimer was not about to show weakness. Turning for McClune he called, 'Good fellow, kindly join us a moment and enlighten Mister Devlin on the matters of law and order.'

McClune trotted down, bull-faced and irate, and Mortimer recited Colum's claim. 'Hear this,' the sub-inspector boomed. 'The government presses for land relief measures as soon as possible. The responsibility falls to the likes of Mr Mortimer here who, whether or not you like it, is in control of Drumloch. As far as I'm concerned, as representative of the government I will assist Mr Mortimer's wise plans. If that means organising evictions, 'tis fine with me. An' those who resist will get the jailhouse.'

''Tis preposterous. Mortimer doesn't own Drumloch.'

'Seems you'd prefer the jailhouse now, is it?' McClune said.

Colum's anger cooled quickly.

'Which is it to be?' Mortimer asked. 'The factory, a packet on the high seas, or jail?' He glanced smilingly to McClune. 'Fair choices, to my mind.' Tom Porter joined them and the three men laughed. Colum turned his back to them and began airing the soil with his pitchfork. 'Plot 22,' Mortimer read out in triumph. 'Land detailed to hops warehouse, construction commencing June the first.' He flicked the eviction notice from his hand. The single leaf floated down to Colum's heel.

The three horsemen spurred their mounts and cantered off, ignoring the clear-drawn path and crossing the corn field, rejoicing in the pulverising thunder of their horses' hooves. When they were out of sight Colum flung his fork down and cursed after them.

Without embellishment Colum related the incidents of the day to Donna in the cottage kitchen. 'Anderson's imminent rising troubles me,' he told her. 'If it is to be this weekend I want you out of Tipperary by Thursday – at least till the dust dies. You must understand your life would be in danger during such a row.'

'I will not leave – not with what you've told me of Mortimer's continued plan. I will not stand by and watch him begin evictions and further construction work. No. I have no intention of allowing your eviction or imprisonment.'

'Life and death considerations must come first, Donna. If the word I have is true Mortimer will not progress far with his weekend evictions. By Sunday the whole country-side could be at arms.' He took her hands and spoke with emphasis. 'A judicious retreat harms no one. You must repair to Dublin.'

She pulled a letter from her purse. 'I am not about to withdraw from the fray with Mortimer. I have here Dermot Halifane's missive from Dublin. He seems properly appalled by Letitia's move and agrees to work for me. He suspects all Mortimer really wants is settlement of the debt I told you about, the debt papa owed him. I am prepared to allow him go on believing that until he gets me what I want. I've told him I need a loan – a loan that will pay off Mortimer and buy Letty out – and he intimates he might, *just might*, be able to find something for me. The tradition of thriving Drumloch appeals to him, it seems, recalling the honourable days of his and my ancestors and their happy associations.'

Colum took the letter and read it through. 'You offer to repay this loan by selling lands and turning rents over to your creditors?'

'It's as good a start as we can make,' she shrugged. 'You have shown how almost half this estate is uninhabited now, so I am not stealing land from anyone.'

'It's a dream, Donna. You would never realise nearly enough money to pay Letty and Mortimer.'

'Hush, and do not complicate matters. Halifane likes and trusts me. So does old Estelle – he may give me the inflated price I want for the best river plots. Do not be pessimistic, my dear. I have tricks up my sleeve yet.'

Colum referred to the letter again. 'Halifane wishes to meet you but says he cannot get time free for a week. He suggests a possible halfway meeting in Athlone this Saturday evening – '

'I have time on my hands. I can wait – '

'No. Go to him. Take your maid and carriage and strike out on Thursday or Friday. Don't worry for me. Mortimer won't gain much in a short few days. You take refuge with Halifane in case this storm brews up and persuade his advice and help as much as you can. McClune has the law in his own hands but there must be devices that can stop him and Halifane will point you in the right direction.'

She pushed the attorney's paper aside. 'But I do worry for you, Colum. I would rather be by your side in time of trouble. Having found you again I will not sacrifice you to uncertainty. You have spoken of a civil war in the offing. If that be the case what difference between Athlone and here?'

'You must listen to me.' He took her hand and squeezed it till she cringed in pain. 'Conducted properly I do not see why this rising should touch the lives of innocents – gentry and farmer. But there are question marks involved. Communication with the political leaders, the Young Ireland Confederates, seems non-existent. Anthony

345

has enlisted the help of Black Hand O'Tracy, and he is bound to bring along his own crew. Right now there is bitter feeling among a section of the old Drumloch people aimed towards the manor house. Once arms are taken up the danger of uncontrolled violence is too high.' He kissed her fingers. 'I want a live lover in my arms, not a memory in my dreams such as I had this last year.'

'A lover – or a wife?' She did not smile. 'What will become of us, Colum? The difficulties of a marriage, mixed as it would be, are obvious – '

'But not insurmountable, now that our family ties are gone and the world has changed.' He took her masterfully in his arms. 'What would you choose for us?'

She detected from his tone that the choice of claim really was hers. This time she would not dawdle. 'We will marry –' she began.

'All right.'

'But first, as soon as the haggling with the estate sorts itself out we must journey to America and face Paul Cabbot. I must be honourable to him and to you. I want to enter marriage without guilt or doubt.'

'Very well.' He kissed her, then busied himself with preparations for their meal. Donna could not resist crossing the kitchen and wrapping her arms around him as he worked.

'This rebellion frightens me,' she said.

'It will be decided quickly, my love. In a day or two at most.' He twisted into her embrace. 'Anderson is brimming with confidence. And you need not fear for me. 'Tis the gentry that are at risk. I will honour the laws of war ... and keep my head down. I have land to fight for, but love to live for.'

'I may not see you for some days, then?' Her fingers began boldly toying with the buttons of his shirt. 'I need something to remember you by.'

On Thursday afternoon Donna arranged her short packing for Friday's journey to Athlone. Colum's portentous talk and Mortimer's glum silence, coupled with fanciful

346

woman's intuition, had somehow eaten into her, fraying her nerves. Something about the day was not right. The air was balmy but too close, without wind or the filtering voices of life. From her bedroom window the view along the river farms was ominously dead. Not a soul walked abroad and no animal or bird drifted into sight. If she craned out she could see the corner of the demolished wing, ugly at any time but hideous now in its desolation. These sights and senses brought to mind a period of calm-before-storm not long ago, and Donna mulled again on the days before the blight.

'I see your game at last,' a sly voice said behind her.

Donna turned and faced Letty. She saw her sister in startling light: a selfish and lonely girl desperate to retain an easy foothold on the good life. They were sisters in name only and when Donna spoke it was as if she addressed a stranger.

'I have no wish to converse about make-believe "games", I am too busy making my travel preparations.'

'It was Devlin all along.' Letty's tone was incredulous. She sat on the bed and watched Donna. 'This dalliance with the farm boy was quite calculated and you came back here to take up with him again and recover this property for both your aims.'

Red-faced, Donna kept about her packing. 'There was nothing calculated about it. You are quite wrong. I came basically to stop this work at Drumloch because, Colum Devlin or not, it was my intention to preserve the estate and see it built back to its former glory.'

'Don't try to tell me my spies have been wrong. That you have not been carousing with Devlin and conspiring with him since the first day you arrived back.'

'It is true that we are close friends.'

'Ye Gods.' Letty whistled low. 'The devil boasts her sins! Whatever would Mr McClune or Major Middleton, our good neighbours, say if they knew?'

Donna spun on Letty. 'What would they say? I don't know or care. Many might welcome an association like this between gentry and farming community. Times are changing, Letty. But whether yes or nay, the relationship stands, and I am proud of it. And do not think its existence secures *your* position in any way. The fact is, I have equal rights to you – so Mortimer cannot go against me. I will never allow his factories, so the sooner the better *you* start channelling his greedy ambitions in another more feasible direction. Otherwise you risk an eternal deadlock position that may have him scrambling off to other pastures, frustrated by me and disillusioned by you.'

Letty was stuck for words. Donna might be prepared to go on haggling for years, but *she* was not. Her future depended on Mortimer's contentment. Already the marriage had been delayed. 'See reason,' she said with sudden passion. 'Mortimer can pay you handsomely and you can build another Drumloch. If this is your sick ambition – ?'

'No. *You* see reason. There were doubts in my mind but now I have come to Drumloch, come *home*, and I know what I want. You must persuade your future husband to find another suitable factory plot in the south. *I* shall pay you, and pay him off if necessary.' She shrugged. 'And you cannot trick me by declaring loving interest in Drumloch, for I know you have hated it.'

'Where do you propose to get the money to pay us off? Can it be Cabbot was all part of your wide plan? Had you and Devlin connived – ?'

'Don't sicken me, Letty. We are not all entranced by the ruses you so love.'

'I will not dissuade Samuel.'

'Then I will use every legal pitch to stop him. I am prepared to linger here just as long as it takes.'

The sisters stared each other like animals in combat. 'I will repay this moment,' Letty promised. 'You will curse the day you set foot back on Irish soil.'

CHAPTER THIRTY-SEVEN

Rough hands shook Colum and he woke to focus on the towering ghosts that crowded the small bedroom. Anderson's fevered eyes twinkled down and the call was there, unsaid.

'A rising?'

Teggie Kelly stepped out of shadow. Colum saw the shimmer of sweat on his brow. The big man was panting like a racehorse. 'It's unco-ordinated and early, but it's off. We must rush to band all supporters. You know where the arms are kept – in the grain shed behind my cottage.'

Without another word Teggie was gone. Colum clambered out of bed and held Anderson, his thoughts wild. 'You said Saturday or Sunday. 'Tis Thursday and – '

'Out of control,' Anderson reported, pale-faced. 'Word is coming in that some of the northern groups have changed their minds and called it off, but nothing is certain.' The distress in his green eyes was clear. 'Seems all we can do is go along with it and try to establish some definite control. On Middleton's lands a group has risen up and Black Hand O'Tracy leads 'em. Some of Black Hand's men have taken the reins here – ' As the mists of sleep dissipated Colum realised what he was saying: on rumour and without confirmation of any countrywide plan local groups were taking it on themselves to hit out. Black Hand was at the helm and Anderson and Teggie, supposed leaders, had been caught unawares. 'Major Middleton's house is under siege,' Anderson was admitting, 'while McClune and a police contingent have barricaded themselves in. That's the danger – that this may become a one-sided series of vendetta battles.'

'This is senseless,' Colum cut in. ' 'Tis the Ribbonmen again, under a politically respectable guise. You've been lured into it, Anthony.'

Anderson would not hear that accusation but the doubt in his face said everything. 'It might work,' he insisted. 'Word will run round fast. Others will take arms. If we can marshall our men and achieve a direction – '

' 'Tis madness without organisation.' Both men were shivering and, mechanically though without purpose, Colum was pulling on his clothes. 'What of Drumloch manor house? If Black Hand's people are in control they will feed on the old farmers' fervour.'

The private fear in Colum's face was recognised by Anderson. He opened his mouth, intent on reassuring his friend, then stopped. A loud report, unmistakably of gun-shot, threw alarm into both men. The implications of its closeness fired both to action. They ran.

Outside their ears were assailed by the cawing cries of men and women, disembodied songs on the cold night air, cheering, urging on. Anderson guessed at the cause and his heart shot into his throat. He began running towards the hill that divided Devlin's land from the manor house. Colum hung back, then his nerve snapped. He charged forward. Another gunshot cracked. *They have started here*, Colum thought. They have heard the call to arms and, like the long-suffering on Middleton's land, have at last given vent to years of oppression.

Breasting the hill, the sight that opened up blinded and stilled him. Anderson stood, shocked, beside him. 'The fools,' Anderson hissed. 'How can they!'

Drumloch manor house was circled by fifty or more wild-voiced people, many armed with muskets and pitch-forks. High-piled mounds of tinderwood had been stacked about the house, and ignited by flaming torches. A furious inferno had powered up in minutes and licks of blue flame slapped the walls. Windows popped with the intense heat and black scorch marks spread towards the roof pantiles, sprayed out as if by magic. Around this the farm folk danced, shouting obscure victory and daring the inhabitants to venture out. Colum looked among the farmers and disbelieved his eyes. Old trusted friends many of them were, quiet-minded gentlefolk whose whole existences had been the soil and the seed. Now they were egged on by crazed rowdy youths, among whom Black Hand's known Ribbonmen were prominent. As Anderson and Colum watched the manor house doorway opened and Tom Porter the manager assisted old Nurse down the steps. Even at this distance their terror was apparent. A shot boomed – and Colum shuddered to see Porter reel back, blood spouting from his chest. Colum darted forward, Anderson stretching too late to grasp him. He tore down the hill, shouting to people he knew, begging, ordering retreat. Behind him Anderson took up the call, following. Colum leapt upon the first armed man he saw and took his sword. As another hefted his musket he lashed down on it, shattering the barrel. 'Get back,' he shouted. 'Retreat! We have no right to arms here!' He ran on for the house.

'Here come the police!'

A welcoming cheer roared and Colum turned to see groups of excited farmers attack the three mounted police-agents who had come on the scene. The new arrivals were hugely overpowered and dragged to the ground. Anderson moved to intervene, then drew back hopelessly.

By now the very door of the manor house was afire. A few of the staff had escaped through the service entrance and Colum ran around to see Letty stagger out, her maid bearing her up. A bullet sped over her head and he ran in rage at the attacker who had pulled the trigger – a dirty-faced gossoon of no more than twelve. The boy galloped off.

Anderson nudged beside Colum. Colum shouted in his ear, 'Donna has not come out. I must get in.'

'I fear we're too late. This will act like a beacon across the whole countryside. The troops will swoop on us. For everyone's sake we had better break up the men.'

'The hell with them! 'Tis their own choice, this devilry. I'm going in!'

'No!'

Colum slipped from his friend's grip and ran back to the front of the house. At the grassy edge of the forecourt he stalled and found Letty lying at his feet, her maid reviving her with a wet linen. Their eyes met, and Letty glared at him. Her mouth moved, articulating venomous words that the growl of the fire tore away. He grabbed her maid's arm and shouted, 'Get her back from here. The fire is growing and timbers may fall.' The girl began hauling Letty away. Colum sprinted into the flames, ducking the gouging shot that pounded the doorside pillar.

Inside the air was smoky and hot enough to sear the lungs but there was little structural damage as yet and only two or three local fires crackled. There was time to take stock but the thunder of the outside fire threatened to break through at any moment. Everything depended on locating her quickly, Colum knew. There was no time to check rooms individually. Screaming her name he ran for the main drawing-room. Here the blaze had spread. The Italian drapes were alight, raging noisily, their flames thrashing the ceiling, worrying the heavy chandelier. As he closed the door the huge ornament worked free of its chains and exploded onto the floor. Somewhere else in the house the ripping crack of falling masonry could be heard. He twisted round to make for the dining-room and found himself facing Mortimer. Instinctively he ducked. Just in time. The iron axe Mortimer brandished glided above his head and sank into the door frame a foot from his ear. Colum realised what was happening. Trapped and panicking, Mortimer was lashing out at the first alien face he saw. Colum drove out a defensive blow that winded Mortimer. But he still held onto the axe, jerking away and trying another sweep. Again Colum side-stepped and again the axe splintered the wood beside his head. 'You're in no danger from me,' Colum shouted. 'Get out, for God's sake, while you can.' But Mortimer wasn't listening. As he came down with the weapon again Colum saw it was life and death, himself or Mortimer. He coiled his body, then leapt out. His head rocketed into Mortimer's gut and sent him flying backwards. Off balance, Mortimer tripped through the dining-room door. As the door swung in Colum saw the new savagery of the fire. The wooden flooring had taken and great wild wings beat the walls. Mortimer crumpled in the middle of this conflagration.

Colum grabbed the doorknob. He stalled, unwilling to leave him to so terrible a torture. Insane in fury and fear, Mortimer had run to the battery of windows, searching a quick way out. But before his shaking fingers tore the first casement latch open the great curtains on either side buckled and collapsed under flame, covering him. A torrent of fierce fire ascended, bursting through the whole room. Colum jumped back and closed the door firmly.

By now the billowing smoke was choking every room in the house. As he made for the stairway in the middle of the Great Hall the foul air, accompanied by intense pulsating heat, brought him quickly to his knees. A rafter from the vault crashed down on him, slicing inches of skin off his upper arm. He crept along the floor, coughing and spitting, trying to keep his tongue lubricated and his lungs full. In minutes he had lost his way in the thick greyness of the smoke.

He fell flat.

An eerie storm of scalding air burst out behind him, rushing over his body and peeling the waistcoat off his back. The flowing blood of his shoulder congealed instantly, baked. He scurried on another yard, strength ebbing, fingernails finding the cracks in the stone flags, dragging him on.

In his mind's eye there was only Donna, but failure chased over him. His fingers found the frame-edge of a door and the moist air of night gushed in. Tears streamed from his eyes and he blinked them back, found the first step, then rolled until the cool gravel of the forecourt crunched under his back.

Hands reached out of the dark and took him, pulling him away, rending his remaining clothes. Gravel bit into open wounds, grime and smoke blinded his vision. The torture was endless, endless. He passed out, wakened, then swooped again. At last wet grass tickled his chest and revived consciousness. The hands turned him over and he saw the moon. Many moons – all transforming into the faces of uniformed men. All around there was shouting and screaming and the relentless thud of gunfire. A battle was running and the jagged bulk of the manor house was engulfed, blazing like hell itself.

Colum heard one of his rescuers – a soldier, he guessed – shout a question. Someone nearby was answering, 'Yes, yes. He is one of them.' He pinched his eyes open again. Letitia, ragged and smeared, propped by two maids, was pointing out the attackers for the troop leader.

Colum slumped back, drained. The impact of what had occurred had not yet hit him. Mortimer dead, the manor house gone, a rising miscarried, the die cast; after generations of simmering unrest, the inevitable explosion; open shapeless enmity, farmers against the gentry. Instead Donna dominated his thoughts, fading bit by bit like a wraith in a dream. If only he had insisted on earlier departure. If only she had never returned! She was gone, dead in the fire, and he would carry the weight of the tragedy forever. Drumloch was no place for her. Long, long ago he should have followed his pledge and taken her away . . .

Soldiers shuffled him to his feet and shouted for assistance. An uncovered cart crowded with roped prisoners clattered towards them. Colum could not stand but they supported him and eased him onto his back in the cart. As he glanced round now he could see in what numbers the garrison troops had turned out. The local men and women, though still engaged in a pitched battle, were outnumbered by two to one and even now more soldiers were arriving. Colum felt helpless and panicked but could do nothing. He wanted to shout out that Donna was still in there, that he had been robbed of his heart, but found no energy.

Amid the din of activity round him a breathless voice called out: 'The rebellion on Middleton's has been scotched, and Black Hand O'Tracy's crowd wiped out. The villain himself's dead.'

'How many have we taken here?' a replying voice barked.

'Twenty-two captured, six dead. I think we've beaten it.'

Colum saw the conversing men, both in the red field uniforms of lieutenants, one no more than twenty-five, his upper arm shattered by the stab of a hay fork. 'Let's shift these for the jailhouse,' the older lieutenant called. 'They've had their fun, and they'll hang for this.'

Colum closed his mind and turned towards the great flames that soared to the sky, then remembered no more.

Word of the disastrous Thursday events at Drumloch did not reach Athlone till Saturday afternoon. At Dubhmara, Halifane's country house within sight of the celebrated Anglo-Norman castle, an officer of the town garrison calling to pay respects delivered the news. At tea Halifane relayed the facts to Donna whose early flight from the manor had been precipitated by the grumbling pressure of Letty.

'Gracious,' Donna responded, 'I can only have been hours clear of the place when the trouble started. My maid and I stayed at Banagher Inn overnight and saw much troop movement, but no indication of any concerted uprising came to us.' Her cheeks went pale. 'You say many were arrested and the dissent quietened?'

'I'm afraid it was somewhat more serious, my lady,' Halifane said with heavy expression. 'It grieves me to have to tell you that, according to my informant, the manor house was virtually burnt to the ground. Your sister is quite safe, I hasten to add, and is staying with Lord Estelle. But Samuel Mortimer died in the row. And yes, many were arrested and will face the severest penalties.' Halifane shrugged. 'There is rumour that the Young Irelanders were behind this, but concerted rebellion it was not. My informant says it was little more than an overblown Ribbonmen skirmish and only remarkable in its fury and in the fact that its main thrust occurred on an estate formerly known as a peaceful and settled one.' The attorney's bland face became sad. 'After our talks today I can see how truly badly Drumloch needs a new enlightened patron like yourself to guide it back to its one-time glory. The warmth of your attitude gives me heart, may I say, and you have won me to your cause. It's sad about Mortimer, but now that he's gone – '

Donna was on her feet, pushing her tea plates aside. 'Let us indulge no premature talk,' she said with tension. She was thinking of Colum. 'I must go this moment and see how grave the damage is. Burnt to the ground! Sir, my heart is sickened and I can sit no longer.'

On Halifane's insistence she stayed overnight but early on Sunday they struck out together, taking one of the Shannon flyboats rather than a coach. With a good skipper the journey was made in record time and by late afternoon the barren knolls that circled Drumloch valley were in sight. 'We shall moor near Estelle's and take horses there,' Halifane proposed. 'Discard unhappy memories of the past and put your confidence in me. Your papa made an enemy of Estelle, but he is still a friend of mine.'

'If I am to reside here, he must become my ally too. He fair likes me and will, I'm sure, come to admire my aspirations. My ambitions may not offer the immediate radical change that Mortimer promised but at least my claim to the estate is legal and decent, and I seek no more than an atmosphere of peace and growth for all.'

The attorney grunted, well pleased. His failure with Bouchard had been an irksome burden, and he was relieved and encouraged to find Donna, so young and candid, resolved to repair the rot and devote herself to reform.

Their reception at Estelle's was brief in the absence of his lordship but they rode without delay for Drumloch, stalling only to ascertain the state of Letty's recovery. Mile by mile their fears grew until, by the time they rounded the fir forest, Donna felt ill and dizzy. Estelle's groom accompanied them and reined in as they turned off the forest path. Donna and Halifane followed suit. All three sat still to survey the ruin that stood before them. Not a word was spoken.

The manor house was now rubble – a roofless frame dotted with the regular holes of one-time windows. Even the coach house was destroyed, its charred timbers still smoking, its great oak doors vanished to ash.

'Beyond hope,' Halifane muttered, shaking his head.

'Not beyond hope, Mr Halifane. There is always hope. Who knows? – the structure might be sound still. With some appropriate redesigning perhaps . . .' She mumbled on without thinking, dragging up all the confident enthusiasm she could find. One happy voice spoke from the back of her mind: Mortimer was out of it, and weak Letitia would not now cling on. Given time, and a loan, the future she wanted was hers.

But that thin voice was shrouded in worry even still. What would be the aftermath of the failed rebellion? How would the farmers resign themselves to defeat and to the tough law measures that would inevitably be employed as penalties? And, most importantly, was Colum safe?

'I must go to visit my friend Mr Devlin,' she told Halifane suddenly. 'He's the son of the old middleman and will know the upshot of the rebellion.' Halifane moved to ride with her, but she dissuaded him and advanced alone.

Inside the door of the river cottage a slim figure jumped on her from the murk and pinned her to the wall. Assuming it to be Colum, she allowed his force and fell back submissively. Then her eyes flicked wide and she recognised Anthony Anderson. His face was sweat-streaked and frightened, his shirt bedraggled. Over his shoulder there was slung a soldier's kit bag, plumply packed. '*My God*, 'tis you!' he breathed. He unhanded her. 'Forgive me, but I could take no chance.' He blinked anew. 'They said you were in the manor house, that you were lost in the blaze.'

She shook her head, eyeing the filth of his clothes. 'What's wrong? You look as if – ' Remembering details Colum had told her, she deduced truth. 'You ran with the rebels and are now fleeing the police? But where is Colum?'

He walked away from her and lowered his gaze. 'Disgust and guilt render me speechless. No rebellion it was, but a travesty that meant nothing. I believed the time was right, I encouraged it, but lack of organisation proved me wrong.'

She tugged his sleeve. 'Tell me, Anthony. What

357

happened to Colum?' A note of mounting hysteria shrilled.

'They took him – the garrison troops. Little time they wasted. He went before the magistrates on Friday along with forty others.'

'Oh no.'

Anderson gave a mournful sigh. 'The method was wrong, I now see. Black Hand should never have been involved, and my association with the Confederation was ridiculously inadequate. I was premature. Colum's wisdom was greater than mine. My fear now is that, in allowing the disturbance, we have damaged Repeal and set our cause back some years. I feel ashamed to face you, ashamed that the fighting turned inward, and your Drumloch was besieged.' He took her hands and she marvelled at the fact that so sensitive and gentle a man could devote himself to warfare. 'Will you ever forgive me for what has occurred? I have destroyed your house and blighted your love, I know. Colum was involved only in forcing entry to the manor during the fire, thinking you were there.'

'And they believed he was one of those out to destroy it?'

'Yes. Letty herself denounced him to the troops after the row. Some were hanged later, but my informants tell me Colum has been sentenced to transportation.'

'Good God.'

'Better than hanging, though that comforts not at all.'

'How . . . long?'

'Twenty years.'

She staggered away from him and collapsed in a fireside chair. 'A lifetime,' she said, repeating the word in a monotone, again and again till its meaning was lost. For a moment she rallied. 'I must speak to the authorities, approach the Castle, make them realise their mistake . . . I can visit McClune, implore him –'

'No use,' Anderson shook his head emphatically. 'The authorities won't waste time. Once sentence is passed, it'll be the first navy brig from Queenstown for Colum and the others. And McClune would be the last to lend aid. In the skirmishes he himself lost a leg and lies abed desperately ill now. If anything he would take pleasure seeing Colum, son of Desmond Devlin, done down.'

'I will not give in, not without struggle. I will not let him go! Not now, not after all we've gone through. Not when my dreams are within reach – ' Composure was gone and tears began. Anderson crossed to her to offer a shoulder and she fell into his arms, sobbing like a child. It took long to soothe her but eventually the breathless weeping quietened and she looked into his jaded face. 'Colum always spoke of you as the dearest of friends,' she said, 'and I have known you as a gentleman. Please – I accept that your associates would know more of such things than ever I might. Tell me. There must be a way to free him? I've heard it said there are groups of people who work in secrecy to make escape channels for transported felons.'

Anderson did not immediately reply. He gazed at her with piercing intensity, his green eyes unblinking. 'I come here today to take away the few pounds and dear possessions that my friend owned. If I do not keep them in good store for him, the Lord knows what will become of them. You see, my heart is heavy today because these are the last hours I shall ever look upon this land. Informers named me among the ringleaders and there is a price on my head. I have smuggled my mother and sisters to Dublin, where I will join them in a day or two. Then passage for America will be arranged.' He slapped his fat bag. 'Here I have recovered from our home all that's worth taking, and we will make a new life for ourselves in New York or California.' His tone became grave. 'There are many friends of Irish Repealers in America, it's said, and some are very powerful.'

Donna brightened. 'Do you think there might be a hope – ?'

He put up a restraining hand. 'I cannot promise much. Who can be sure where Colum was sent? The authorities have been withholding such information these last four months. He could have been sent to Canada or America – but he could equally have been taken to the godforsaken wilderness of Australia.' He waited till she acknowledged that with a little nod. 'If he's in Canada, there is hope. Our compatriots there will be sympathetic and, yes, there are organisations for tracking transportees down.'

Donna thought of Paul Cabbot, of the overdue duty that lay before her. In a roundabout way she told Anderson her story. 'I can travel and meet up with you in New York. Together we can work to locate him.'

'In my heart I was committed to trying to locate my lifelong companion Teggie Kelly,' Anderson admitted, 'and I confess to a similar debt of friendship to Colum Devlin. So, if you desire it, I will help you. We can join forces, and pray.'

'In the meantime I can summon help here in case a ship has not already been arranged or some other delays have occurred. It's worthy of a try –'

'Perhaps. Anything is worth chancing, but I doubt you will find luck. The machinery of transportation once started will not slow down. Colum will be long gone in some barque of her Majesty's navy, and on the high seas by now. Anderson examined his hands. 'You must also give thought to the future, to the wisdom of confiding in certain people. You say your aim is to wed Colum and build a new type of life on Drumloch estate. That may not be so easy now. The husband you seek to return here is, in the eyes of the law, a felon.'

'His innocence will be proven.' She paused and swept back a tear. 'And anyway, memories are short.' As she spoke already her mind was preparing for Halifane and Cabbot. Intimate details must not yet be chanced on Halifane: the man was good-hearted and on her side, but a firmer relationship must be founded first. Anderson's caution was wise, but the history of Ireland was checkered with civil unrest and so often this year's dissenters were next year's heroes. In a month or a year Colum Devlin's criminality would be buried and forgotten. One thing she knew for sure without questioning herself: in the last days she had seen the two things she so truly wanted within her grasp; now she was resolved to settle for no less than those. 'I shall use my wiles and secure my position at Drumloch,' she said. 'But I will find and return Colum Devlin too.

Nothing will stop me. I lacked courage and almost lost them both before. I will not lack courage now.'

They talked on for a half-hour, agreeing a plan and exchanging addresses and information, then Anderson left her alone in the dusty little house, alone to her memories and the dignity of unchallenged tears.

CHAPTER THIRTY-EIGHT

There were no options but to follow the agreed course of action. Careful inquiries through Halifane's garrison friends elicited the truth of Anderson's claim that the deportees were already gone, so there seemed little point in beseeching the police and raising waves. The way to Colum lay overseas. Shunning Mortimer's funeral and vesting authority in Halifane to pursue her interest in Drumloch and prevent any further stranglehold from Letty, Donna made her preparations for travel. In mourning for her husband-to-be, Letty had repaired to Lurgan – a move designed as a tactical side-step, no doubt – but after her treachery in handing over Colum Donna could not bring herself to face her. After a day or two at Dubhmara she made straight for Queenstown and joined a Cunarder out of Southampton. Departure stabbed her heart in a way it had not done before and the voyage was a misery. To have been so close and lost so much proved almost unbearable.

America greeted her in its perfunctory grimy way – smoke spewing, whistles shrilling, too many carriages in too few streets – and she fled to Fifth Avenue and was grateful to find an unprepared and serene household. Refreshed a little in an hour, Josephine's arrival from an uptown business meeting soon induced a return of tension. She made no bones about her disapproval of Donna's unplanned trip and professed herself insulted that no fore-notice of return had come. 'Whatever will people think?' she said. 'The Cabbots have many friends in this town, lots of them involved in shipping. If they see you travel alone in this way with no suitable greeting party at the dock they will suspect a groundless rift. I will *not* have it.'

'You would perhaps like to know the result of my venture – this legal problem concerning Drumloch estate?' Donna spoke with a barbed tone.

'I wish to know *nothing* of your private whims, m'dear. Nor of Ireland. I have had quite enough of it for now. My fingers have been burnt and I have no desire to allow it occur again . . .'

The old lady ranted on. Nerves shredded, Donna decided not to defend herself. Better to confront Paul first, and acknowledge the greater debt and obligation to him.

On Josephine's orders they dined together and during coffee Paul Cabbot arrived from his Coney office, anxious and aglow, all-eager to embrace her again. They had taken their beverages to fireside chairs and he crossed to kiss her forehead and welcome her effusively but Mamma Josephine lingered on, full of chatter about gifted seamstresses and golden wedding gowns. 'Would you mind terribly if we had a few minutes together?' Cabbot finally asked and Josephine, for once, complied without hesitation. As she passed from the room she made a show of whispering to her son and Donna distinctly heard: 'I'd not fuss to please her, Paul. The girl demands more of the whip to teach her her place.'

Cabbot waited till the door closed then pulled her up and hungrily hugged her. 'My love, how wonderful to have you home! Disregard anything mamma says.' He laughed and kissed her ear, a trifle guilty in manner. 'She is merely perturbed that the pomp of the wedding she had been so looking forward to was postponed for three months. But worry not, I explained everything away very convincingly and assured her *I* had recommended the voyage.' A tremor of passion took him and his lips moved over her décolletage. 'Thank heavens you return. I was on point of journeying after you. My patience would hold no more.'

Donna eased him away and returned to her coffee with self-conscious deliberation. At first he noticed nothing amiss and poured himself a celebratory brandy. Very succinctly she reported the encounters with Letitia and Mortimer, and the incidents of the rebellion, making no mention of Colum. Before she was fully finished he interjected, 'But if Drumloch means so much to you and money is the heart of the issue – why bother to waste a minute on this Halifane? The desires of a wife of mine must be borne out! Obviously, in the wake of this civil disturbance, it would be unwise to invest any more time or effort there now, but in a year or two – '

'There is something I must tell you, Paul. It pains me, but the truth must come out.'

The buoyant gaiety vanished and he sat before her heavily, like an old man. His smooth face became tragic, grim. 'There are certain truths I would choose not to know, Donna. Tell me as much or as little about Ireland as you really want to – but spare me stories of . . . of romance.'

'You knew – ?' She was not surprised.

'I recall your farm boy.'

'I see. Then you have guessed that my . . . affection for him has not ceased?' She found his eyes bravely. 'My life has gone through big changes but my heart is where it has always been – attached to him.'

Cabbot flinched as though wounded. His brandy glass clinked loud as he crashed it down. 'You must be sensible. He is impoverished, of peasant blood – '

'No.' That argument was worn out, and weighed nothing against real love. 'We only differ in beginnings. What wealth could *I* bring to him now?'

'You may feel confused, but give us time. You and I are well suited. We cannot perfect a friendship in weeks or months, but *it will grow*. Believe me.'

'But one must examine one's heart, Paul. Does one want it to grow?'

He mulled a minute, chewing his knuckles. 'But you have returned to me. That reveals something of your heart. Outwardly you may feel – '

'I return merely to offer you the courtesy of thanks and to explain.'

363

He became deathly pale. 'So you wish an end to our marriage plan? This . . . peasant is accessible to you again and you seek his company? The vow you made at Christmas is forgotten?' A current of anger strung his words together and he fought to keep his voice low.

Donna shook her head slowly. 'All I wish to say is, bearing both our happiness in mind, I believe we must now say good-bye. I do not know what gesture I can make to repay the kindnesses you have given me. You have given me my life, even.'

'And you have helped give me the Coney deal. That is good. That is how sound relationships should be – give and take.'

'I cannot believe that, Paul. Above all there must be one ingredient – selfless, self-satisfying love. Love of the body and soul.' She watched his eyes and saw blank bewilderment. 'Don't you understand that? Don't you understand that love is not arranged and dispensed like a business contract? It's no emolument for good deeds done. It's a nerve that either throbs, or doesn't. And one must settle for nothing less than it.'

He was silent a minute, his clean ageless face no longer animated. 'You wish to go back to Ireland?'

'Soon – yes.' She looked away from his sad face. 'There lies a steep road ahead for us, but I will rebuild Drumloch. I will succeed.'

In silence, Cabbot sat by his escritoire and withdrew some papers, his expression icy. As he dipped a quill he spoke at last. 'The Cabbots have never been romancers like the Irish, I regret. But one may learn as one grows old.' His eyes were on the papers before him. 'You are lovely and desirable, Donna. At first, it's true, I was attracted to your . . . suitability. But then, after learning to want you, I learnt to care. Learnt to love you.' He concluded writing and looked to her. 'In the three months that have passed I came upon emotions I never before experienced. I may be losing you, but I doubt if I will so readily lose these treasures you've brought to my life.' He walked to her chair and handed her a folded paper. 'That is drawn on my

English bank and you will cash it, I'm certain, without trouble in Dublin. I shall write a covering note to London tonight. If you need immediate currency Blake, my New York banker, can honour it.'

She opened the blue paper and saw it was a cheque for three thousand pounds.

'Paul, I cannot accept this.' There was irony: After Halifane, an approach to the Cabbots had been the reserved second barrel of her gun. If all else failed she had planned to come to Josephine or Paul and beg assistance; a sound debenture would have been drawn up and she would have toiled relentlessly to repay that loan. But here he was offering a gift, giving more than her wildest dreams could have drawn.

'You should not be forced to live like beggar. You deserve a sweet life. Please. Please allow me to contribute in this indirect way to your future happiness. Rebuild your Drumloch and do what you must do.'

She stood before him, torn between satisfaction and sorrow. 'It would be dishonest to accept this magnificent offering were you not to know all the facts,' she said. 'I should be ashamed to admit this, but I am not: you see, I am with child.' She held the cheque up. 'I will think no less of you should you wish to take this back. You *owe* me nothing at all, Paul. How good you have been already! And now I must go to find my destiny with the man I love.'

Without the flicker of an eyelid he stood above her, considering this startling news. At length he said, 'When will you wish to leave?'

'Soon. I await communication from an Irish friend who has offered his company. My heart's in Drumloch, Paul, and I will not be content till I'm back there.'

'Stay in comfort here as long as it pleases you,' he said, and he cupped her hand, crushing the cheque back into her grasp. He kissed her then without looking back turned to leave the room.

The chance seemed too good to miss: that very night Donna drafted two long letters to Letty in Lurgan and to

Halifane. Without referring to Colum Donna offered her sister an immediate outright cash settlement in respect of her interest in the manor, to be negotiated forthwith via Halifane. It was impossible to guess at the kind of financial provisions Mortimer might have made for his wife-to-be but Donna's optimism was keyed up by the fact that Letty so obviously detested Drumloch. To Halifane she detailed her move, revealing little more than that the 'friendly loan' had come from the hospitable Cabbots. She did not doubt that, in his mind's eye, the attorney probably envisaged all sorts of promising relationships, but she offered nothing to lend false hope. It was vital, she pressed on Halifane, that advantage should be taken of present circumstances and a swift deal agreed with Letty. It seemed reasonable to begin the bidding at two thousand, she suggested, but such details she was sure could be safely left in the attorney's hands.

That done, the period of waiting for Anthony Anderson began. Emma disappeared to Milford and sombre gloom descended on Fifth, but Donna was determined to keep her heart high. Blessedly Anderson's first communication came within four weeks. His family's flight to escape had been tricky and protracted – but successful. At last a convenient base in a tenement block on Monroe Street had been found and the settling in had started. Next day Donna stole out to meet him at a Broadway eating house and he outlined his excursion through the Tammany world in pursuit of the renowned rebel sympathy groups. Delight fired his talk.

'I've met more Irish here than I ever did in Tipperary,' he told her. 'And the intriguing thing is that the voice of harmony among them is so strong. They are organised – rightly and properly. There are the militia – the Hibernia Guards and the Emmet Guards and God knows how many others. Then there are the rights societies like the Irish Emigrants' Protection Group. All the various strata gathered together under the solitary roof of the Tammany. If only Ireland herself could see the value of this oneness.'

'Have you found any group that organises escape channels?'

'Not yet, but the wardheeler – leader – of a local Irish precinct has promised to instigate inquiries. He says every emigrant, criminal or citizen, is listed and known by his organisation. He could speak with no great confidence about felons, but he says if Colum Devlin has set foot on American soil his people stand an excellent chance of finding him. What better start can we ask for?'

Back at Fifth neither Paul nor Mamma Josephine now showed their faces for days on end. After another fortnight the stifling silence was such that Donna felt she could impose no more. To occupy herself she prepared final packing and began seeking out a suitable boarding house in Manhattan to transfer to. A day later the scant note from Anderson arrived, detailing the local wardheeler's information. The joyous message was brief: it said Devlin had been located and was currently in the Bellevue Hospital.

CHAPTER THIRTY-NINE

The salt-and-pepper façade of Bellvue stood out against the New York skyline like a monolithic gateway to hell. In a city of stark newness its appearance was ancient and time-less all at once. Donna hesitated in the cab, apprehensively examining her destination, and Anderson shook his head sadly. Everywhere there was the evidence of emigrant poverty and illness – cripples dawdling on the pavements, beggarly children in the Georgian archways, blotched faces, disease. 'I cannot believe that Colum could find his way here,' Anderson whispered, 'unless some grave illness took him and they transferred him from the Staten fever hospital.'

Donna steeled herself and went inside. On the ward-heeler's instruction a German surgeon was requested and came to them laden with day-books and fever records.

While ailing children eddied about his tiny office and fussing nurses wove through, the surgeon surveyed his endless lists of patients, reciting, 'Deaton, Deegan, Derman, Dervane . . .' Presently he stopped and pulled off his pince-nez, nodding, grim-visaged. 'Devlin, yes. Regrettably unsafe to see. He should not have got through the Staten Island medical check, but he did.'

'I must see him.'

The doctor regarded Donna seriously. 'I would not advise it. He has cholera, we suspect, and though the worst of it seems over there is always an element of risk.'

'Perhaps it would be best if you waited – ?' Anderson started.

'No, I would rather see him now. Just for a minute or two. It is very urgent. You see, he was a servant of my family's – '

'Very well.' The German sought no details. He rattled a brass bell.

'Can you . . . tell us anything of his arrival here?' Anderson asked.

'One in a thousand?' The old man's bushy brows shot up. 'I involve myself only in patching up their infected and damaged bodies. Pauper and criminal, they are all as one to me.' As he spoke he fitted Donna with a gauze mask but as he moved to do the same with Anderson Donna pressed her friend's arm and shook her head. 'All right,' Anderson agreed and he declined a mask. 'I shall await you here.'

A nurse came and led Donna through corridors that crept into the distant heart of the sprawling, noisy building. Rank smells abounded. Walls stood lined with posters praising Dr Sweetzer's $5 panacea and advertisements for Mother Soap. Melancholic nurses pushed trays groaning with dirty food plates and sparkling instruments. Patients crouched, sat and stood at corners: women disfigured in smallpox, grey-faced children, skeletal old men. And all the time the largo deadly medley went up: disembodied screaming, the rasp of Hey's saw, the crack of amputating knife. Donna shut off the part of her mind that evaluated what the eyes saw and the ears heard. Instead she fixed attention firmly on Colum, wondering at the course that had led him here. It seemed unlikely that he was still under military or police guard and the notion that he had escaped suddenly thrilled her and quickened her step. Cholera, the doctor had said – but he was alive, and through the worst of it.

The nurse pushed into a narrow ward at the end of a deserted corridor and slipped up her face mask. The attendant inside conversed quickly with the girl then pointed down through the row of beds. 'Last one,' the attendant said. 'Name of Devlin.'

Donna walked down alone. Suddenly she was conscious of the chill in her belly. All around were the faces of dying men. Bed after bed, strained faces, flung-out arms. The area was hot – airlessly hot – and as silent as a tomb.

He must see her courageous and cheerful, she told herself. There must be no tears, no smallest hint of defeat. Cholera was like typhus, and she had beaten that devil. Now the burden was on him, but he would not succumb. It *would* be beaten. She would nurse him, take him from this filthy hell . . .

She approached the last line of grey-clad beds. Two children, an elderly man quite dead . . . then Colum.

He was lying on his side, away from her, and something in his humped posture alarmed her. She gasped relief to see he *was* breathing, his shrunken shoulders heaving intermittently.

'Colum?' Her voice was a pathetic whisper.

He stirred, twitching awake, and edged over. On impulse she took a retreating step. She glimpsed purple-veined cheek, the parched pallor of disease, bruised lips. 'My God!' she muttered, holding herself from stumbling back. '*My God.*'

'Donna . . .'

The man before her was not Colum. It was Rob. His fingers spread and his right hand groped for her. She recoiled. 'I am your father's friend,' he mumbled in fever. 'They cannot punish me. What I have done was for him alone.'

'Be still.' She sat. The lifebloood seemed to drain out of her. She had been foolish to hope, to believe. It had all been too swift and simple. Her mind focussed on Rob and she tried to hide her distress. He looked aged and broken, a hideous ghost of the full-bodied man he once was. His weight seemed no greater than a child's and his dark eyes were sunken in pits in his face.

'You come to take me away, to see that I am hanged for murder,' he raved, 'but I swear I did it for the love of Letty and your family. The courts will hear me out.'

'I thought you to be Colum,' she whispered.

'Colum? But this is not Ireland – is it? Colum cannot be here in America. Your venture is wasted. He is away in Galway or Athlone or –'

'There was a rebellion. Colum was unjustly tried and sentenced to transportation . . .' She went on mechanically, telling him the tale in simple language, taking the time to reassert herself after the shock of disappointment.

His eyes blazed. 'Then he lingered on? Even depriving him of his herd did not deter him. The fool. He should have seen what future lay ahead at Drumloch.' He stopped suddenly and swung over the bed's edge to retch drily. Donna remained frozen, unable to move. Rob slipped back on the pillow and recovered himself. Now his voice lacked emotion. 'I cannot see why you bother with him. Why did you not find yourself a clever husband? Ambitious, strong-minded, far-seeing.' His eyes closed. 'Letty should have seen. It could have been so right for us. But I wasted it all, wasted my time. How could I set to marriage with her? How, when the truth was known?' He petered out, exhausted, but his eyes rolled back to her. 'Can you get me free of here?' he urged. 'Any way? Explain to your father, anything. Say I killed Adam Rossitor to defend her, to help her. You must –'

'I don't see there is anything I can do at this time.' There seemed no sense in trying to explain all.

'I could help you with Colum in return.'

'How?'

370

His brain was suddenly sharp and alert. 'You seek a transported man, and wish to secure his freedom – yes? When I fled from Dover I sought the help of those who could guarantee me a safe passage. By chance I encountered a group whose sympathies were entirely with Irish political prisoners. I explained my case to them – suitably slanting my facts, of course – and won their support. They got me to New York without trouble and fixed me in lodgings at Cherry Street. I was free – until the sickness came.'

'These are the people who operate escape channels?' Her heart was slamming.

He nodded and demanded, 'But you must help me out of here, and back to your father's side. I am not done yet. I am fit and . . .'

Donna had sympathy for him, for his suffering, but it was controlled pity, remote and undemanding. Was there a way out for him? She hesitated, staring. Obviously this limited quarantine would have to go on. But later, if he recovered . . .? *If.* She reconsidered the damage Rob had done to her relationship with Colum. For that he owed her something – and she must place her own needs first in contemplating his future. Though fully unsure of her commitment she said boldly, 'All right. I will do what I can to help you out of here.'

'Your father – ?'

'Do not worry. I give you my word. When the quarantine is over I will assist you. But now I need this address.'

Rob looked at her with diminished suspicion. 'Next time I will not fail,' he sighed. 'Fate stood against me with Letty, but I will waste no time in getting back a good standing. I *must* succeed.' Donna said nothing and he resumed, 'Take down this address. Go and say I passed you on.' He rattled off an address near the park behind South Street, a tough area. 'Tell them you seek the release if possible of a man charged with treason against her Majesty. And you have money? That combination will surely win them over.' He laughed until the rhythm became a gurgling bloody cough. Frightened, Donna stood. He gripped her wrist, his fingers

371

cold and wet. Fever was back in his eyes.

'Your father bears me no ill feeling, does he?'

'Why should he? I thought you and he were excellent friends. That is as it is.'

'Yes, yes we will be friends. Best to say no more. Just friends.' He was shivering and panting. 'Heed not what I may have said. It is fever. I seek nothing but a post by your father's side.' She nodded. 'And Drumloch?' he went on. 'Is it gone at last? – this rebellion you spoke of, the fire?'

'Yes, Rob. It is gone.'

'Good, good. We need never return.' He lay back, peaceful. 'When you find him, tell Colum I assisted. Tell him, whatever I did to aid the stealing of his accursed herd, I have made up for.'

'I will.'

'Tell him you found me well – not in a poorhouse hospital.'

'Yes.'

He said no more but lay in repose. The even movements of sleep inflated his chest. Donna gathered her winter wrap tightly about her, as if to ward off the evil demons that cluttered this foul place. She said no farewell but blessed herself and drew a cross in the air above him.

He needed no good wishes. Diseased and in pain, he bore a rigid smile on his face. In defeat he was a victor. Thrown from good society, he had won back a foothold. He had made a bargain, found an important friend. Everything had its value. Even lowly associations and the face of illness. Even honesty and compassion.

But death had done.

'They say our best chance is to go to Sydney Town.'

It was five days later and Anderson spoke across his beer in the Broadway cafe that had become their daily rendezvous place. When Donna's brow furrowed he pressed on:

'These people are professional operators of escape routes. They know much about the transportation system and have friends in Colonial offices. They say quite definitely that neither America nor Canada are taking Britain's felons any more and the men sentenced after the aborted Tipperary rising have gone to Australia.'

'Where in Australia?'

'Maybe Van Diemen's Land, maybe Sydney. They were not easy about surrendering details. They interrogated me for many hours before they satisfied themselves that I was an ally and did indeed support Repeal and reform in Ireland. Later I discovered that whilst they detained me in South Street an inquiry agent had been sent back to Monroe to establish the veracity of my story.'

'They are Repealers, then?'

'Hardly that. Many among them may be genuine enough, but others are mercenaries and they wasted little time in stating the essential requirement of money in procuring an escape route. I paid them the twenty dollars you gave me, and now they seek twenty more before they can put me in touch with the Sydney merchant who controls the Australian link.'

'They believe Colum could be freed?'

'Every man can be freed – but the reason or the price must be right, they say.'

'You know my position. The money will not trouble me. But Australia is round the other side of the world.' Donna pushed her port aside and gazed onto the dusty Broadway pavements. She sat in silence for many minutes. Qualms of fear beset her at the prospect of so arduous a journey in the middle stages of pregnancy. She had not yet confided her condition to her friend and the convenient fashion in full skirts allowed her secret still. But the alternative to taking this new challenge appeared just as daunting: unable to tolerate the Cabbots' home a day longer, she had already moved to an expensive $8-a-week suite at the United States Hotel; nothing more suitable for a single lady with maid had been found, so, unless an active course was followed, depressing weeks of cosseted languishing lay ahead.

'Australia it must be,' Anderson interrupted, grinning. 'But do not for a minute contemplate your participation in such a journey.'

She did not challenge him for a moment but said, 'What about your family here?'

He shrugged. 'You are right. I am mindful of my responsibility to them. They are safe and well in Monroe now but – alas – it seems to me that America will not hold them. They pine for Ireland so, and the close walls of a tenement are no substitute for the scent of summer over fields of corn.' His chin jutted determinedly. 'I recognise great tasks that lie before me. I have discovered the way to Teggie and Colum, and I must travel to find them. Then, despite the glories of pretty America, I must return to lead my family home. After all that happened in Ireland it will not be easy, but – as you said – memories might be short, and a new life can be found somewhere.' He gave a short tired sigh and looked out to the windy pavements. 'I'm not saying it was a mistake to come. America has provided us with a convenient refuge. But all along in our blood we knew that home was home. We have had our temporary escape.' He laughed. 'I begin to sound like you! Who'd have thought that Anthony Anderson could profess himself a sentimentalist?'

Donna reflected, wondering about the child within. A voyage to Australia was eight or nine weeks, and the babe was due in seventeen. If the job of finding Colum was devolved entirely to Anthony there would be no remote chance of greeting him with the news of the joy to come. 'Your loyalty is much appreciated,' Donna said. 'But I am not about to shirk my commitment now. If the path seems a sure one, then Australia it must be for me too. I am young and fit and another sea trip will not reduce me. I will go with you, and we will set out as soon as you can purchase a passage and get this contact name from the South street people.'

Anderson seemed unsure. Sheepishly he said, 'You must know what you are saying, Donna. Australia is a primitive desert where they say five men in ten die and five become kings. The sun beats down with ferocity in winter and the earth freezes in summer. It is like nowhere you or I have

374

ever been.'

'I am not afraid.' She drew herself up defiantly lest he saw through her thin mantle. 'We shall voyage as brother and sister for ease.'

'You are brave. Devotion to love such as yours I have never seen in any woman.'

She gazed away. 'Not brave. I merely hunger for adventure.'

He stared her, his eyes full of a mysterious depth that added to her embarrassment. Bare admiration was evident. 'Before walking down Broadway I had resolved to dissuade you from accompanying me at all costs. But now I am glad for your decision. There will be long weeks of tiresome travel, and your warm-hearted company will be truly welcome.'

'I'm flattered,' she laughed.

It surprised and thrilled her to see him blush as though some intimate sin had been confessed. He winked at her, and the bond of their friendship and trust was confirmed in that split second.

A gnawing sense of duty drove Donna back to Bellevue before boarding the *Victoria*, Sydney-bound from the East River, some days later. In her heart, there was little interest in her exchange part of the agreement with Rob. But the visit absolved her from the promise of aid. Rob was dead and buried.

The German surgeon directed her to the paupers' cemetery a mile uptown. She did not go. She quit the hospital quite clear-headed, without blessing or prayer on her mind. She would remember Rob as she had always thought of him: under a shadow of obscure roguery, callous and self-interested, manipulating human beings like cards on a table in hope of winning his ends. She recalled the mystery of his jealousy of Colum and spitefulness towards her. It wasn't surprising that in the end jealousy – the alleged jealousy against Adam – had precipitated the final flight that denied him the *haute monde* for ever.

There was little else to do. The runners had already

taken her luggage to the docks and Anderson was to meet her at the cafe on Broadway. With a half-hour to spare she took a cab to Fifth, but the mansion was slumbrous and the reception from the housekeeper cold. Paul Cabbot had travelled on business to Michigan, Donna was told, and would be gone till the New Year. As she resumed her cab a maid came running after her bearing a letter. Immediately Donna recognised Halifane's seal. On the way to Broadway she opened and read it.

In reply to her letter of eight weeks ago Halifane wished to triumphantly announce that Letitia had agreed a sell-out deal – for the specified two thousand. A sense of victory and his new-found fondness for Donna encouraged flourishes of detail: Letty had proved difficult to deal with; she had tried a hard barter, but the attorney's 'inside' information regarding her financial position enabled him to call the tune. Truth was, Letty was broke; Mortimer's money was to be divided between no less than three illegitimate children and his true beloved, Miss Amelia Prendergast of Lurgan, so said the will. Thrown to her own devices, Letty had taken up with the magnificent but miserly Sir David Villers and moved to London. Halifane phrased it most exquisitely but his letter expounded the certainty that Donna's two thousand had come at the vital time, permitting her sister to become the independent mistress of a promising politician and not a paid whore.

'I am quite excited that events have resolved themselves in a way that will please you,' Halifane concluded, 'and, like you, I look forward to Drumloch estate raising itself once again to pre-eminence. With the fund available to you for settlement with your sister I acknowledge your need for further monies for rebuilding, but to date no suitable loan agent has been found. But I will persist . . . '

It didn't matter. All that was important now was that Drumloch at last was hers.

She met Anderson at midday and by three o'clock was standing amidst the touts and runners and aspiring passengers on the East River quay, awaiting the *Victoria's* gangway. Bounding with joy and expectation she clung to her friend's arm.

CHAPTER FORTY

The first few days under sail were gayest. The sky was clear, the shoreline breeze that washed off the Americas soft, and the company aboard pleasanter than any Donna had experienced before. The only mild unease stemmed from the fact that men outnumbered women five to one but that uneven state was palliated by an infectious mood of merriment. Not a soul aboard, save the gregarious old captain, had ever set foot on this 'nether land' that was their destination, but optimism was high. The young officers going out to join the marines spoke of welcome sunshine and cheap women, families of grantees day-dreamed about the empires bestowed on them by the Crown and down-at-heel young gentlemen indulged fantasies about sheep farms and gold. It was hard not to make friends; harder still not to abandon care for gaiety and wallow almost sinfully in this cradle of hope.

Under the watchful but tolerant eye of Midgie – unquestioningly dedicated now to her friend and mistress – the comradeship with Anthony Anderson grew. When she reflected on their past associations it seemed incredible to Donna that she had once viewed him as a colourless character. The ready traits of humbleness and taciturnity certainly played their part but they distracted from a personality that was fired by passion. Their for'ard cabins were side-by-side, linked by a common parlour, and, when not walking the decks, they joined there, exploring each other conversationally like newly-weds. Donna learnt of Anderson's lifelong belief in social reform, of his true conviction to rebel action and of the subtler traits that inspired him. He was a man of considerable sensitivity, devoid of base emotions and guided by decent moral principles. Though goaded to rebel work by obvious injustice, he somehow lacked Colum's intensity and, the more one got to know him, the more the dominant feature of kindness emerged. After a day or two the make-believe of travelling as brother and sister was no strain; as solidarity and familiarity grew it became easy indeed to look upon him as a brother-in-blood. This strengthening closeness made those first days all the happier.

On the fifth night out a full moon broke and the captain announced occasion for celebration: his creaking vessel had, he estimated, just crossed the hundred thousandth mile of its career and a wassail-cup was called for. The spirit of jollity rippled out. In the great captain's dining-room admidships ham, rye-cakes and syllabub were packed on the tables, wassail-bowls were spiced and heated and the eager voyagers gathered. The steaming hot draught was passed around, songs were sung, toasts were called and the past succumbed to confident future. A flute and whistle materialised and enthusiasm supplanted order while the captain himself danced a wild Scotch reel to loud-voiced encouragement from one and all. Mindful of her unborn child, Donna gracefully declined the invitation to join the dance and, after a cup too many perhaps, made for her cabin shortly after midnight. Midgie had found a fellow Bostonian to engage her and the party was still in swing but Donna was glad to get back to the quiet and cool of her empty quarters alone. Her head was woolly from drink but a pleasant sense of wellbeing lent relaxation. As she stripped off her petticoats to climb abed the rounds of her figure reflected in the looking-glass caught her eye and she paused. The face and body that looked back at her sent a little shock through her veins. How one's psychic vision of oneself can be surprised by the reality! Donna stared at the figure in the mirror and felt satisfaction in her blood. She peeled off her chemise and drawers and regarded her flesh, soft and clear as cream. How splendidly she had grown to womanhood, the bony hollows of her body richly padded, the breasts standing full and high as ever, the thighs once

378

inclined to fat now tight under muscle. And whatever immaturity or self-doubt existed inside her head was no longer borne up by expression and poise. She gazed into the blue eyes and saw unwavering confidence. Mature courage, no less. In terms of art, in terms of overheard adult conversations, in terms of what she sensed about men and women and nature, she knew that looking glass reflected sheer beauty. The excitement of that thought rendered her dizzy for a moment.

Anderson's voice called out from the parlour. Hastily she wrapped a gown around her and walked out to him. His eyes blinked wide when he saw her state of undress, but in her mood she wasn't troubled. He clasped a bottle in one hand and crossed to take some glasses from the Dutch dresser. 'A good-night celebration,' he said woozily, splashing out some wine. 'Everyone's dreams have been toasted tonight, except ours.'

She sat by him and they clinked a toast, but when she tilted her head to sip he did not follow suit. Instead his attention fell to her hand on the glass and he set down his drink and reached for it. His fingers caressed her plump wrist and hand and it came to her suddenly that he was more than mildly drunk. 'How pretty your skin,' he said. 'Without wrinkle or blemish, indescribably coloured. A shade between snow-white and sunshine perhaps?' A distant voice of better judgement urged her to pull away but when she did the folds of her satin gown slid apart and bare thighs were exposed. Anderson stared a minute, then reached out a nervous hand. The hardness of his flesh against hers made her gasp. He traced a line upwards with a forefinger. 'See the lustre, veined finely like the petals of a flower . . .'

The ship's movement, the wine and an awareness of her body conspired to make her giggle. Encouraged, his hand fell firm onto the broadest part of her thigh.

'A happy night like tonight is not complete without this,' she smiled, tipping her wine.

Anderson appeared to misunderstand. His face became pale and his mouth grim. ''Tis the loneliness of so long a

379

voyage,' he said mysteriously. 'I feel hunger too.'

His quizzical, insistent gaze should have warned her, but she merely replied with a grin. This was the first time in her life she had felt this way, her body running hot in alcohol, her brain melted. It was many minutes before she realised his posture on the couch had changed and his hand was between her legs, languidly advancing without hindrance of any sort. He kissed her, and she swooned to enveloping sensuous pleasure. Then, like a hurricane wind sweeping through her she understood his desires. Before the kiss was finished she lurched out and pushed him off.

'Please, Donna – no.' He crushed back on her, begging. His arms gripped her tight and he struggled to resume the kiss. 'Do not torment me in this way. Please. Allow me – '

The grappling fight sobered Donna and she slapped his face hard. He released her instantly, springing away until half the room separated them. The cosy feeling had left Donna entirely and a sense of disgust flooded her. The smarting pinch of his grip on her thighs and belly shamed her and she turned away from him. 'I am tired and it is late,' she panted. 'Kindly permit me to retire unmolested.'

'You . . . you must understand – ' he started.

She left the parlour brusquely, slamming the cabin door so that his protesting words were drowned. Alone again and despite herself she started weeping; but the tears were not tears of contrition and disgrace against Anderson, but the voice of a lonely, hungry heart.

It was lunchtime the following day before he cornered her again, this time charged with remorse. She had avoided him since breakfast, absorbing herself with fellow travellers whenever she could and making excuses to keep to her cabin otherwise. When at last she promenaded on the fore deck and he confronted her their embarrassment seemed exactly equal. The American coast that had stayed in sight for days had now disappeared into mists, and the sky was darkening. Before the bows the silver Atlantic stretched out, unwelcoming. The atmosphere of cheeriness was no more. The serious business of difficult voyage lay ahead.

'They say a good beginning is half the battle,' he said. 'And I am ashamed to say my behaviour has undone the opportunity for a good battle!'

'The weather has been kind till now. The signs augur well, I should say.'

He saw that she was endeavouring to side-step and realised his persistence would cause more embarrassment. Keeping his gaze from her he said, 'I can only apologise for the silliness of last night. Unaccustomed to alcohol in large quantity as I am, I fear a madness overtook me. What I said and did were reprehensible indeed. I hope, in your wisdom, you may see that nothing of my *true* attitude came out, for indeed I admire and respect you greatly and you hold a position of high honour in my thoughts.'

Deep within her she longed to answer him, to grant forgiveness and confess that she too had been unexpectedly transported, but rectitude and guilt stood in the way. Quite simply the moment of intimacy appalled her. With Colum such sacred moments were, it seemed, legitimate. At very least she knew him, had grown in their bond and declared love; but Anthony Anderson was a stranger, someone who had stepped from the shadows of childhood to assist her, who had won her over with the honesty of his friendship. It was shameful that he had broached the caress of love, all the more so when he was touching a woman pregnant by another's seed.

But then, how could he know about the child? She had held her secret carefully, considering it too personal, a factor closely wrapped up in her affection and ambitions, something that could not concern him. But, with all his involvement, was that fair?

Her resolve crumbled and she turned to him. 'Anthony, the wine overtook me just as well. I regret –'

He held up a hand to stop her. 'Do not distress yourself further with discussion and surmise. Just tell me . . .' The boyish eyes drifted to hers. 'Tell me you can forgive me. And forget.'

'You meant me no harm.'

381

'Dear Donna, if you could only know. Since we were chldren together I have looked upon you, and looked up to you. I would sever my right hand rather than hurt a hair on your head. . . .'

'I know.' Her tone was soothing. '*I* reacted as I did because – '

He would not let her speak. 'That fiery ale the captain brewed is vicious poison. Another drop will never pass my lips, I swear.' He went on heatedly remonstrating himself until she began to doubt that the guilt he confessed to related to the previous night's encounter at all.

Shrewd Midgie had overheard part of this exchange and later, when Donna and she supped together at dusk, the old maid plumbed for frank details. Suddenly eager for a confidante, Donna splurted some truths, alluding to the romantic advance.

'It is no more nor less than I expected,' Midgie said. 'To an old-timer like me the writing was on the wall ages ago. Isn't it as obvious as anything the man's in love with you?'

That was nonsense, of course, but it lent food for thought for the long voyage, flattering and confusing Donna all at once.

CHAPTER FORTY-ONE

After a lifetime of ashen skies and mountainous waves arrival was sweeter than paradise. One moment the horizon was straight and bare as it had been for two months; the next, Australia was upon them, unrolling with the magical splendour of a child's painting-book. Passengers and crew crowded the decks and Donna held loyal Midgie's hand while Anthony Anderson sighed satisfaction. The sights were like nothing any of them had experienced. As the *Victoria* whispered through the headlands at full sail they saw huge scarps tumbling with karri and eucalyptus, lush waterfalls spilling through silent gorges, blue hills, silver mist. White-painted cabins dotted the greenery and everywhere bark-and-bough shelters showed signs of life. Parrots of every colour squawked around the harbour lighthouse and exotic sea birds floated over the sails, basking in the brilliant sun. 'It's a punishment to be sent here?' old Midgie joked. But Anderson's face turned up to the sun. 'Chain a man's leg and let him toil under *that* for six months,' he said. 'Then see how delightfully novel the world seems.'

Disembarkation was swift and painless but once ashore Anderson's caution proved too quickly true. On the parched back streets of Sydney Town the Australian summer soon absorbed all their energies. There were few runners to carry bags so Anderson was obliged to seek some transport. Leaving the women in care of their trunks he trekked off to search and returned after a half-hour with an incredible contraption in tow. Donna gave vent to huge laughter when she saw him approach. For five dollars he had purchased the only readily available conveyance – a tottery ox-dray. Loading their luggage in paroxysms of laughter they struck out without delay and found a boarding house near the town centre just as the short cold night came down.

In the morning Anderson awoke Donna with a fistful of pebbles on her window and, leaving Midgie in charge of the dray, they sauntered into the heart of the township to breakfast and locate the escape line agent referred by South Street, a ticket-of-leave man called Gunning who operated a provisions store.

A wisp of a man with hard living carved into his thin face, Gunning greeted them like old friends and waved away their letter of introduction. They sat together on his veranda and sipped beer while uncouth redcoats marched the streets and chained convict groups laboured before them, at work on a new military barracks. A philosopher to his baccy-stained fingertips, Gunning asked no questions but discoursed like a king. Transported twelve years ago from England for theft, he had come to revere Australian life.

The balance was right, he claimed. Here was a land of treasure trove prospects, religious toleration – but rigid authoritarian control. The harsh control was vital, because since '25 more than a third of the 300,000 immigrants had been criminals transported. Gunning had met them all – Scots Reformers, Tolpuddle Martyrs, feckless gentry, Irish rebels – and had welcomed their impact on society. Above all their presence tempered the quality of life, softening the strictures – moral and otherwise – that made life in Britain increasingly difficult.

Anderson refrained from querying the loopholes in Gunning's rehearsed philosophy and got down to asking about the newest shipment of Irish rebels. The ticket-of-leave man was confident from the outset that Colum and Teggie could be found and freed. Then it was only a case of coming to a satisfactory agreement about shipping them out. Such financial matters could be discussed later. He aided Donna to her feet. He would get to the business immediately. There were people on the Governor's staff who would help, and redcoat overseers who signed in the new chain gangs. It might take some time, but given determination and cash, there was nothing that could not be achieved.

Handing him the address of their lodging-house and promising to await news there, Donna and Anderson withdrew with Gunning's assurance of some word within a day or two.

It took three full weeks, but the Irish transportees were found. The settlements of New South Wales had, as Gunning guessed, turned them away and a hurricane off Van Diemen's Land derouted them. Overfull with felons but engaged in massive construction and roadbuilding ventures that ate up labour forces, the province of Victoria had finally taken the new troupe. Gunning could report with certainty that ninety convicts – some from England – were landed at Melbourne and headed north to join a bridge-building project on the Murray at Albury.

Excited, Donna clapped her hands. 'I am grateful beyond words, Mr Gunning. Whatever payment you need for these investigations will happily be given. The next step is to go to Albury?'

Gunning curled his grey lips to whistle, impressed by Donna's verve. 'It's no pleasure trip, Ma'am, but I reckon it'd be best. I've got a man here called Nathan, former marine lieutenant. He's well known and well loved by the Melbourne garrison people. He's the man who'll rig or purchase an escape for your friends. Your best route home then would be via Melbourne. Sydney's too well manned by the military and there are problems for us.' Gunning drew out a pouch of black tobacco and a meerschaum pipe and lit up. 'There is one small problem,' he added. 'Might delay things a mite.'

'What problem?'

'Reports say there was a mutiny on the new transportee group. Two escaped and the existing team was split up.'

Anderson cursed. 'So our men might no longer be in Albury? Indeed might have fled to freedom?'

'Long shot,' Gunning observed cooly. 'An' if they're not in Albury on the bridge, they won't be too far.' He scratched his stubbly chin and blew white smoke. 'Only thing'd alarm me would be the prospect of part of the group – the part with our friends – repairing to Sydney.' He nodded towards the chained workers engrossed in the building work across the street, under close supervision of twenty uniformed soldiers, all armed. 'Always easier in the outback, or in Melbourne where we've many friends. Not so here.'

'What if . . . if one or both of them has escaped?' Donna's voice broke. 'How would they survive?'

Gunning breathed deep. 'Well, there ain't too many places to go to put yer boots up round here. Likelihood would be slipping into the camouflage of an area already heavily populated with ticket-o'-leave men. Maybe take employment on a sympathetic ranch, an Irish ranch. You know.' He shrugged. 'Don't worry. Ol' Nathan'll trace 'em down. As you travel south-west he'll have lots of important contacts to make, lots of in-the-know people who will put him in the right direction.' Gunning produced a military map and prodded a finger at Sydney Town, then to tiny Albury. The sketched dark of the Great Dividing Range separated them. No pleasure trip indeed. 'This is the course Nathan will take – towards Lambing Flat, a hundred and fifty miles to the southwest, then down to Albury. You'll need provisions for some weeks, and an ox-dray or two.'

'That we have already,' Anderson put in.

'And the fee is a hundred and fifty now – and six hundred dollars at Melbourne when a boat is fixed up.'

Donna drew a breath. Of the seven hundred pounds she had drawn on Cabbot's English cheque in New York almost everything was gone. After paying Letty there would be little more than a kitty to survive on for a few months in Ireland. But she opened her purse and paid Gunning in American dollars.

'My man Nathan will call tonight to arrange travel.' He crumpled the money carelessly into his shirt pocket. 'God bless you both, then. You'll need His good fortune for the journey ahead.'

As they strolled back to their lodging-house Anderson said to Donna, 'You look drawn and tired. Might it not be better to wait here while I move on with Nathan?'

'You heard what Mr Gunning said. Sydney is the greater risk for convicts. If I stay on I'm only lengthening the time until I see Colum again.'

'You could take a ship to Melbourne and meet us there. That might be a lot easier.'

'No.' she said, almost in anger. Nothing was said for a moment and the unmannerly rebuff had clearly offended him. She slipped her fingers into his. 'I'm sorry. I don't mean to sound ungrateful. You are right – I am tired. But that is not all. Maybe I have been unkind in not explaining the true nature of my impatience. You see, time is running out for me. I must get to Colum soon. I must see him before . . . before our child is born.' As she spoke she pulled her hand away and diverted her gaze.

'I know.'

'You *know*?'

'Midgie confided the secret. Oh, don't blame her – because I was the one who suspected and pestered her for the truth. Growing up in a household of women and with

386

many cousins and aunts who have yielded fit children, I know a little of these things.' He grinned boyishly. 'Sickness in the mornings, the disguise of fuller skirts, that flush of expectant thrill.'

'Say no more. You embarrass me.'

'I envy Colum.'

They came to a forced stop at the end of the street, blocked from crossing while a troop of redcoats tramped by. He turned to her and found her nervously hiding her eyes. 'It's sinful to say what I've said, but I do envy him. You are beautiful and fearless and at peace with the world. I –'

'Please, Anthony. No more. No wild talk that we may later regret.'

When they walked on he took her hand firmly and did not let it go.

They set out in the enervating heat of January, a wagon train of seven people, counting Nathan's scouts. Once outside the township dry winds lashed, whipping grime dust clouds that blinded the eyes and parched the tongue. Populated regions shrank away and the plains opened up, devoid of all life. The last skeins of cirrhus faded from the skies and the sun drilled. Anderson tried to wet his tongue but the salt rivers of his sweat increased the discomfort. He rode ahead with the scouts while Donna lay in the covered dray, the top buttons of her bodice undone, all modesty forgotten. Even under canvas the choking dust was overwhelming. Old Midgie sat by uncomplaining, marvelling at the devotion to service that lured her on this escapade.

The second day took them to the Parramatta toll-gate and through the leery cheers of the ticket-of-leave men who gathered there to ask employment of farmers and grantees bound for the arable plains beyond the mountains. More days of sun and grit passed, then the craggy slopes of the first mountains stretched before them. Nathan and his scouts had crossed the mountains several times, so the safe quick pathways were known. Up they went – up through spiralling peaks that flattened into sandy deserts, then descended into mist-wrapped canyons. Climb and descent, climb and descent. Ridge after ridge was conquered, and still red pinnacles towered ahead.

Donna stayed cheery, but Anderson and Midgie could see that the journey was taking its toll. Sharing the task of driving the dray, withstanding the constant hip-breaking rocking, remaining alert to pot-holes and ravines – all the strain showed in her sagging face.

After seven days the grassy spread of the interior was at last sighted and as the final descent began they camped for their last night in the mountains. In the still of night Midgie tugged Anderson awake. 'Her time is here,' she whispered, eyes sparkling fright.

Anderson shook off the disappointment he felt for Donna. 'Can you cope?'

'No choice, but the poor darling is weak. She has much pain and fears the baby is premature.' Anderson took heart from the fact that the old maid was an all-rounder, the type of proficient practitioner more common to Irish farmhouse life. 'Build a fire quickly,' she said. 'And get me hot water.'

While lamps were lit in Donna's covered dray and the sound of her gentle moaning drifted on the night Anderson busied himself setting a raging fire. Watchful but uninvolved, the scouts and their leader stayed in their shakedowns, their repose interrupted only by the swirling persistence of hungry mosquitoes.

A slow hour passed and Anderson did not move an inch from his fireside spot but sat still, concentrating on the pulsating noise of her agony. Then a tumult of pained cries crashed out, succeeded by silence.

He waited.

The dray canopy slid back and Midgie scrambled down. Anderson found reluctance in his step, but he crossed to her. 'Yes?'

'There is a baby. Alive. Much premature, but we can but hope he will live. A pretty boy child.'

'And Donna?' Anderson stuttered. 'Is she – ?'

The impassive old maid allowed a ghost of a smile. 'She is weak, naturally. But well as might be expected. She swooned to sleep, which isn't surprising with all that brandy I'd given her. It will do her good.'

'This will sadden her. She wanted so much to see him again, to allow him the delight of expectation and present him with the gift of new life.'

Midgie ladled warm water from an extra pot on the fire and poured in a measure of brandy. She sipped it down and enjoyed its sting. 'What matter, once the child survives and she is well?'

Anderson nodded. 'Yes, that's all that's important – once *she* is well.'

They did not move camp for six days but Nathan and a scout rode ahead for Lambing Flat, intent on making contact with some military friends and investigating further news of chain-gang movements. After a wavering start the child's grip on life strengthened and Donna took the time to sleep and recover. When they were ready to resume their journey Nathan was still absent, but the scouts knew his course and there seemed little point in dawdling.

Apart from the briefest of conversational exchanges, Anderson did not discuss the disrupting events with Donna. All of a sudden his own emotions confused him and he found himself looking upon the child with a grudging fervency that almost amounted to jealousy. He chalked it down to infectious disappointment. He had promised to give her what she wanted and failed. Had he been faster in leaving Ireland, faster in researching the Tammany, faster in dealing with South Street ...? But self-arraignment would not redress the situation and the strange growing discomfort persisted.

They had almost arrived in Lambing Flat many days later when Nathan met up with them again. Their train had stopped to cook a midday meal when the scouts shouted out his arrival. Donna was nursing the child under cover of the dray, fresher and fitter now, with her hair neatly plaid and new bloom in her cheeks. She watched Nathan dismount and chat with Anderson and suspected from his animated urgency that some worthwhile news was forthcoming. She called out, summoning them, but only

Anderson strode across. 'Tell me,' she reared up. 'I can tell by your expression and by Nathan's excitement that something has happened.'

'It plunges us into something of a quandary,' he confessed. 'I am unsure whether to feel exalted or distressed.' He took a deep breath and rushed it out: 'Nathan's secret intelligence source in Lambing Flat has come up with all the information we need. Teggie and Colum have been positively located.'

'You mean it?' She gripped his hand, her eyes afire. The baby in her arms stirred and grunted out of sleep.

'It's not quite as straightforward as it might be. Much of what Gunning told us was right. The chain-gang was split some months ago. A part of it stayed in Albury on the bridge project, but the other part transferred to road work in the Wagga Wagga district. Then one month ago they trekked back to Sydney, bound for eventual shifting to Van Diemen's Land.' He paused. 'They were the Irish group of prisoners.'

'You mean – ?' Her heart skipped a beat. 'We have crossed paths with them, and lost our opportunity for seeing a quick escape?'

'Maybe. Nathan would not promise any fast routes from Van Diemen's Land. He says the best chance would be to return to Sydney at all speed and implore Gunning to try some tricky bribes and get away on the first merchant trader.'

'Well, let us do that. Now! If Colum is there –'

'Colum is not there. 'Tis Teggie alone we may pursue in Sydney.'

'She edged back, scared. 'Colum was among those who escaped the gang?'

'Fear not. Yes, he did escape – but Nathan's men knew where he was. He is forty miles beyond Lambing, working a farm.'

Donna frowned and shook her head. 'A farm? But that cannot be surely? If Nathan's men knew so easily, why wouldn't the authorities have recaptured him?'

'Seems Nathan's men *are* the authorities. They are members of the marines like any others. But, according to his story, Colum Devlin of Tipperary, having broken free and been run down to this sheep farm . . . paid them off. He purchased his own freedom, and settled to work a farm.'

'Purchased with what? I cannot believe it.'

'You trust Nathan and Gunning?'

'Nathan more than Gunning. He is fond of the Irish and a man of simple nature. I quite admire the man –'

'Well, that is half of it. The other half is that, without my prompting, he described details about Colum – his appearance and history – that only we might have known. The full story of aborted rebellion even came back to me.' He nodded decisively. 'No doubt, Nathan's friends know where Colum is.'

The first real smile Anderson had seen light Donna's face in weeks flashed out. 'Let us head for Lambing, then. I am strong in body and spirit. The boy is growing every day –' She halted and examined his bland face. 'Colum is found, safe and free, but you worry for Teggie – is that the quandary?'

'Nathan advises the quickest possible return to Sydney. He proposes we set out on horseback – *now*. Alone, he is quite prepared to undertake the venture, but my identification of Teggie and my presence at the port might aid an escape.'

Momentarily Donna felt despair creep over her. But why should she feel gloom? Colum had been found, and lay only fifty or so miles away from her. And she had in her arms the ultimate gift for him, the blossom of their love.

She wormed into her petticoats and drew out a wallet. She passed a wad of notes to Anderson .'You will need ready money to secure Gunning's aid. Take that, which should cover it.'

'Perhaps if I delayed it a few days – a week – just to make sure all goes well with Colum?'

'No. You said yourself. You are a man who honours his word. And you gave your word to Teggie as much as you did to me. I have Colum. Now you must jump for the chance and ensure Teggie's release.'

'But –'

'Please, Anthony. It would be better if I went on . . . alone. I want to. When I think of it, I would rather be travelling alone for our meeting.'

'Very well.' He smiled with warm affection. 'I shall await u, or word from you, for as long as possible in Sydney?'

'Yes. But do not jeopardise your own or Teggie's free-dom in doing so. I have Midgie and I will be well. If there are delays or problems I will get word back on Gunning's grapevine, I'm certain.'

There was a second's silence. He gazed in his tragic, ponderous way. 'Then we might not meet again . . . till Ireland?'

'I thank you,' she said simply. He reached forward and kissd her at the corner of the mouth, then craned to kiss the child. At that moment Nathan walked over. He nodded smilingly to Donna and chucked the baby's chin with evident pleasure. 'My scouts can safely guide you on to Mister Devlin's farm,' he told Donna, 'should you wish to strike out directly?' Donna said yes. 'And you, Mister Anderson – do you choose to accompany me to Sydney?'

'I think it's – as you said – wisest.'

'Good. Then we can mount after food, and ride for the military encampment at Bathurst. I have friends in the township there who might direct us . . . .'

One of the scouts called that food was ready and Nathan excused himself and moved off. Alone with Donna, Anderson offered no fuller goodbye. 'I had better gather my belongings,' he said. 'And you too, if you wish to head south immediately.' He disappeared into the second dray and she did not see him again until, with Nathan, he galloped off for the mountains in the east.

CHAPTER FORTY-TWO

Once Midgie and the child were safely settled at lodgings near the Lambing Flat sheep station, Donna wasted no time. On horse back and with the necessary minimal supplies, she headed out with Nathan's senior scout, guided by a scrawled map supplied by the friendly captain of the local Cowra troop.

It took eight full hours but finally the last bushy hills were crossed and the map markings re-examined and there below them, in a clearing beside a serpentine stream, was the farmhouse.

The old scout was shocked by Donna's sudden anguished tears at the culmination of a quest which, like all others he partook in, he understood only in terms of challenge and search, simple success or failure. 'This be your husband?' he asked.

Donna did not hear his question to reply. She nodded forward, speaking in a dream. 'There he is,' she mumbled.

Below them there were skinny sheep wandering the fields and chickens in an enclosure. In the distance two young boys hammered up a palisade to ring the little house and corral the animals. And in front of the veranda Colum stood, stripped to the waist and shoeing a palomino. Donna sat quietly and absorbed every line of his body, every flutter of muscle, every familiar move. Had it really only been nine or ten months? It seemed like years, all the more so because in appearance he had changed and, inside, she had too. He had grown up. Gone was the girlishly soft visage, the longish brown hair, the impression of vulnerability. Now, browned from the sun and his hair tight-cropped, he appeared more man than boy, a muscular, hard-living warrior. And how had she changed? What lessons of ambition and spite had Letty and Rob taught her? What lessons of humility had Cabbot given? And what had Anthony Anderson contributed? She thought about Drumloch manor house. Colum and the manor – she had come to want both. Wild unbridled love and honourable independent power. The food to change the world! To make things *right*! And yet, how fickle a friend righteous ambition really was. Witness papa, witness Rob. Who can change the world, or redirect the tides? These things just happen, under Fate. In that moment Drumloch's thriving future receded from her brain and only Colum stood before her. All that really mattered in this universe was the soul satisfaction of true love.

The scout dismounted to sit in the grass and, saying no more, she jabbed her horse and picked her way down the fertile slopes.

Colum did not see her until she was only yards away. Then he glanced carelessly up, as if expecting another, and his expression twisted from calm to open-mouthed incredulity. He dropped his mallet and released the horse. Donna climbed down and leant against her animal's flank.

'*It is true*,' he stammered.

'I come for you.'

He walked towards her with an unblinking gaze that stunned her, strangling all the words she had planned. 'They told me a woman and a man sought me. Friends from home. I could not believe. I thought you dead, lost in the manor blaze.'

His arms looped round her and they held each other like children in a storm. 'I had left a day earlier for Halifane,' she explained. 'Anthony told me your story. Oh my love, if only you could have known! What distress you must have been through.'

'How did you journey? Did Cabbot help? How did you find me?'

'We have time to talk forever.'

As their mouths met a throb of life that had lain dormant within started, filling her with excitement. But the kiss was too short.

A voice from behind, a nasal Australian lilt, clipped: 'You want us to fence the stream bank, Mister Devlin?'

' 'Tis all right,' Colum replied. 'Just finish the high land and band the sheep together, Tim.'

The boy strode off to join his companion on the hill slope and Donna looked inquiringly to Colum. 'My land,' he smiled, but some vague guilt unmanned his confidence. 'I bought it from some squatters, fair and square.'

'Bought it?'

'You know much of what occurred? The passage, the chain-gang?'

She nodded. 'You escaped the chain-gang with another man.'

Colum laughed. 'No sense in wild running. This district, between here and Wagga Wagga is about the best for settling in.' When the boy Tim had moved out of sight around the shoulder of the weatherboard building Colum squeezed and kissed her again. 'I came here with a Chinese convict called Kao who'd been charged with the manslaughter of his best friend. He had been assigned our chain-gang, but knew Australia well as he'd been here six years as merchant and farmer. The row that saw his conviction had allegedly been over a woman, but Kao confided that it had concerned a secret gold find made by his friend which, under their agreement, should have been shared. I liked Kao and when the mutiny occurred we luckily escaped. Kao's intention was to trace down the cache of his friend's and buy off his freedom, but he had been wounded in the mêlée of escape and died later. The gold he'd found he gave to me.'

'You should have made for Melbourne and bought a passage home.'

His voice faltered. 'I couldn't know you were alive. And I would be safe on no British ship as an Irishman headed away from this country.' He pressed a finger against her lips to silence her questioning. 'I cannot believe you have come,' he said. 'My brain will not function. When we sailed from Ireland I wept my heart out and gave up hope. I knew there could be no future in hoping.'

'But there is, there always is.' She went on to give him a rushed, garbled account of Cabbot and Rob and Nathan, but said nothing of Anderson or the babe.

'The voyage tired you,' he said. 'You look pale and thin. Come, come into the house and let us drink.'

It was an austere building, decorated with incongruous pieces of mismatched furniture. Scraps of undyed woollen carpet were neatly squared on the floor and pretty blue curtains framed the windows. There was no filtering dust, but a healthy perfume of soap and food. The atmosphere was unexpected, unsettling. Colum poured her coffee from a pot that had been steaming on the stove and sat beside her on a fat settee. She felt disoriented, and could not bring herself to move closer to him. The threads of their conversation were resumed:

'So Paul Cabbot's gracious gift enabled me to follow you, and will permit me to purchase Letty's interest in Drumloch.'

'I'm glad. I know you wanted that.'

The stark answer unnerved her. 'And now you are wealthy?' she rejoined.

'I have some money. "Desert" money they call it here. Nothing is asked and nothing is spoken about it.' He spread his arm. 'But I have a farm, and that has kept me busy and content. Good animals, fenced pasture, prospering outlook'.

'Yet no substitute for home.'

'Home is where ambitions lie.'

She felt herself choke, bemused by the portentous feelings in her heart, by this manifest chronicle of change. 'And your ambitions now lie here?'

'Regardless of the injustice of it, in Ireland I am now a wanted man. And there is the famine and endless conflict between gentry and farmer.'

All of a sudden the neckband of Donna's bodice was too tight. Sweat dribbled between her breasts and her breath was short. Somehow this inkling of impending sorrow had crept into her the moment her eyes met his again. Somehow she knew.

'. . . You must see,' he was saying, 'that when I came here I was forced to reconsider my future. Then, escaping, I saw the sensible way out, what so many had done before me.'

'An easy way for you.' She felt her tone brittle, beginning to crack. She was not fearful of what he might say any longer, but stifled by futility, by the wastefulness of it all. Why hadn't she found tell-tale signs in the past? – his indecision when their first plan of elopement was made, Desmond Devlin's warning? 'I want to go back, Colum. I know where my roots are. I want Drumloch because it is part of me.'

'It is gone, Donna. Burnt down and ended. What your father, nor the Ribbonmen, couldn't do has been done by blight. Drumloch and its folk are altered forever, finished.'

'Maybe its salvation lies in that change. We can start from beginnings and build up a new kind of estate –'

'Think of it. It isn't feasible. We could not live there, tormented by our different origins.'

'You said you wanted me –'

'I still want you. As I did from the first day, as children, we met.'

'Forgive my mood.' She shook herself tartly. 'I am just shocked by the fast decisions of change you have made. It seems only yesterday you made love to me and we spoke of a life in Drumloch –'

'No more, please.' His head slumped into his hands. 'Do not torture me with talk of what might have been. Australia is my home now and I have the freedom every man needs. *My own* plot of earth.'

She understood, but it gave no comfort: in Ireland he had suffered and struggled under the shadow of many troubles – the complexity of his desire for her, the uncertainty of his tenure, the call of rebellion. Everywhere there was restriction of movement, difficulty of decision, threat. But here there was void. Newness. Men reborn in an embryonic society.

'Perhaps my trip has been in vain,' she said and on

impulse her fingers stretched out and touched his cheek. 'I have loved you so much, but I fear I could not settle here forever. My home would haunt me.'

'I'm sorry.' He kept his eyes from her. 'You always urged me to act more decisively. Here I have followed that advice. I have chosen a calm life and . . . cast you aside. It is too late to go back.'

As he spoke the door opened and Donna drew her attention from him. A slender blonde girl with the robust look of an Australian prairie animal about her stood before them, a basket of wrung washing cradled in her arms. She looked eighteen, not a day more, and had not the social grace of knowing how to respond to this odd spectacle of a prim noble lady seated in her parlour.

'Oh, didn't know y'ad company, Colum,' she stammered, scraping licks of dirty hair from her large beautiful eyes. He stood nervously before her, wordless. Like a whippet she retreated.

'Your wife,' Donna whispered, seeking no affirmation, no denial. Enough had been said. The intractable gulf was forged.

And still she had not mentioned the child.

Colum was gaping vacuously, now holding her gaze, begging response. But she put down her coffee cup and stood. Then, avoiding his flexing, unsure hands, she walked to the veranda door.

Outside the sun had slunk behind black-hearted clouds and in the distance the fog of thunder-rain masked the mountains. Days ago Nathan had warned them: when the storms came most of the mountain paths were unsafe. So Anderson and he would hold up at Bathurst tonight. Tomorrow might be finer.

The scout was dozing and she stirred him. Together they mounted. As she took the reins the tramp of a boot behind made her turn. Colum opened her saddle-bag and slipped a small pouch inside. Impatiently she scooped it out, tearing the cord that bound it. Her thumb flicked sandy-coloured clumps of dirt inside. Gold. Maybe hundreds of pounds worth, maybe more.

'Desert money,' she said.

'It can help you try for the Drumloch you want, help you build.' Over his shoulder his wife watched, wary of the sadness she could not understand.

'Your kindness is appreciated but –' She threw the pouch back to him, and he flinched as he caught it. The lapse that harried ambitious resolve as she arrived at the farmstead twenty minutes ago was passed. Drumloch loomed large again. 'It would be too easy to accept, and I fear I have not truly learnt your lessons yet. I seek no *easy* life and no more charity. The future I want I will work for. There is stubborn Bouchard blood in me, it seems.'

He stood away and she whipped her horse. She did not look back. The crazy dance was over. Childhood was gone in the shedding of a tear, the passage of a few months and the birth of a baby. The future lay ahead like the open barren plain – as empty as her heart. And yet in the desolation there was one beckoning voice – the faintest echo of simple true love.

When they reached the tableland track she told the scout: they must make Bathurst before the rains died; it was important they caught up with Anderson.